The BRoKen WoRLD

Tim Etchells is a writer and an artist whose work reaches across boundaries from fiction and critical writing to performance, video and visual art. He is the writer and artistic director behind Sheffield's internationally renowned theatre ensemble Forced Entertainment. His previous books include *Endland Stories*, *The Dream Dictionary (for the Modern Dreamer)* and *Certain Fragments*. *The Broken World* is his first novel.

The BRoKen WoRLD

Tim ETCHeLLS

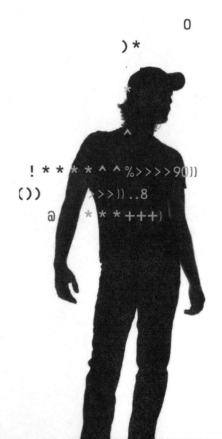

WILLIAM HEINEMANN
LONDON

Published by William Heinemann, 2008

2 4 6 8 10 9 7 5 3 1

First published in Great Britain in 2008 by William Heinemann

Random House, 20 Vauxhall Bridge Road,
London SW1V 2SA

www.rbooks.co.uk

Addresses for companies within The Random House Group Limited
can be found at: www.randomhouse.co.uk/offices.htm

The Random House Group Limited Reg. No. 954009

A CIP catalogue record for this book is available from the British Library

ISBN 9780434018338

The Random House Group Limited supports The Forest Stewardship Council (FSC), the leading international forest
certification organisation. All our titles that are printed on Greenpeace approved FSC certified paper carry the FSC
logo. Our paper procurement policy can be found at www.rbooks.co.uk/environment

Printed and bound in Germany by GGP Media GmbH, Pößneck

for Vlatka

Very little is known at the start.
As the story unfolds, more will be revealed.

Starting OUt

When you first start *The Broken World*, you'll see just normal logos and after that you will see a field of ordinary black and then the title music will start to sound softly.

This is the first walkthrough that I ever wrote and I hope you can forgive any error in my advice or in the English. I guess that's how it goes. I must have been in *The Broken World* about 600 times (or probably more) and tho many times I came back dead or badly injured I know it better now and sometimes come back alive. I think I know some towns in there better than the back of my own hand—at least that's what Tory says. Oh yeah. I dedicate this guide to Tory. Hi, Tory.

The black will slowly turn to the white and the sound will rise and when you push the Start all things will begin. Be patient. This guide helps in every place and makes it easy to fight all the bad guys and find a good way thru—so PLEASE read the guide.

*

When *The Broken World* begins all is quiet and well until a dark, ominous shadow appears overhead. The shadow will navigate its way through a forest, possibly hunting for something, or someone . . .

Then the scene will change to Ray—the hero—who is stood by the bank of a river (with forest behind) and watching the waters below. Ray is the main one, the tall one, the one with darkest hair. He looks pretty cool standing there.

After some time at the water, you will gain control of him for the first time. If you turn him round you can see the same shadow I mentioned before—turning and twisting at the edge of the forest. There's a voice shouting which Ray must run toward. Get the feel of moving him around and practice the Kicks. He is not always easy to control, at least not for a beginner. Now you are Ray. Get use to that coz you will be him in *The Broken World* and you have to get to know him better than your own self if you want to succeed in the game. You are Ray and have to make all his decisions, solve all clues and fight the good fight as he (i.e. you) goes from town to town. I'll try to guide as well as I can.

*

The scenes in the caves at Tora Bora are not there anymore. They were there in the first version of the game and now they've been taken away. Also the freaky weapons that fill the air with explosive petroleum particles and burn everything to pieces are not there anymore coz everyone got killed. But one favorite part of mine—where the enchantment potion can be collected in the Motel Room on the edge of the Fourth Town—is still there. And the part with Mirrors of Truth and Mirrors of Untruth is a new part that was never there before. I'll try my best to guide you thru the game from one town to another and complete all the missions etc. That is how it goes.

*

Ray runs toward the voice that he hears from the forest but the shadow is still moving out there twisting and turning. Ray is drawn into the shadow and cannot fight it—when he gets close he stumbles and goes down falling and his vision goes and then it is scary, bro, coz all you can hear is the voice and the sound of wind in the trees that I already mentioned. The voice you can hear says "Ray, Ray, come back" and then another voice (I'm not sure who it is) says "Life is so precious Ray, even right now" and then the screaming woman and the forests fade to black.

*

The scene then changes to a ship, sailing on high seas. From an aerial shot we zoom at Ray, who is looking at the ocean and staring again like he is thinking deep about something. It's not much action yet, bro, but soon there will be enough action for anyone and triple Bonus included. You cannot tell what Ray is really thinking when he looks in the ocean like that but from the look on his face he is one Troubled Motherfucker.

GARS has taken everything from me . . . My home, my contentment . . . Everything . . . This will be my last chance . . . my only hope for freedom . . .

Rachel, the game's other main character, stands in the background looking out at the ocean as well. After a bit, she walks off . . .

(NOTE: Rachel is not actually there with Ray onboard the ship—at least not in the same way like I am sitting here at the computer or in the same way that Tory is lying right now on the sofa watching *Killerwatts* on TV in the other room—no, Rachel is a figment in Ray's memory or like a ghost of the past that is haunting him.)

(2nd NOTE: Also, you do not know who or what in hell GARS is when the voice mentions it at this point but do not worry, man, you will find out soon enough.)

I will not give up . . . This will be my Ultimate Adventure.

When the ship docks you will be in control again so if you need more time to practice moving Ray around you should do it now on the ship where there is no one there intent to harm you because after this it is no party. Get used to crouching and RUNNING (you will NEED this, I promise you—doesn't matter how brave you are). Get used to all the commands. I heard about one guy who couldn't control Ray good enough even to get off the freaking ship up the gangplank and he lost all his health and life force just stumbling and wandering around while the big clock ran down.

*

First Town (kind of small and gray/green atmosphere) has Monsters—ugly motherfuckers but not too difficult to kill. There is a hospital in the northeast corner, where the Doctor can heal any wounds you have accumulated, and a Nurse can save the memory of what you've seen or learned so far which is not so much at this point, I guess, but you can come back if you need to at any point in the game (or find another Nurse to save Memory). That is the best advice I can give.

Also, there is a shop in the northwest corner, where you can buy healing potions, maps, magic dust, and a green potion. You can also sell "meat," which you find aplenty, as you defeat all the monsters.

There is a fountain in the middle. Go there for water supply. Some strange kids are playing near the fountain—be careful. The boy has a Ring—trade something out of your Items for this coz you will need it later. The Ring is important and PLEASE remember: you can always Trade for stuff you need.

The game is a whole world. That is what Venter says and if anyone replies that it's JUST a game he says no, INCORRECT, it is a whole world and I agree with him. One afternoon in the summer we tried to map all the levels, places, and options—but we cannot. There is so much territory and not enough paper even if we totally covered the floor of the place he was living in back then. That's when I decided to write this walkthrough. I will try to explain it all.

There is an old run-down house in the southeast corner of First Town, which will reward you with some good supplies if you snoop around. But here is a warning: they do not make it easy. There is Bad Atmosphere in the house maybe coz it is a place where somebody died and Atmosphere will affect you, taking away Life points. Do not stay in that house longer than you have to – and bro, PLEASE watch out for these places all thru the game. Bad Atmospheres is a nasty way to die.

You need the torches, the knife blade and the ammo that is lying on the ground. Get those and Move on bRother; get out the house and get on the road. Also, please remember: anytime you kill anybody or Monsters or anything CHECK THE BODY. Remember: CHECK THE BODY. CHECK THE BODY. That is the best advice you are ever going to get. Clockwork told me that once and he was just repeating it over and over and over and over and over and we were all laughing. CHECK THE BODY. CHECK THE BODY. CHECK THE BODY.

I'm now officially insane from the endless nights of hard work I have put into the game.

*

There is one last task to accomplish in First Town. Head to the Warehouse in Southwest Area. Use the Map you bought and figure out a route. HEADS UP. This town still has some residents who are human. You can hear them trying to escape and even witness them being attacked and eaten by Zombies. Ignore them as most of them are not important. Just check their bodies if they are dead and hope you get something for free. Avoid Parks and Playgrounds. Stay away from Supermarkets.

If any Zombies come near you use the Kick Attack. The Zombies are more easy here than anywhere else in *The Broken World*. Think of it as training. Only use the gun if you have to: the noise of it attracks more of them and before you know it you are in a full carnage situation.

At Warehouse get Keys from the cabinet and also Lighter Fluid from the table. Go to the top. You are Ray now. Check the way they do the reflections in the steel doors at each floor—you can see your new face—Ray's face—very cool. When you get to the very top do what you must (?). I cannot explain it better. Then open the Cabinet with a small Key, take out the book that has passage underlined (= clue about Rachel), and return down the stairs.

Check the dead guy lying in a corner by the Exit—could be the Janitor, who knows? Anyhow, check him for the Shotgun, which can replace that other gun you had at the start. Don't worry, there are bigger and better guns to come. After that, head out. Use the big Warehouse Key to unlock the side door and go out down the alley and onto the main road again. Time to leave First Town and don't waste time. You need to find Rachel and it's gonna be hard.

*

It will be snowing on the road out of town. The snow will be falling softly and they do the light very beautiful and soft and gray, and as well as the snow there is mist, a soft mist that means the houses and stuff look like they are hidden in veils.

A cool thing: turn around when you have been walking and you can see your footprints there in the snow on the ground. This is a good way to see where you have been so if you get lost just replace the steps. One day I showed it to Tory and she made me stand there for ages on the road until the snow had covered the footprints. It took nearly 12 minutes, which was really the longest time I ever stood still in *The Broken World*. Tory said this was the most beautiful thing she ever saw in the game. The stillness on the highway that day and the snow and the way the footprints were slowly covered.

Again. I want you to train your eyes and pick up items, notes, diaries, maps and other stuff by yourself. I cannot tell you everything because it is too much. Judge the value of items you want to carry, for there are many items you may need. Be a good judge. Walk out of town. Keep walking.

Second TOWn & BEYOND

HEADS UP: There will be figures in the mist at the side of the road and they will call to you to come with them and be real free and Happy but do not listen to them because that is a false direction. I think they are like Mermaids or Sirens or something. You are Ray now and you have to have good direction.

Once Clockwork was involved with his stepbrother in stealing a car. Cops chased them but they got away. He said it was a real blast. We've been friends since I don't know when (mostly) but I can't say he's a best friend because 1) what would that actually *mean*? And 2) if I said he was a Best Friend it might cause offense with Venter, Brainiac, or Dieter. I guess

The Broken World is a big thing for all of us, except Dieter who doesn't really play tho I try not to hold that against him. Hi, Dieter. And Tory of course I mentioned before, she doesn't play either or care that much about the game.

*

Ray walks through the snow on the lone straight road. After some time (I don't know how long, the time is hard to judge in there) you come to a right turn, which leads to the next (i.e. Second) town. After this things get more difficult.

You find yourself at the crossroads in the town. This is the first dilemma. Which way to go? If you go right it means trouble and suffering. And if you go left it means suffering and trouble. It looks like the only items on the menu are suffering and trouble. For now you just get to choose the sequence—that is all you need to know. You take Ray to the left or right—I am just here to advise. Just walk through the streets and take what *The Broken World* can throw at you. Behind you will hear the sound of gunshots in the night but that's normal by now. And ahead is the future, and Rachel waiting, somewhere, if only you can find her.

The scene in the Mineshaft comes next, I cannot write about it all. I don't understand how or why they make it so dark in there. It's worse than that dark when you're a kid and people say you can see monsters only there it's your uncles teasing you and here it's totally REAL. In the Mineshaft you have to locate Fake Papers (also, I am not sure how they get them in there in the first place). Then comes the car chase in streets of that town. (Second Town has FOUR areas: Red, Blue, Silver, and Gold.) Escape by driving over the most eastern bridge then crash the car and torch it somewhere. Get rid of evidence. You do not want them to find you. (I am talking about GovCorp agents and GARS.)

Try moving Ray slowly sometime; keep a track of where you are. The game gets confusing—they do it deliberate (?) to make it very hard. Pass thru the Funfair with the shootout in the Hall of Mirrors (not the Mirrors of Truth and Mirrors of Untruth that is later). Then at Haunted House some guys (i.e. agents) will check your fake documents and most likely let you thru. After this there are puzzles—the Puzzle of Electrified Fences and the Puzzle of Rune Letters. Also Puzzle of Trees, Puzzle of Choosing Daughters and DNA Sequence Puzzle. All in Puzzle House. I try to update it. Some people get frustrated with the puzzles but even Venter admits in private that Ray is not ALL fighter—he sometimes has to be a thinker too.

Do not be scared in the game. It's like Ray can tell somehow if you are scared and things start to go wrong. Rachel makes an appearance in the Funfair sometimes and she is screaming again but it is not in real life, like I said before, she is just a figment haunting Ray's mind. Rachel screaming—that hits the spot and drives Ray on. I guess you hardly know who RaCHEL is at this point. It's all just starting out, but you will know, you will find out, BroTHEr, she is important. I sometimes think that for Ray and Rachel their world wouldn't work without the other one. They are so connected like those twins so joined onto each other that it takes nine-hour surgeries to separate them, only with Ray and Rachel it is a connection of souls (?) not bodies of course—they are kept apart so much by the cruel Fates and Hardships of *The Broken World*.

Follow clues (from underlined book out of Warehouse) to scene in a parking lot of Second Town. Respect to Brainiac who found the solution for this part = you need the Ring you traded for at the fountain back in First Town. I really hope you got it, Dude, because without it you cannot get thru and that means you have to go back and get it and that means the Golems will be waiting and that means you are in Very Big Shit at this point. SO do what the guide says and keep track of all things. I admit that Tory is making fun of me sometimes coz I am such a hotshot high score at remembering stuff in *The Broken World* but how come I do not always remember that I am supposed to take out the trash for example or that I made an agreement to get groceries or how come I forgot her birthday one time? She was mad and left a note for me, went out with BugMap and Dieter (to the Palace Bar), and did not tell me where they were. I admit it here, right at the start of this walkthrough, that I am not a perfect person. We just do what we can do, bro, like I say to Tory sometimes in my defense; we do what we can with the brain cells we are born with.

After the parking lot cops will try to hunt you down. They are not real cops but GovCorp agents or Thugs working for Chang, and they have Special Powers of Arrest (ha ha). (Again. OK. You do not know who the fuck Chang is right now but you will find out what can be known soon enough and for now please take my word for it that you do not want these guys to catch you.) Chase over roofs of the buildings (nearby) and PLEASE avoid all cracked-glass and broken roofing panels. Also remember to drop down at the end. DROP AND ROLL. What a blast. DROP AND ROLL, brother, just DROP AND FREAKIN ROLL, as Venter likes to say. DROP AND FREAKING ROLL! Venter was asked to leave the Subway sandwich place in Easton because he was yelling that too loud. He has a big mouth sometimes and a lot of noise can come out of it for such a little guy. Lose them cops in the alleys by the Ice Factory. Rent car. Find laser mechanism. Take package to Lawyer and get payment in return. You need the cash. Pick up clues from garbage cans outside Chinese takeouts. Like I said, they make it confusing. Rushing, rushing, rushing, and always the sound of helicopters hovering up above the town (?) and the sound of Time ticking onward thru the game. Things go so fast sometimes I hope you can follow and survive.

Once you are all done with this stuff Ray must get on the road again only this time at night. Head to freeway – the 105 – and do not delay coz those Chang mfkrs will be hot on yr trail.

*

Later. Tired. In a dumb predictable rhythm Tory came home and I went out to work (yes, bro, sadly it is not all sitting on the fat ass and playing computer games—I have other shit to do). Now it is late night and I'm back again. Sun comes up. Sun goes down etc. Outside the sky is dark and you can see the lights of buildings thru the branches of the trees. This walkthrough takes a lot of dedication when it has to be combined with what people call real life. It reminds me how in *The Broken World* Ray must keep track of so many things—missions, enemies, and intelligence—as well as fighting for his life almost 24/7. It's a Tall Order sometimes, bro, but I'm strong enough to take it on.

When I got back after work Tory was sat with Rolo who you can think of as the inevitable and not-that-interesting roommate—human back-ground noise—sorry, Rolo. Or whatever. I guess Rolo will not be reading this walkthrough. Anyhow, Tory and Rolo were parked on the big TV chairs watching *Doors of Power* = "a nine-part miniseries about a president that goes crazy" (*TV Guide*) and "a Los Angeles turkey stuffed with has-been/wannabe actors" (Rolo's version). Rolo had some Grass and he and Tory were a bit high but they both seemed hooked on the show, esp some part where the President was having trouble memorizing a speech. Tory was laughing so much but it didn't seem that funny to me. I think it was the grass making her laugh like that. I am rambling, dudes. I will try to do the good job and get you through *The BW* and before anyone starts to complain. I apologize for this break in the actual walkthrough. Maybe I am like some guy that bothers you on the street—first he wants spare change then he blabs unwanted info on his private problems? Apologies, apologies. Trust me (ha ha), there will be no more interruptions to the service.

*

You are standing by the road (in the game, not a real road). Cars are passing and none are stopping. If you want a LIFT from a driver (yes—you *need* that) you better struggle down the bank in the dark, bro, and find the discarded old baseball cap that is lying in a ditch by the road sign that says EXIT OF SECOND TOWN, POPULATION 2,321. Wear the cap and don't worry if it doesn't look cool and bears an old familiar slogan like THE EXON—this is no time for vanity. Cap covers Ray's long hair and somehow make him look less threatening—better chance of getting a ride. Only you can guide Ray thru *The Broken World* and get him out alive.

Oh yeah. There is a funny thing about that POPULATION sign which I heard from a kid called Jo Bo, on a *BW* Internet discussion board where people post their deep thoughts as well as hints, tips, and cheats for the game. I do not know Jo Bo in real life, but that is not the issue here. I'm getting to the point. Jo Bo said once he went out of Second Town and back in again coz he forgot to get the laser mechanism that I already mentioned about or something—I don't remember. Anyhow, when he was back in there he got jumped by bad asses who tried to rip and hang him from a streetlamp. He got a blaster (an 8-bore—you can get it in the Swamp House) and blew them all away ha ha ha and when he got back out of town the sign then said POPULATION 2,317—because the ones he killed already were mathematically deducted from the total. I never did that; I am only repeating what Jo Bo said. But me and Clockwork were wondering about Ray tho? I mean, what if Ray gets killed—does the population of that town go down (i.e. by one)? I don't know if Ray counts as a population—he is just passing thru but he is still a human being. I don't know.

Anyway, what matters is: A) get the baseball cap (to do the "civilizing the hair" thing) so you can maybe get a ride, and B) hit the road jack and don't u come back no more no more no more no more no more, hit the road jack and don't u come back no more, hit the road jack and don't u come back no more no more no more no more no more, hit the road jack and don't u come back no more no more no more no more, etc. I will stop there—I am not a crazy person.

*

While you stand there by the roadside in the headlights of the oncoming cars with your thumb stuck out there are flies you can count and even raindrops—they do a lot of detail and it helps pass the time. Do not worry tho, the cars will stop once you have the cap. Choose a good ride and get out of there. Do not get a lift with Red Trucker (in red truck) or in Family Holiday Wagon (you tell it from all the kids in the back) or Gay Trucker (unless you think Ray likes that kind of thing, I mean it does not seem like a very gay game. But then I admit I was wrong about that before – for example: Ashton. More about him later, I guess). Anyway. There are plenty of good rides—try Francis (an importer and exporter of goods = boring but he will not hurt you) in a black BMW, or try Sharlyne in blue-color Ford Focus (sales and marketing). She is going a long way and lonely. Fuck, there are probably 1,000 other rides also possible—I didn't go in every freakin car. There is too much else to do, like killing bad guys and avoiding different kinds of disaster and saving the world. I will update this part of the walkthrough with good information and clues. Meantime, just use your *judgment* and *intuitions*, I cannot stress that enough and I cannot be around to tie all your shoelaces. I am talking to you, GoblinHead and Jose30—I cannot answer your emails with tiny questions abt this stuff at all times of day or night just because you are in a hurry or stuck on some aspects.

*

When you do hitch a ride and finally get to Third Town then you have some major acts of retrieval to perpetrate. (That way of describing it comes from Sleeptalk. Respect to Sleeptalk. He may be more goth than is healthy but he knows his way around in *The Broken World*.) At Third Town just take stock using a Map then get to work. Town has 4 ammunition dumps or stores/supply areas (i.e. 1. supermarket, 2. mosque, 3. gun club, 4. liquor store) plus a place for food and other type supplies (Mega Mart)—all marked on the Map. In Southeast Corner there is a bar—i.e. good place to pick up gossip and news. There also you find a Shrine to the local River God where you can make a sacrifice or say prayers to bring good luck—some players think it really helps to succeed.

A cop car just went by outside. Very fast and all lights flashing. Sometimes I try to think that Ray is out there (out in the neighborhood), shooting and running—what would people do?

And another thing I think sometimes: What would happen to me in *The Broken World*? Would I have the strength to survive? I do not know. One thing I noticed is that one guy in the background near the start of Third Town looks a lot like Brainiac's brother. Paul is his name. Tory once had this thing with him but it ended when he moved away. Sometime later she and me got together. I do not mean to say personal stuff. I apologize. SOmetimes I see Brainiac and I say stuff to him up like, Hey, I saw your no-good brother Paul looking blurred in the distance of that car chase or something, and Brainiac just looks confused.

I am starting to ramble again which is a sure sign that I am tired, bro. Also, PLEASE REMEMBER that in *The Broken World* Ray needs rest sometimes. Otherwise he gets slower in fights and problem-solving and can even die of it, tho I only heard that once—from some cousin of Tory's who kept Ray walking for weeks coz he (the cousin) was a no-good speedfreak. NB: 1) If you can rest in a dark place you recharge much faster, 2) Try to rest with the shotgun still there in your hand—I guess I don't need to explain why. You can leave Ray resting an hour or more but NB again: If you leave him much longer he might get sick (like those guys who stay in bed all day. Yes, Brainiac, I am talking to you. That shit is bad for you).

When Ray is resting you can do other stuff (i.e. you in the real world not you in the game of course). That is OK. But do not go out of the apartment, or too far from the computer. In this situation you can think of Ray as a baby over which you have soul responsibility. I.e.: YES you can go make coffee and eat foodstuffs or call friends or watch TV (etc) but keep an ear out for the sleeping and/or precious one, even if in this case he is a big motherfucker with a gun in his hands. It is common sense—DO NOT think Ray will be OK if you go out to some party or like leave him for half a day. Ray needs you there concentrating 100%— acting like an adult with Duties, which is exactly what they told Clockwork's sister when she had a kid and was acting like a fool. Please. DO NOT LET RAY DOWN.

THIrd TOwn Lucky

On the streets of Third Town beware of birds that flock to attack. Also
Hydraworms (?) and VIGILANTE groups that are basically mobs of
redneck motherfuckers looking for somewhere or someone to vent
their grievances using a crowbar or a baseball bat, I think you know
what I mean. If you hear these guys coming or see them it's best for
Ray to hide (try doorways, porches, underneath or in a trunk of a car,
in the shade of a church, or in the parking lot of a grocery store). There
is no shame in hiding, bro. And note: Don't bother killing Rednecks
unless it is strictly demanded—they are not worth much in points and
can do Body Damage as well as losing you out on the all-important-level
time Bonus.

The going will get tough from this point. Next stop after picking up ammo and supplies should be Lumberyard where you can trade up for a Sword. Then GO to Magic Shop and purchase Snake Illusion. Bro, if you have no money you must steal it coz you NEED the Snake Illusion. After this go to Schoolyard (West District). Use Sword (from Lumberyard) to open gate. There are kids there at Schoolyard—1) fool them with that Snake Illusion, and 2) continue. If only real life were that simple—kids are supposed to guard that playground but get totally distracted by the rhythmic swaying of a fake plastic and multicolored snake. Easy.

On the ground at the western edge of the playground you find a complicated puzzle written in chalk – numbers, math, and letter substitution. (This is really something for Clockwork—I think I only got past it by a fluke, I don't know what I was doing.) Write down or remember the solution—you WILL need it later. And again watch out for Rednecks—those baseball bats are not made of rubber.

Your main destination in Third Town is the Shopping Mall (go east, thru park (?) and housing projects) and remember this visit is not because you are going to get all stocked up on knitted ties or gift-wrapped fancy bathroom goods. Ha ha. What do you think the fucking HUGE amount of ammo that you collected before was all about? For a handguns amnesty? No. It is for killing.

NOTE: One other thing. If you try to carry all the interesting items you find around the place you will quickly run out of space and get totally loaded down by the sheer freakin amount of it. Ray can look insane carrying five or six suitcases of "useful stuff" like some psychovagrant that you see sometimes on Delgado or Bryce complete with Shopping Cart of Life. Also, you don't have to be a genius of combat-training camp to imagine how well Ray can fight the bad guys when he is loaded up like a homeless donkey. You do not want it. You do not want it. One good solution I have found is to store spare items in dressers of the Inn rooms you stay at. Still can't believe that all the times I did that no one ever messed with my stuff—not even if it was months later when I came back and needed to pick up my Lock Pick equipment or Vibrogun or whatever. I did lose some stuff when the Hotel Ricardo burned down in some battle in Eighth Town but that is a different situation. Did they make it like that on purpose? I mean, it is pretty weird that in *The BW*—full of thieves, robbers and murderers—somehow those cabinets in the Inns are totally safe. Is it a mistake? Some people say there are no mistakes in the game—that everything is planned. I do not know. You can also leave stuff in lockers at the Train Stations in 39th Town but for that (just like the real world) you would need to buy a token from that man in the Booth.

*

Right now I am sitting at the computer. If you can imagine an Ikea table with a old computer and the table covered in music CDs and data CDs, coffee cups, soda bottles, etc, then you have imagined the scene. A big mess is how some people would describe it, I guess (Hi, Tory), and I admit that I am not such a high score in tidiness. Also, imagine a kind of bulletin board on the wall behind the desk that has one picture of Mom and Dad at River Basin and another of Tory and her sisters. Hi, Linda, hi, Shay, I guess you will not be reading this walkthrough either. Then the scene is complete except the sound of the TV plus now some girl goes jogging by outside on the sidewalk in the jogger's uniform of pulled-back hair, shorts, T-shirt, headphones, and not a glance at the world.

Apologies. This is all getting a bit random and I should NOT be talking random stuff right now—I mean, I set myself a task of getting to an end of the next part of the game before now and it did not go well because too much trouble arrived. Trouble 1 was at work—yes, I have to do some as I already mentioned. Yawn. It is enough to say that my "job" involves putting circular cooked items in square cardboard boxes and then giving most of them to an asshole (yes, Stentson, I am talking about you) dressed mainly in black leather from head to foot and some kind of full-face helmet. Welcome to DOMENICO'S—if you are over in the neighborhood please do everyone a favor and be totally sure to avoid it—there are more pleasant places to eat nearby that do not carry a bad risk of food poison. Domenico's was trouble 1 coz the oven was not working properly—"IRREGULAR HEAT" was a note pinned to it from yesterday's nightshift (thanks for that info, you guys, it was REAL helpful and such good preparation for how it turned all cooked circular food into an impersonation of a napalm attack). Motherfucker. I would like to get out of the cooked circular food business and no mistake. And the way that "BOSS Number 1" (Miroslav) and his dumbass brother "BOSS Number 2" (Branimir) looked at me today when they saw all those burned circular dinners I could get my wish pretty soon. Trouble 2 came from Tory who was in some kind of all-purpose bad mood and grunting round the apartment "moving Rol's crap out of the way" and "moving my crap out of the way" and looking at me with Eyes of Evil Intent that she said was not that at all and would I please not be so on edge around her these days. I do not get it. Trouble 3 was some total loser drunk guy coming in to Domenico's and hassling people for free cooked circular food making a claim that last week we gave him a wrong topping. "Wrong topping," he kept saying, like that was going to argue his case. Ashton thought this guy was hilarious. Feels like suddenly I am trouble central for the whole area. Even Tory's parents were getting in on the act (to make my life more difficult) when her dad Joe phoned up with "a little Question." Oh man, he likes to do that a lot and it can mean LOTS of extended distraction, like they think I'm in some kind of contest. The topics vary but this afternoon Joe called to say they have some problem with the garden thing, the hedge strimmer or trimmer (I don't even know if there is a difference) and asked if maybe *I* know how to fix it? What the fuck? Help me, bro. Do they really think I have a collection of manuals and crap in the house for the maintenance of terminally outdated garden equipment? What kind of a place do they think we have here on the East Side? We do not even have a yard, and esp not even a garden, or even a box on the ledge outside a window. Do I know how the strimmer/trimmer might be wired? And what voltage does its alternator require? Man. The questions they come up with. They are crazy out there in the suburbs. Crazy crazy crazy—and plz don't forget: You read it HERE first.

Apologies. I'm getting distracted. We did not come here to chatter. We came here for the TSZ.

*

So. When you and your kickass burden of guns, knives, and ammo finally get there to the Mall in Third Town it is called the Total Shopping Zone. I guess they should have just called it a Total SHOOTING Zone. TSZ. That place is a BLOODBATH and no mistake, because it's crammed full of Zombies and yr task is to clear the area by any means possible. Bring it on. Load up. Take off the Safety and Go To Work, baby. We got Zombies to kill. Brainiac say this part of the game makes *Montezuma: Aztec Sunset* look like a kind of Barbie theme picnic. Anyhow, Tory will not even watch anyone play thru TSZ. She says it makes her feel sick to her stomach and sad for all those Zombies getting slayed. Last time I went thru it she sat at the window ledge, looked away and waited, drank a beer til the noise of it ended. The violence is totally justified by the fact that Zombies are taking over the town. You cannot negotiate with Zombies. Everyone knows that.

Some good advice before the carnage starts is to *take the high ground*. There is a glass elevator like a Cinderella carriage in the center of the Mall, which goes right to the top. Use Number Key for the elevator—code is the numbers from the puzzle in the Schoolyard. See how stuff from one part helps you later, bro? That is how it goes all thru the game. Anyhow. *Take the high ground. Take the high ground.* The Mall is in the form of a cross. Watch out for Security Guards (west-pointing arm of the Cross) and watch out for Riot Cops and Lethargists (I don't know the right word for these guys but they are Bad News). There are Bonus points for the blind couples (2) and the Girl Guides (I counted 12 but could be more, they are so small and hard to keep track of), the Krishnas (24— likewise could be more and anyway all the same), the tourists (14? You can tell them by digital cameras) and Double Bonus for the guy that crawls away the whole time whimpering and trying to save his own life (mostly Zombies in any case). Spare no MERCY. Shoot, shoot, shoot.

*

The Mall has a big outdoors/equipment store for extra supplies and Grocery Hall of Dept Store for foodstuffs, tins, bottles etc plus a good gun store for even more weapons (remember: you can never have too many weapons, bro). (I guess I will try to make a map of the whole Mall later in a Maps section that I plan to do sometime i.e. WHEN I get round to it. Please do not mail me and ask, Hey, dude, where are the Maps? There are not enough seconds in a minute, minutes in an hour, hours in day, days in a week, weeks in a month, months in a year, etc, as Tory's dad used to say before that heart attack kind of slowed him down.)

Some ppl are complaining that there's not enough fighting back in the TSZ—that it's too much just like a slaughterhouse. Whatever. The most important thing is that afterward, when you walk the floors there, there's a strange feeling of calm with the blood dripping and the noise of the fountain. THAT IS a kind of peace you should take time to enjoy. Ray moves slow and tired past the wind chimes that stir in the draft of the air con. Maybe it's true what Venter says—you have to know that feeling, that PEACE, just to know Ray and understand the game.

Note: people on assorted *BW* blogs and discussion boards (Grinning Cat for example and also Yoko898) claim to have completed *The BW* without the big slaughter in the TSZ or anywhere else (i.e. Battle of Arandale, Bickers Field, etc) that is very well known for being superviolent. Grinning Cat wrote about having a dream one day to find a total pacifist solution to *The BW*, i.e. a way thru it all without any show of violence—but even she admits it is a loooong way to go before THAT is gonna happen. Here's the deal. I guess OK, if she says so, she has got thru the TSZ without creating a bloodbath etc. OK. OK. Maybe that is possible. You can certainly try this. But listen up to what is true. ANY PERSON RAY DOES NOT KILL HERE WILL COME BACK 200 TIMES STRONGER IN THE NEXT TOWN AND WILL BE HELL-BENT WITH DARK HEART AND MURDER IN THEIR EYES TO TAKE RAY OUT OF ACTION FOREVER. It is not a pretty way to go if the Zombies get Ray, believe me, because I tried and Ray was pulled to something that looked like McChicken pieces (?) and eaten alive. "You do not want it," as Clockwork and me like to say. "You do not want it." "You do not want it." Or another good advisory: *Kill now to survive later.*

*

It is later again. That real world (remember it?) keeps getting in the way. I was writing for a while then Tory came in to depict in great detail some confusion about her gym membership, a message from the janitor of the building concerning what he calls Trash in the hallway (wtf are people supposed to do with BIKES?) and some plans she made to get drinks at Palace (probably) or No Slime with Dieter on Friday. No Slime is a new bar I've not been to sounds kind of stupid with that name but Tory gets bored of the way we mostly go to just Palace, Palace, Palace.

I tried to make a joke about her parents when they called before and the whole trimmer/strimmer questions, but Tory just looked at me blankly and made a sound that's like a sigh but she said it was just breathing. She soon left the room and was later reading quietly (a magazine) which I guess meant she was feeling OK.

*

I am back on topic. On the third level of the Mall in north-pointing arm of the Cross, there's some kind of security room or guardroom or whatever. In there are some things you may need i.e. swipe card and walkie-talkies. Also take the Polaroid camera (I cannot explain now. Just trying to help).

When you've got everything just take a second to look at the security monitors. You will see the TSZ all quiet, with the slicks of blood and the debris. They do the flicker of the screens real good. If you stare at the monitors long enough you will soon see other things too—i.e. Glimpses of the Future and Glimpses of the Past. Look and be patient—then you will see. Like Clockwork says—it's only a Glimpse of the Future or Past, but that's more than most people get. You might see a glimpse of Rachel in a subway station (past) or on a stony beach, hair wet and looking scared (future). *Good Luck, Ray. Good Luck.* At least I think that's what she says—the words are way too quiet. Just glimpses, but take what you can. Take what you can. (= a quote from Spider, the main roadie with Centurion, but he was talking in an interview about drugs. Still relevant here in the spirit of what he was saying at least.)

I think it gives Ray strength and Inner Hope to see these pictures of Rachel, just like some guys with a picture of their kid(s) or girl on a computer desktop. Brainiac had his girl for a desktop too once, but the picture he used was not really good enough quality so her skin went all kind of laminated, with weird scales from the pixels. I think that's how she got that nickname she didn't like so much at all, and why she left Brainiac for some other guy. Pixels was nice—she had a good smile. No one sees her anymore, especially not Brainiac. I miss her sometimes, the way she used to laugh. I guess he misses her too.

Ray slows down in the Security Room. Take your time there. It's a welcome relief after all that fighting and speed and you soon see the health readout come rising up again.

*

I'm thinking about ways we have to go fast and slow in our lives. That sometimes SPEED is really needed—to think QUICK and ACT NOW. Other times you need the slow and considered pace of things—for changes that come over months, years, or longer. With Ray it's the same. Yes. I mean yes, he has the SPEED and the energy like Venter— that is a good thing. But he has to find his own different method and rhythym (I cannot spell it) in The Broken World—more subtly and slowly, like finding the way across a darkened room you've never been in before.

Venter said it took his mom three years to decide to leave. Then she just packed a bag 1 nite and left. It was a combination of slow and speed. I try to think how these things play out on the keyboard—what keys you hit for different things, different speeds or energies. It would be like:

A = speed. Where speed is the essential item.

B = slowness and more delicacy. Where slow move or CONTEMPLATION is needed.

And then a combination move: *B* then + *A*, which is A with the Special Key pressed at the same time = slowness *then* immediate speed. Like Venter's mom, the thinking and the sudden leaving.

I'm also thinking about the other (reversed) combination: *A* then +*B*, which would be speed *then* slowness. I don't really know what occasion you would use that in. I'm no expert, but I think maybe that's the key combination for regret. Something you do fast and then u have 4ever to think about it. Don't worry. I'm not going to get all philosophical here. Maybe A then + B is the key combination for Ray when he walks thru the Zombie corpses at the end of the killing in the dead fluorescent light of the TSZ leaving footprints in the blood only there is no falling snow in here to erase it away. Or it could be the key combination for how me and Tory first got together. On a rooftop at a party in Baslake. Speed and then slowness. That's how we were then, I guess. Or maybe it's just another combination for describing what went on with Venter's mom, only here it's different—more like *fast leaving* and then *slow regretting* even now. He had a postcard from the valley once but it had no writing on it. Thought it might be from her.

*

Listen up. After the TSZ comes more in Third Town. I think the notes I wrote about it are in some blue notebook that I left at BugMap's place

(?) or maybe in another notebook that is possibly lost. Fuck. Goddamn it to Hell. Now I'll have to skip some things. I've looked everywhere for the notebook. I remember the cover and have a definite picture of it sitting on a table kind of half under some magazines. Sometimes my good work just gets wasted—like the time Sleeptalk lost my Map of Exits from the subway in 17th Town or when Tory's parents went to New Haven but lost their train tickets.

After all the action in the town is complete it's good for Ray to rest. Just think SAFETY and find somewhere near. Plz be careful. There are bad guys everywhere and like Dieter says sometimes when he puts on his EVIL Voice: "It is MAINLY by other people's mistakes that we prosper." Dieter has such a good Evil Voice and used it well in those prank phone calls he got kind of notorious for making last summer—so watch out. He loves to mess with people. I will try to tell about those crank phone calls another time but there is too much to write now about *The Broken World*. No time for it all.

There's silence when Ray sleeps. Peace, peace, uneasy peace— that's a proverb from where my family came from, like way back. But uneasy peace is the best you can hope for in that Broken World where I seem to spend so much freakin time according to Tory. Hi, Tory, again. I guess she's sleeping now. I think she went to bed.

When Ray sleeps you can also take some rest. Take a look out the window, i.e. the real one in the room where you are when you are playing and/or reading this, not the room or whatever where Ray is resting. Look and Listen. Bro – if you do not see anything interesting then maybe you don't know how to look. Everything is a clue. I mean EVERYTHING. If you cannot understand that you will certainly be dead before the game can get to an end.

FINDING RACHEL / LOSING Rachel

Well after midnight. Some tips while I can still keep eyes focused to write. Please pay attention. Track of blood can lead you to those you have to slay. Noise of squeaky floorboard (in room above) can warn you of Ninja's approach. If cobwebs at Beer Shack are broken come back another day. This is random again so I apologize. It is just stuff on my mind.

Also. There is a good defense called Slow Time. Venter told me about it. Thanks, Venter. I mean, he is more for the Slash Attack but he knew I would like this. Slow Time makes all the rest of *The Broken World* go slow and you stay fast. Kill enemies while they step in across the room like sleepwalkers. When they fire at you it is funny coz the bullets come

so slow you can nearly dance with them as you move out the way.
Beautiful. Beaut-E-Full. Like they say.

*

I got interrupted from a call by Branimir (of Domenico's fame) in a long
supposed conversation about what shifts I'm doing at the big D and can
I swap with Ashton on Tuesday and "further than that" if I can trade an
evening next week(s) for a morning coz Cookie who mainly works the
day shift cannot be there because of a gynecological appointment. (Too
much information. I don't know where she's going for her excuses to
take time off but this starts to sound desperate.) Yeah. Hear me—
Branimir is a great guy and knows it's totally cool to call his low-pay
workers anytime, day or nite, he has a scheduling problem on his mind.
I mean sure, why not. I call him at home after midnight all the time.
Jesus. Anyhow. It's NOT an enthusiastic thing for me but I'm agreeing
to all his extra shift requests because 1) I need the money and 2) if I do
some good things maybe it can help cancel the inevitable offenses I'll
cause in the future at Domenico's by having a sense of humor and not
respecting the cooked circular food as a way of life. Man, the REAL
trouble with the phone call is that even agreeing with Branimir can be a
hard enough job esp at this time of nite coz he is completely unclear
and circular in his statements (kind of like the food) and because in the
background Miroslav is providing a constant bad-tempered, half-drunk
chorus, grunting alternative suggestions and ideas apparently
at random. For example: NO TUESDAY or NO—TUESDAY or
MOUTHFUCKER WEDNESDAY. MOUTHFUCKER WEDNESDAY. He means
MOTHERFUCKER but you get the idea, I guess.

*

No time to waste, bro. For you (i.e. Ray) the NEXT OBJECTIVE = Fourth Town and now really FIND Rachel because Chang is closing in and time is running out. It sounds easy just written like that, but really IT IS hard and if those guys get you at this point it is GAME OVER.

Possible routes into Fourth Town: 1) Blocked Highway, 2) Forest Path, 3) Dry Riverbed. Watch out for Vagrants, Survivalists, Con Men and Scorpions. Remember to collect the Screwdriver Gadget from some dude's Log Cabin. Also, the Enchantment Potion can be collected on the edge of the town in a Motel Room—like I mentioned, a favorite part of mine—including the puzzle of Magical Knives.

Once in town you have many possible directions and none of them too obvious. Use your nose (intuitions) and explore. Fourth Town feels like an old-fashioned idea of what's modern—packed but clean. Weird. If you get stuck try the Shadow Neighborhood (east of the River) for clues and orientation. Shadows are friendly, so long as you don't move too fast, but I don't get the back story with them—freaky see-thru dudes that seem to shape-shift. I mean, if they are shadows, where are the people they belong to? I asked Clockwork how they even make those Shadows and he just went off on a long unstoppable rant concerning optical vectors and ray-tracing diffusion filters (?). We were in the Starbucks on 9th Street and I did a good job of faking it that I understood what he was talking about. If you get CW talking like this he gets excited like never for anything else—you can see it in his eyes like he's gonna melt down. For Venter it would be the same amount of enthusiasm he gets for jumping off the Big Bridge in summer. He loves that rush. For Sleeptalk it would be Skeleton at High Volume. And for me, I don't know. But CW, his head is a science class. He loves to talk about the workings of things.

Measurements, codes, numbers. Like the pyramids. He can tell you how high they are and how far it is to the moon and how many times in a minute a cricket's legs are really moving.

They make Rachel hard to find, but bro, get used to that. If things get tight use the subway to beat the time limits. Subway has six routes and only three stations have Bonus health points. I don't know why.

As you go across town, ignore the Ghouls coz they're the lost souls of dead people and will not hurt you. But if the Demons come (in the form of Kids) smash those motherfuckers with the rifle butt til they drop then keep on smashing til they do not get up anymore. NOTE: bullets do not work on these two-legged freaks so do not be afraid of some hard labor. Heh heh. You can probably imagine the conversation round here sometimes—Sleeptalk and Venter on the PC and someone calls to say what's happening and they just laugh, "Oh you know. Smashing freaky kids up with the rifle butt again. That's all." No wonder some people think Sleeptalk and Venter are Disturbed and should get some Help.

The place you're looking for is a neighborhood Gas Station but on arrival things are typically complicated i.e. *Broken World* style. Check it out—hoodlums are holding up the Gas Station and Rachel is their prize hostage along with the idiot semi-retard guy that works at the counter, the manager (who is just about to retire, it's her last Shift) and a classic random fat guy/customer. Shit. With GARS to fight and a vicious crackdown by GovCorp agents etc what you really need is two armed petty thieves probably looking for Crack Money. What next? Ray has to sort out a wave of pickpockets or an invasion of evil DVD pirates? Even worse news is that the cops have TOTALLY surrounded the place and (yes) the cops are very (i.e. 1000%) likely to be in pay of GARS. So—you do not want Rachel in there as a hostage and you really do not want her "rescued" by cops. Welcome to *The Broken World*.

There are several solutions to this part of the game. One involves crashing a tank in there from the front, snatching Rachel and driving right out thru the back. That is Venter's favored way. I guess anything where you can drive a M1A1 Abrams tank fitted with a 120mm M256 gun down a four-lane freeway full of commuters and blast at anything that gets in your way is fine by Venter anytime.

I prefer a different route. By one of those lucky coincidences of the game there is a microlite hidden in a Storage Unit not far away. See Map (later). HINT: The Gas Station roof is an OK place to land if you have skills, good judgment, and are lucky with the winds. If you are quick enough neither cops nor dumbass crooks will know WHAT THE FUCK HAS HIT THEM. It is so cool. When Ray bursts in thru the polystyrene (?) ceiling tiles the classic random fat guy/customer looks like he will be needing extra Prozac for the rest of his natural.

*

Rachel looks good when you rescue her. I guess she always looks good. There's nothing wrong with the kind of all-in-one motorcycle leathers/ catsuit thing that she wears in this part of the game. Nothing wrong at all. And long-haired brunettes are also hard to beat. Yay. Apologies to Tory. Rachel is not real so I guess there is no grounding for jealousy if I say that she is HOT.

Now here is the bad news. Rachel has somehow lost her Memories. As Ray approaches she is suspicious and hardly recognizes anything at all. *Who are you?* she says when you try to take her to the Microlite. You have to teach her all about the past and especially the part about you (Ray) and her and what happened before (I mean WAY before in the story that happens before the story). Rachel is in fact Ray's girl if you did not figure that out already (or he is her guy. I know, yes) as well as the fact they are like a Team in the fight against Chang, GovCorp, GARS, and the Archduke.

*

Tory drifted thru looking beat and stared at me a long time while I sat here at the screen. I guess she's trying to tell me something. It's two in the morning. When I got off the phone to Branimir's-After-Midnight-Shifts-Hotline she called her sister (Linda) who just got back from traveling (Asia maybe—I didn't follow closely). They were talking all this time with the door shut. It's hard to say on what topics. I just heard the shape of it—some laughing, some arguing—pretty typical sister stuff. Fuck. There's too much to do and not enough Time in the day.

*

It's strange all the pieces and FACTS that make up a life. All the evidence, stories, and threads that build a picture. Lines of code. Ray has to tread Rachel back thru it all, bit by bit and memory, collecting clues and info, like a 10,000-part jigsaw that must be assembled by Ray, the pieces scattered in First, Second, and Third Towns. But you need to get back on the road.

Rachel is a suffering traveler, like a stranger in her own EYES. To me it's not clear why she lost her Memories but by the look on her face it was probably a bad experience in the Brainwashing Department at GovCorp or GARS. You can see Ray watching her with the Look of Love as she leafs thru the photo albums he has to collect (hidden in attic— old house, Third Town—you need Key from somewhere but I cannot remember where). His heart is beating all the time.

The hardest part is in a Motel (back again in Fourth Town) when all clues are assembled in a sequence and you have to convince Rachel about love. While you are talking she will move away from you and lie on the bed and cry, and then she will turn her face to the wall. Ask her what is wrong. Ask her to believe. Look in her eyes. You can see flecks of green in the brown pixels. Who would not fall for pixels mixed like that?

This is a sentimental part but I think it works well. Some guys (hi Venter) say that it sucks major ass and please pass the Weapons Manual but I don't agree. *The Broken World* has different levels and complexities, which is a good thing. Also NOTE: If you did not kill the Zombies in the TSZ then HERE is where they will all come back—rushing into the bedroom and causing all kinds of Mayhem. You Do Not Want It. So plz kill the Zombies when u are back there at the Mall.

Rachel will listen while you talk and ask questions and then she will reply but it's inaudible. I've turned the speaker up many times, but I can't hear what she says when she cries so much—it hurts to hear it, she is so confused. While she cries you should lie beside her and stare at the ceiling—watch the headlights that spin on the wall. Try to count headlights and see the pattern. It can be cracked with the pattern. Yellow light and the cast shadows of objects outside. When you know the pattern wait for an interval of darkness and then stand. Fate will favor the one who is patient and strong. (That line is from Sleeptalk. True, bro. True.)

Tell Rachel that you're going out for ten minutes and that you'll understand if she's not there when you get back. Say you will love her anyway and anyhow. No matter what.

Even if this part IS sentimental it still punches straight in the heart and I always remember the time that me and Tory had an argument in an Asian noodle place and were both crying but couldn't talk. It's not easy to admit but these scenes are what happen in my life. That is my experience and I have to express it to you here. I'm gonna stop now (immediately) before it gets embarrassing. The game must go on.

Tell Rachel that you are going out for ten minutes—like I said—and that you will understand if she's gone when you get back. Say you will love her anyway. No matter what the hand of fate will reveal.

*

Morning. Tory just came and stood in the doorway of the bedroom like a replay of last night, only this time in her sweatpants and an old T-shirt coz she was probably doing situps in front of the TV. She has the phone in one hand and is mouthing the words SORRY, SORRY SORRY. Fuck, fuck—her parents again. Like I'm advertised as a technical helpline for Parental Units. This time it's NOT the strimmer/trimmer question, but a not-so-quick quiz on the topic of water filtration, i.e. Tory's dad asking Do I know how they can check that the water filtration *is actually filtrating* (is that right word?). I don't know why they think I can help with that particular question and (maybe worse) I cannot even understand why they might be thinking about it in the first place. Maybe Joe is forgetting to take his medication? I don't know. I'm afraid to think about it anymore. In any case—they are going crazy out there in the suburbs. Remember, you read it here for the second time, bro, and this time it's serious.

Tory asked again if we should fix Palace or No Slime for the drinks with Dieter but I just said I thought we'd decided already and she walked off because I think she remembered she left the water running in the shower. Her latest temp gig is in some big law firm office and she says she can't discuss the cases and stuff she learns about in the photocopy room or what she overheard in the elevator, which must explain why she's quiet. It's not big Crimes these guys are discussing anyhow, just evasion of traffic offenses and Injury at Work.

*

Outside the chalet (of Motel, where you are in the game) you will see someone running away. The bad man runs and you have to follow. It's probably an agent working for Chang (or Cheng? I don't know) or some guy from GovCorp. But anyhow, as you go round a corner the DUDE is waiting for you with those kung-fu things—the sticks and chain—please can someone tell me what these ARE? I always forget and I want to call them Nuggets, but I know that's not the right name. Anyway, the DUDE smacks you on the head with the kung-fu things and Ray goes down. Darkness spins and spins like the beginning of time. You lose control of the game and are Powerless.

You see Ray getting bundled into the back of a truck all wrapped in chains and strips of duct tape on the mouth. Clockwork said he feels sick at this point of the game. Sicker than whatever. It's bad enough that Ray is captured like a wild animal, taken off to a cage of who knows where and what. But worst of all is that Rachel will lie on the bed and maybe she'll wait for him and be ready to say yes, yes, I believe in love, in what happened, I BELIEVE in love, and wrap her arms warm around Ray. But of course it cannot be. Ray is captured and cannot come back and Rachel will wait there alone for DAYS and then decide that Ray has betrayed and abandoned her etc.

Maybe they'll both Go To Their Graves with this feeling, never see each other again . . . if you cannot succeed in the game. That is what is so harsh. I don't know why it has to be that way but I didn't write the game. I'm just the one that played it and now it's my unfortunate job to break the bad news to you. Ray captured and tied up alone. Rachel left in the Motel and thinking he doesn't care. You can get out of this mess but you will have to SWEAT IT, bro, I swear to God you will have to Truly Sweat.

Ways to GO

There are so many ways to buy it (i.e. DIE) in *The Broken World*, it's hard to recount them all. I mean there are the obvious ones, dude—run out of LIFE points, get shot in a Blaster, step on a Mine, fall into a Mineshaft, get caught in the explosion of a portable nuke, get shot in the back, drink poison, be lacerated and stabbed to death, get pushed off a building, miscalculate a jump between swinging bridges, answer questions wrong in Quiz of Death, get staked out in front of an ants' nest or left in the burning sun, get shoved in front of a speeding Bullet Train, etc. But there are some not so very obvious 1s too like in one part you can get a Shivering Sickness from the Jungle of the Amazon, or parasitic organisms can make a host of Ray's (i.e. YOUR) body in Ninth Town (?)

or you die of love (I am not joking. It can go that way with Rachel if you don't fix things up good with her). You can also be executed by Government Law, lynched for being in the wrong place at the wrong time, given a Lethal Injection in Texas. Ray (i.e. YOU) can get smashed in a car crash, dissolved in acids, or get a plague from Out of Space. He can also get Uranium Sickness, Chemical Sickness, and Fever from an infected werewolf bite. He can breathe in Chemicals or the Mystery Fog. Or get poisoned by Archduke or by Rialto or by someone else. Or shot by agents of GARS. Or executed by a guy called Fulton or Transmission or by a guy whose name you didn't catch in a Boiler House or a Canning Factory or in an Amusement Arcade. Or get smothered in sleep by the gorgeous and untrustworthy Natalie, Sophia, or Juliette. There are so many ways to watch that red bar of life get smaller and smaller and smaller in the left-hand side of the screen and at a certain point to know that it will not get better, that you will not make it to the next health pickup point, that there are no Potions in Ray's bag that can cure it this time, that there is no Doctor of Medicine to help things out. There are so many ways to buy it in *The Broken World*.

And there are worse fates than those deaths. If things go that way, you can get caught in a Internment Camp for example and there you can get interrogated half to death for months and months until you do not even know what Ray's name is anymore or until Ray does not know his own name anymore or until Ray thinks he knows your fucking name which would be totally impossible. Or you can be forced to take witness protection and live yr whole life in the game undercover in a faraway town from that point on—no more fighting, no more missions, no more adventures. Just a stranger's face looking back at you (Ray) from the mirror, and a life you hardly understand in suburbia, your hands feeling so wrong on the Garden Cutters or the Lawnmower handles when they are more used to holding a gun. It can go like that too or Ray can get sidetracked/lose sense of his missions and end up fat and listless, sitting in some bumfuck place watching reruns on the TV and wondering what became of his life. Or he can get addicted to some drug or another (there are lots to choose from in *The BW*), and end his days on a filthy mattress, and nights stealing items to sell for money to buy more of that drug. Like your whole life going down a drain.

And things can get worse still, believe. One time I was playing the first level—some place in Third Town there was a bar fight that was not even part of the main action and things got out of control. Strange the way even the smallest thing can drag the whole game in a unexpected direction. It's so big like that, and unpredictable. Ray got sprayed in the face by some guys (using Mace but not actually Mace). It was OK afterward for a while and then Ray was driving south on a freeway (near the place where he sometimes meets a Soothsayer) and then the screen started to go black. I had to pull the vehicle over on to the hard shoulder and within a minute or two the whole screen was utterly dark and Ray was blind. I don't know how to get out of that one. I was panicking. At first I thought it was a monitor error but it wasn't. If anyone knows any clue please tell me. I managed to get Ray to kick open the door of the car, but still couldn't see a thing. Brainiac and Clockwork were laughing at me. Ray was stumbling around on the hard shoulder (I guess—I mean—I don't KNOW what was happening because you can't see a fucking thing, right). I was blundering and then there were some voices from behind saying, HEY, BLIND GUY (very funny. They put some real intelligent punks in *The BW*), and HEY, LOOK AT THIS HEADLESS CHICKEN (like I said before) and laughing. And then they pushed Ray (I think) and pushed him in the road (I think) and then there was a noise like screaming of brakes and a thud that sounds like when you drop something heavy off a bridge and maybe Ray got hit by a big truck and then it said the words you don't want to hear—GAME OVER. That is for sure a bad way to go. Like you get to die but don't even get to even fucking see it. I was in a bad mood after that for a week and didn't feel too good. Tory said I was hard to tolerate then I had to apologize. Ray dead and fucking blinded.

Venter met some guy on *The BW* discussion boards who said he had been blinded like that too in the game. Only this guy kept Ray alive that way for several months—all blind and stumbling around with only the sound to guide him. That's extreme behavior if you ask me—I mean, why not go back and start the game again? People need to recognize that some situations are like Lose–Lose. The guy said blind Ray even made a couple of friends in there who were helping him, leading him around and explaining things to him and stuff and how he was living in a squat somewhere near the Airport, trying to learn Braille, but then the "friends" changed personality (that's what the guy said) and ripped him off, beat him and left him for dead. I don't even like to think about that. Would it be possible to survive in there and even complete the whole *BW* as blind Ray? Maybe. But who can tell? I think if he gets blinded with the Mace that is not Mace it's probably better that he dies right away there on the hard shoulder. Why should he stumble through life totally blind, getting ripped off and abused and then die anyway with just a dose of extra suffering between? I mean—The Purpose Of Life Is To Maximize The Relaxation. Tory had a T-shirt that said that once but she didn't wear it too often.

*

Tonight after I was all done at Domenico's I went out to Tory's parents on the bike to take a look at the strimmer/trimmer. I know—I'm a sucker and this will only encourage them. But what can you do? Joe said that after giving it some mental attentions he didn't recall if the strimmer/trimmer had EVER really worked since they bought it, which set me off to a downhearted start but after ten minutes with the box and the instructions I had it working OK. Hint: You have to set the Mode switch otherwise it does not Operate. Plz do not be mailing me with these kind of stupid domestical maintenance questions about Items in your household. I am talking to you, Leviathan12 and The Macho Mucho. This is a walkthrough for *The Broken World* not a blog about consumer goods Troubleshooting.

I wanted to get out of the suburbs pretty fast coz I didn't want to get drawn into a follow-up water-filtration topic, but anyhow couldn't get out of the door or down the driveway to the electric-operated gate thing before Barbara was offering food and Joe kind of cornered me to sit down for one of those thought-provoking chats he likes to have since his Heart Attack. Don't worry, I'm not gonna get all philosophical. Trust me— I'm not ready for that.

When I got back, Tory's dishes were stacked neat in the sink and I guessed she'd left already to go meet Dieter at Palace as planned. I kind of slumped on the sofa and let the TV wash over me and somewhere around the point that Rolo came in and went out again I lost track of time. Later when I got to Palace and Tory nodded the kind of hi like I was some guy she'd maybe met before but wasn't exactly sure when, and I was going to explain where I'd been (i.e. with Joe and the strimmer and her mom's Southern-Style biscuits—why are they eating that Soul Food? I don't get it?) but it didn't seem worth the effort. Dieter was already in full flow telling sarcastic stories abt guys at work (he's a Motorcycle Courier) and then Tory was complaining about all the slackers in her law firm gig. It's like even if she's only there two weeks she still wants to do a good job. As one of the Lazy People on this planet I don't get that attitude, but Dieter was nodding along with Tory and making jokes, doing an impression of some stoner dispatcher guy at work and saying "Yeah, yeah. I know THAT guy exactly" when T was describing her boss at the current place. Dieter is cool like that and even asked about the walkthrough and "How is it going?" before he started making untrue jokes about how I live in *The Broken World* but just keep an apartment here in the real world so that I can visit on occasional weekends. Not funny.

Before we'd been there long Brainiac came by unexpected. He sat at the table and ordered a drink, but then didn't really join into the conversation and left before his drink even arrived. For the rest of the night there was this Sierra Nevada sitting on the table next to Brainiac's vacant spot and no one wanted to touch it until finally Dieter did what he called the Honorable Thing and drank it. Brainiac never came back. And I don't know what's up with Tory. Mostly it's all OK and then suddenly the mood changes for no reason, like I said something bad or didn't get ice in her drink or the glass they gave me at the bar is dirty, and we end up in an ongoing argument conducted entirely using the weapon of silence—in this case The Silence That Says I Am Not Talking to You v The Silence That Says I Don't Care If You Are Talking To Me or Not Asshole.

*

I'll try to continue. There are so many ways to buy it in *The Broken World*, it's a wonder sometimes that anyone ever gets out alive. There are slow deaths (think about Organ Failure) and there are Fast Deaths (so many car crashes, so many bullets flying round). Now the phone is ringing.

*

Jesus in the Heavens. A nice way to end a night like tonight is to get a stupid call from Branimir and have him beat me up in the ears for supposedly missing the Late Shift which 1) he never offered me, and 2) I never agreed to do, and 3) he never mentioned at all, i.e. not when he called me after midnight the day before yesterday and not today when I was there working the whole Afternoon shift and he gave me all kinds of bullshit for stuff that Cookie and Ashton had done and how Stentson delivered some cooked circular food to the wrong House or Apartment Number and then there were complaints from some Mexican guy, i.e. LIKE AS IF ANY OF THAT HAD ANYTHING TO DO WITH ME. Stentson was making out that I told him the wrong House or Apartment Number but that is BS. I mean—he cannot hear properly if he doesn't take his helmet off, I think that should be obvious to anyone, even Branimir. All the while B was on the phone he was talking at me nonstop and in the background Miroslav was again kind of grunting like a weird echo saying MOUTHFUCKER LATE SHIFTS and MOUTHFUCKER TIMETABLE and all that. If he didn't exist, Ashton once said about Miroslav, it wouldn't be necessary to invent him. This is a true statement.

Fuck. I even have the paper where I wrote my shifts down. It's some-where here. There is no way he offered me the Late Late. I am so fucked up in the finances department that FOR SURE I would have taken it.

*

So many bad things can happen to Ray in the game. I mean, when Tory and me walked home from Palace tonight we nearly tripped over this homeless thing (a person that you couldn't tell was a man or a woman). I was just stood there, staring at this lump of blanket, groaning with its legs stuck out a doorway and then Tory kind of pulled me away by the arm.

Fuck. I was trying to write about the different ways that you can buy it in *The Broken World* but now I'm heading downwards like Brainiac on one of his bad days. There are lots of ways to die in the game, that's for sure. Maybe this Fact just serves to warn you again that "Life is precious even right now." I don't know. The things you value don't last forever. I'm not talking about ITEMS and such—many times I'll say to you plz collect the Wire Cutters or don't forget that Parchment (of Ecelentia or whatever) but these are only Items. The feelings and thoughts that come out of the game are more important.

Now I'm getting too full of Philosophies, like Tory's dad, which goes against the promise I made before. I'm trying to keep it light, bro. No one needs an unnecessary depression. I don't want to end up like Joe. I mean, he could see I was heading out tonight when the strimmer/ trimmer was solved, but still he called me over to where he likes to sit in the window that looks out on the decking, and then without warning launched into a long speech about what's wrong with the people and what's wrong with the world and what's the deal with the universe? Then he went quiet like some men do when they are worried about things. I guess he was more upbeat before the cardiac stuff, but I couldn't get a word in. Then when the silence came it seemed better not to interrupt. I felt a kind of duty to do my time in the hot seat by the window next to him. SOmetimes while he was talking Joe picked on *The Broken World* coz he heard me mention it, and the more he talked about it the madder he got, even tho he's never played it and even when Barbara (Tory's mom) said firmly he should surrender his drink and calm it down on account of his heart. I don't know if what bothers Joe is all that violence people are normally complaining about in the game. It seemed more like he was mad that someone could get so "addicted to another world" and spend so much time there. It's not reality, he kept on saying. That is not reality. You have to think about reality.

Yes. I know. And that is true. But is it reality to be a purchasing manager of a Supermarket Corporation? I asked him that but he didn't want to answer. Is it reality to be sitting on the Deck and watching the pool boy fish out leaves? Is it reality to be even asking if it's reality in the first place? I mean, I personally like Joe, in a strange way, but I don't care if Joe likes *The Broken World* or not. In the end *The BW* is just a part of reality. It is in the world—a part of the world. That's all there is to say.

People ask me what is it with *The Broken World*? What is Ray's quest? In other games it's clearer—like with Talin in *Jerking Stone*, he has 30 days to reconstruct his Time Machine and get home to save the future—that is clear—or like with Caroline Hearst in *Beyond Good & Evil* her mission is also totally clear, but with Ray it isn't. Ray has missions, he has goals, yes—to defeat GARS or Chang, to attack the Archduke, bring down GovCorp and kill bad guys, and to win various races and chases (in daylight and at night) and solve different puzzles, collect Maps and various Amulets or Rings with Powers, to travel the towns in sequence and reach the place called Far Lands, to save some towns from Zombie or Automata takeover, to find/save Rachel, etc, etc. I could write a million-page list about it. But in fact his mission is simple—Ray has to survive.

I don't know if this makes any sense. It's late. I'm tired, maybe I'll come back to it in the morning. Tory's aunt always says you shouldn't do too much thinking at night. But somehow the night always presents itself as the only available and best time for thinking. I guess that's the trick of it—the night always tricks you that way. Anyway. Ray has a quest. I don't know how to answer all the questions it asks but that's why it's a good game. There's no point in a game where you know the answers already. I'm trying to be a good guide. This is my first ever walkthrough and I'm tired now. It's night and I'm probably beginning to repeat things that I've told you before. It's best not to think too much at night. I'm going to write this sentence and then go to bed.

A NOTE from the Customer ServIces / LAO PI

When the game starts again you're facing a nearly black screen. Ray must have moved somehow (from the truck and chains) because the chains are gone and so is the truck. It's so dark you can hardly see Ray, he's just a shape all bundled in the blackness and laid on a floor.

There are footsteps. Ray struggles to get up but realizes he's tied to a radiator. That's the bad news. Just try moving and you will find out soon enough. A "guard" comes to put a bowl of water on the floor, looks at Ray with Menace in his eyes, then leaves with a shrug of shoulders. Get used to that guard. For a long time he's the one, only, and Big event in Ray's world. A kind of Metronome that brings water and occasional kicks to the ribs. In light that spills from the hallway you can make out the small room you're being held in, without windows or furniture, but when the guard closes the door it's total darkness again. Try moving— it's impossible. Try yelling—the gag is too tight.

It will take time—days or longer—for your vision to get used to the darkness. Slowly Ray's eyes adjust to show the full extent of that kingdom in which he (i.e. you) is now trapped. Looks like a cellar. The walls thick stone. The floor dirt. The door rusted steel. A landscape of desolation and Ray tied like an animal.

My guide will help you every time. Here is what to do: 1) stretch and kick repeatedly to loosen bindings, and 2) when wrists are loose enough reach for a small stone that can just be seen on the floor—half buried in dirt approx 2m away. NOTE: You need the Stone that looks like an arrowhead/horse head and not the one that looks like a distorted kidney or the one that looks like a dirty giant bogey.

Brainiac says this bit is a good example of the ultimate Humbleness of Mankind. I mean, once Ray had a whole goddamn warehouse of weapons and Items—blaster, sword and hand grenade, photos, papers, maps and potions. Now he's stripped naked and has only a stupid dirty stone. That's all you have—a stone. Fuck. But listen—in the right place even just a stone can be the most perfect thing in the world. It could even be funny but it's hard to keep up a sense of humor when you cannot see and can feel only pain. Just check the Levels—they are maxing out the circuitry.

*

Tory went out to the temp gig, which tho it is dull, short-term and slacker-full is also WELL paid which is good news concerning life, rent, and bills since Domenico's is still subscribing to the idea of a Minimal

Wage. Ha ha. Thanks to Branimir & Miroslav for that "joke" and the fact that the oven is still doubling as a nuclear furnace on the brink of dangerous meltdown, so we're fielding complaints from customers who don't like the new chargrill effect on marinara cooked circular food. Food tastes are sooo conservative in this town is what Ashton says, like he knows anything just from watching that *Gay Chefs* program. It is true tho that the new Scorched Earth cooked circular food may take a while to catch on.

Later in yesterday's shift, the 2 of us were joking that they're gonna bring in the Atomic Energy Authorities or whatever to investigate the sudden hike in radioactive emissions from the neighborhood, and we were picturing these scientists all staring at a giant illuminated map with the exact spot of Domenico's ovens glowing orange at the center and how they would be thinking what the fuck.

All the while we were talking and laughing abt this, Miroslav was there and like keeping an Eye but not really able to complain coz it wasn't so busy and WTF we were only talking. But you could see that the way we were having some amusement was bothering him and in the end he had to come over and say What? What? but we could not explain and Ashton told him it was something a customer said and Miroslav nodded very enthusiastic and kind of half spat the word back—Customer. I mean, if there's one thing he likes less than the staff it's probably a customer.

Anyway. I'm remembering the time me and Clockwork, Venter and Brainiac and BugMap were fooling on the waste ground after the river by the big bridge (not the very big one, the other one). BugMap was balancing on some old chair that was left down there and he kept standing on it and tipping it over by stepping so it fell like in some clown circus routine—and he was always raising his arms to say "Thank you my friends!" and doing it again and we were laughing and laughing.

Those were the dayze, as they say. It must have been summer because it was late yet not totally dark. (OK. I'm getting to the point.) We were fooling like Kids, BugMap just doing this thing with the chair. And then suddenly he fell and cracked hard on the ground (his head) and the blood came out fast and red and I used some Starbucks napkins to catch the worse of it. And BugMap was groaning and the expression on his eyes—which is the whole point I'm coming to—was JUST LIKE the expression you find on Ray's eyes in that Holding Cell. Something like dead shock or horror fear. That is how Ray looks and it is not a good look and that is how BugMap looked in his eyes on the waste ground that night before he started to cry like a baby and the blood was EVEryWhere and no one knew what to say.

The doctor put six stitches in it and told BugMap he was a fool.

Word up. I get complaints from dudes who say like shut the fuck up about stuff like all that Memories and stuff abt Tory and just get on with the GAME. But I'm trying to be a good guide and that's a hard JOB. What can I tell you? It cannot be the good guide I want it to be if I cannot communicate what it's like, what it reminds me of. I don't know. I'm walking the path. But even if you follow my footsteps, it's still not the same. It can be different. Sounds crazy. Yes. When you are Ray it's different. When you're the one that breathes in him, looks out of his eyes, then it's different. How can I be a guide for that?

*

OK. Rain outside. Reality check. I mean Reality back in the game. Back in that tiny cell (approx 4m by 4m). Motherfucker. What is strange is that sometimes you can get Ray thru a whole complicated town using only 5 instructions of advice and a piece of good luck, but this small Cell could have a whole fucking guidebook of its own. It's like a whole earth in itself. The stone. The dirt. The gray light that changes so that more can gradually be seen. The crawling bugs to Eat (disgusting but you need to survive). The bindings and radiator code (I'll explain later).The sound and rhythm of Steps, the keys etc, but that all still to come.

*

Another time me, Clockwork, Venter, and Brainiac were down there by the Bridge again. This is also way back. Two years? Probably longer. We were watching boats go by and how they churn up the river. Clockwork was doing some writing and stuff on the wall of the bridge. Venter and me were talking about some movie we saw with a speed chase in a Toxic Gas Refinery and a big explosion at the end and Venter was saying he thought it was kind of unrealistic and Brainiac was just staring into Space. I don't know why I'm remembering all this stuff.

*

Once Ray has the stone, start banging on the radiator. That is your only hope.

Knock in a pattern. - - - - . . . ——(= Morse code for Yes?)

When an answer comes work slowly to make a code of communication with person next door. Plz don't worry. An answer will come. There is hope even in the hardest world.

In every version of the game the code must be different—i.e. I cannot tell it to you. Use bangs and silences. The code must come from you—from Ray and the person on the other side of that wall. Only then can you make plans for escape.

OK. And hear me. Please, I'm begging you—don't start emailing me NOW to say that oh Ray is stuck in a dark cell naked and can I please send you a cheat or a code to get him out of this mess. I *cannot*. Read my lips: *cannot*. Are GoblinHead and Plexi2005 listening to me here? Start from one knock yes, two knocks NO and the rest will follow from there. And please remember (this goes for Brainiac also and BugMap who can sometimes be impatient)—Rome WAS NOT BURNED IN A DAY.

*

It's later now. Tory is out at a movie with little sister Linda who, like I said, just got back from Asia. I'm not a jealous or possessive person. I can have my doubts about Linda, but it's good that Tory connects with her after what happened last year. I mean, she's still her sister no matter if she is a nut job.

Rolo has gone away for the long weekend with his girlfriend, so I'm alone. Work is done—a usual mix of avoiding 1) Branimir, and 2) any effort at all. There is nothing on TV and I'm too broke to go wasting with Venter, so it's my perfect chance to get writing. I want to set myself an Official Task to write to the end of the First Level before the end of tonight.There are 9 towns left. I guess I shouldn't speak too soon coz many times I sit down to write and get completely interrupted. Dude— when it comes to that, Rolo is the fucking "high-score roommate from mystery"—always coming and going with more unpredictability than those particles they research in the high-level Physics Labs of *The Broken World*. I don't know him at all really. I know he works at managing some "project" for a useless software firm and that he often has grass, which makes him popular with some people (Tory—you know who you are). Strange to be more like a half-assed acquaintance of someone that shares your bathroom. I mean, the only other things I know for sure about Rolo are that 1) he's even messier than me, and 2) he turns up when you least expect it. This last fact can lead to some embarrassing situations—I spare you the details but the words ME and TORY, FOOLING AROUND and NAKED may give you a clue. Too much information? Yes. Too much information.

OK. I'm sat here again and outside are all the usual trees, tall buildings, houses, and cars (just to set the scene). But I won't be looking out there tonight. I'll be looking at the screen—I have Tory's laptop to write on. I also have my computer running *The BW*. HAL 9000 is what I call it (my computer), ha ha, named after the crazy mean computer in *2001: A Space Odyssey*. My computer is starting to look like it was made for a prop in that movie, i.e. Old. Whatever you are reading this on is probably better than HAL. I mean, HAL does OK apart from choking on the graphics in *BW* sometimes, and if I'm honest I don't use it for much except the game, email, and messenger. One day Venter came around and I was using Excel or something and Venter made a joke like "OH MY GOD. HAL can do that too . . ." Like all he EVER saw it do before was running the *BW*. Yes, I'm getting on with it in a minute.

*

Lao Pi is the name of the person held in the cell next to Ray. When you get the radiator codes working (i.e. bangs and silences) you 2 can soon figure out an escape. HINT: Pay attention to rhythm of changing of guards. Also: Herb that grows in damp corner of Lao Pi's cell has a strange effect like chloroform. Also: The third guard (they call him Kaveco) has a bladder problem—that guy is always taking a break to go pee. He's worse than Branimir. And LISTEN: When the time comes you must act. FAST AND ONLY FAST with Lao Pi. Please, I'm telling you— make no hesitation or PHILOSOPHICAL contemplations because you have been sitting on your ass in the dark for some weeks. GET OUT. Cut bindings (using stone). Guard has gold keys (you NEED THEM so GET THEM). Collect two Invisible Cloaks and also two Daggers from Lockers (not the Justice Daggers, they are somewhere else, these are the different Daggers). Wear Cloaks to slip past extra Demon Guards (near special fortress doorway) and if any fucker raises up the alarm then slit the throats and move. You are Ray. You have to succeed.

*

Shit. Tory called to say she and Linda are in a bar and they gave up on the movie coz L thought it sucked or had seen it already and can I PLEASE go join them coz Tory didn't take a jacket and it's cold. They are at Palace.

Strange SKIlls

There are many times when you will need Skills. I'm not just talking about normal things like Stealth, Agility, Strength, Wisdom, or Aggression etc. Those are things you need pretty much all the time. I mean other important stuff that you do NOT need all the time but then later—i.e. when Ray gets in a really tricky situation—then you need it so freaking badly that without it you cannot succeed. For example: you will need Limbo Skills to get under laser trip-wire security fences in high-security places and you will need Flying Skills BIG TIME if you get in a battle against various Dinosaur Bird things and YOU HAD BETTER GET Obfuscation Skills if you ever plan to get thru the City of London (I only did it one time and I wished I had the Obfuscation).

Some skills take a lot of training to acquire, bro—you cannot just go into a Store to purchase Hypnotism Skills or Extended Reason. Or take, for example, shape-shifting, and Interrogations or Muscle Attack (?)—they all take training to achieve. Venter hates anything with training. He's too impatient and always wants to find a way round it. Like maybe there's some gun he can buy that does the same job, or a chemical formula, or a magic amulet—anything so long as he doesn't have to practice, train, and level up the hard way. Sleeptalk is very different, like he kind of excels at those things that take loads of patience. Where you really have to work a task over and over until you're good enough to move on. Languages, shape-shifting, sales technique—Sleeptalk is very good at all that.

Everyone agrees that Invisible is a VERY tough skill to acquire but you need it in parts of the game where a "magic solution" or Stealth just won't do. Invisible needs a lot of practice. I wish I'd had it last night at Palace so no one could see me standing next to Tory and Linda when Linda was making such a big exhibition of what a great party girl she still is.

Anyway. To get Invisibility you have to walk down a whole crowded street without being noticed at all. No matter when you think you have finally got thru to the end there is always some nosy Kid passing by or an Eagle-eyed Motorist that spots you and fucks it up.

Grinning Cat says that to succeed you have to "see no difference between yourself and the actual street" (?)—you have to be "truly a part of it." That is true Invisible. Some kids in blogs and on the *BW* discussion boards are saying this is just a bit too much like that stuff they put in kung-fu movies to fill up time between the fighting. But I'm willing to keep an open mind. Those kids are fools already. Hear me, Conquest19 and ZuluBabe—when you can walk down that street unnoticed then you will know what it's all about and until then you can shut your much-too-noticeable LOSER mouths.

Other skills that can come in useful—Tongue Twisting, Subterfuge, Harpsichord Skills (to charm ladies at Masked Ball). Also Ninja Stars, Anarchy, Fraud Skills, Shit Eating (can be used on almost any occasion, ha ha—I'm not joking) and "Vibrancy" (I don't know what it is so please, anyone, I could use your help on this). Also, plz don't forget Anger (I don't really think you can call it a skill but VEnter disagrees—sometimes I think he just likes to take the opposite position in any conversation), Distortion (also not too sure what kind of skill it is), Listening, and Sympathy. Also Marauding (?), Hope, Desolation (Brainiac is good at it), Mediation, Grief, Virtue, Hostage Negotiation (3 levels possible and NO, Nightmare and IcePack, the Trick from before with the Tank or the Microlite that I wrote about in Gas Station Hostage Episode does NOT qualify), Balancing, Surgery (3 levels), Advanced Sorcery, Water Dowsing, Dream Interpretation, Conscious Dreaming (?). There are many more. I will try to add them all later.

*

It was like special "Easy Saturday" at Domenico's. Not busy and they apparently fixed up the ovens so there's no more Scorched Earth. Roll out the weekend and a Free Extra topping of Cheese and Minor Accidents to go. Later, for no good reason, we went with Clockwork, Brainiac, and Venter to a party at some house out of the city on the South Side, perhaps a mile or so into suburbia. It was just a party we heard about from a friend of Venter that turned out to be just some guy he met at a bar and there was like a general feeling of Whatever. When we got there the guy Venter supposedly knew was kind of saying Oh well in fact it's more like his kid brother's party or something and Venter didn't care anyway he was jumping around to the music and the whole scene was like a flashback to the usual childish madness of an irresponsible summer—people and other stuff were getting thrown in a pool, this kid brother of the guy whose parents' house it was was getting upset, some girl (or maybe 3 girls) crying, some guys acting tough etc. Brainiac was supposedly not drinking because of the car but at least he was more social than before—talking to some person he knew from somewhere. Tory said she was going to sit on the steps and try not to feel old. Me and Clockwork found this place in the kitchen where no one was really standing and just got talking—the game, Domenico's, the way some kids look like they are trouble, etc, whatever. It was late night when we started to even think about getting home and collected Tory who was still sat on the steps but had accumulated a couple of guys with dope and then we were in the car and neither Brainiac and certainly not Venter or anyone else was really good to drive (as they say) but we were in the car anyway and off we went. Someplace north of the freeway we got in a accident with a road sign at an intersection. That fucking sign came out of nowhere was the commentary afterward from Venter, ha ha. Venter was laughing but Brainiac was freaking a bit coz it is his brother's car that he's only really looking after until someday when Paul wants it back or needs to sell it. In the middle of it all Tory started getting texts from Linda saying "Hey, what's up?" and do we want to hook up. This is like 3am already and in any case no thanks. There was only slight damage but the road sign was all bent and at first the car was kind of attached to it (the sign) in some way that none of us could figure out.

No one was hurt but after the crash and the immediate BS there was a whole panic scene about what to do and how to get home—if we should risk driving in the car with the hood not closed properly and everything, and what if the cops were coming while we sat there arguing abt what to do etc etc. I think everyone was less cool than they thought they maybe might be in a situation like that. Only Clockwork kept calm to some extent and Venter was certainly the one that twisted the sign off and tied up the hood (a belt) so we could leave and meanwhile Tory just sat in the back sending a few texts and watching it all. She was a bit high (thanks to Rolo or the guys she magically accumulated) but it was something else. Much later (i.e. back at home) she said that she was kind of watching and thinking about the qualities different people have. How they deal with stuff, like how our group of four drunk idiots on Earth were dealing with the crashed car situation. She said she was watching the whole scene unfold and then drifting and spinning outward, like endless thought-bubbles as she sat there in the back. Thinking about how her parents dealt with the death of Joe's brother (it was not natural causes) and how they dealt with Shay's move North and with Linda's various divorces etc etc, and how she herself dealt with different things, even how she was dealing with the whole car thing by just sitting there and spinning off like that in her head. It's one of the reasons I love Tory, I guess. That under the sometimes abrasive side she can be thoughtful. I will stop there before it really gets into freaking love-blog territories.

*

As well as developing Ray's skills to level up you will sometimes have to choose other people with the right skills that can help him. I mean, for sure Ray normally plays a loan wolf but in some parts of the adventures he needs a team of talented persons to succeed in the goal. For example, if you go to Void House (12th Town) or Manor Club (10th Town) you will need a thief. Yorba is good for this or the Manchurian Guy, or maybe Villain, or the Nightclub Bouncer or even Fingers from Senegal. He is a world-class thief but not always reliable.

In some other places you also need a Mystic or at least someone with healing and "ocular" powers. Be careful who you choose tho coz Mystics are notoriously WEIRD in their behavior and can damage a team with the way they act. Lisa is one (a Mystic). She works in a Fifth Town Pet Store but can easily be recruited if you tell her about your mission. She is not interested in rewards (unlike Thieves who always are) but only in the glory of the quest. Lisa says that Mystic is not a *job* for her but more like a calling—i.e. she is not in it for the money. Trouble is she will for sure freak out the others in yr party, esp any Thieves—Thieves and Mystics do not get on. Lisa is a good Mystic tho esp if you go for the wasted albino type (I am talking to you, Sleeptalk). On most missions it doesn't matter so much that Lisa has a bad attitude to hygiene, authority, and other people coz she is definitely a hard worker. Another Mystic is Horsewain but he won't work unless he is drunk and it's not good to have people with a drinking problem in your team. Yes—just like in the real world, bro..

Everyone has diff abilities. Venter can be a Practical person and has good Strength. Clockwork has Logic and the Technical Skills. BugMap has some Reasoning, Persistence, and a Sense of Humor. Sleeptalk has Music and Honesty. Dieter has Charm and Humor again. I mean, they all have good skills. I am not so sure about me and Brainiac tho. Sorry, Brainiac. I think I am a Watcher person and he is more a Worrier type. They do not name those skills in the game. I don't even know if they are really skills in like a true sense of the world, just like Anger is not a skill according to me. I mean, it's hard to see Ray saying, "OK, what I really need in my team is a Furious Lunatic." Or if you think about the Worrier type Ray does not make an announcement like "I really need someone that will worry and freak out and get depressed so he cannot function any longer etc." or "What I need is someone that makes everyone else

TOTALLY doubt what they are doing and where they are headed in life."
Or when it comes to Watcher skills he is not thinking YES, what I want
is someone that will come along on the mission just to watch everything
and think about what might happen and maybe write it down in a
confusing way for other people to read abt later. He does not say, "I
need someone just to be there with a notebook to make all spidery
handwriting notes and later either lose the notebook or type it in a
computer so that geeks who are too lazy to figure things out for
themselves can read it." No.

Me and Brainiac. Maybe the skills we got have no use in *The BW*, it's
not clear. Or maybe we're even pretty useless in any world. I don't know.
I didn't see much cooked circular food in *The Broken World*. Freakin A.
I mean what the fuck. Even I am starting to sound like Brainiac now—
he's supposed to be the one with mental problems not me. Take a look
how many times those words—*I don't know*—appear in what I have
written already. A sound bite repeating to eternity.

I don't know.
I don't know.
I don't know.
I don't know.
I don't know.
I don't know.
I don't know.
I don't know.
I don't know.
I don't know.
I don't know.

etc

They will write it on the tombstone Tory will have to purchase from Target, using her Amex (if there is anything left on it) after her Lovely Sister Linda has bought clothes and flowers and organized all the catering or whatever).

From CASTLE TO NOWhere

Searchlights kick in from the top of the Castle (?) as Ray and Lao Pi make their Exit. The lights are glistening everywhere on the cobblestones and narrow streets and Sirens are making a huge sound so go as fast as you can from that place. Head out of the North Draw Bridge then tread down the stone steps. Head west, keep going and do not look back, there is some kind of enchantment they put there that freezes you into something like salt. HINT: Plz avoid the 3rd and 6th steps coz they have BLADES that stab thru the feet. ALso: Lao Pi will be weak from imprisonment so help him if you can in the fights with Guards and the I-Wanna-Be-A-Hero peasant-type Townsfolk that also try to stop your escape. Another HINT: If you steal the cart from outside the yellow building (maybe it's a hay barn?) you can wheel Lao Pi along.

Looking back over what I wrote before I can see that I've even lost track of why I started writing about SKILLS in the first place. The thing I wanted to get around to is that Ray must use the skill of Subterfuge in this part of the game. That is the skill you really need, so try to level up.

Head to top edge of town—it doesn't matter about route but do not go to Cemetery or Stadium. Take candle from window ledge to navigate yr way. Town seems to be divided into six districts, but I've only ever been to three of them. It's all very shadowy with winding streets and has some Bad Atmospheres. I don't like it even if Sleeptalk says it's cool.

Before long horsemen belonging to some guy the locals call the Archduke will come after you using Seek spells for direction and Thunder Hoofs for speed. Do NOT panic. Archduke seems to be like a local franchise of GARS. Not really GARS but bad enough. The Locals put up Parchments with pictures of Ray and Lao Pi that accuse them of being Sorcerers and offer a reward. You will need Subterfuge like I said before. Use Footfalls (potion) to soften your tread and Silencia (vial) to help with whispering. DO NOT speak to locals, esp friendly ones coz they are spies of the Duke. If there is trouble, as usual, shoot first and ask questions later. The cops have it right on that one ha ha. Drink Mead for health and follow local customs. At Serpents Inn please trade for Items and more detailed Maps.

HINT: Give money to the Beggar who stops you on exit from the Inn—Blind Pete or something. Any kindness to him will be REPAID later.

Lots of people argue about what TOWN this is exactly—is Ray still in Fourth Town where he was with Rachel and where they captured him in the truck? Or did they take him off somewhere else like to another town? It certainly seems pretty different from before. To tell the truth it doesn't matter much where he is at this point coz all he really has to do is get the fuck out of there as quickly as possible. That is exactly what Dieter said about Minnesota when we went out with him that other night. He said it was definitely a good place for getting out of and he was doing his Evil Voice, pretending to BE Minnesota and saying Get Out of Here and GET OUT OF HERE, GET OUT OF MINNESOTA, etc. Me and Tory laughed so hard the beer was coming out my nose. OK. Back to the game.

Go to Doorway at the walled Exit from Town. Why is there a wall now? Can someone explain that to me? I don't remember it from before. Maybe there are walls that come from nowhere in this town? The Gateman will ask to see your papers. Don't panic—just tell him you left them at the Inn and head back in that direction. As you walk you will hear the Archduke's horses come thundering down and a sound of great commotion. When you reach the Well wait there a while (i.e. DO NOT go back to Serpents Inn)—blow out candle and sit patiently in darkness. Blind Pete will join you. Thanks to your previous kindness he gives you the false papers you need. Pass the Gateman by same route you attempted before.

*

Truth is I made another deadline to reach the end of this part once b4 today but things didn't go well with the plan coz of more trouble at Domenico's, the shift ending late and "general mental annoyance." The afternoon started bad coz the Thermostat of Doom was fucked up again but then the guy (Micky) came to fix it and Big D's was not busy and mostly me and Ashton were just hanging out behind the counter, trying to step on Insects (do not tell the guys at the Dept of Public Healths) and making up new tagline names for Domenico's. "Home of cooked circular food" was a favorite and "Purveyors of fine pizza since ten months ago" was good as well and "Traditional Pizza from the Urals" was also a contender. Ashton can be mean and funny, but I tell you, man, he doesn't mix his fooling around with any quality like wisdom. He made a sign with the slogans on it using a marker pen on the backs of some delivery boxes. You could tell instantly that Stentson did not approve when he saw the sign. There was one regular customer came in and was laughing a lot and I think Ashton really intended to take the sign down before Branimir or Miroslav came back but we must have got complacent. So at 6pm when Branimir lumbered in, his expression changed from pissed off (= basically the default expression mode) to very pissed off. I was trying to get out of there at the end of the shift but he was keeping us on with a loooooong lecture concerning responsibilities and Attitudes and basically yelling at us way beyond time. It was maybe 7 before I got away.

Coming home I stopped by at Brainiac's (I admit a huge detour is not really stopping by) and hung out with him a while instead of going home coz T is out at some movie again with Linda, I don't know why, but in the end he was too low-key and again not great to be with for whatever reason. I don't know—there is no reason why he should be so obsessively worried about the car. It's just a set of bumps, bends, and deep scratches according to the quotation from the garage. So I came back and tried to get on with the writing in the walkthrough but that didn't last for long coz there were phone calls (I am a Mexico City State lottery winner even tho I never bought a ticket ha ha ha) and some persistent guy wanting to talk to Lorraine (dude, there is no Lorraine that lives here, there never was one, and I do not think there will ever be one). After a while there were even Mormons at the door (I'm not joking, I don't understand how they even got in the building) and then Brainiac was IMing me to say sorry he was no fun before. After that he and I were just chatting—sending lines of text backward and forward in that way, exchanging nothing much and "views on the day" and other stuff only Brainiac would somehow think to bring out in conversation, like a story he saw somewhere about how bees navigate using magnetism. Weird.

Halfway in the chat Brainiac changed his icon. At first he was his regular icon—this old picture of him, his face, I don't know where it came from, he looks drunk in the picture—but then later he changed it to a zoom on the same picture, just a zoom on the eyes so he looked kind of intense and like a different person. Then after some minutes he started to go thru all the cartoon icons they give out with the chat program. So with more or less every line he wrote in the chat his picture (icon or whatever) was different. First he was a quizzical and purple-looking rodent. Then he was a lime-green dopey-looking bird. Then he was an earthworm with crazy eyes etc. I was joining in also. Normally I just have a dumb picture from a year ago—something Tory took when we were out with Dieter in the woods. So I changed my pic a few times—to one of me sleeping that Tory took another time and then a picture of my shadow in the park that I took, me all thin and stretched out, just a shadow on the grass. After a time we were going faster and faster and it was like we were paying more attention to the picture changes than we were to the chat. Around the same time Tory called to say she and Linda skipped out of the movie again (*Car Rental? Rent A Car? Rented Car?* I never heard of it) and how they were now having cocktails somewhere. Good job Tory took a jacket. Back in the chat Brainiac started using even more pictures, ones he'd found on the Internet (?)—a man with a gross distorted head and another guy with a fake fake-looking smile like from an old-fashioned dentist ad and he was just typing stuff like "Hi I am

Brainiac" or "Help—My Teeth are Glued 2gther." OK. I'm getting too distracted.

*

How big the world must seem to Ray and Lao Pi when they escape from prison in that Castle. How vast the sky must at first appear to them and the Earth itself and how bright the sun at sunset must seem to them too after all that where they mourned and ached the loss of light. (OK. I admit that sentence before I have copied off a website about *The BW* but I cannot resist coz it captures that part so well.)

It reminds me of the feeling when Tory and me went to Vegas after her sister's wedding (not Linda, the other one—Shay) and we were spending all our time in the casinos, in the Luxory Pyramid or whatever they call it and the Castle in the Air and then after a long weekend we drove out on a day trip into the desert. It was kind of terrifying. I mean, I love a desert like anyone else, but it seemed so big after all the people and the noise. The sky was so empty and the *time* of it all out there was so still and slow. I don't know if Tory likes it that I can be weak (?) like that, I was kind of freaked out by the desert that day. Maybe I shouldn't write that kind of thing here.

I'm also thinking how cool it must be for Ray and Lao Pi to actually speak after the weeks of nothing but the code they made by banging on the pipes. It's hard to imagine how cool that sound of voices and WORDS must be. When Ray first gets out of that prison he seems to me kind of nervous or jumpy, like all his moves are out of scale. I guess that isolation can really get to a person before too long.

Descend away from the walled Castle/Town and try to find a subway station. (Entrance down the road some way.) If Ray walks Lao Pi will follow. Find a good route. Now is when you need the Subterfuge again. Answer riddles to earn Tokens for the subway or force the turnstiles using swords if you want to be more like Venter. Then go down the escalators in silence (because of surveillance). On the waiting platform there is time for some whispered conversation with Lao Pi to share facts and say thanks to each other for the efforts of the escape. Ask Lao Pi about Maps of *The Broken World* and any rumors he has heard concerning weaknesses in GovCorp. Ask as much as you can and take note of all. Remember—ANYTHING IS A CLUE.

Do not take the first train marked BOREDOM and do not take the second train (i.e. the next one) marked UNTRUTH (trust me, you do not want to go there). Instead you must wait for the train that is marked DESTINY to town of NOWHERE where Rachel must be found again. Lao Pi must take his own route in a different direction to face the Veil of Darkness (that is what he says. I don't understand it either. If anyone knows what he is talking about please tell me.) And don't worry—if you're lucky there will be the chance to meet again, some way down the road.

The subway journey is long and as you ride the train slowly fills up with guys that look like Japanese salarymen with their briefcases etc—you cannot understand what they are doing there or what any of them are saying or where they are going dressed for work like that and the train becomes a massive crush. It is maybe one of those parts when the people that wrote and coded *The BW* got a bit lost in their own heads, I don't know. But that's how it is. Salarymen, 100s of them. And talking Japanese.

*

OK. Dudes that only want to hear talking about the game please go ahead and skip these next paragraphs. But LET ME WARN you—you will inevitably miss some stuff because in the end it all amounts to the same thing. I try to be a good guide, to explain what I know about the route you can take. Sometimes it's not so obvious as just to say Kill the Monster and take the Golden Fucking Key. You have to be smarter than that and learn from different things.

Now another random chat from Brainiac. Just short conversation like:

Hi.

Hi. What's up?

Not much. Gaming. LOL.

Then he went right back into the changing-the-icon thing and the pictures he chose got more and more intense. He started with a 5,000lb naked fat guy with layers of fat rolling off him, and then switched to a snapshot of some lost-looking kid in a desert (?) and then to a picture of a body in a totally burned-out building all shot up and stuff, some insurgent or something, I don't know, whatever. I mean, these are pictures you can easily find on the Internet if you want to look, but it is somehow disturbing when the picture is supposed to be like a chat icon for your friend. Sometimes I just don't know what goes on with the Brainiac—he can definitely act like a freak sometimes.

*

When you reach Nowhere it looks like a place in some old communist country they built but didn't want to put on any maps. It's certainly not stretching a miracle in the graphics department—I mean, how many colors can you make using concrete? There are a few gypsy women (near the Train Station) who have handy magickal items for sale and can identify magickal items for you, as well as training you as an Apprentice in Prowling. The town has a big problem with WOLVES and in many places you need to run from them or be prepared to fight. Wolves are not as easy to fight as like the Zombies you already encountered, esp coz these Wolves seem to be radioactive. (I'm not sure exactly—they have luminous stuff dripping out of their mouths.) Try Bossanova (nightclub) to find some guy Henri (?) who can help you with lucrative side missions.

NOTE: You will find that some items are "hexed" (evil) and must be dealt with by a wizard before you can use them. A good test to determine if an item is hexed is to try picking it up. If you hear a nasty humming noise and the ground under Ray burns in the pattern of a fiery pentagram it's hexed, brother, and you want to put it down. Do not delay in any case. You have work to do.

*

Finally B was changing his picture so much it was like that experience when someone is messing with the TV controls and flipping thru channels when u are trying to watch it. I mean, Brainiac was spending more time on searching for crazy new pictures and changing them and stuff and not really giving a damn what he was saying or what I was saying, so I was just thinking fuck it and I had to say OK I'm going now and catch you later. I mean—it's not so friendly to do that but some people (hear me, Brainiac) have to figure out that they cannot act the fool all the time, no matter if they have a history of issues.

*

Shit. Shit and Motherfucker Shit. Half past midnight already and I can hear Tory by the door on the street below. Looks like I can only get the nine towns done to the end of Level 1 if I pull an all-nighter. Maybe I will chill with her for a while, talk about the latest half-a-movie she saw and then come back to writing when she goes to bed. At least the good news is it sounds like L is not coming up. Yes. Normal service will be resumed as soon as possible. Do not get impatient. I remain your servant and will probably return.

TRACKING Rachel

Think about it this way. Now that he has escaped from that dark prison cell and the walled town etc, Ray really needs to find Rachel. It doesn't take Einstein, Darwin, or even Colombo to figure that the first thing he should do is head back to the Motel and see what he can find. Maybe she's still there (yes, dream on, bro) and maybe there are some clues (yes, yes, there are some clues—there are always clues).

So Ray has to get from Fifth Town back to Fourth Town. Take a route. Any route. By air. By land. By sea (I'm joking—there is no sea here). You can go by the bus even, as long as you can figure out how their ticketing works. It doesn't matter how u get there but plz do not get in trouble on the way. There are those that like to go off and just randomly find missions or things to fight, and yes that is totally an option at this point just like any other. There are GovCorp conspiracies to be stopped with Resistance in Sixth Town. There is a big mystery with some UFOs and an alien life form on the outskirts of another place nearby. There are a million things you can do. But at this point I recommend a structured approach—go back to Fourth Town. On the route Ray should try to sleep and get his energy back. Press your head against the glass and let the world go by. If you want to win in the game you have to sleep, even if it is Uneasy Sleep. I guess that's all there is in that world.

*

Thinking about it, things were left a little weird at the end of my shift at Domenico's today. Things there are hotting up somehow. Miroslav is such a High Score Asshole—he was in some huge argument with Stentson all afternoon. All the while he (Miroslav) stood in the entrance so that no other person could pass; not in and not out; it didn't matter if they were customers or "staff" the route was totally blocked. The whole time he was yelling I could see at least two people show up, take in the whole scene including the fact that Miroslav was obviously 1) crazy and 2) not gonna turn around to let them enter the premises and get food in any foreseeable future, and basically decide to leave. I was whispering to Ashton that well, it is his freaking money that he's wasting. Stentson took the verbal assault in typical style by standing totally still like a robot and not reacting while Miroslav ranted, and best of all by not once even flipping up the visor so that Miroslav could see his face.

*

When you get back to the Motel first locate and question the Hispanic Maid—she is probably cleaning the rooms or smoking out back—and she will say that Rachel has gone and long departed from that place. (She speaks a kind of bad translation weird.) Afterward hold your ground and insist that you talk to the Old Guy, the guy that runs the place, I don't know his name.

Old guy will be suspicious—*he does not like strangers*—and he will say that she (Rachel) was *never* there. Show him the photo. He will totally deny. After this go back to the road and walk away from the Motel. Find the Phone Booth. You need a coin from somewhere—if u don't have one in your Items just go down main street of town and ask people until you succeed. You can even have some fun making up a story concerning why you need the money—like those guys that hang around in the station. Anyhow, once you have the coin, call the Motel and ask for Rachel and they will deny they ever heard of her again.

TIP: After calling, wait at the Phone Booth. Wait five minutes—phone will ring. The caller will be the Maid again, feeling too guilty that she covered up the truth but also scared to talk. If you play it right she will give you a clue concerning where to go next. Easton she will say but that is not the name of a place, it is a name of a GARS controller you must find and fight in the upcoming towns—if you beat him in fair Battle he can give info to help find Rachel.

*

After this things come thick and fast. Here are some notes on immediate next towns but due to the circumstance (i.e. it's LATE and some of us have to work again tomorrow and don't have time to play a computer game all night anymore like kids wasting away in college) I won't go into full detail. Like always I'll try to come back and add more information if there comes a good time. I hope that's clear and understood. JarHEAD, I am talking to you. I am doing the best job I can. There is a long road to follow and I will try to help you at all points. Now it is just notes I hope you can follow it:

Sixth Town
Forensic collection. Pass "Liars Bridge." Defeat GARS controller (Easton) (Rachel clues).

Seventh Town
Fight contest (Ray). Buggy race. Also watch out for Sniper quest. Ray in Motorcade. When you get the signal you know what to do.

Geographical Town (no number)
Clue collection. Fault lines. Storm warnings. Predictions. Security Puzzle.

There is a phone ringing in the apartment downstairs (not in the game—here—in the world I am actually living in). It has rung about five times in the last hour—rings for ages and then stops again and starts again, like someone really wants to talk to the guy that lives down there. I hope it doesn't wake Tory.

Eighth Town
All in darkness.

Ninth Town
GovCorp conspiracy (1–6).

10th Town
Sewer chase. Target practice (Ray as the target. Keep head low.
Wear body armor).

Hidden Town (no number)
Gray adventure. Maze of Increments.

They kind of slow it down on the Rachel thing. I don't know why. I mean, Ray
has so much else to deal with, so many situations he needs to help out in,
fights he has to fight, mysteries to solve. Some people say he does not
give a Shit—that he forgets about her but I don't think Ray forgets about
Rachel, that's not possible. Anyplace he goes and no matter how severe
the challenges there is always some small part of it related to Rachel—a
clue, an Item that you need to find her, a Fool from GARS or whatever you
can trick for some Information. Ray does not forget. You can tell that, even
in the thickest firefight or where he has to abseil off a clifftop with a knife
between his teeth, he is still thinking of her and determined to get back.

11th Town
Jungle Adventure. Schizophrenia attack.

12th Town
GovCorp conspiracy (7–12).

The phone is ringing down there again. I don't even know who is in that
apt anymore. It is where the Jones and Christie and Trent and Bosnia
were living, but they moved out.
   Bear in mind at all times—use common sense and intuitions. You
have learned the basics now and should be able to get thru. In the

Motorcade try to stay behind the secret service men and in the clue collection remember to bag and tag *everything* no matter what you think about it—so many times the investigation founders from lack of all proper evidence. In the hide-and-seek try hiding in the cupboard under the stairs as well as in the Garden Shed and also under the bed with the blankets pulled down to hide you better. No one ever thinks to look under there, it is so obvious, but you can really succeed. In the sewer chase cover MOUTH with Handkerchief to stop poison fumes and in Schizophrenia Attack take tablets as prescribed by doctor but avoid going outside for three weeks (game time, remember).

*

Just a note to the smartasses who are emailing to tell me, Dude, You mention a part of the game with e.g. GovCorp and some freaking nine-part conspiracy but then you don't explain it. Or, bro, You talk about how one part is where the Hotel Ricardo burns down in a big battle (in Eighth Town or Tenth Town or whatever) but when it comes to that town you never mention it again—no hotel and no fire—no fire and not even the frickin hotel. Or, Man, there is always like a long list of scenes that are supposed to be cool, but half these places you don't give info about them or make anymore mention of it in the rest of your walkthru. Or, What's up? You say I will need that Screwdriver Gadget from the desk in some dude's log cabin "later" but when is that later? You don't mention it again, motherfucker. Do I need it or not? Don't be telling me to get stuff and carry it about with me if I don't really need it. I cannot carry the world around on my back.

OK. What I have to say to you various assholes (and all the rest whose complaints I cannot repeat) is this. Of course you can find a whole town or adventure or whatever I missed. There are like 100s of them, maybe more—the game is a world, remember. Do not forget that. And do NOT forget I am not covering all the bases. I am getting you thru. I cannot write it all—I am not a typing pool. It needs time. And the other only thing I have to say to you is check the fucking small print (Tomahawk esp) and get off my back—remember the two important little words it says: UNDER CONSTRUCTION. I am WORKING ON IT, dude. One day this walkthrough will be so perfect that you will see your reflections in it but for now PLEASE GIVE ME A BREAK. Also try to recall (again) that there are many different roads and routes through *The Broken World*—I cannot keep a track of it all and I'm not claiming to be a genius (I leave that to you smartasses) so of course things don't always add up. I do the best I can here with the brain cells available.

And the other only thing I have to say is Yes, DrunkenApe or Naplam50 or whatever you call yourself now—the one that mailed yesterday—you NEED that Screwdriver Gadget from the desk in that dude's log cabin especially to shove it right up your dumb ass. And when you have done that you can carry it around in there for six months, then whip it out, lick all the pixels of shit off it and use it to undo the screws in the drainage ducts in the prison of Gangis in 16th Town if you end up there which is when you will really wish you did carry it with you on your back or up your ass like I said already.

*

Near dawn. That kind of light that it is probably impossible to describe, so I won't even try. I'm feeling more awake than before. It doesn't matter that Branimir is always saying that I look tired already when I get to work and plz will I stop putting my head down on the counters like that to rest, because it will spread infectious diseases. I think I have more to worry about from the counters than they have to worry about in my direction if you get what I'm trying to say. I feel strangely awake, I guess, in the soft lights spilling out the window and from the sky.

Soft light from the screen also. On the desktop (computer desktop), all documents scattered. In the chat program that is running in the background I can see that B must still be sat at the computer because he is changing his icon from time to time. Not chatting, just changing. Yeah. There he is again. A crazy irregular metronome. Just killing the time. Just shifting from one picture to another. Now he is a porn-star face with that Botox mouth and too-wide eyes. Before that he was a burned guy sat strapped up in a fighter pilot chair. A car crash. A victim of a medical experiment with all swelled-up eyes. Like he's set on some sort of random mode of horrors and I am playing tunes from the Music Player. Also random.

*

Now comes the final part of Level 1. You need the Utmost Concentration and clarity of Thought for this part and now seems a good time of day/night to write about it. Soft in the light and a bit of chill in the air. First you have to retrieve some Jewels from an Ivory Casket (Apartments of Afterward) and get them back to a woman that people call Alice in Olympic Village or Princess Alice (she can give you clues on Rachel's movements), then you have to sharpshoot some playing cards at the town's saloon (aim for Aces and don't hit Kings) and then face off against the local fucking bad guy, a certain Mr Duros, who for no good reason takes a special dislike to Ray.

This whole last part is certainly weird—we seem to have moved in time a bit? and I have no clear idea how they are justifying the plot at this point—but please don't blame me, I am only the messenger. I'm talking to you, Torpedo. I don't really know what happened with Ray trying to find Rachel at this point either—welcome to *The Broken World*. I don't make the game, I only tell you about it. The thing with Duros comes to a natural end with a totally KICKASS Duel. They do the field very green and the dawn was very beautiful. A faint dew is shimmering everywhere. Duros chooses the longer sword, which is also lighter so he comes at you with speed, and can strike from a distance. You can choose the slightly heavier sword or the one with the magick jewels/inscription—both of these are adequate for the task of killing this pretentious ass—but like BugMap said one time "Personally I prefer the AXE" because it saves messing around.

Just a hint. If anything goes wrong here—in the part called Apartments of Afterward or in the Olympic Village with the terrorists or in the final Duel with Duros—it is OK to use TIME GRENADE. These can be found and collected from part of that Armory in Sixth Town and I really Hint that you go there even if the battles to get there are hard. But plz remember the time grenade is for emergencies *only*. I.e. I mean— if Ray gets shot up real bad or cut up or impaled in the Duel and if his Symbols go into Code RED during Gray Adventure, that is to say, IN CASE OF VICTORY BY DUROS or other SERIOUS AND UNSTOPPABLE CRISIS/ EMERGENCY ONLY then you should make use of the time grenade.

The phone has stopped ringing downstairs now. It hasn't rung for quite a while. It's very quiet now. Tory is still asleep.

Apologies for so much badmouthing the complainers back there. I didn't mean to offend most people using this walkthrough. Remember to leave thanks or at least understand how much work it is to do. I guess sometimes stuff just gets piled up inside me like a system overload and then I have to rant and flame. Apologies. Like they say in the movies: Let's try to keep it calm.

Time grenades look just like handgrenades (I'm sure you all remember that from weapons school ha ha) but they don't cause an explosion in "material things" but instead an explosion in *time*. Take out the pin and throw the grenade at the part of the game that has gone wrong (at the gun that shot Ray, toward the person that discovered him, in the direction of oncoming Storm Troopers or Duros and his rapier or whatever). Throw in the time grenade, throw low and right toward the center of the Bad event.

NB: Ray must be close—i.e. in the shock wave of the time grenade—but NOT TOO CLOSE to the explosion. It works in an obvious way—the closer he is the more he will be affected by the explosion and the ripples in time.

I heard from Clockwork once that he had Ray blow up a time grenade with it still in his hand and Ray went all the way back to a six-year-old boy. Whoa there. That is bad. I don't know if I can even imagine that. When I look at a photo of me when I was like six years old then the main thing is how thin and totally weightless my body was back then—not meaning light, but without history. In those pics of me in Belltown there are no marks on that body—life did not press on it in any way. And in those pics of me at Lake Windermere (in England, asshole) I look like I'm just pressed out of the pod. That is what Tory said about them. She was laughing (I think in a affectionate way). She said I looked straight out the pod. HARd to imagine Ray like that. Without the scar(s) and that tattoo of a bar code they gave him in a prison sometime in the backstory. Hard to imagine his eyes when they don't look like they saw *everything* already. Ray innocent. That is certainly hard to imagine. It's strange what time does to us.

Clockwork said that the 6-yr-old Ray didn't last long in *The BW*. It was certainly a big mistake to stand so close to the time grenade. The 6-yr-old Ray couldn't do the kicks really or the other attacks. He was low on Bravery and low on Cognition and also had no strength and no defense and no aptitude and basically no fucking chance at all.

Tory is still sleeping in the gray light that comes. I got up to get water and just stepped in the room to look at her. You can see that time took its marks on her if only just little marks. She is not old like Justine who Ray sometimes meets in 12th Town but at the same time you can see she is not a teenager. The skin is not all taut. It is soft sometimes, looser. And there's the scar above her eye that was a car crash. Or there's the other scar on her stomach where she cut herself on coral in Florida. Coral is beautiful in the water but not so pretty when it comes out into the light (or into the air?). It is also sharp, as Tory discovered back when she was nine. (Suddenly I am writing a nature guide? I'm sorry.)

Strange. In a body like the one Tory has or mine or even yours, you cannot use a time grenade. Time does not go backward. At least unless you have a spaceship that can fire you toward a black hole with you inside it and all crap like that, but for any realistic purposes at this point we can safely say that time only goes in one direction—forward—and that you are stuck in it. Stuck just like me or like Tory sleeping, like Brainiac sat there at his computer too early in the morning changing his icon like he doesn't know who he is or who he wants to be, like Dieter, Venter, or Clockwork. We are all so fucking fragile. I am breathing and I try to imagine you also breathing. Maybe your mouth—without speaking—makes the shapes of the words that my fingers are writing on the keyboard. I guess that you and me are alone together. So fucking fragile, going forward in time(s). I don't want to get freaky but I think you get the point I'm making here.

In so many words: If you have to use the Time Grenade with Ray to get thru the Duel with Duros at the end of this level that is OK. It turns back the clock to before whatever went wrong and off you go—just do the section again and MAKE SURE that you beat the Duros motherfucker the second time around. There are only 3 time grenades in the whole of *The Broken World*—that means three big chances. Don't waste them just for a scratch—there are many more dangers ahead.

The DOUBLE Moons

The next level starts in a different place and Earth seems like a long long way away. You look up and there is a black black sky complete with unfamiliar stars. It's not really clear if you're supposed to be on Venus or Mars or on some imaginary, undiscovered planet many light years away, but one thing is for sure—the planet has TWO very bright moons.

You move your legs and go bouncing upward (lower gravity?) toward the high ceiling of the Landing Station/Base or whatever. Only by grabbing one of the emergency ladders (at the side of the walls by the fuel tankers) can you stop from floating all the way to the top. Assuming you do not float away entirely (ha ha) make your way to the white sliding doors that lead off the central hangar. You can see landed spaceships and technical crews working on them. At the other side you can see the doors that are all identical except the one that has a radioactive (nuclear) symbol on it. That is the door you have to go thru.

Head to the end of the hallway. There will be a lot of busy people that go by—but many will notice you and stare. Get the impression that no one new ever comes to this colony? Correct. Ignore them and get to your destination (at the end of the hallway) where you need to collect yr Identity Badge, Geiger Counter, and Space Gun. A guy will arrive in a Buggy to drive you to a briefing. Do NOT miss this otherwise you will have no clue what the fuck in Hell is going down. Be warned tho that even getting there IS a serious challenge esp since there is one big design flaw in the WHOLE space station which is that it all looks exactly the fucking same. The place is on a vertical axis and it's hard to know this but you are on 19th level in the west quadrant. Walkways, hatches, sliding doors. Hangars. Jumpsuits. All the freakin same and all of it white white white. No wonder the captain of the space station, Lt Walitano— a huge black guy—looks pissed off all the time. Just try to get to the briefing on time.

Went to Palace with Dieter and Tory plus a friend of hers from the new temp gig—Sissy, I think, or Chelsea. There was a lot of talking, laughing and complaining. Chelsea (I remember it was Chelsea) was moaning her bad luck at having the same name as an ex-president's daughter which leads to inevitable teasing and Tory was moaning about the constant friends-rotation in Temping World like always having to get to know six new people and be nice to them for three weeks or whatever and then move on. I guess I was also complaining about Domenico's on all/any topic.

It was already late when Venter passed thru on his way somewhere else. Brainiac was in tow, in a strange mood and again not really talking to anyone. I don't know. Hi, Brainiac. Please don't take it all so SERIOUSLY. Venter and Brainiac. Mr Up and Mr Down is what Dieter said. Mr Up and Mr Down, he said, they are like a cartoon. Tory laughed so much about that.

All night Dieter was flirting with (the kind of attractive) Chelsea in a motorcycle courier kind of way. Chelsea made excuses and left and Dieter was making jokes about himself and showing off some not too convincing moves in the mini bowling lane they have in the back and making out that those moves (trick shots that did not even knock any pins over, but did cause drinks to get spilled) were always a surefire hit with the ladies and we were laughing at him. Funny tho. With Dieter I always get the feeling that he is gonna be alright. Out of everyone I know he's the most sorted out even tho he's kind of killing time in his job and is pretty much a waster. He's the kind of guy that probably makes teachers and parents and all those kinds worry. You know "so much potential" and "he's just coasting," enjoying the sunshine while it lasts. But you just know he's going to be OK. I mean—if doubt more or less hovers all around Brainiac, in the air somehow, the opposite feeling travels with D.

*

When you get to it the briefing is pretty much a long info overload. Hear me—GARS or Enemies of the Provisional Government (?) or Chang or someone (Archduke maybe, or some other guy or the Zorda) is trying to take over the known world (which is pretty obvious anyway by this point), plus some stuff about random snipers and a complicated political conspiracy of some kind to depose the President. You guessed it: Clarity is not a strong point in this briefing, which is done by someone called Lt Col Xavier. The guy looks like he is out of his mind. The briefing also contains a lot of info on enemies/problems you might encounter and how to combat them—the kind of genetically engineered Werewolves you have already dealt with, plus variations on the thieves, witches, assassins, Golems, and Rednecks etc that you know about of old from other towns, and a lot of new menaces that only feature in space—alien predators called Rashamons (I don't know if I am writing it correctly) and metallic drone weapons that follow your movements and then kill you in an instant by dropping from the sky, also space storms involving magnetism that trash all your instruments and throw you back to the Stone Age for fights where you end up using like 2-million-dollar laser equipment as a beating weapon or cudgel. Cool.

The last part of the briefing is all about your mission. On one of the moons there is a mining colony and according to this Xavier guy things were established there three years ago to mine out a rich uranium ore that is good for bombs i.e. valuable. At first things went well and the mine was productive, then things went wrong. There were a series of accidents and rumors that the people there were seeing ghosts. Finally there came strange radio messages from the colony and then total silence. Your mission is to go there and find out what happened—kind of like when Branimir couldn't get a answer from Domenico's one Saturday and he went round there to Investigate, only to find that the whole place was locked up coz Cookie was working alone and got a call saying her housemate got admitted to a hospital with schizophrenical delusions. I don't think it's gonna be the same when Ray gets to the Planet Moon—he's not gonna find the whole place locked up and the lights off and a note taped there with a Band-Aid saying Sorry Gone to Hospital.

*

A newsflash on Domenico's is that Stentson got fired. Here's what happened. First of all he was saying that he would no longer deliver to certain of the Projects because there were too many bad guys hanging around. Then a few days later he was saying that he wouldn't deliver to another area for the same reason—like he heard something on the news that there was a probable drive-by or something and there was "inadequate street lighting". That was the argument I saw, I guess, but I didn't know it at the time. Some time after that he told Miroslav he wouldn't deliver to another place because he was getting a bad vibe about it. And then he wouldn't deliver to some other other place because he'd dreamed it was a dangerous building with Bad Guys living there. And this went on. I mean—it was like the map of the neighborhood that Domenico's was able to make a delivery to was getting smaller and smaller and smaller and smaller on a daily basis. Like D's was the laughing stock of the Pizza Delivery Community. In a final straw Stentson saw some program about Crime Statistics in the whole East of the City and told Miroslav flat out that he wouldn't go there anymore, he didn't care how much they were paying him. So Stentson got the boot and no more is the Man-in-Black-and-Full-Face-Helmet to be found hanging round looking moody and jibing about how the pizzas were cold when he GOT them and how the FUCK can he be expected to deliver them warm if he gets them that way (COLD) in the first place and no wonder that customers are complaining.

Stentson finally rode off on his bike after standing silently on the sidewalk for a long time, looking at who knows what (the visor). Then Miroslav called Branimir and said that now there would be the Big Time of Changes (at Domenico's I guess unless he has converted to one of those cults).

Ashton said to me with his like best slow-motion TV horror-show expression—You know, Stentson worked here ten months and in that whole time I NEVER ever saw his face.

*

Go to the landing decks in South Quadrant. Level 6. But when you get there don't waste time looking for Lt Walitano—he's not there to meet you for some reason, maybe he got lost or succumbed to Space Madness, I don't know. Instead there's another guy, I don't think he has a name. I once tried to do screen grabs of him to look at his uniform identity badges, but when you zoom you still can't read it—I guess they thought that no one would be looking that close. How can you be a person without a name? I don't mean like Clint fucking Eastwood in the classic (i.e. old) western where he has No Name. In that *it is his name that he has no name*, he is The Man With No Name. But I mean just to have *no name*—not even random letters. No name? The name is what makes a person.

Anyway. He—the guy on the colony that has no name—looks at you (Ray) and says: "Here is a bit of lite reading," then he hands you a big motherfucker folder that weighs about a TON containing More Information Concerning the Mission. Then he smiles (?) with a raised eyebrow and says, "Your ship is ready, sir," and nods toward the flying space transit vehicle that is right there in front of you.

*

Figure out the launching process and log a route with Space Traffic Control. Then take off without wasting further time. Look out from the window as the ship moves thru the cosmic blackness. They do it totally awesome. Later, when u are done with the heavy tome of reading try playing chess against the ship's computer (the more chess you win the more ammo you have when you get to the other end). Careful tho—if you keep on losing at chess the weapons in your stash will start to disappear and you will be defenseless.

*

Echoing vaults of never.

That is what is scratched on the walls of the corridor in one part of the ship. I don't know why.

Life sucks. That is what someone else wrote in the dust by an airlock on board. Maybe Brainiac would like to agree—he called before and left a voicemail in which he sounded like life sucked. Tech support is not a good way to earn money—talking on the phone all day to idiots who don't know how to start up after a crash. I'm talking to you, DoubleTrouble or whatever your name is. DO NOT bug Me with those questions. It's not my department.

Anyhow. There is a gym on board the ship. Go there to practice all your zero-gravity combat moves. Ray tumbling and twisting, striking out at invisible Zorda, floating, kicking, falling but not falling.

*

There was a bit of a scene involving me and Tory and an argument about money and time. Seems Tory does most of the work around here and brings in most of the money. I didn't know we were counting it like that, but it seems like all along she was and she had plenty to say. I should do more shifts. I should stop the loser fucking pizza job, coz that's what it is however I try to cover it up making "jokes" about Cooked Circular Food, and I should not look at her like I was looking at her etc. Discussions here in the apartment last night over Beer and Tears then again this morning at like 8.30am involving the normal kind of door slamming and small reconciliations. Now she's gone to work. I think it's going to be OK. Everybody has these kinds of situation if they've been together a while. Before the conversation was over she went out of the room and called Linda and talked for sometime, then it sounded like she wasn't feeling too bad about it all.

*

Land the ship at the colony. Please don't forget abt the retroblasters.

According to the file that you probably read already, the last radio broadcast came from Dr Gincha—a senior researcher with specialist interests in drilling or tunneling etc. Dr Gincha (it's a woman and oh yes YES YES already you can tell from the hologram in her Sec. File she is CUTE) has her lab away from the mine itself, nearer the center of the complex.

You need an access code to move around the complex. Get this from the Number Randomizer Puzzle (Airlock). There are also Items to collect (as usual)—only now it is Oxygen (without it you will DIE) plus Protein Pills etc. The colony seems normal (whatever a normal space colony is like—I don't know) but the few people you see walking around are not too friendly. BugMap called it "Day One At New School Weird".

Go to Dr Gincha's lab. Watch out for faulty electrical installations (HAZARDS) throughout this building—getting a shock off these is a good way to lose a lot of health very quickly. At first Dr Gincha will not want to open the door, but just find an excuse and start asking questions. She has that look like she just got out of bed and an English voice, blue eyes, blond hair like she belongs in an ad for something. Also she is biting her lip a lot and looks like she has forgotten something the whole time, or is just on a verge of remembering it again. Hear me tho. Don't get too distracted by her appearance or the eye contact she gives you. Ray needs a lot from this situation but getting laid is not really on the agenda. If you show enough interest in the mine and the ore and problems it has been having Gincha will invite you on a guided tour. This is what you want. Don't seem too fucking curious tho or like you are snooping. Remember: Softly softly catches a monkey.

*

I think it's OK if me and Tory fight. I mean, I'm not writing an advice column for Gamers In Love or anything like that but if there are Negative Emotions it is better to let them out, no? Otherwise it can probably cause cancer, I am pretty sure Tory said that one time.

*

Probably designed with some sort of "spirit of utopia", in true life the Space Colony is a very grim high-tech shanty town, assembled by off-worlders in spacesuits and crucifying heat and now gathering space dirt. At least that is what Gincha says to Ray when she is driving him around at high speed in the Transport Vehicle thing. Cool. The colony is sweaty and cramped and the remaining miners/colonists look fucked up and frightened.

Apart from the informative commentary and the cute guide, the tour comes complete with an attack of moon vermin (use Sonic Attack), usual hazards and some tough-level zero-gravity puzzles. When it's done it's best to get some rest in Ray's quarters. ALONE. Venter and BugMap have got a bet going to see if either of them can get Ray to seduce Gincha. They've been playing it like that for a long time, always sending Ray round to ask her questions and making him stand too close and staring at her and making unprompted personal revelations and arriving at her living quarters at unexpected times of the night looking "sensitive." Venter claims that one night Ray went round and Gincha, just out the shower, answered the door wearing only a towel with her blond hair all wet and starlight in her eyes, but I don't know if I believe it or not. Just remember: 1) Gincha only has a certain limited amount of info and no matter what takes place between you that cannot change, and 2) there is Rachel to think about. I don't think it really does Ray good to distract him with other girls. Think about health points and emotional levels. Think about the kinds of diseases you might get on a colony like this one. No matter what I say, Venter and BugMap keep making Ray try it on with Gincha. I don't know. I'm not responsible.

*

Listen up. There are TWO glitches I spotted in the Colony Section including one in Ray's room where he should at this point be resting. (Hear me, guys.) I mean, there aren't as many glitches in *The Broken World* as in some games (check out *Back to Endland III: Reality Strikes BAck* for the ultimate glitch-fest. It is freaking ridiculous).

About those glitches. Here goes. Ray's quarters are cramped. There is a cot, a chair, and a table with a vase containing a Moon Orchid (BugMap says it is plastic, not even real). On the far wall you see a pretty non-spectacular porthole/window. You cannot see much out there, only moon buggies stacked high with ore and a few Rogue Drones (?) headed off in random directions. But if you take a close look you will see a pixelated shimmering by the left-hand side of the porthole. Bro—it is a tiny gap (maybe one pixel) between the texture mapping of the window and the green stuff below. OK. I am not an expert but when I showed the glitch to CW he told me that cool green line you can see is a part of the wireframe, i.e. the skeleton that they build the whole world onto. Texture mapping is how they make the porthole look like it does (with colors, paint, and textures, etc). Anyway. Look hard between the two and into that gap of darkness, and you will see it is somehow different from the night. My friend, when you look in to that gap you are seeing right thru to the nothing that the world is drawn onto. HINT: Do not spend too long looking in there coz you soon start thinking much too much about that nothing. Like what is it? Or what would happen if Ray could get inside it, i.e. not if he went out thru the porthole into space, because then obviously he would die (unless he was wearing a spacesuit)—but what would happen if he could somehow prize open the tiny gap in the world and go inside there, into the nothing that the world is drawn onto? Where would he even be then? These are the kinds of thoughts that can send you crazy. Ask Brainiac. He knows more about it than is good for anyone.

# MORE GLITches

Round two of the all-state Door Slamming Contest was this morning. I should apparently not do that thing I do sometimes when I whistle a tune under my breath. And I don't know what a conversation is, apparently, which is total BS since I don't spend *my* entire time with my head buried in a magazine.

*

There are other glitches in the game. For example, you can see artefacting (clumps of bad pixels that make the picture look wrong) in at least one Arctic glacier. Another example—the audio drops away during parts of Terror Motel. Also. Sometimes on the moon base when Ray washes his hands they do the water real good as it flows over his hands and into the bowl, just like water should do. But when he takes his hands out of the sink or whatever all trace of that water is immediately gone. At first I was thinking it was some special/magick kind of water they have there? But then I figured it's just a glitch and I was kind of disappointed. There is a full list of *BW* glitches that Yoko898 is working on—maybe coz she and Grinning Cat and El Nino etc think that the glitches have some deep fucking significance. To me they are just errors, not part of some big plan. It only takes a one and a zero to be switched or as Clockwork says "they only have to put an incorrect modifier between two output command lines" and you can get a spectacular effect glitch. No, I don't know what the fuck he is talking about either. But *The Broken World* can certainly be unstable.

OK. Listen up. Now I got an instant messenger from BugMap who insists that he got Ray and Gincha to way past first base. I think that is a sign of a sick individual—1) that he is doing that in there anyway, and 2) that he wants to broadcast it to me and anyone else here. BugMap. Go take a cold shower. And leave Gincha alone. She's got work to do Saving the Colony, dude, and she doesn't need Ray's help in that particular way.

*

With Stentson gone the scene at Domenico's is pretty weird. Business is slack "because it is Quiet Time" therefore Miroslav is personally doing the delivery in his "car" (it's an old vehicle made in Germany, a vanlike thing, you cannot really call it a car). Most shifts I'm just there with Ashton who is operating the register more or less in actual slow motion and for some reason doesn't speak that much these days unless spoken to. I guess the End of Stentson has set a worrying example of how things can go around here and has kind of cramped Ashton's style. That's the problem with these new guys—ESP the Gay ones. They start out with attitude and energy but the System grinds them down and they get to be gray faceless compliant assholes. Hi, Ashton. I know you're reading this. I'm only joking.

*

Anywhere you go day or night you can observe the true misery of the colonists and miners on this desolated moon. I mean, life on Earth can be hard (see previous abt Door Slamming) but it's better than the Colony Station. I mean fuck, that is not a life – breathing processed air with added fluoride, eating only artificial Meat and keeping up Morale Levels by telling crappy stories about Home. Gincha may be cute but the miners/colonists are 1) not getting laid and 2) half crazy. Just stare in their eyes for just a second and you'll see what I mean—the pixels there are in a non-standard arrangement (that is how Clockwork used to call his bedroom when his stepdad told him it was a mess and to tidy the motherfucker—a non-standard arrangement. Ha ha. I always think about that).

HINT: Head to Ninth Quadrant of the Colony. They do make it complicated and I don't understand how there can be more than 4 QUADrants. Why don't they call them sectors? Surely there can be an infinite number of sectors, but only four quadrants? This is one bit or thing I don't understand. Can someone help? Send a mail. I will credit any help in the guide. Also. If you want to put this guide on your website that is cool, but OnlY if you write me and get permission. DO NOT copy my work and think it's OK. The guide takes a lot of work and leads to pressures in my life (e.g. Domenico's and Tory) so give credit where it's due. No one should steal the fruit of my endeavors.

*

Colonists will stare at you if you say that you are going out there to Ninth. "Hey," they will say, "this guy is going to the Ninth." "That place is trouble." Even Gincha will warn you. No one in their right mind from the "technical stratas (?)" would go to this district alone at night, but guess what?—that is your mission.

Hear me, bro. There are lots of rumors at loose in the Ninth. Check bars like the Drill Bit or the Ore Miners Wetdream. You can hear rumors about GovCorp. You can hear rumors about a big Shipment of Metals that's due to come in. Pretty soon you will hear the stories of a legend that only one weapon can truly defeat the Zorda—a magic crystal (or something like that) that is buried in the heart of the mine. Hint: Ray has to find that Crystal Weapon, with help from Ghosts and also from Gincha. Info: The Ore Mine is on the site of an ancient mining colony, and Zorda are descendants of creatures that wiped out the colony, ghosts of those colonists from long ago. And their battle continues—Ghosts will make an alliance with the new colonists to defeat the Zorda. Only with help of the Ghosts can Ray find the Weapon etc. You get the idea.

*

Some news on the Tory situation is that the all-state finals of the Door Slamming Contest is at least on hold or maybe even canceled for good. I am joking—things are OK. She has gone off on what can only be called a nice camping trip with Linda. Oh Linda—not the friendly and even OK sister

Shay, but the one who's unsettled at all points in her life and exerts an influence of instability in any direction she walks, esp concerning men but also including other people and esp family members. I guess you see where I'm coming from when it comes to Linda. Anyway. Tory was meant to be temping but the firm that hired her for three weeks filed for bankruptcy sometime yesterday. Bro, it was freaking hilarious. They all got one hour to clear their desks, tho the Chelsea person was apparently not too delighted. I mean, for her this is not a Temp Gig it is True Life. Of course Tory claims this set of events was nothing to do with her, that the firm were in financial hardships already way before she even arrived. (I guess if anything T would have somehow improved their chances of survival.) Anyway, there was no realistic chance of anything else coming up to fill the gap at such late notice, so Tory called Linda and together they made a vague plan that got less vague pretty fast and (this morning) they took off. Since eight it's been just me here all alone. Music blasting and sun almost shining.

*

There are lots of Card Games in the Ninth and in many you can win useful stuff, Health Points or Items or whatever. The best card game (and the one you need to find) is run by a dude called Markham but the game is always moving so I cannot tell you the location—plz ask in bars and you will get the info. ALSO: Try not to seem like a cop—no one likes GovCorp or its paid stooges around here, plus there is no purpose in wasting Health Points by fighting colonists drunk on local hooch.

Wherever they are playing it, Markham's Game has some regular players to watch for. Check out Cindy—a miner's wife who's had plastic surgery to look like a doll from the 80s—and Rodrigo, a tough and lonely-looking miner who keeps himself to himself. Check out the

Brothers—two black guys who don't bet much but are constantly talking French. Also the dude with the filthy tuxedo, looks like he hasn't slept in a Million years—he's apparently trying to win enough cash to buy himself a one-way ticket on a star freighter home, but the way he plays cards that's gonna take some time. And of course check Markham himself, the son of an Alien who keeps one eye on the girls and one eye on the game and another eye looking out for trouble.

Remember—this is NOT VEgas. They play Black Jack with Space Colonist Variations (threes are wild because of the fact that apparently most spacecraft have three Fission Engines, plus some other rules—there is a full guide that Jo Bo is working on—I will try to post a link to it when he's done). Instead of chips they use little Blue Pills. Buy 10 of these pills (which is all they will sell you anyway as a newcomer to the game). Then start to play.

*

I have to say I don't know about Tory and camping—to me it's a strange combination because she doesn't even like domestic spiders, let alone the bugs you find out in nature itself. Fact: Any part in *Broken World* where Ray has to fend off horrible crawling creatures or whatever she nearly throws up. Also, once in college a wasp came into the room when Tory was doing exams. She got so distracted that she couldn't finish the paper. OK. It doesn't matter. Concentrate.

*

Your aim is to win 50 pills. Bet slowly and get the hang of the game. NOTE: Do not go high against Tuxedo Dude—he NEVER bluffs. When you have won 50 say you're gonna leave and that YOU WANT TO KEEP THE TOKENS (PILLS) instead of cashing them in coz you're gonna come back later. This is just so much BS, but bro, you need the PILLS more than you need the money—all will become clear later.

On the way out of Ninth Quadrant be careful coz you will soon face a big problem—his name is Rodrigo, the silent lonely-looking miner from the Markham Game, who will follow you to try and take back all your winnings. He's big and mean and will come at you without warning so Beware. Again, use the Kick attacks and watch out for a weapon he has—a big-ass piece of drilling equipment. Fight, fight, and fight again. Hint: If Rodrigo is winning try using slow time—that's a good defense and gives you the chance to rethink your strategies.

When Rodrigo is defeated he'll fall over. Bummmpphhhh! Crrraaaasshhh! Then something shocking comes. His body will shimmer and tremble and then a green light (plasma is what people call it) will rise up from him and hover in the night. The plasma stays there a moment then goes burning sideways at high speed, out/away toward the exit. Congratulations—Ray just saw his first Zorda. Rodrigo has been taken over, like so many unfortunate others (?) in the game. Check the Body. Check the Body. In the pocket of "Rodrigo" (= an empty shell of a dead person) you'll find a Map of the Mines. Take it, my friend. You will need it.

*

I mean, the good thing about Tory being gone is that I can really concentrate on this writing and get some work done, so plz expect more regular updates. Also, while she's gone I can make more effort to get extra Shifts at Domenico's. I don't mind working hard. By the time she gets back I can make some payments on the credit cards.

Two messages on the voicemail, one from Mr Up (Hi, Venter) and two from Mr Down (Hi, Brainiac), one from some computer voice to tell me I'm a Big Winner again, ha ha, plus one more from The Guy Who Is Looking For Lorraine. I have told you, dude, like a zillion times. There is no Lorraine. Or Lorraine has given you this number coz she hates your fat loser ass. It had been pretty quiet from Brainiac, which can be either a good sign or a bad sign. When he did eventually speak on the message—very quiet and superhesitant—it was only to say that he was thinking of going to see a movie but couldn't decide which one and I should call him with suggestions. Sounded like he'd been maybe wondering about which movie to go see for about a week. I don't know. In these moods an everyday decision can take him forever. Clockwork once timed him at the Pharmacy—Brainiac was stood in front of a shelf containing various toothpastes, reading and rereading the packaging on like 40 different brands to make the "right choice." He was there for 37 minutes and 17 seconds, which is probably a record of some kind.

I called B back and after maybe three times hitting voicemail we finally talked and made vague arrangements to get together tomorrow or something. I don't know what we'll do. Maybe call up Dieter and go to Palace again. It's just me and the apartment to consider so we can go anywhere.

 Seeing VOices

Here is an example of deductive reasoning that you can use. Fact: There is sunshine all over the apartment. Therefore: It is sometime in the afternoon. Therefore: I must have slept way waaay late thru the alarm. Thus: It looks like Domenico's can go to hell.

*

In some guides they are always using spoilers that give away the story, but in this walkthru I will only tell you the end when we get to the end. The story has to unfurl in its own time. Not faster, not slower. The clock of *The Broken World* is ticking. Its air is moving in that warm breeze of the mineshafts. It moves the hair of Gincha as she is driving the Small Jeep and Ray is watching her and keeping an eye on the Geiger readout. You can make some small talk—it helps to pass the time, but is probably not important in the Schemes of Things. Patient is the Warrior. Strong and Patient.

*

Make a checklist of stuff to take down to the depths of the mine then meet Gincha at the Vehicle Depot. There is a range of vehicles to choose from. I mostly prefer the Small Jeep coz it handles better, but there's also a bigger jeep if you like that and some scooter-type things. Load up with yr chosen equpMNt and get going.

In the mine there are the usual hazards of the colony—electrical stuff, mud pools, and drastic chemo spillages. But as you go deeper down there are also small Rodent creatures with red eyes and sharp CLAWS. These guys will jump at you so Beware. Rodents can be killed with handguns or with the poison-dart thing, but try to save the Laser for the Zorda who become more increasingly frequent as you go deeper and can interrupt yr progress for serious battles round any corner. Purple Zorda are the powerful guys so be careful. There are so many ways to buy it in *The Broken World*—I said it already. Sometimes I think it's a miracle anyone ever survives.

As you descend in the dark, Ray and Gincha will need to wear the Nightvision Goggles. In Nightvision the mine goes all green grain and colors and everyone's eyes look weird, staring, empty. Check it in the driving mirror of the Small Jeep—Ray looks like a cool green ghost but do not be complacent. You are thousands of Miles from Earth, on the moon of a unknown planet, miles under ground, relying on a stranger, headed to Zorda, Ghosts, and maybe worse. If nothing else, like Skeleton has in the lyrics to "Tampa," this is an easy place to die.

*

A call from D's but I didn't take it. I knew it was gonna be Branimir with an awkward type of question like Where The Fuck ARE YOU? Best to say nothing.

Brainiac was OK enough the night before last—the not so down side of Mr Down. We arranged to meet at Palace but were only there like five minutes when he decided some guy that he didn't know, or thought he didn't know, was staring at him. Every place we went to from that point on there seemed to be some problem. Too crowded. Too quiet. Too full. Too empty. You know how it goes. Too many assholes—that last description seemed to cover many bars. We moved a lot of times, so many that no matter how often I texted Dieter, he only caught up with us at 12. By then things were already a bit strange. In Bam Zak Brainiac introduced himself to some girl as A-Man-Driven-Nuts-by-Working-in-Phone-Support-and-Here-to-Drown-His-Sorrows. She didn't last long, which I guess was OK coz then there was a stool for Dieter. Before long Brainiac started in on trying to persuade him that even he (i.e. Dieter) could work Phone Support with ten minutes' training. Ten minutes. That's all B said he needed, but Dieter was skeptical, esp since he has like NO technical knowledge. Come on, Brainiac was saying, let me teach you etc, and in the end Dieter had to agree. It was a blast. Brainiac exclaiming his way thru this whole list of set phrases and Dieter repeating them, starting with "Are you sure you have the Item plugged into a power supply, ma'am?", going through red lights, green lights, pull-down menus and software versions before getting to the punchline, yelled across the crowded bar "I will have to speak to my supervisor."

*

It's a long route down thru the hidden levels to the place where the Crystal Weapon is. Zorda circle more and more but as promised Ghosts come to help, leading a way, fighting off some Zorda and blocking tunnels to trap them behind. The Small Jeep will only go so far and after that Ray and Gincha must continue on foot.

In the last level of the mine you have to save the Nightvision battery by turning it off and walking in darkness where possible. If the ground is uneven or dangerous go fwds with Ray and Gincha sharing a Nightvision kit—same way like scuba divers are sometimes sharing those oxygen tanks—passing goggles from person to person. Let Gincha lead because she knows the mine. I got mail from people who don't like letting a woman take control. Ha ha. That's the way to survive in this part, bro— get used to it.

*

The apartment is starting to look like a deserted disaster area now, with no one in it for days, except me (obviously—because I couldn't possibly be writing if I wasn't here). Yay. Seems that without Tory to stand in my way (ha ha) I can enter my name right back at the top in the Book of High Score Untidiness. I'm living on the tins, pasta, and breakfast cereal that's left in the cabinets. That's saving money the easy way, plus it's really healthy food, bro, plz take my advice. Oh man, now I'm like a freaking dietary guide blogger or something hideous. I'll get back to the game.

*

Sometimes in the journey downward thru the mine a Ghost will show up, bringing more bits of map to show hidden levels and to present a series of in-depth infomercials concerning the Ancient Colony and ten centuries of struggle against Zorda. This stuff is exactly what you need when you are 6 miles underground and scared half to death (check the health meter, dude, I'm not joking). In any case, I don't understand why there's so much talk e.g. about the history of the colony movement, its phases and leaders, evolution of its politics, and great battles of the planet etc. Agggh. It's sad, stupid even. Maybe that's the point. Ghosts are completely obsessed with the past, obsessed with stuff that happened already, but you (Ray) have to live in the present and get on with actual life. If anyone finds out a way to disable those Ghosts from the lectures plz let me know as soon as you can.

They do a lot of work on the sound down there in the mine. It shifts and moves with like inexplicable noises that come from who knows where in the thick green darkness. Hard to tell if these are hallucinations—I'm not an expert in sound—but they are upsetting anyhow. Venter had a cat that would totally fucking freak whenever this part of BW got played—scratching and hissing. It's on the edge of hearing what they do in there but it does the job OK coz NOTHING feels more tense than this part. Later the cat (Toby) died when it ran under a garbage truck, but that was nothing to do with the game.

*

Tory called from her camping trip. Hi, Tory. In fact she called from a nearby motel. Sister Linda is still camping, or maybe not, T didn't exactly make it clear. Anyway, there were apparently some problems with mud and rain and bugs the size of Rats living in the trees near where they pitched the tent. Probably just flies. But I got a laugh out of it—Tory facing flies and Ray facing distorted Rodents and Zorda. Anyway, despite the problems, Tory and Linda are staying away for some time, so I still have plenty of time to get on with this writing, except for all the extra shifts that I plan to do at Domenico's, not counting the accidental no-show I did today. Bro, it was maybe 3am when I came back here after last night with Brainiac. I cannot keep pace and the headache/nausea is in full freaking Payback Mode.

*

So far so good, so far so good. That's what the guy says when he jumps from the window of the 69th floor and is falling downward, past each floor with the wind in his hair. True. But here at the bottom of the mine—when you see the final chamber in which the Crystal Weapon lies—it's a different story because the freakin sidewalk is not a good friend at high speed. Yes. There is good news *and* there is bad news. The good news is that after all the obstacles you have found the one true weapon that can slay the Zorda forever. The bad news is that Gincha is really a Zorda and will turn on Ray here.

You see the Crystal Weapon in the Last and Final Chamber. You step fwds to get it. Then you lose control of the game.

Gincha steps back as you enter the chamber. She pushes Ray forward, smashes him on the skull with the butt of an exhausted Laser Rifle. Cool? Not at this point. Gincha starts to glow—Zorda colors seeping in her skin, red, green, and yellow, and casting a strange light on the whole scene—she looks at Ray where he has fallen, laughs, then locks the door so that he—battered, unconscious, and maybe even dead—is left trapped inside.

Gincha leaves and as she does there's a strange kind of echoing noise that reminds me of the graffiti Ray saw scratched somewhere on the walls of the spaceship bringing him here. *Echoing vaults of never.* Maybe this moment, this terrible terrible sound as Gincha leaves, is what that graffiti back there on the ship was really all about. A premonition. I don't know. Gincha takes the Rifle and the Nightvision kit with her, as well as what little remains of the supplies.

GETTING OUt / GETTING in

Ray lies trapped in the Mine. Unconscious.

*

Branimir called from Domenico's once more, but I let the machine take it again. I think I can probably skip another day/nite and claim to have flu—there are so many people sick with it I don't think a short absence is gonna seem weird. Cookie or definitely Ashton need the shifts. I can do a few doubles later to make it up financially and (for a last excuse) I'm pretty sure that Tory won't notice. (Hi again, Tory.) It's Cheerios for lunch here for the 3rd time, and for dinner there's a bagel I found inside a paper bag at the back of the ice box.

*

For a long time there was a kid on *The BW* boards (Hooper64, I think, or 56, or 69) always saying that he was gonna find a way to get the Crystal Weapon somehow—maybe without any help from Gincha, or that somehow he'd get the weapon and TRAP HER INSTEAD inside the empty Last Chamber.

BW discussion boards and blogs are often full of that kind of talk and people claiming they "defeated GARS using only a knife" or they have a cool new route through Impossible Town or have discovered a way to take off Rachel's swimsuit at a Pool Party etc etc. When asked to prove these claims it seems people can't quite remember how their great solution worked. Some admit they made an error of judgment and others just wipe out their entire profile and slip off into a night of Internet anonymity. Mostly it's just the boasting and emptiness of young guys. (Sorry. It's like I am suddenly 100 years old, but I think you get my point.)

Anyhow. It was like that with Hooper64/56/69 and the big idea how he'd get the Crystal Weapon first without getting trashed by Gincha. To start with came his big announcement of plans and then just a lot of sad reports on his failures. No matter how he tried to achieve it, the ending for the mine section was always the same—Ray dead or Ray trapped by Gincha and left to die there alone. All plans coming to nothing.

It's like this—a kind of catch as they call it or unavoidable Fate—1) you need to find the Crystal Weapon and 2) you can *only* find the Crystal Weapon with Gincha's help and 3) when you *do* find it Gincha will betray you, crack you on the head, and leave you locked down there to die.

*

I called Dieter to see if he wanted to get drinks or hang out later but he said no he had other plans. I was spacing and said OK I better go, but then he was laughing so I said what and he confessed that he's meeting the freakin Chelsea person from Tory's Temp Gig for drinks.

He has a date with her. Man, that took me by surprise. I told you he (Dieter) is gonna be alright. I thought he was making a idiot of himself with his stories about the lean, mean lore of bike messengers and all his close scrapes and his late deliveries, but all the time he was secretly planning to get her number. I'm impressed. I don't know how he does it. I guess girls can spot the survivor types in a dangerous profession like his—some kind of genetic radar. Dieter and Chelsea. Tory will think that's hilarious. Kind of wondering when she's back. She hasn't been so big on the specifics.

Today I had some music channel on too long, and the whole time they were playing the same freakin songs again and again, and all the songs were on the exact same topics—i.e. Love and Loneliness. It's as if there's nothing else in the world. I cannot stand it anymore. I cannot find the remote.

I was just thinking about the time Tory and me broke up. It was something like three (?) years ago—we'd been together a year—I don't know, I'm not equipped with a working calendar function. She met some guy at a party and they were flirting. Then he mailed her a lot. Nothing happened. But one time I came into the room and they were IMing each other and T was like laughing and closing the window real fast when she noticed me, and I was like OK, let's take a break. Abt a week later I went on some half-assed road trip to see Hunter who had gone to college somewhere. It was a weird trip. BugMap came along and I was basically freaking about Tory and what was going on. I was thinking a lot esp abt the IMing—those little messages going backward and fwd between her and that guy. All those bundles of words and phrases. She has that flirting thing down pretty good. At night I always went to the spare room at Hunter's and shut myself away, thinking this is the best place for me, no distractions—just time to think it thru.

*

When you first wake, long after the Zorda formerly known as Gincha has left the building, plz take a good look around in what they call the Last Chamber. I guess the name of this place isn't exactly optimistic, but don't panic: I am here to help.

Firstly, it doesn't take long to figure out that there are no easy ways out of the chamber. The walls are hewn of granite stone and the door is twenty inches of solid steel. Here we go again. What is it with Ray and confined spaces? Sometimes I think he likes to get locked in, just so he can prove how good he is at getting out again. Secondly, since the Crystal Weapon is like a powerful tactical/portable Nuke, it probably seems like maybe *that* can open the door. Ha ha. Very funny. I admit that BugMap and me tried it one time. Man. After 4 hours in the darkness trying to figure out the controls there was suddenly this gigantic sound and everything in the vicinity was totally ATOMIZED. When the sound died and the destroyed surface of the moon was visible thru the swirling dust, Ray was left lying on his side in a crater two miles wide, and he didn't have a Health Readout anymore.

*

No word from T, but there was a call from her parents who are now apparently concerned about her and Linda being out there in the middle of wherever the fuck. I was saying like it's OK, they're grown women, you have to let go of them sometimes. And all the while I was thinking about Tory checking into a motel and leaving her sister out in the wilderness. It will be OK. Nothing to get concerned about.

So Tory's mother talks to me for a while then Joe gets on the speakerphone with a "quick" Question. Here we go again. Today it was the regularly occurring Special Bonus Round Question of "an issue with the TV." They had like a new cable system installed just before the summer, which was already the subject of numerous Questions. Anyway, ever since the installation Joe says there has been a problem with Channel 89, which is, as he describes it, a Dead Channel. Maybe (he says) it's a channel where they only broadcast at certain hours of the day or night, and he's never got it on at the right time, but now he's starting to wonder if that's possible. Or maybe (he says) the company that paid the license to like broadcast on that channel has actually gone bust and out of business—that would explain it of course. He's not convinced though, and *now* (and this is what he wants to ask me), NOW he's thinking maybe there's some kind of defect in the way that the guy was installing the whole set up—i.e. that there is something there on 89 but he just can't fucking see it. I mean, T's dad has like 200 channels and the idea that there is something on Channel 89 that is really cool is what's bothering him now. I mean, he's losing sleep over it—the dead fucking channel—what is he missing? What is it? What is it? That's what's slowly tormenting him into hellfire. And the Question is—yes, I know, it takes a while to actually get to the Question this week—the Question *is* "DO *I* think it's an installation error? And do *I* know what should be on 89? And is there *anything* that *I* could do to help fix it?" (Which is three questions in fact, a change in structure for the bonus round.)

You've read it here before already, my opinion that the people out there in the suburbs are CRAZY—I offer this as further proof. Why can't they just buy a TV guide? Or call the frigging cable guy? Or the gardener or the pool boy or the cops or the maid or a fucking shrink or something? That would be simple, but instead they decide to call me. What the fuck. In the last three years I've became like a Dr of Everything. All scientific, electrical, domestic felony-related, and philosophical questions answered. I don't know. They are crazy out there in the suburbs. Don't forget, you read it here already.

*

Now the sun is leaving the apartment. Same pattern every day. TOOK ME ABOUT TWO YEARS IN THIS PLACE BEFORE I KNEW THE PATH IT WOULD TAKE. (The caps lock sticks sometimes. It's not my deliberate intention for the last sentence to be in capitals. I'm not awake enough to deal with technical malfunctions so if it happens again, please ignore.)

*

Yes to everyone sending complaints. A big apology for all the diversions that keep you from the much needed solutions. PLEASE RELAX, take some space to breathe, rest or do Interweb shopping or whatever.

When I came back from Hunter's, Tory and me made up. I guess when things are bad I still have doubts and think about back then. It's like that with Ray too, and what happens with Gincha's betrayal. I mean, even if you get out, take revenge on Chang, bring down GovCorp, and like even make it all the way after the Gincha trashing, it is never the same etc.

So much for the Tough Guys—when it comes to the girls they are not all so tough, ha ha.

*

HINT: To get out of the Last Chamber you have to start thinking more laterally. HINT: Check thru those items that Ray got on the colony and try to think what might be of some use. Bro, sometimes it happens that you stare and stare at Items in some desperate situation, thinking like WTF, and then suddenly—ping—the answer comes and you know what to do. HINT (in this case): What about something you might eat?

OK. I cannot HINT anymore. I am just gonna tell you. What about those BLUE PILLS Ray won in Markham's Game?

Take them out. Examine them. No writing, just smooth and blue.

When you pick up the pills there will be a flashback. You will see Rodrigo, back in Ninth Quadrant, trying to take Ray down and get the pills back, like they're important. That is the flashback. Then look at the pills again. It's weird, now, because after the flashback, like a magic trick or sleight of hand, there *is* some writing on the pills. The words say something, very tiny: EAT ME.

*

One time BugMap took the peyote his brother was hiding in his closet. At first it was amusing. BugMap came round to Domenico's and was laughing a lot and talking shit (so what's new?!). (Apologies to BugMap.) But then it wasn't so funny, when BugMap claimed to be transported back to a primal land of the Ancestors or something, which in his case would be like Sweden or Norway. He was freaking out at all the cars on the expressway and then talking about things that are "before language" (don't ask me, I didn't write it down) and then he was just crying and crying and crying like he was a hemophiliac, only with tears instead of blood.

For this reason (and others) I'm not keen on taking strange drugs you've won in a game of cards on another planet. (Hear me, BugMap—this is true and good advice.) I'm also not so happy abt drinking random potions that happen to be lying around even in *The Broken World*. The brain is a delicate machine. You can rearrange the 0s and 1s in there quite easily, even if you just put a very powerful magnet next to your head or stick your face over a can of the strong adhesive (the one that Sleeptalk, Cordy, and the Jones were addicted to) and breathe deeply. I take a dim view of that attitude/behavior. The 1s and 0s are hard enough to keep track of at the best of times—ask Brainiac about that, he knows too much about it. I don't like them rearranged at random.

But in this instance, with Ray in the Last Chamber and a moon so far away, I always make an exception.

Word up, bro. Take the pills. Take them all. Then lie on the mother-fucking floor and wait like a baby for the consequences to begin.

Sometimes it's not so much about getting *out* of someplace or situation, but going further *in*.

OK. When the blue tablets take hold, Ray's vision starts to swim—the blackness of the Last Chamber shimmers round him, like the light that's reflected from black mercury (?). Ray is sweating. He staggers and falls. You see him from above, and his eyes struggle to focus, like he's looking at something in the air up beyond where the camera is. But of course there is no camera—there is no camera at all. I can't understand why I'm talking like it's a movie—of course anyone can see it's not a freaking movie. Anyway. The non-camera (whatever) moves closer to Ray. His eyes widen and the shot goes closer, zooming in thru the eyes—into the splash of pixels and the screen goes bright, bright and then very very dark. You lose control of the game.

THE CROWDED EArth

When Ray wakes it is in a crowded city street and you know straightaway
that the drug has brought him back to Earth, but it's not the Earth of all
lonely hick towns and minimalls that he left behind, and not the Earth of
deserted-type desert motels or isolated research facilities that are near
the North Fucking Pole, or the Earth of Castles, flaming torches, and all
the goth stuff that Sleeptalk likes. Instead it's a big crowded Earth that
Ray has gone to—like the biggest city you can imagine, with the crowds
and "permanent clamor of human beings in the air." (I got that last bit of
description from Janka—thanks, Janka. Respect.)

There is sunlight bouncing on office buildings made of glass, and
nearly mile-high corporate-type structures, and you can also see kind of

cool grand hotels that almost break up the clouds with pinnacles (?) that look like radio or maybe satellite masts. All around you the street is so full with human life you almost cannot believe it. Man, you do not want to do your Xmas shopping in this—it's out of control and the crowd is pressed really close and flowing in so many directions that you cannot properly keep a track of it. There are like thousands of people crammed between the buildings and all of them apparently having somewhere to go except for Ray who is just standing there, eyes blinking in that street. For the first time in the game he looks just (i.e. only) like a person—not like a hero anymore—just like one more guy, one more human body. This is the Crowded Earth and—just a warning, dude—it's one of the hardest parts they ever made in the whole of *The Broken World*. It's so hard to make it thru alive.

Ray says something you cannot hear. Then he looks around at the advertising hoardings high up above the street. On one you can see a slogan for the New Gap and Consolidated Nike, and on another it just says in thick black letters: I DID NOT KNOW THAT DEATH HAD UNDONE SO MANY. Maybe that's the name of a band, or a tag line for some movie, or just like a private joke of the guys that coded or rendered this whole scene, or maybe it's just a side effect of the drug. I don't know, but somehow it fits with the whole freaky situation.

*

At this point in the game a lot of people are saying like "Who can I shoot?" Or "What about a cool puzzle to solve?" Or "Let me at the Demons." My advice is that when you regain control of the game, just stay still. Wait and watch the crowds. The rest will come.

Lots of people wonder about the blue tablets that Ray took back there. For example—how EXACTLY does it move Ray to the Earth? Is that even possible? Or maybe Ray is not really on Earth at all and everything he sees now is just a hallucination? Etc.

I just want to make it loud and clear that in this walkthrough I will not answer these kinds of questions. I also won't answer the bigger questions that people are asking, like is this truly EARTH or is it just someplace that looks exactly like it? And how could anyone tell the difference? Hear me, bro—to all such questions I just say a big almighty "PASS" or "NEXT QUESTION." Many have focused their brains on problems of philosophy in *The BW* and did not find a good answer, and I will not follow them to run on a road I cannot even walk. I'm more for the game and shooting and the prize than for that kind of thinking. I take the simple approach—I say Ray is either there, on Earth, or he is not really there—whatever way you like it—it still has to be got through. That last bit is the most important part and do not forget it. I don't much care about making long metaphysical distinctions with those kids that probably do too much Weed and Ludes and think that Sine Evaders are a really good band. No way. I'm done with that. Let the game continue.

*

In the Crowded Earth you have to stay alive in usual ways—i.e. Ray needs shelter, food, and rest, plus you need to keep watch on Health and Energy Levels AND stay out of lethal danger. In a big city where you are a total stranger that's not so easy. I mean, there's no ZOrda chasing you or crap like that, but try looking for a chance to work without the proper legal papers or getting hassle from Gang Members or negotiating a price for food at the street market or sleeping on a park bench or in a Homeless Hostel, and see how you like it. The first few days in that city are hard and they have randomized the game here totally—this part goes beyond the beyond. No cheats and no pattern. It is chance—all chance, all of the time.

For this mission Ray needs to find a key, not an olde golden lock kind of physical key, but a key made of 27 numbers. Your problem is that just *one* person in the whole Crowded Earth can give it to you. Nightmare. Ha, ha, ha. "Oh they REALLY did it this time," as Brainiac said, and because they randomized it *I cannot give you one single clue on who it is.* In a game that is already pushing the limit, the Crowded Earth truly takes it to the edge. It can be any one of those thousands of people passing you in the street—any one and ONLY one of them knows where the key code is. Any *one* of them can be your savior or not. Just watch the crowd and think abt it. It can be that girl over there, the one laughing, or the old guy that opens up his briefcase on the bench by the tall glass offices or the kid that brushes next to you that's wearing pink and red sneakers, or that other kid with the blue and curious eyes, or that woman sleeping in the sunshine near what could be a Library, or the traffic cop wiping sweat off his face and directing traffic at one of maybe thousands of busy intersections in the city, or the construction worker that leans on his pile driver, his ears protected by those things that they wear—I don't need to go on, I guess, I think you get the full idea by now. There is, for sure, no easy way to win.

*

I still haven't been into Domenico's since T left. Ashton left a sarcastic voicemail in which he hoped my illness was incubating nicely, but you could tell from his expressions that he didn't really think . . . whatever. Thing is, the more I pretend to get sick the more I think maybe I am sick.

Like I'm listening to his message and kind of rubbing my forehead like I'm aching.

*

Every now and then comes a rumor or a bragging idiot (hear me, Yakuza333) who says they have "discovered a system" to beat the Crowded Earth etc. But anyone that's truly played the game and all the real *BW* crew on all the discussion boards and blogs and in any other place you can find out there on the Internet are totally agreed that you CANNOT CHEAT IT. We are talking needle in a haystack, dude. You can only do this part the hard way. And yes—it's nice to believe all these fairy stories, but brother, the world is not Disney. Everything does not have an easy answer that can be sung in the words of a rhyming song from a cute animal with a chorus of dancing plankton.

Only with the number code can Ray get back to where his real body lies—in the Last Chamber back there on the moon, so far away where you left it—and escape. Without those numbers he will die for sure—body in the mine and his soul (or consciousness or mind or whatever you like to call it) probably wandering the Crowded Earth for eternity. *Bring it on, bring it on* is what we always say, but how can you bring it on in a part like this?

NOTE: 1) Do not Panic. Ray knows somehow if you are panicking and then things start to get worse. 2) You will quickly notice that there is something special abt the crowds in this city. I don't know exactly how they make them so much better, much more real than they look in other games. I mean, Clockwork once told me that they do the crowds in a special way for *The Broken World* and esp in this part— "fractal generators" or something else out of his Dictionary of Big &

Technical words designed to Confuse innocent people. I'll ask him about it.

(OK. There is no immediate response from Clockwork on IM, so I'll come back to the whole thing with the crowds.)

*

Bro. While I'm writing abt the crowded streets of that Earth and all the people there, I'm in the middle of a great Emptiness in my life. It's just me here and a landscape of the apt that now has like 5 days of dirty dishes and even more of laundry. Rolo is still away seeing his brother who got back from one of the Occupations. I didn't even know he had a brother, let alone one in the Infantry. And Tory is still at loose in the world with the Princess of Wacko Linda. Rolo's stuff is everywhere as usual tho, despite the fact that he's gone. I mean, HE is like molecules—you cannot get rid of him no matter that he's been away for two weeks. My crap is here and there too and Tory is also there—I mean her traces and clues are everywhere. For example, a picture of me and her in Vegas, on the floor her underwear, and a magazine she was reading by the couch etc.

*

I took a timeout to drink some colas and Clockwork called with the lowdown on the crowd thing, so I'll repeat it here just as he told me, but I make no guarantees for anything lost in "translation." Clockwork says that now in most games (or movies) they do the crowd using "generator software" but in *The Broken World* it's done by hand, each person done separately, not even in batches. Crowd generator "works on a set of basic human forms, giving them height, width, body shape, posture" (I wrote that bit down) and then gives them movement (motion) and "a certain amount of averaged agency" (don't ask me. I am just the messenger. Use Google if you want to find out more.) OK. Each person in generated crowds has a "standardized departure from a mean" (that is the average), and the software just creates faces from a set of overlapping morphed templates. Whooa! My heart is pounding, either from the colas or all the Big Words. In fact, bro, I have a depressing feeling that no one really understands this except Clockwork and the ppl that wrote the game. He loves this stuff.

CW says a decent crowd generator works like a cabaret magician. The main trick is sleight-of-hand distractions—waving frantically with the left hand so that people don't see that the right hand is secretly getting handkerchiefs, duplicate playing cards, doves, or girls in a leotard out of a box. I mean, if you're watching what's happening in the foreground, you won't really notice that the background isn't real, that the crowd isn't full of people but full of Shapes. The trouble starts if you *do* look closely, then you start to see defective repetitions and patterns—figures or maybe types repeating. Check the crowds in *Mob Rule VII* or *Forensic Detectives of Woodstock* and you can see it immediately. Sure, there are no obviously "repeated persons" . . . but you still sense the crowd is not right.

When it comes to the crowds, *The BW* is in a league of its own. Straight up you get a feeling how wrong all the artificial crowds you ever saw before in movies and games really are. You can tell that it's hand done. For a test just pick any one person from the crowds in Crowded Earth and try to follow/interact with them. It is way cool. They do not 1) fade into nothingness when you get out off the main thoroughfare or 2) conveniently exit into an office building or behind a razorwire enclosure where you cannot follow. They all have what Clockwork calls "permanent integrity'—which means they do stuff all the time and have proper characters, they're not just background Shapes. That's enough from the Big & Technical book for now.

*

According to the most recent call from Tory, she and Linda are now both at the motel and the camping is totally abandoned. Ha ha. I think I know whose credit card is getting maxed. Not Linda's. Things aren't so good now between Tory the Queen of Mazes and me following a stupid conversation on the phone where I suggested that Linda was mostly interested in her—i.e. Tory's—cash support and the Queen of Mazes said I should mind my own business esp when it comes to Financial Management and I said OK but blah blah and blah your fucking blah blah and she said blah and what the blah blah blah and blah. I guess you can imagine the rest of it. But this is a walkthrough and not a blog about dating. I know that's not what you want. You want the game and nothing else, right, CurveBall? Sure. I guess I'll tell all about Tory and how she got her Queen of Mazes nickname some other time. Whatever.

*

It's cold tonight but the heating is not on for another month. The whole apartment feels like that deserted mountain town in a Hidden Level somewhere, the place where everyone has been evacuated in advance of a murderous Children's Army. I am Ray, me, walking about, discovering it all after everyone has gone, in the scattered ruins of life that once existed in this lonely apartment. Like I'm the first on the scene of the crime, only I'm also the crime and *The Broken World* is also the crime but like there is no crime in the first place. Fuck it. I don't know. Or maybe, like I'm the only person left in the world and I have to sit here in this apartment and write it down to try and figure out what happened coz I'm the one with the freaking writer skills. I guess I don't really make any sense. It's late. I'm thinking too much and going in circles.

*

Around ten-thirty I couldn't take the hunger pangs anymore, so took a chance texting Ashton to ask if I could liberate some CCF at Domenico's. Seemed like a perfect plan. Sure, he said. They will get me a Siciliana with Olives and other stuff ready all I have to do is go over to collect. But as soon as I put down the phone I started to think it might be a trap, and Branimir would be there waiting for me. I got halfway out the apartment then came back to sit and think about it. I mean, Branimir or Miroslav is never there at night unless there's a break-in/emergency. So why should this night be different? Just to make sure tho I texted Ashton some questions, like were the Brothers in today? And did they for sure leave already? It's freaking ridiculous but I don't want to be dealing with Miroslav late at night yelling Mouth Fucker Mouth Fucker or something in the Middle of the Street.

Gone 11 I finally got up the courage, found an old coat I don't wear anymore, and went in the long way, looping around the back of the store so I could see if the Miroslav transport/van was outside. No sign. When I went inside Ashton could see I was nervous and was making out that Miroslav was just heading back for some reason, but I was pretty sure he was Bullshitting me because he couldn't keep a straight face. There is NOTHING straight about Ashton. Anyhow, I pretty much took the pizza and ran for the hills, at least if you think about the apartment like it is some kind of hills you can hide in.

Oh yeah, one other thing. Since yesterday there is FINALLY a new delivery guy to take Stentson's place. The new guy is called Danny, but to keep things simple I'm just gonna call him Stentson 2.0. I only caught a quick glance of him but can confirm that he is just like the previous model in the Stentson series i.e. dressed in Black from top to toe and Full-face helmet. According to Ashton tho you can have an actual conversation with this new one, so they must have improved the design of the sociability function. In a week's time or in a month the 2.0 will have more depth, but for now I don't know. He's just a shape I saw outside the store on his bike. I think about Rolo again and how I hardly know him even tho we've shared the apt for so long. He's also a kind of shape, only half filled in. Or what abt the other people in the building? Or the ppl that I pass in the subway? I don't know.

*

There are some dudes writing to me constantly to say listen up you Pussy y*ou cannot even call it a walkthrough* if there are major parts of the game where the Author just says "there is no solution—go figure/you have to work it out for yourself." Like these guys are implying my work is a CRIME against the very idea of a walkthrough.

Well, that may even be true if that's how you want to call it. Yeah. Bring it on then, all you lazy Assholes. I cannot deny. You can nail me to that and fly me up the top of a tree. Go ahead. *The BW* is too complex and I say right here and now that you cannot walk it through, not step by step like that in training pants. You have to live it. You have to sweat, Motherfucker, that is what I say and what I'm trying to do with this guide. I have no time for all you whiners that cannot truly take the pressure.

So now, just in case you've been sleeping or not paying attention in class, here's a reminder of the bad news. There is no cheat for the Crowded Earth. The game has a complex and unpredictable AI engine (thanks, Clockwork, again for Big & Technical) and the crowds are as real as unreal can be. YOU *cannot* cheat it. You have to find the key/number code. The whole thing is randomized. You CANNOT cheat it.

The WISH-Less WAITING

Branimir called again but I thought I'd leave it one more time for the voicemail and maybe skip some more days saying I have Jury Duty. It's not implausible and legally they have to let you take time out for Jury Duty, PLUS Ashton doesn't care (if I'm not there) and I'm sure the new Stentson 2.0 can get on just as well without me. I can do doubles later to make up the difference.

I'm thinking of Tory down at the motel, wherever, probably lying in the sun by a pool or something—she was vague at describing the scenery when we last spoke on the phone. They've been gone seven days now, by my count. And while she lies there, I'm sitting here in the freaking gloom with the curtains all drawn against the day. No sign of life in the apt except from me. The whole city outside so quiet now. Not even a noise from outside or downstairs. No dishes done. No calls. No TV. No light coming in from outside except just like tiny cracks to remind you that it's probably still day out there. I can hear a pin drop of water. But it does not drip and it does not drop. Like, absolutely Nothing.

Also got a call from Brainiac but flipped him again to voicemail. I wish I could stop thinking of him as Mr Down. But I cannot deal with it now. I need to focus. No distractions.

*

To succeed in the Crowded Earth you must find a way to be OPEN to all that happens in that city. Drift. And be open. That's my advice.

Do not find a place to sleep and like stay there the whole time. Do not find a place to hide and barricade the door. "Get out there and ACTUALLY MEET PEOPLE" like they say on all those dating/ personality-transplant shows. Get out and walk the sidewalks. Breathe. Get on the subway. Walk. Ride the escalators—even just up and down is OK. It doesn't matter. Move around. Bro, sometimes THE ACTUAL CITY ITSELF IS THE THING YOU ARE TRYING TO SOLVE. You can even find graffiti that says those exact words of advice, right there in the Crowded Earth, on the handrail of a escalator down in the train station, scratched beside more regular (i.e. not so useful) graffiti concerning FAGGOTS DIE and REDS FOREVER, REDS FOREVER, REDS FOREVER.

*

Fuck. I spent like 30 minutes turning the entire apartment over to find something to eat but there was only 3 freakin rice crackers in a packet in Tory's gym bag. I don't want to think how long they were there. A nasty taste. Ughhhhhhh. That doesn't really count as food, but I cannot risk Domenico's again. The day is still young and I'm already confused. The clocks in the apt are either showing the wrong time or else flashing 0:00:00 like after a power-out, but I'm not fooled coz I can still tell what time it is, bro, just from looking at the TV. I MEAN, DEPENDING ON THE KIND OF PROGRAM THAT'S ON on DIFFERENT CHANNELS YOU CAN PRETTY MUCH TELL THE TIME LIKE IN THE OLD TIMES WHEN PEOPLE USED TO LOOK AT THE SKY TO TELL THE TIME. (OK. Capslock was jammed again—if this continues to get worse I'll have to finish the whole freakin walkthrough in SHOUTING mode.) I'm really gonna have to go out sometime and find some proper freakin food. Feel like a vampire in the dark in here, bro,—forced to scour in the city by Night for what I can find. Maybe later I'll just have to go to Brainiac's, confess that I'm still on the planet and see if he has stuff to eat. Not that he's known as a genius of cookery, but at least he has a job that pays over minimum wage. And anyway—I CANNOT risk Domenico's again even for a jumbo Siciliana. It's not good for my sanity.

*

One good method is follow people—pick on strangers and walk with them. Go where they go but don't let them see you or they'll freak out. I don't think I'd like to see Ray following me in the street (ha ha)—I mean, he looks pretty roughed up from the mine and the fight with Gincha and everything, with his own dried blood all over his face and torn Space-Combat clothing, it's not exactly what everyone is wearing. Anyways. Get out and walk. If you don't know how to choose a route in the city just look for random clues—walk from one red thing to the next, or from one blue thing to the next—could be a plastic bag that someone is carrying, someone's scarf, a billboard—doesn't matter. When blue gets boring switch to orange, red, or gray. Doesn't matter. Or look thru the trash on the street and take some random route clues from that—call phone numbers on thrownaway napkins, call the hookers on the calling cards in phone booths, follow the hand-drawn maps that you also find on thrownaway napkins or paper blowing in the wind. Man. They do the wind real good—in gusts and spurts and gales. It's a fucking masterpiece— better and more detailed than the crowds. I love how they do the wind. Read my lips again. You have to let go. You have to lose it, dude. Find a way to stop thinking (?).

NOTE: When it comes to people in the Crowded Earth, remember that anyone can be useful, anyone can be the one you're looking for. Do NOT discount suspicious types, or what you think are ugly people, or crippled dudes in wheelchairs, or chicks you wouldn't normally trust, drunk or sober, or stinking homeless bums that lie sleeping under cardboard, or crazy demented old hags or retarded kids or boring-looking old assholes of indeterminate gender that sit playing on a park bench or whatever. You have to leave ALL your ideas about people behind if you're ever gonna succeed. And all your other ideas.

*

A lot of people on the boards are always saying stuff like Ray is a man of action, an action Hero. What's he doing walking around like a fruitcake or like a freakin homeless guy rooting in the trash? Or they say Where can he get a big-ass weapon? Or what if he could like smash his way out of this world and back to that faraway Moon using a combination of a homemade Dimension Portals and a Quantum Bomb? Or whatever crap like that. OK.

HEAR ME. ANY WAY OR "METHOD" FOR SUCCEEDING IN THIS PART
INVOLVES A KIND OF GIVING UP. (That's not accidental capslock this
time—it's deliberate.) You need what Grinning Cat once called a state of
wish-less waiting. Or if you want that in simpler language, a bit less like the
kung-fu movies—you might just have to lose control. It's a case of search
and you will not find. Look and you will not find. Drift and it will come to
you. On this one thing Grinning Cat and Yoko898 and Me and Brainiac and
Clockwork and Venter (Etc) and even roughhouse shoot-em-up-type dudes
like Crispin and Helium and Scat are all in agreement. And there is, FOR
SURE, no one that you need to shoot, no Demons, no bombs to detonate,
no traps, no Puzzles. Not this time, and not like that.

I guess a lot of people that give up on the game are doing it here. I
mean, I'm not like a market fucking researcher but I would bet actual
money that *this* is the place where the weak get going. It's definitely a
turning point.

In her 1st post about the Crowded Earth—after she got thru it the first
time—Grinning Cat wrote only one line of advice—I mean, other people
are writing complicated stories, ideas, and how they did it and what a hero
they are for being first etc, and GC just wrote that one single line that is
maybe still the best advice you can possibly get for this part of the game,
I give respect for that. She wrote—"Keep that Don't-know Mind." Respect
to GC. REspect to those that find the ways. It's like a quote, maybe some
proverb from a cracker barrel, I don't know. This might be the only time I
ever agree with her, but it's true. You have to keep that don't-know mind.

*

NOTE: There's a good story on *The BW* boards from some guy who *just
waited at the spot where Ray first entered in the Crowded Earth and*

got the whole solution from there—without even moving. He had Ray wait there and simply not move for three weeks. Ray not eating or sleeping. That's so cool. Standing. Refusing to move around. And then after the period of three entire weeks, Ray was delirious, starving, a freaky figure in the crowd—and there came, in the blue sky above, a fucking *airplane* going right right overhead, *skywriting* to spell out the 27 numbers. Cool. Cool. Cool. But when Brainiac tried it the same way— just for a test, to see what would happen—oh, then it wasn't so cool. Ray stood there and stood there and stood there and finally died of Hunger.

It's random. Keep that don't-know mind.

*

No sun in the apt now. I don't know where the sun is these days. I drew the curtains closed so I can concentrate and see the screen better.

You can see that Ray himself gets kind of tense and edgy sometimes in the Crowded Earth—maybe the lack of violent combat starts to get him down, or his body isn't used to the Gravity, or he's just tense tense tense from waiting for an enemy that never appears. I guess peace can be like that, if your norm is War.

Just realized there are messages from Tory on the answering machine. (And a new one from Branimir. I'm writing this on Internet, Branimir—have you heard of that, ha ha?) Tory is still out there some- where with Linda, only, according to T, now they've hooked up with some guy(s?)—she was non-specific—or Linda hooked up with some Guy (?) who is Fun and showing them the sights. What kind of sights are there? I don't know, I cannot picture it. Is he Fun with a capital F or just an ordinary one? If there was just some way to send a warning to that Guy. Like to keep his hands on his credit cards, balls, and sanity so that a certain person cannot get her hands on them.

*

Branimir called AGAIN. Still no pickup from me. I mean, I know that I'm probably getting close to the point where I need to DEAL with the missed shifts and everything—you can tell that by the temperature of his voice— but I need to be in the right frame of mind. If I talk to him when I'm not in the right frame then it will just backfire and do more damage than good. I can handle this. It's nothing to worry about.

*

Some people say that Ray can find Rachel on the Crowded Earth but that's not true—no one ever found her there. (Hear me, WiseAss. You are free to look but I'm not gonna hold my breath. That is not the purpose of this part of the game.)

NOTE: One last thing I noticed about this part is again concerning glitches. When Ray enters some rooms here, there's a glitch to the graphics where the landscape jumps or stutters somehow. E.g. Ray checks into a hotel and opens a door to his room. The room is small and tidy, with folded sheets, a chocolate on the pillow, and flowered curtains. As he steps into the room it all kind of jumps or flickers. Funny, they have so few glitches to the graphics I wonder why there is one here, in this stupidly simple part? I mean, they make such good petroleum explosions and cartwheeling blood carnage and splattering mayhem and swirling symphony of Zorda attacks, but this scene—the motel room with its door open to the sea just outside and a "sparkle of light"—somehow they cannot get it. How come simple things are suddenly the hardest?

*

When the key code/number finally comes to you (Ray) it can be in many different ways altho the skywriting as mentioned before must be the most spectacular that I've ever heard of. Be ready at all times. The number could get passed to you on a scrap of paper by some person you just met, or whispered in your ear during a taxi ride, or told to you in a phone call from some near-total stranger that you just happened to encounter. Or it could come ringed by a stranger in the numbers of your bank statements or written in the sand by a girl that Ray (you) is slowly falling in love with against all his better judgment, or chalked by some dumbass kids on the wall at the end of a long long garden in a house that Ray just happens to be staying in when all hope is almost gone etc. There is more or less no actual limit to just how the code can come through, but one thing is for sure and certain: you will only get one chance—so plz PLEASE write it down when you see it and keep it safe.

*

Weird with the curtains drawn the whole time. I just opened them to look out, but I guess I totally missed the day. It's night again. I have to somehow break this spell.

I'm trying to picture Tory again, but I can hardly get the thing started in my head. Somehow I just see a standard motel and a standard guy at reception and a standard blue sky. I cannot get the detail, she didn't tell me enough. A standard picture of Tory and Linda. A standard picture of some guy (or guys?) they met. Not enough in the detail. I can hear Tory's voice tho, not her phone voice, but the sound of her voice, the texture of it—that's in my ear, or lodged in my mind somehow.

Tried Dieter on the phone to see if I can snap out of this mood but he's busy again tonight with this Chelsea person. They're going to some show. I don't know. Seems like they became quite the inseparable Item, those two. I thought he'd gone quiet on me.

Also tried B coz he called before. Now there's no answer. I'm still here in my deserted mountain town. Starting to think this wasn't such a good idea. Tory away doing I don't know what with I don't know who. Me here alone while the world got stuck in some kind of loop. When B called he left the exact same message to the one he left before about going to a movie. I know I did NOT just replay the same message I already listened to—it's a new message, but it just says the same thing.

*

Back on the Crowded Earth things change once you have the code, like the Earth is moving from under Ray somehow, shifting in different ways. Don't panic, assuming you get this far. It's gonna be OK. Some parts of the game end quickly but the Crowded Earth goes slowly slowly like a fade-out, or like the last effects of the blue tablets are distorting Ray's perceptions of the world.

You will notice in the Sleep Levels display that Ray needs to sleep more and more and when he does it takes longer to recharge him. Soon his DAYS WILL GET SHORTER, AND HIS SLEEPING NIGHTS MUCH LONGER (capslock) and in time it will reach the point where he has to like grab sleep wherever or whenever just to keep on going—sleeping on the subway or a bench or at a table in a café. Sometimes even a cop or a waiter will notice Ray and push him on the shoulder saying *Hey man. You cannot sleep here. Move it along.*

In the end—days after you first get the code/key—Ray will just pass out/collapse in some public place. This is the start of the end. People nearby will panic and start calling paramedics or whatever, yelling Get Help and asking if anyone round here knows some First Aid. But Ray doesn't need First Aid—it's just what happens when he leaves that place forever. There is no route back. The Crowded Earth will shimmer and glisten round him like it's "only a dream" and then the screen will go dark. This part is done, and like it says in that graffiti you can see on the toilet wall at Macy's in the Crowded Earth (third cubicle from the entranceway door), "We walk a circle in the night and are consumed by the fire."

*

Oh man. It's late now.

After that last bout of writing, I hung around in a kind of brain-and-starvation coma for a while then decided I had to get the fuck out of here before I fainted or turned into a vampire. I put on clothes (I wasn't naked before—just not dressed properly), then headed to Brainiac's looking for food/moral support. It was dark outside and raining. From the traffic and the people on the street I couldn't figure what day it was. Thursday maybe? Friday? Instead of the moral support (?) at Brainiac's I found computer games and reheated Pasta with Paul Newman Type Sauce and bottles of beer. Maybe I can get some sponsorship for the walkthrough by endorsing foodstuffs?? Contact me here if you want to discuss this. I'm serious, ha ha. I can make it like a real long list of stuff I like to eat.

When I got over there to Brainiac's he was killing time on *Broken World*, but not really following a Mission, just finding tasks or puzzles to do. He was turkey-shooting Cyborgs then trying to catch a lucky fish in some lake in 42nd Town, making morphing spells and doing target practice etc. We talked a bit and I didn't mention all the weird shit he's been pulling lately, but I was watching him the whole time, trying to see "how he is under the surface." Bro. I hope he's more organized in his head than he is in his apartment. It looks like a total bomb site, worse than my own landscape of Oblivion back home. Oh Brainiac. I don't exactly know what the problem is with him, but his name alone gives out a pretty good clue. His mom said even at the age of five he had such a deep-sea THINKING look to his face they were worried the muscles there might get strained. I guess that's why they gave him that name.

B was playing, so I was in charge of reheating the pasta and throwing the sauce on it. (I even WANTED to get away from the screen—I've been staring at it too long.) I enjoy cooking. I don't often do it, but at times like this I can see why people get into it. After we ate, B came to some place in the 19th Town, which I wasn't sure I'd even seen before. There wasn't one piece of pasta left in the pan—we ate the whole lot. Anyway, there in 19th Town B found this "office" building where you (as Ray) get trapped by Operatives of Chang and out of which (kind of obvious) you have to escape.

At first there seemed to be no exit at all—the door is like iron and totally locked and the window has bars and would be wayyyyyy too small for Ray to fit thru unless he could miniaturize (no—he can't). But word up. Plz don't despair if you come to this situation. Instead LOOK UP HIGH to the ceiling where you will see that there's a skylight. I have to admit it took us like nearly forever to spot that. Sometimes the simplest things can be the hardest to figure, even when they're staring you in the face.

To get out you have to pile all the furniture etc in a certain puzzle/arrangement i.e. building a tower to the skylight to get higher and higher, then climb to get out. First we worked as a team, but in the end we were kind of competing to see who could build up the most twisted and unlikely arrangements of furniture and stuff. We played on this part maybe four hours straight, making the craziest towers we could possibly get to balance. You have to think of a pile with a little coffee table and folding chairs at the bottom and other chairs, one on top of the other, in the middle and then a sofa at the top with a desk balanced on it to complete the arrangement. Neat. Brainiac said the whole thing was like the tests they made him do when he was a kid and his mom took him for a Mental Assessment (with inkblot tests etc) and the longer we worked at it the more we were laughing big time at the sooo many different unstable ways you could build it up, right up to the skylight, and escape.

But here is the thing. In the end I kind of lost interest. Maybe 4 hours is my limit for making towers of virtual furniture, esp when the beers have run out. So I started drifting, watching TV (*Killerwatts*) and thinking of stuff like the Future and Tory all that way away, about the thing she had once with B's brother (Paul) who she never really talks abt and how it only really ended coz he left for Portland, and how T doesn't like it when B gets weird coz it reminds her too much of those days which was when B had his 1st breakdown (not the right word), and then I was thinking more about me and Tory and more about Brainiac like where he's headed on his cycles of up and down right now—just drifting, like I said, but also going round and round in circles. And all the while I was kind of watching B play and getting this sense off him that something's wrong even tho he was playing with his back to me and not really talking. I mean, I was Phased Out but B—no way—he just would NOT stop. He went on and on, sat alone in front of the computer and staring intently, saying "Man, man . . . " when he had a good arrangement of all that furniture or "Motherfucker, motherfucker" when it started to collapse.

I must have semi-crashed right there on Brainiac's sofa when it got really late. I remember staring at him thru half-closed eyes and Brainiac (as Ray, in *The Broken World*) taking books off the shelves in that office/prison and piling them one on top of the other, making something like a house of cards (only with books), the whole stack getting higher and up toward the skylight like a huge and impossible ladder. And all the time he was talking under his breath, working on it, superconcentrated, and anytime the stack started collapsing he'd just go right back to the start and begin building again. I think I drifted off to sleep there for a while. I was exhausted and pretty drunk and when I woke up Brainiac wasn't at the computer anymore but fast asleep on his futon thing, and fully clothed and *Killerwatts* had finished a long time ago and now it was some documentary about a golfer that had to have hip surgery. B's computer was paused where he had ended playing the game. I looked at the pic—Ray in the flickering strip-light of that office, looking light as air on top of the highest stack of books you ever saw, Escape Map in his hands, reaching out for that skylight and the stars.

I got up. Dude, I was cold. I stole Brainiac's jacket and left to walk home. I was thinking B is so resourceful, so fucking determined in something like that—the divergent thinking escape test or whatsoever—how come he can't be like that out here in the world? It took maybe 20–25 to walk home and all the time I was thinking about Brainiac.

The RaIN MAZE

Tory, Queen of Mazes, has returned. I was half woken by the noise of the door around 5am, and then when I woke properly (9, half an hour ago) she was there beside me—back in the picture like she never left it, asleep in bed wearing T-shirt and panties, comforter pulled close to her face.

The apartment is still like a micromuseum with spilled samples and crumbs of stuff I ate in the last days next to other exhibits of Dirty Clothing, Magazines, and Dust. Tory's bag is dumped right by the door. No sign of Linda.

What caused this sudden return of the Queen remains a total mystery and will have to stay that way until she wakes—the rest is just guessing.

It looks like it was a looong trip though, at least from how deep she sleeps. I'll let her stay that way till noon or so. The sun is bright and sky is all clear, flat and blue.

T's parents called, as if they knew by kind of biotelepathy that Tory was back, but I didn't mention it, just to gain her a few hours of peace before the explanations and interrogations concerning Where Is Linda? And What Happened to Linda? have to start. In any case, they weren't explicitly looking for Tory. Instead Joe wanted to speak to me in my role as notorious freelance Dial-An-Expert. The big new question concerns a virus on their computer that's causing emails to be sent out randomly to different people in their address book. Do I know how they got it? (The virus.) Of course I do NOT know. I guess they're opening the emails that say Subject: Joke and then inside a file called Is It About You? or the other ones that say Subject: Important and then a file called Please Read As Soon as Possible. Ha ha ha. Of course Tory's dad denies that he opened any attachments like that. And Tory's mom also denies it. But privately they are both accusing each other. Do I know how they got the virus? No. Do I know how they can get rid of the virus? Run virus scanner would be a good start. What can they do to stop getting viruses in the future? Stop opening emails with the Subject: Secret Report and a file called How To Get Rich. Chances of this happening: probably none. (Repeat after me—the people out there in Suburbia are going crazy crazy crazy.)

This afternoon I will reluctantly be accepting a nice invitation to go into Domenico's to see Branimir about my recent absences, repeat bout of serious flu, and Jury Duties. I am also invited to take a Sick Note from a person in the medical profession, which will now have to be written and printed by me, and signed by the Queen when she wakes up. Yes, I'm looking forward to that. The lies are piling up, bro, but I guess they have to if I want to keep the Domenico's job. I'll get extras shifts for the week ahead and make up the ones I blew out while T was away.

*

When Ray wakes again he finds himself right back again in the Last Chamber of the Mine. PLEASE. Do not get depressed. At least now you have the important key—those 27 numbers—that can get you out to meet Destiny.

Enter the numbers in the door-lock keypad. Make sure you put them in the right sequence. The door will open.

When Ray gets out take him back thru the tunnels of the mine. Follow the map Ghost gave you (second map) then head for the place marked Abandoned Excavations. (Remember to take the Crystal Weapon with you coz that's needed to defeat the Zorda.) The game moves fast at this point. There are plenty of Zorda to fight, complicated hazards to jump over, get around, or demolish, plus some Rodent creatures etc to kill. It's just like old times. By the end of the battles you will be dripping with large amounts of Zorda slime. Cool, as Scat and Helium like to say. Mmm, man, that is Fingerlickin good. (NO. The slime is poisonous, dude. You cannot put it in your mouth unless you want to get trucked out of the mines in a body bag.)

When you get to Abandoned Excavations there are two doors. A green one that says Staff Only (ha ha) and a red one that only says Danger No Entry. There are no prizes for guessing which one Ray has to go thru. It's the story of his life. He is Danger No Entry.

Immediately thru that door is the Bad Maze. It soon becomes clear why they call it that.

*

AT FIRST THE MAZE IS ALL (fucking capslock). At first the maze is all corridors and tunnels and mineshafts etc just like before. But after that it constantly transforms in diff ways. Sleeptalk says it's like an endless flat plain that goes on to infinity and beyond, in shimmering green color. BugMap says it's just about freaking impossible. I guess both of them are right. The endless shimmering plain has hidden/invisible-type walls and if you so much as touch them we are talking Game Over. Thanks, guys. This is the Bad Maze—bad because you cannot even see it— hardest one of all in *BW* or in any game I ever heard of.

NOTE: 3 players have so far published solutions to the Bad Maze. That makes this the 4th I guess. I didn't check the others but from what people have said on the boards I salute SuckIt, Ishbel97, and of course Gimp. Not like I know them except by reputation. Respect. Gimp was the first to get thru the long empty green shimmering that is called the Maze of Endlessness (other people call it Puzzle Maze or Diamond Maze or Bad/Psychotic Maze, like I said already, but it doesn't matter—it's only a name).

I should say respect to the sleeping Tory, Queen of Mazes, for her help in this part. I never could get thru it without her. Bro, the first time I came to it (last summer), I admit it, I was getting majorly pissed off and stuck, getting lost like a baby. Always having to go back, save, and restart just to keep Ray alive. At that time no one had posted a solution on the boards, in blogs or anything. I was getting demented.

To make it worse we had boiling days in the city and I was sitting there in my underwear the whole time (too much information), no AC and sweating like an animal. Branimir even closed down Domenico's five days straight coz he and the Miroslav agreed you could NOT work there— that's how hot it was. Even the grunting slave drivers had some compassion. Anyhow. One afternoon at the height of the heat, me and

Tory were both home and she was reading but really half watching me over the shoulder coz I was getting so mad with the game, going round in circles many times, Health Points dripping away like shit. In the end she came over, put down the magazine and stood behind me for some minutes, real calm and quiet, just watching me twist and turn like a legendary idiot. Then after a time she put her hand on my shoulder and said all matter-of-fact: "No. You went that way." And I was like "Uh?" and she said, "You went that way already. Just go left and fifth right, and then first left and then straight and third left and straight and sixth right and then you should be pretty much out of there." And it was true. She went straight back to her magazine. And I sat there like in cartoons with my jaw dropped on the table. Motherfucker.

Ever since then, if it ever comes to labyrinths I always call in Tory—official Queen of Mazes. Bro, I would even give the controls to her if I thought she could operate them. Tory got me thru that big maze in the Black City (32nd Town?) and the Ice Maze somewhere close by and thru another one really like it (I forget the name) and also thru a maze that you can find sometimes in the Gardens of the Overlook Hotel (in part of the colony, Ninth District—best to avoid).

They make those mazes mean, but they cannot beat Tory. They make them like a pattern of veins in human skin or like a city grid, or like a network of interlocking tunnels built by prisoners in a war that has not happened yet. That cannot beat her. Some have force-field fences, and some have mirrors and kind of horrible repeating architecture so you cannot tell where the fuck you are going, and others stretch for what feels like a million miles, but even that cannot beat her. Wherever space is unwinding and unfolding or twisting about on itself in like many fucking knotted directions—that is just like second home to her. She cannot be beaten in there.

Some people draw maps for the mazes. Other dudes on the board suggest that Ray should drop Items or torn-up Paper or Bread or other crap like that to leave a trail, but Tory doesn't need a thing, no method, tools, tricks, devices, and no trails. She just looks and walks and looks and walks and not too much later she *knows* the way. Brother, she just *knows.*

*

Here (below) is the route based on my notes from last time I went thru. For now I don't have time to write it out properly. The apartment is too much of a mess and I have to 1) tidy up some and 2) go get breakfast food unless I want to feel the wrath of the Queen when I wake her. I think you can figure out the route from what is written here (??). If not, I will update it later. It's hard to know sometimes if I should just continue to go forward in the game toward the end, or else go back now and try to fix some places where I said I would add more detail. Apologies.

7 South
2 East
5 South
7 West
8 North
16 West
7 South
12 West
3 South
2 East

Ray will often need to sleep but you mustn't let him. Use extra energy.
Also Reserve Energy.

56 West

21 South

7 West

7 South

1 North

2 West

8 North

12 East

Where is the Queen of Mazes when you need her? I wish she was awake
to check the directions.

19 East

23 South

52 West

12 North

2 East

2 South

22 East

Ray needs to sleep and this is a good place. You can let him sleep now,
but only on condition that he stands and keeps his eyes open. It is
possible to achieve this, but it really takes practice. Rest and let the
levels go up. Then continue. After this things get very hard. The maze
gets more complicated.

8 North

3 West

12 North

3 East

30 South

12 West

8 North

36 West

12 South

18 East

4 North

3 West

12 North

7 East

5 South

4 West

5 South

2 West

34 North

1 West

32 North

3 East

33 West

2 South

77 East

It goes dark at this point for twenty (20) seconds. Try to count. When the seconds are up just fire the blaster in any and ALL directions and keep it shooting til all the ammo id done. Id done. Ha ha. Id. I should have written "is." Ha ha. After you have fired it all, take a Flare from one of your Items and light it. Just count the dead Zorda in any direction, lit up by the burning purple light.

    9 WEST
    10 EAST
    5 North
    6 West

Darkness. Like I said before. I don't know why they make it like that.

    *

Tory is kind of stirring in her sleep. From the bedroom I can hear she is partly talking but I cannot hear the words. I even get scared writing the mazes. I mean, for me they are like the hardest part and this is the Mother of all of them. Would like to wake her just so she can help me check thru.

    *

    5 North
    45 East
    2 South
    ~~7 South~~
    ~~1 North~~
    ~~2 West~~
    ~~8 North~~
    ~~12 East~~

~~5 North~~

~~6 West~~

~~18 North~~

~~16 West~~

~~3 North~~

These ones are crossed out in the notes I made. I don't know what I meant by crossing them out—I guess it's a bad direction. But I put them here just in case it's useful or relevant.

THERE IS THE SOUND OF RAIN FALLING NEARBY/OUTSIDE (in the game *and* in the rw).

(= real world)

9 WeST

Unrest.

23 South

9 North

set forth.

4 West

best.

3 North

Make a rhyme to make it easier to remember.

18 West

19 South

*

Tory woke so I took a break. We had breakfast by the window. The rain I mentioned before was not in fact real rain—just in the game.

Turns out Linda took off with the guy they met down there. Mike. Possibly not his real name. Probably a dentist. Linda and Mike were going on a road trip (?!) and Tory apparently didn't want to be part of it. They swung by to drop her off and oh yeah Linda borrowed 200 before saying goodbye—which plus the motel bills and other Amex means she made a good profit this time. Tory was quiet on the details of the trip but I put that down to the tiredness. IN fact she sounds basically pissed off at how it developed, esp at Mike's repeated joking (but not really joking) hints about a possible threesome when Linda was out the room. But she said it was good to see Linda. Good to see her having fun at least, even if it was fueled by the usual "Linda Diet" of Weed and Mixers. Mmm.

*

7 East
23 South
1 West
2 North

Not far to go.

When we first beat the Bad Maze it was two summers ago, not last summer as I said before. Tory and me were deciding that it was Love with a capital letter. SO I STILL REMEMBER (fucking capslock) she and me sat next to each other walking Ray thru the final parts where they make the maze out of rain. We weren't in this apartment then, in another one, on Reece.

The noise of that rain is amazing and it falls in sheets to make walls of the maze. Ray has to walk and stay dry. They kind of dissolve the mine to a secret world—first with the invisible walls on an endless (?) plain and then with the Rain Maze. Ray has to stay dry. It is dark and the rain is visible only in moonlight. You have to go carefully. It's one of those parts where you wish they could really do smells and tastes in the game coz the smell would be wet and DEEP STICKY BEAUTIFUL IS WHAT WE USED TO SAY. THE SMELL WOULD BE LIKE THE BEST NIGHTS OF EARTH, THEre on that moon far away, we said, where Ray is outside but he cannot be outside because there is no oxygen there.

For the last parts the notes are becoming unclear. I think it goes like this:

12 West
13 North
29 West
1 South
~~7 South~~

(Again, it's crossed out in the notes but I have left it here in case.)

5 North
6 West
2 East
33 South
12 East

You see a wall the color of rain with a door the color of rain. Open it and step thru. Ray emerges into a exit tunnel near the Main Station at the Lunar Base, the Crystal Weapon at his side. The maze is done.

*

Just a newsflash concerning Brainiac who has ramped up his weirdness, at least if you count the number of times he called yesterday. Way to go, Brainiac. Bring it on. I had maybe 16 (?) missed calls and 6 where we spoke. That is an average of nearly one call per hour. Even back on the COlony Ray doesn't have that level of radio contact back to Lt Walitano or Melange (the communications officer that BugMap said is probably French). As well as more frequent calls thru the day, Brainiac's messages also got more and more miserable and increasingly unclear coz of the way he mumbles the whole time.

Motherfucker. I don't know why he takes so much on board, all the "worries of the world" on his shoulders. Talking to him is like sitting near a endless fountain of despair and even over the phone you inevitably get splashed with the stuff from it (the fountain). The bad news. The massacres. The guy from down the street. The fact that it's so dark at night etc. No good asking Brainiac to take it easy, I guess. He's our personal ticker tape or Reuters or Associated Press Agency of only the bad news and hosting a special news show edition each freaking night called The Glass Is Half Empty. You certainly couldn't hire him to do a kids' birthday party. Mostly on nights like this when he starts to get bad (and I say this just as a warning for what can come) you can only do two things—1) listen and 2) ask politely if he is still taking his medications.

*

Outside the maze there is the dark sky and the stars etc but across the landscape you can see a shadow running, sliding, spreading on the surface of the moon that reminds you of the shadow that Ray chased right back at the very start of the game. He looks out exhausted, at this far-flung planet/moon. And gets ready for what is to come.

*

Last parts of the level. (Just notes. I'm sorry.)

Trip to Boss Mountain.
Discovery of Tapes.
Colonists Town Meeting.
Off-world Wrestling (Interlude).
Zero-Gravity Tag-Team Mystery.

Arming the Crystal Weapon and delivering it to the Zorda Nest with the help of an underground network of colonists (resistance). When the queen Zorda are dead the rest of them weaken, turn into gray-green slime.

(Arming sequence for Crystal I will explain later.)

Exit Puzzle. (Time Flight Potion—do not neglect to collect.)
Moon Orbit (Interlude).

A huge explosion at the heart of the Zorda encampment. Invisible poison radiating out to Zorda everywhere. Celebrations across the Moon. Board spaceship—*Invincible* is OK but *Ratcatcher* is better, faster.

*

On board the ship to get home to Earth. Handle blast-off and launch sequence. Set course and fire Distance Engines. Check ship meters and subroutines. ATTENUATE LEVELS.

Mix the cryogenics formula (you need ingredients from store's lab, and formula from ship's mainframe). Inject it in veins. Lie back. Set timers, alarms (sequence as directed from mainframe).

The cryogenics kicks in and you lose control of the game. Cut to a wide shot. Looking down on Ray (from above). He lies, curled kind of fetal, in the sleeping pod, eyes open, looking upward. Maybe he thinks about all that's happened since the start, since he set out on the road toward First Town—about the battles and trials and tribulations he's been into since then. I don't know. You cannot ever really tell what Ray is thinking. I mean, I'm not a mind reader. But when u see him and look in his eyes he does seem to be always thinking about something. At THIS POINT HE has a certain look, like he's sad enough to weep at the FACT that the world is in troubles and deep under threat from the Archduke and Chang. Or maybe he's just worried about Rachel, you cannot tell. He starts to close his eyes in sadness mixed with the approaching sleep of chemical oblivion. The ship breathes a darkness round him and his vital signs trigger a kind of symphony made of bleeps, blips, and LEDS. Cool. He sleeps. On his way back from a planet far away. And as he sleeps the whole Earth's fate lies in the balance. The level HAS ENDED. FATE WILL TWIST AND TWIST AGAIN. (That is the problem with allcaps again—not deliberate.)

Some MajOR Changes

I'm sat here at the computer (HAL) with notebooks and Coke bottles and everything all scattered around. I've been sitting here a long time, thinking about the next part and how best to explain it. But the more I think about it the harder it is to find a way to break it to you gently. SO, here goes, dude—You are Rachel now.

Remember those brown and green eyes with pixels to die for—they are what you'll be seeing the whole world thru for the coming months. Rachel. Rachel. Rachel. Remember those sparkling and like utterly mysterious eyes—they are what you'll see into when you look in a mirror or other reflective surface. Rachel. Those eyes, that face, those legs, that butt (and the rest of it, YES) are all yours now.

Or more precisely they ARE you now—there is probably an important difference.

I say it again. Rachel. Oh man. This comes as a Biiiiigggg shock, I know. There are gonna be some major changes around here (in *The Broken World*). Ha ha. It's no joking matter. For the next levels you are Rachel. You cannot be Ray, coz he's fast asleep in the Deep of Space, and now only Rachel can carry the game forward toward victory, bringing death to Chang, GARS, GovCorp, Archduke, Zombies, etc.

*

T was only back maybe 30 hours and already got sucked back downtown to keep her hard-earned reputation as Best Temp in History/Since War Time/in Living Memory. They called so many times to offer gigs when she was away, I lost track and stopped writing them down. It's fucked up we couldn't hang out more.

Meanwhile, this afternoon, as planned, I finally braved the music at Domenico's after my high score of unaccountable absences. I was hoping by a Miracle of Unknown Reasons this could be a day where Miroslav and Branimir were NOT going in, but instead when I got there they were both waiting like heavies in a movie where they intend to break the legs of a little guy that owns money to them, or where they will cut off one of his fingers to show him a lesson. Cookie and Ashton pretended to be busy working hard on something in the background while Branimir led the attacks with lots of questions and jabbing the air. His whole speech would have almost been hilarious if it wasn't also what you could call a First Verbal Warning, and also coz Miroslav was constantly repeating aspects of his Brother's statements. What about Tuesday? Branimir asked and in the background Miroslav grunted YES.

TUESDAY. Or when Branimir said How come you didn't even answer the phone? Is it a wrong number? his brother was grunting YES, MOUTHFUCKER, WRONG NUMBER? I survived this interview of doom and made assurances that in the future, since I'm over my illness, I will be more like a good drone worker. I could hear Cookie laughing out loud at that, but thankfully I don't think Miroslav knows the word drone.

OK. In the end it wasn't as hard as some days at Domenico's can be, and gave me the chance to check in with the Stentson 2.0 model and how it's dealing with the pressures of the job, heat and chaos. Bro, I think the technical team that works on the Stentsons should be congratulated. The first pickup I saw him do he had the helmet on and the visor closed in like 35 degrees of afternoon-and-kitchens heat. Way to go. Way to go. I don't think the 1.0 Stentson could operate as smoothly in conditions like that, and I'm looking forward to reading the full specs and getting the lid off somehow for a good look at all those hydraulics.

*

You pick up the story way way back at the Motel—right back there in Fourth Town—where you remember Ray got snatched by Agents and Rachel was left all alone. Of course, Rachel waits in the room when Ray goes out the door and says he's gonna just be gone for like 10–15 minutes. But hear me—when he doesn't come back she doesn't sob and linger like a high school girl who's maybe lost her boyfriend at a theme park or in an unfamiliar shopping mall. She doesn't sit there looking sorry for herself or sniveling and looking at the telephone and waiting for it to ring. She waits a couple of hours and then she bites the bullet and signs up to be a realist. You see her leave the Motel and take a look around outside. Whatever. It's all pointless. She doesn't seem to see the tire tracks and scuffle marks in the dirt from when Ray was taken away, and soon you see her go back in the chalet/room and sit down on the bed. There's a close-up of her face and she counts to ten. It's like the ten seconds where everything changes. Ten seconds to think the world thru in the harsh new way—ALONE—and figure out what to do.

1-2-3-4-5-6-7-8-9-10.

Maybe every life has seconds like that. I guess for me it was moving in with Tory. I don't know. Anyway, when she's done she says "OK" and you see her stand and stuff useful belongings in a bag, throw the bag on her shoulder and head right out the door. The world is not a perfect place or even a good place, but Make the Best of It while you still can.

It's pitch dark outside there at the Sandy Beach and at first you think you will get control of the game as soon as R steps out, but you don't— *The Broken World* is full of surprises. Mostly they keep the movie bits short but here they make it go longer to Heighten the Drama. You watch Rachel head out to a big four-wheel drive, take a can of gasoline from the trunk, head back to the room, throw gas EVERYWHERE, and then torch the whole fucking thing.

As she drives away from the Motel you can see the fire spread and various minor players in the history (or population? I don't know) of *The Broken World* come spilling out of their rooms all flushed out by the alarms. Everyone is wrapped in towels or robes or whatever and they are sheltering their heads from the downpour of the sprinkler system. They do such DETAILS. You can see the hairs on the arm of some hooker-looking chick. You can even see the title of the book one surfer dude is carrying—*Ubik* or something. You are in the fast lane of the freeway when at last you gain control of the game and you are driving North.

*

Me and Tory took some time to chill. We even went for a walk, at least if you count it as "a walk" if all we did was deliberately go to the further (bigger) supermarket and not just the closer (smaller) (Mexican) one. They charge too much for the produce there, Tory says. Didn't go near the computer for most of the day, which must be a record of some kind, and didn't answer the phone either, except when T spent an hour on there to her parents who are now repeating the computer virus questions with an increased level of urgency. They also enforced an invite for us to visit them "anytime", i.e. at the weekend. If this turns out to be some genuine social Impulse full of love for Humanity and family in general or if it is just an excuse that I should take a look at their computer I cannot say for sure. But I have my doubts, bro, I have my doubts. In any case, an invite from them at this point really is "a pleasure that cannot be refused," like in *The Broken World* when Ray meets Dr Kaos and if things go badly Kaos prepares Ray a poisoned beverage that he must consume or he will be forcibly injected with a lethal substance.

*

I try to get on. Remember: You are not Ray. You are Rachel now and there are for sure a certain kind or type of *BW* players (i.e. Idiot Guys) who will SWEAR by ALMIGHTY GOD THAT they will not go further than this part of the game, but to me that is dumbass stupid. These guys say stuff like "it's not right" and "not the same" when they have to be Rachel, that they don't like the shift to another body or "vision," I don't know what to call it. Some of these are the same dudes who also make a fuss in other parts of the game if Ray gets transformed into an Eagle for some shamanistic magic reasons, or they don't like it if Ray changes into a Lab Mouse (for dangerous experiments). OK. The truth is that these guys REALLY do NOT like to be inside a woman's body at all, at least not in *that* way. Sure they like to be inside a woman's body in a more obvious way, but I leave that to your imaginations (and theirs). I mean, they are freaking out abt how they have to BE a woman now and not Ray anymore like it makes them totally Gay or something or transvestites and people will laugh at them now. But listen up. It's no big deal—and anyway, there are NO other solutions. You have to be Rachel. I'm making a personal appeal that you Idiot Guys plz lighten up.

Also. Just because you are Rachel does not mean the whole game is Gay—i.e. at least half the cool *BW* players are girls and they are not ALL from like the Grinning Cat/pacifist lesbian school. Hi, girls. I mean, look at Vengeance who hangs with Scat and Helium or look at Miss Kittin. She is NOT a pacifist player—I believe you can tell that from her actions in the game and from her comments in the comments section on *The BW* discussion board.

*

Word up. I will not talk about it like an issue anymore. Being Rachel won't be as easy like you think. You are used to being Ray and making his moves. Ray is heavy and strong. But Rachel has her own special tricks. She can do the Turn and Stab, the Molotov and the Necklock, none of which is possible for Ray. Sometimes she also seems stronger than Ray, tho Clockwork says that is Objectively Incorrect and mentions some statistic he read about before. He always has something he just read somewhere. But I don't know. I've seen plenty of girls that can kick ass in fighting—at least when I worked bars before I hit the rock bottom of Domenico's. Rachel is like that, a born fighter—except she doesn't have to get drunk before she'll fight, and in target shooting she's 10 out of 10. Even Ray is only 9.8. You have to be Rachel from now on.

And, dudes. A note that is JUST IN CASE you are like a TOTAL idiot. There is no good stopping the car and running into the woods and taking all your (Rachel's) clothes off so you can touch the new parts of your body. You know what I'm talking about. Do not even try to go there. The game will not let you do that, at least not in this part for sure. Rachel is brunette (tho according to some people maybe auburn is the color of her hair) and she is buff and trim, but I'm telling you do NOT get too interested in what she looks like underneath all those skintight leathers, asshole, coz the clock is ticking and there is fighting to do.

*

You have to live as Rachel, breathe in her skin, or you will not survive. Keep driving the 4wheel North from the Motel. That is my advice. In the dash of the 4wheel with the compass you will find several Items of use and interest. Best of all is a diary that belongs to Rachel where she has written about her life and about Ray plus clues they've found concerning GovCorp, GARS, and Chang. Read ALL these and keep the diary safe. Only from the clues in there can you (Rachel) figure what to do next. Here is my Number One HINT: At one place in the diary there is the same name written down—underlined and ringed many times—12th Town. 12th Town. 12th Town. I guess that's where she should be going. And GARS are not far behind. Of course (I am talking to ZuluBabe and

Scatterlogical) you can go anywhere. It is a world, not a game of snakes and ladders. But my advice is you take the hints and go to 12th Town. I will try to get you through.

*

All thru today's shifts Branimir was super pissy pissy pissy for all the obvious reasons I will not go into it again. He was also raving about the world and stuff, which he seems to do more and more often these days. I mean, at first he was just in a bad mood coz I came late—some conversations with Tory that dragged on etc—but as soon as I get there he starts poking his finger at the TV news or whatever and ranting like some bitter fucked-up dude from the Bible. Then he starts complaining about the mess out back where the big garbage containers are. Personally, I don't get any connection at all between these topics, but for him it looks like two halves of the same big deal. Even Miroslav says that since the summer Branimir has "ants riding up in the crack of his ass." Ha ha. I admit that no one wants to clean out near the garbage containers though—it is DIRTY and for that reason alone a class-one Unpopular Item on the duties rota. We dodge and we use what stealth we can to avoid it, but from time to time Branimir most likely will fixate on the filth and squalor out there, announcing "There will be rats if we don't act" (which is true, I guess) and then lay down a Law that we all do unpaid overtime to clean it up. I have seen the future and it hurts.

The way this story goes I am headed for a not so subtle/disguised punishment for all the skipped shifts, which means I will soon have to put mop to bucket and spade in the great piles of indistinguishable shit (garbage) out there. I mean—what is the word for that kind of mud that gets left when cardboard and random food waste is mixed with rain and drain water and then neglected for a very long time? You get the picture.

Plz God spare me all these long boring afternoon shifts with "Ants-up-the-Ass" and his brother hovering like vultures while Me and Ashton work like maniacs. If they could put that atmosphere in a can they could sell it to Prisons. That's what Ashton said. Even after the brothers were gone we were stretched so right up to the limit with orders for cooked circular food that we hardly had chance to hang out with the Stentson 2.0.

In the quieter moments Ashton gave me the lowdown tho and from his report it seems like the 2.0 is working out pretty OK and gives good value in jokes, basic laziness, and toilet humor. He's also (according to Ashton) a closet goth when it comes to music, a nonsmoker, and (the music aside, sorry, Sleeptalk) a total improvement on the previous unit from the popular Stentson series. Fax your orders now, or book online at the-stentson-series.biz ha ha.

*

Maybe what Tory says is true—that I cannot take ANYTHING seriously at all. I guess I don't want to work in Cooked Circular Food for the rest of my life, but at least it pays part of the rent. The way things are going I won't be there long. Things go better for a day or two, like once I even got a compliment off Miroslav for being one of the good ones, not like the Ashton he said. But then at a vital moment I always get the urge to fool around and make a joke out of some disaster, like today with the Rota of the Oven and the Order System. I would bet money that if the business takes a dive again next month and B&M are looking down the list to see people that they can rather get rid of, then my name will be near the top of that list.

It's weird having Tory back, I mean in some ways. Not just coz she reminds me that I'm basically a slacker. But also coz I got used to her being gone and now she's back. Like this constant negotiation of space and how to behave and how long to leave the dishes and the laundry. Somehow Love Levels and Happiness seem to be running low. I guess you get points for Eye Contact, proper conversations (shrugging or grunting doesn't count) and the Intimate acts, but we're not really doing so well at any of that stuff since she returned. It's NOT easy to share space.

*

The Broken World is definitely complicated for Rachel at this point. When she reads thru her diary on the way to 12th Town it describes a life she lived but cannot remember. Like she's not quite herself but then she's not any other person either.

It reminds me of Brainiac once complaining how he couldn't imagine ever BEING the person he was when he wrote his diary 3 years ago. He was really into Speedcore at the time and was doing crazy stuff and writing it in there. Crazier than now. But reading back it didn't feel close to his heart. HE could not identify. Sometimes I wonder what reaction I will have on this walkthrough when I read it far away, like maybe three years from now. Will it even make sense? What I'm talking about is a problem that comes with Watcher skills or just from writing stuff down. I'm not an action person. Action like Ray or Rachel is just to do it, man, Let's Kick SOME ASS. It's not to make notes or dwell so much on the imaginary consequence of things that are not real or which might not even happen.

*

One question that inevitably comes up is why Rachel burned the whole Motel back there like that? Wasn't it enough that she just upped and left? Is it just so the computer graphics people can have a lot of fun and show off all their skills again in rendering the fire? Or is it because big fires are by definition cool? I don't think so. I think the REAL reason is that Rachel wants much MORE than to move on and forget what took place there, forget Ray and his big speeches about Love that came to Nothing, forget the time they spent there. She wants to move on but ALSO to DESTROY that memory—to burn it from the actual world. Like when Venter's dad started up a freakin bbq with family photos when Venter's mom left without warning and he made steaks for everyone. I mean, Jesus—every photo they had from like 17 yrs.

Whoa, Rachel. Like she would so hate for anyone to be there in that Motel and imagine for even one second that a scene of "happy life" was ever there in that room or that bed that she burned up in the fire. I guess she's mad with Ray because he went away without a word. She doesn't know that he was captured. That's the terrible thing. They make the game so sad, and this is just the start of that.

 PROBABLY 12th TOWN

A general complaint is that I cannot keep good track of the numbers of
Towns. Also, what are they really counting as towns and what are just
places not towns? Seems confusing. Why do some places have names
and others not? And then when you go back there again later in the
freaking game the name has changed anyway? It's like being in a chat
room where people are chatting but all of them start writing as several
different identities and fooling around and it gets more and more
complexified until in the end no one can figure out who is who or what
is going on. There was like a wave of this last year sometime with
everyone logging into MSN and pretending to be different people and
spreading confusions. Man, as you can guess the Brainiac was totally

King of it. He could be like 9 different people: The Count, Hippie Jesus, Werewolf, PapaDog5, The Dallas Hilton, Saddam, Wherther, Prez90, and Omega Man, and still Brainiac at the same time and keep track of what they all said and the different personalities. I could never do that. I guess the best character he was was the Werewolf. All Werewolf ever did was log on and then say:

Aaaaaaaaaaaooooooooooooowwwwwwwwwww!
Aaaaaaaaaaaoooooooooooooowwwwwwwwwwwwwwwww!
Aaaaaaaaaaaooooooooooooooooooooooooooooooowwwwwwwwwww!

*

While we're on a subject of Brainiac, there was KIND OF word from him. I mean, what is it with some people that they can fill the whole 3 mins of a voicemail and still portray the feeling that they didn't get close to what they wanted to say? I should try to see him again before the shit really does come out and hit the fan. I know some people get depression in winter when the sunlight disappears, but for Brainiac it seems more the other way round. Life Sucks, like it says way waaay back on the walls of that spaceship, I think that more or less sums it up.

Venter said that some days ago the lovable Brainiac let slip his great theory that the dead are somehow lucky to be out of it. He's hilarious that guy (ha ha). Like I can just imagine Brainiac walking Venter on a route past a graveyard on purpose, just so he can point thru the fences and say, "Hey. Look, dude, they're the lucky ones. They are out of the whole stupid game by now."

I know he doesn't think that really—it's just a chemical imbalance, in the brain or whatever. Just a kind of glitch in some lines of code to do with feeling things, a glitch that means he doesn't think straight. Only a small thing has to be misplaced—a chemical formula or a number entered incorrectly and then things can go so wrong. Change this < for this >. Or this // for this /. Replace an "if" for a "where," a #232 with a #345. A 12 for a 22. A zero for a one. A one for a zero. Then everything is suddenly different.

Mostly I don't like it when Brainiac cries. He's not at that stage yet. But crying on the phone is worse than when he's in the same room. Maybe crying on the phone is harder to stop somehow, like you are not really there with him, so you cannot totally comfort him, only listen to it. Like when you watch people screaming and yelling in agonies on TV. It's worse somehow than if you were really there.

(OK. Now I got IM from some guy who says this is *not* true. It's apparently worse if you *are* there—he was there in fact, for a long time, at someplace with the bombing and people burning/screaming in agonies and he invites me to swap places if I really think what I wrote before is true. I'm going to say, OK OK. I take your word for it, bro and thanks for the correction. I don't want to turn the conversation into a flame battle—I have other stuff to do. So just ignore what I said before. Consider it deleted. And keep your head low. Nothing lasts forever.)

I again try to continue. When Brainiac is depressed it's like with the glitches. Something in his brain is probably displaced. I mean, it's probably just a simple thing. But then for weeks it's like he's seeing right thru to the nothing that the world is drawn onto. Most of us don't have to experience that in our whole lives, or like maybe for just a short time—if someone dies, or if we get psychotic (I'm not counting the time that I mentioned already when BugMap took the peyote Sleeptalk's brother had been hiding in his closet). But for Brainiac there are months on end when he's looking into the cracks of the world. You do not want it. You do not want it. As we say.

*

Went out with Tory and some other people to see a band (Evicerator—it was not very promising, even with that name). It was meant to be a kind of welcome back from the camping trip, but for Tory I think it was just a good excuse to steer clear of Palace for one more night. When we got there though it turned out Tamiflu were supporting and they were OK. Tory seemed uptight, then relaxed after picking a fight with some guy who stood on her toes, almost getting everyone thrown out of Deca-Dance. It's a stupid venue anyway. Once Evicerator started their set we kind of pulled back from the front and went nearer the bar, away from the push and shove. Dieter was there and on Fine Form, making with the jokes as usual and even better new and improved ridiculous routines, coz he has an audience he brings with him (Chelsea). Tory was teasing him when Chelsea went to the bathroom, calling him Fast-Worker and Stud and stuff like that, but he took it just fine, not rising to any provocations about how he was randomly seducing Tory's friends from her temp gigs and how (according to Tory) there were some cuter ones in the data-processing pool at the new gig she has and was Dieter interested in getting some emails or phone numbers, but then Chelsea came back before he could reply. Dieter says he likes her. Chelsea says she thinks she's in love, but she only said that quietly to Tory, and only after the third or fourth round of drinks, so I don't know if it counts.

The bar thinned out some more once the Evicerators were all done and the smell of sweat and leather kind of dropped off—a relief to everyone except Sleeptalk who's friends with the bassist. Too many beers. Got kind of locked in a conversation with Brainiac—who showed up after the bands—so while everyone else was laughing and Dieter was continuing his role as like the most amusing guy on the planet with Tory and Chelsea, both nearly helpless with laughter, I was bending my ear real close to Brainiac who was riding on a freaking total wave of negativity. "I don't know, I don't know," he was saying and claiming that his whole personality doesn't work, that the whole world sucks, that his whole personality is still in testing, that he's not a finished person, that he's still in pre-public Beta, that he will never be a complete person. I guess you have to see what he looks like these days, and see how he is when he's saying this stuff to really know that it isn't funny at all. Plus the fact that with the noise of the bar and the freaking quietness of his voice, I couldn't even be sure just what he was saying for half the time and then he got in a like bad mood how I wasn't really listening to him anyhow so he went off, leaving his jacket on the chair and then he came back to collect it but just picked it up and left again, didn't say anything at all.

*

Bro. It is strange how quick you get used to being Rachel. Her walk. Her eyes. The world in her colors, textures, shapes. Tory even said once that I acted different when I played the game as Rachel, but I don't know about that. Maybe people are less solid than everyone thinks they are. I mean, I do not believe that life is like a spirit or a fog that can be poured from one vessel to another like they say on freaky Low Budget Preacher Channels on TV late at night. But I do think it is officially "complicated" how at home it can feel to be Rachel.

Me and Tory had a game once (a kind of private talking game) where we'd tell the crisis events from our sad-fuck-past-lives and then the other one would have to say what they would have done if it had been them and also guess what they thought the other one did. I mean, like a test on how well we could imagine each other. Tory was pretty good at guessing me but I think her decisions abt what she would have done in my place were completely strange. My confession: 1) I was terrible at guessing her, and 2) thinking back, I guess most of my decisions on what I'd do in her situations were pretty unhelpful. Violence is not always an answer, dude. It is not always an answer.

*

Rachel's journeys to 12th Town is long and there is a lot of ground to cover. I cannot do it all. If you take my advice that longer route thru Blue Town, New Jerusalem, Leningrad, 99th Town, etc, is the best (i.e. safest) one. DO what missions you need for survival along the way, but do not linger around like a weirdo at a Bus terminal—things are about to get seriously strange again. If you do get in firefights plz: Check the bodies, check the bodies. I cannot tell you enough times. Do not go to Houston where the GovCorp has a clampdown and all resistance is thrown in jail. Do not go to Doncaster. Do not go to Rome. There are weird things happening in those towns.

At 12th Town you can meet a guy called McSham, oftentimes he is down at the Harbor, watching the ships. I don't know why. Tell McSham who you are and offer to buy him a drink. There are plenty of bars down there at the harbor. After two or three drinks the McSham dude starts to talk. He talks about money and things flowing from one place to another, about the War that is coming, spilling from nearby 13th Town about Human destiny and how it's caught up in the story of Money, and also the Fate of Nations and about the truth of cash and Destiny and the ultimate

falseness of all ideologies (etc etc). He likes the sound of his own voice—
that much is clear. To be honest tho, they make it pretty confusing at this
point, but then what d'you really expect? It's a fucked-up world, bro, and
I can only add "Don't Ask Me I Only Work Here" as it says on the special
T-shirts me and Ashton made for working at Domenico's last Summer
until Branimir asked us to stop wearing them.

At first the conversation with McSham just seems like an info
dump/waste of time but when you get up to leave he will say that since
you are obviously traveling, might he ask you to pay a visit to an old
friend of his—a woman who lives on South Side of 13th Town who's
apparently on her deathbed? This may not exactly sound like a barrel of
laughs but plz say yes. McSham wants you to take his friend a gift. DO
NOT worry what they say about not accepting packages from strangers
to take on an airplane. You are not going on an airplane. McSham will
give you a small parcel. Keep it safe. I won't spoil it by telling now the
surprise of what is in there but plz keep in mind that it is important. I will
warn you if there are spoilers in the walkthru.

Once you have left the McSham guy you need to collect some Maps,
Ammunition, and Medical Supplies from all over that 12th Town. It's a bad
place. It has a stupid one-way system that makes it very hard to navigate
and in general a nasty atmosphere. There are lots of Idiots to fight and
GovCorp is VERY strong there too. Check the dudes with the Dead Man
tattoos and the cops with webcams for eyes. Shoot first and ask
questions later.

*

NOTE: As you exit 12th Town there is a place on the outskirts, a trailer
park out by the Lakes where Rachel can get some much-needed rest.

MOST TRAILERS (CAPSLOCK) are lived in by families that seem to have almost as many crying kids as they have barking dogs etc. Seems like *Broken World* also has a welfare class. In the east of the park you will find a Blue trailer that isn't occupied. Force the door using Pen Knife from Items and step inside. I guess this place must belong to some Old Couple—like a vacation place, I don't know. You can see pictures of them stuck to the refrigerator with those magnets, also pictures of their grandkids, tabby cat, etc.

The whole scene just serves to remind you of the kind of life that isn't possible for Rachel or Ray—a life of peace and ordinary concerns that the fight against GovCorp, Zorda, and Archduke etc has destroyed for them, probably forever. I mean, Rachel certainly looks out of place in there—in her skintight leather bike gear and boots and weighted down with the Kalashnikov. There is tinned soup in the cabinet and Barley Water also. Eat and drink to replenish Energy. Take off your boots and lean the Gun by the door.

Even if Rachel (i.e. YOU) is out of place, she can feel OK in this tiny, private space, with jazz on that radio they have or a program about Weather and Anticyclone systems—there's lots of stuff on the radio there. I sometimes think about the person who coded that part. How like, just to make this caravan seem right, they put all that different stuff there in the radio. I mean, no telling even if Rachel will even turn it on but if she does the DETAIL is in there, ready and waiting.

The trailer is cool and quiet and soon your levels will be restored. I guess Ray wouldn't sleep so easy in a place like this, not like Rachel does, with her head next to the floral curtains and dreaming many things.

*

B came by the apartment looking for his jacket. I was like what do you mean? And he said I left my jacket in Deca-Dance, on the chair, and Tory was like no you came back to get it and ignored everyone and B was like no, I did not, and then it was quiet and it seemed no one could really think what to say anymore and B left.

*

When Ray sleeps it's like someone threw a switch. Doesn't matter if he's like lying in a jungle hammock, or on the floor of a boat, or curled in the back of a speeding car, in a dark cave, a hotel bed or a prison cell. Wherever he is, he might twitch while sleeping or mutter WORDS but he doesn't dream. Or if he does the dreams are kept private and you cannot know.

But Rachel often dreams and you can SEE them. It's way cool—she twitches and her eyes are fluttering in that REM sleep and they do the dreams like strange little movies that flicker all over the screen. If you leave Rachel sleeping you can watch the dreams but you cannot control her when she's sleeping—you cannot control the dreams.

*

Here are some things I saw in the dreams at different times. I don't know if this is Useful Information or not. I certainly never found out a use for it, but I don't think everything in the game has got to Mean Something. Maybe Rachel's dreams are a screensaver of her mind:

I saw Ray walking on desert sands, carrying a Petri dish of microbes. Cities on fire. Two dead dogs. Rachel in a swimsuit contest, sweating badly. Faces in fog. Rotten food. A jigsaw that Ray was trying to do but with 200,000 pieces and the picture showing soldiers covered from head to foot in mud so you couldn't tell which were dead or which were alive, all tangled together and covered in the mud. Flight attendants, whispering to each other. Dust. A library built on a circle. Some guys chasing after Rachel (or Ray—I cannot be sure). Once I thought I saw Stentson (1.0 not 2.0) from Domenico's but that's impossible. Insects. Dissolving letters. Oppressive silence at a Night Picnic. Car crashes. Two kids running around. Two older-age women, one of them blindfolded. Blue Sky. Sand pouring out of a glass made from water (?). Someone trying to take a photo of a white dog against a landscape of snow. Etc. Etc. There were more dreams but I'll have to keep them for another time, there are too many. Most scary of the Dreams I saw was Ray killing Rachel—he was murdering her again and again—but I don't think that dream was standing in for anything. It was just a dream.

*

This afternoon Tory and me took our tired/hungover and basically snippy asses out on the compulsory trip to the Burbs and I can confirm that they are totally Crazy out there. It is the kind of thing that makes those dreams I was writing about look totally normal. Fact number one: Tory's mother has noticeably had face surgery since we saw her last time (maybe 6 weeks ago?) but kind of denies it in a huge performance of critisicing (I cannot spell it) all her friends and all the people on TV that have apparently had the same face surgery. Tory even goes along with this and was blanking me if I even raised an eyebrow. Bro—her mom's eyebrows are now always in that permanently raised position. She looks totally surprised by the world. It's a shame, I like Barbara and I know she's in there behind that mask somewhere. Fact number two: The food they eat is freakkky—

combinations of stuff that shouldn't be allowed together. Strawberries on a Pizza? What's next—Potatoes and Ice Cream with Gravy? Matter and Antimatter? I'm serious. It gets weirder every time. Fact number three is good, it's so good I've hardly stopped laughing about it since we got back. Until Tory more or less asked me to stop. OK. Here goes: At first during "dinner" there was like a lot of conversations about the Virus Problem and Tory's dad Joe saying a lot of times "Would I like to take a look at it?" (Answer—No, I would not *like* to look at it at all, but you don't have to be in a remake of Colombo to work out where this is headed.)

Eventually when the food is all done I'm forced into the "office" where they have got the computer in a teak cabinet on like a big grande olde desk. I mean, I swear to God in Heaven they would have a mouse made of oak wood and a mouse mat made from Victorian Velvet if they could purchase them like that. Crazy. Anyway. I fixed the virus thing—they had the one called Afterwards which some Croatian kid wrote, I remember reading abt it, he was 14 or something—and I also updated their Definitions (I'm no technical Expert—I leave that to Clockwork—but any fool can run a virus check). Anyway (I am getting to the point). While doing all that I'm getting lots of whispered prompts from Tory who came in a couple of times to say like would I please sort out their computer some more—not just the virus, but would I please do a good proper job—and I was whispering back like WTF, how would I know what other problems they're incubating on there? So in the end I was also looking about in their email on the computer to see what the source of this virus might be—attachments and stuff—and I came across a whole folder FULL of spams. I mean, I'm not talking about just a few spam messages in a Junk Mail folder. But like thousands and thousands and thousands of them—like 223,437 messages in one folder and mostly unread.

It is a miracle their Mail program can even operate anymore. It's like a Spam Magnet or Spam Museum, in fact I'm surprised their freaking computer can even function. Most of the messages there are the ones that sell Viagra and other Meds, Remortgages, Insomnia Products, Witchcraft Paraphernalia, Instant Diplomas, Unbeatable Investment Opportunities, Stocks that are going to go Crazy, and All-State Licenses to Practice as a Surgeon as well as the usual Rampant Teen cams, Asia-Dildo Festivals, and Austrian Anal Action, as well as many other incomprehensible offers, all written in various Korean dialects etc etc. It's like a whole folder full of stuff that is no conceivable use to anyone EVER, and I'm starting to get a feeling that it's weird and even freaky that they are saving all this stuff, kind of like a *Twilight Zone* moment I'm having there with the folder open and staring at the 223,437 messages. That's when I get the idea that they are really crazy out there. And I say to Joe, "Er, you could do with like throwing some of these away," and he says, "No, it's OK. We like to keep things. We keep all the promotions and special announcements in case there's something useful for the future." I was like "OK, Joe. OK. OK" and shut the folder and got up from the desk real slow and careful but very determined. Crazy. Crazy. Crazy. You read it here. You read it here. You read it here again.

*

OK.

There is no easy way to say this last thing I HAVE TO DO NOW (fucking capslock) so I'll just do it in one quick go and get it over, instead of ignoring it and pretending that nothing really happened.

When we got back from the Burbs just now there were two things waiting for us. One was on the doormat—a postcard from some guy Tory apparently "made friends with" on the camping trip. She didn't want to say much about it, WHICH IS 1) UNDERSTANDABLE (capslock) and 2) not making me feel great, but the tone of innuendos in what he wrote pretty well spoke for itself.

The other thing waiting was stuff on the answering machine. A messed-up and rambling message with bad news from Venter and then another one—completely hysterical—with the same news from the Chelsea person. Turns out that Dieter was not so much a survivor at all—he was working in the afternoon taking some delivery across town on his bike and got hit in the traffic and smashed against a wall, then dragged along by the tailgate of a Chevrolet truck delivering to Wal-Mart until there was no life left in him. I guess no point in sparing any detail. What's done is done.

POSITIVELY 13th Town

Leave the trailer park early and check the Mist on the green grass, which they do very beautiful. Take the main road North but when you get to 13th Town ditch your vehicle and trade in (i.e. steal) for something else. Agents are following—it's best to be safe.

Man. 13th Town is for SURE in a bad way. Like it even proved unlucky for *itself* somehow and when the war started all the people living there must have really wished that they relocated to the other coast. It's a big fucking Mess. Even a look at the buildings can tell you that this place is bad news—they are full of scars and explosion marks from the bombs and machine-gun fire.

It's just Rachel's luck that this friend of McSham's, supposedly on her deathbed, lives in this freaking town. I mean, why couldn't she be lodged up outside the city in a nice place with a garden near a river? I guess that would be asking too much. Anyway, like Venter says when he is imitating that Roadie dude from Centurion—this place takes the fucking biscuit. Everywhere you go in 13th there are like random checkpoints run by drunk, stoned, and armed teenagers and a certain amount of fighting your way street by street is inevitable. Warning: These kid mfkrs are VERY volatile and plz handle them correctly—learn to judge the mood. Sometimes it's good to make conversation or share rations and other Items (cigarettes) etc but other times it's better to keep your mouth well shut and your profile low. Those kids are certainly jittery with their guns and Rachel's (i.e. your) appearance kind of freaks them out. You cannot really call them kids. To be honest, the combination of drunk, stoned, and holding Kalashnikovs does not seem like a good one for kids—er, excuse me, but don't they have schools in this town? Or break-dancing contests? Even though those guys don't like to talk that much they are certainly fond of rape, murder, and firing their weapons up in the air, which seems to make EVERYONE get very excited in these parts. It's like the Fourth of July every night—there are so many bangs and flashes in the sky.

Throughout the city there are also troops from the Transitional government going everywhere in commandeered vehicles and buses and pointing their weapons at everyone for target practice. Anywhere you look there are burning cars, minefields, and booby-trapped properties, and altho EVERYONE says that the shelling has stopped (it has, kind of) there are unexploded RPGs here and there and anywhere— embedded in the trees, walls, and riverbed, etc, etc and any of them can get set off by the smallest movements. Tread carefully, dude, you do not want to blow your sweet ass to kingdom come. There are also snipers operating in most of the town. When you first arrive it's puzzling to see how a lot of the residents have like a weird style of walking—crouched and making like a zigzag on the sidewalk even when they're just going out to get milk or ribs or whatever—but after a few close calls with the snipers, or seeing heads get blown out like fucking watermelons right next to you, you soon get the idea and start walking in a zigzag too.

*

I am fucked up about Dieter, bro, but I just don't want to write about it. A truck. I cannot believe it.

*

Good advice WHEREVER you go in *The Broken World* is always pump any bartender for info, and 13th Town is no exception. The best place for gossip is Café Libertine or Café Bargano. Or try talking to people in the Market or in the long depressing queues that you find at the Petrol-ration depots all over the place—you will certainly have time to kill in those lines. Main topic will be the 4 Generals who are locked together in a deadly combat of war. These dudes are so badass that people will only whisper their names—General Die Die, General Rambo, General El Terminator, and General Dare-to-Execute. Weird names, I know—but they certainly give an idea about the personalities involved. There are such terrible rumors circulating about these guys that soon you'll get sick to your stomach. But hear me—you may as well get used to it coz the war is seeping like a kind of poison from 13th Town to 14th and 15th, "sending ripples of insanity thru the rest of the game." I stole the description from Crispin. Hi, Crispin. I guess this is his favorite part.

ALso. Some good advice I learned from Venter is to think twice before claiming allegiance to any one General. It's a well known trick for example to get killed when supporters of General Dare-to-Execute are encouraging you to sing a bad song about General Rambo and then laughing and then revealing that they are really supporters of General Rambo and then shooting you in the legs, the abdomen, and the head. You have to go easy and real real slowly in this town. It's not a bad idea to learn some French. A lot of the soldiers only speak French and some African language (?). I don't know French except the word for love coz they use it so much in songs. You don't need that word in this Town.

*

No point pretending otherwise—the news about Dieter hit everyone hard. I'm not being funny, dude, and that is not intented as a pun, this is not an occasion for that and as USUAL PLZ anyone that doesn't want to hear about the real fucking world, can just skim on downscreen til they see the word RACHEL again. All the actual human beings can read on and take the bad news with the other stuff, the real world and the broken one together. A truck. A motherfucking truck. I don't know what to write. Tory and me were so stunned that the Domestic Irritation levels seemed to subside (for a while?) but then she picked a fight about a pile of clothes in the bedroom that was not even very high or dispersed, and the row went on for hours. Things are a mess. Both of us are fucked up about it. I mean, Dieter, not the bedroom. We hardly even mentioned or talked about the postcard from the guy she met camping. There is more to say abt that later no doubt, but I can't deal or think about it now. I think we both agree about that but for Tory it's more like Wall of Silence mode.

Last night until late and then again today there was a kind of phone circus going on, with Venter, BugMap, Me, and a kind of reluctant Tory relaying plans and news and then a long extra loop of calling going out toward other people incl Sleeptalk and carefully back toward Chelsea who didn't know Dieter so long, I guess, but who saw him most and in most close-up the month before he died. Jesus, enough.

*

RACHEL!

All thru 13th town there are small adventures and distractions you can get involved with, many of which earn Points and Bonus Equipment or Skills. Keep a good eye for clues to locate this dying friend of McSham's but meanwhile check out the assorted ambushes, robberies, thefts, and lynchings, etc, in which you can either save people or choose to participate. They seem to abandon any real solid or strict notion of "sides" at this point so it makes sense to kick back, load up, and go with the flow. Bro, once me and Venter had Rachel set up a checkpoint of her own. She was looting Items from every fool that came thru there til some Rebel General had her stopped, questioned, and shot. (Hint: Be careful.) Throughout the town there are also puzzles to solve—for example Missing Persons Puzzle, Body Bag Puzzle, House-to-House Searching Puzzle, Roadblock Puzzle, Intelligence Puzzle, Missing Journalist Puzzle, Dead Messenger Puzzle (I'm not serious abt that last one and I am not joking either. I don't know what to say).

NOTE: You will find there are blank pages at the back of the notebook/diary that Rachel got out from the 4Wheel. Anytime you are in big trouble and think that all is LOST YOU ONLY HAVE TO CRY ON (FUCKIng capslock—hasn't done that for ages but now it's started again). You only have to cry onto one of these blank pages and a clue will suddenly appear—fading up from out the page. Tory says it's like Rachel's Tears are a wish—that there is no god in *The Broken World* but at least you get some wishes. Each wish answered uses one page. 10 magic pages = 10 wishes, so don't waste them.

*

Dieter's funeral is planned for Tuesday in the St Something or Other Funeral Home or whatever the Fuck. Fuck. Fuck and apologies—I can't write things that make any sense. F.U.C.K. Apologies if this is all kind of disintegrated. I don't even know how much I ever explained about who Dieter (or who anyone) was (I mean, concerning interconnections of the past etc I didn't really intend to be writing about any of this anyhow) so maybe now is the time. Yeah. When it's too late to really mean anything at all THAT is the best time for explanation. Dieter was at high school with Brainiac and Venter. Then he went "home" for a couple years. Then he came back to stay with his mom, but then he got hit in the traffic and trucked against a wall etc—like I said already, no need to go through it again, not like I didn't replay it already in my head 1 million times.

I hope it's a good Funeral Home that D's ma has organized to sort him out for the casket, because it probably wasn't very pretty. Venter spoke to Dieter's mom a couple times, with sad wishes and the offer of any help with the plans. She lives in the Burbs. Anyway. I can't write about it. I guess I was hiding in the game to a certain extent and would like to get back to that. I apologize. But sometimes a coward's way is the only way. There is also maybe Skill in that—I have some cowarding to do.

*

I just had a memory from like last August when we all went out in the woods together—Dieter, Brainiac, Me, Tory, Venter, BugMap, even Sleep-talk (out on south edge of the city where the woods are very big and cool and you can walk and fool around with no one there to bug you)—the trip where the picture I use as my chat Icon got taken. We had good times—he was climbing trees, Dieter, with that expression like he was always gonna be OK. Going so high. I would never go that high.

*

Don't forget to collect useful items whenever you can esp the Healing Rain that collects on rooftops after rainfall. When black smoke fills the streets the soldiers use it as cover to search out and kill any survivors of the Zeppelin (?) crash. Oh yeah, I maybe didn't mention it before. A Zeppelin of Time Travelers apparently crashed nearby and everyone is out to kill them. It's hard to keep track of all the things happening and I get confused with the Time Travelers, if they are important or not. I don't think they are. Maybe people just want to kill them because they're so confusing—no one knows what they're doing in *The Broken World* anyway or why they chose a Zeppelin to travel in.

*

Tory and me were sat together at the screen and she had her head on my shoulder while I was typing. I don't know if it's a normal relationship, like they write about it in magazines. Doesn't matter. As we sat there I had some IM with Brainiac—to talk abt the Dieter thing—coz he wouldn't come to the phone. Oh Brainiac. Aside from anything else this fucking death is REALLY not what he needed. At first we chatted OK—making plans for the funeral and an idea to go out and see Dieter's mom sometime before then. But then he got locked in this big circular thing about Dieter, asking who has to clean up the mess when someone gets slammed by a vehicle like that? I could sense that Tory wasn't liking this conversation but I couldn't turn it around and soon it was a torrent of Brainiac questions. Does the guy himself, the driver, have to do the cleanup? Or do they have a special crack team of cleaners at the van rental place or at the police station that only do it once the forensics team have done their part? Or is there like a contract team of cleaners you can call in on a freelance basis?

Before long he was fooling with the icon thing in the chat program again. He will not let an amusing idea stop until it's flogged and beaten into the ground. Good old Brainiac, he was spinning off his regular picture (where he looks a bit drunk) to stupid pictures like a Bald presenter off some TV show, a jellyfish, a snowman, and then through what is by now the usual NASTY stuff like open wounds of plastic surgery, a vivisected Donkey, some corpses—I'm getting tired of it all.

I typed: Cut it out.

And Brainiac typed: ?

And I typed: Stp th FOOLNG w th pctrs.

And then it said that he was typing a message but for a long while no message came and then it said:

FRTJCLIojkpjiuhytghijokpj[ihuogyftdf

Like he had slowly pressed random letters or just smashed his fingers on the keyboard.

Tory let out this kind of pissed-off sigh and lifted her head off my shoulder, leaned forward a bit, stretching, like she wasn't here anymore, not it in it anymore.

And then came the climax to Brainiac's stupid costume/icon changes—he switched his icon from the picture of a dead dog hanging by a rope in a tree to a square of nothing but black. Venter didn't call him Mr Down for no reason. I don't know if that's a real "black square picture," or whether Brainiac just zoomed in close on a dark part of that drunk-looking photo that he always used to be in the Chat—the darkness in the background of the bar or whatever.

I didn't type anything.

Then Brainiac typed: LMAO

Which is Laughing My Ass Off.

Then there was nothing for a moment, and that was when Tory got up and went to bed. Looking back from the doorway she said, "Sometimes I really wonder about you and your freaky friends," which is kind of crazy because she knew Brainiac way before I ever did on account of how she was with his brother. Doesn't matter. Anyways, she went off like that and left me to deal with him alone. A black square.

We didn't chat much longer. Who wants to talk with a square of total blackness? Too depressing. I cannot deal, bro. He sees straightaway how some people would REALLY like NOT to talk about a certain topic and he just has to go there. I mean, the phrase "DO NOT GO THERE" was probably invented just for him. "Do not go there" I typed near the end, do not go there, but he wouldn't listen to that, he was just asking, "How did they clean up the mess that Dieter became?" Again and again. Hold on at the back there. It is going to be a bumpy ride.

*

In *The BW* there is never any cleaning-up. I don't think I ever saw anyone fix or clear up anything, except maybe a time in one adventure when Ray had to mend a crossbow he made using tree branches and vines. There are so many explosions and detonations and all the rest, buildings collapsing, oil tankers bursting into flames, doors and furniture broken, bottles, ornamental vases, and all kinds of old crap getting smashed repeatedly over people's heads, windows getting blown out, cars going off bridges, pylons crashing into houses and swimming pools, sewage pipes bursting and spraying shit everywhere all over the street and people, and bank vaults detonating to send millions of Dollars raining down in the air, fireballs are roaring through subway tunnels, freak accidents are happening on oil platforms, walls of flame are devouring anything in their path. But you never see anyone come back around to pick up, clean, or rebuild. It's pretty funny (more amusing than HA HA) if you think of it that way. I mean—if the game goes on like that pretty soon there will be nothing left, just a universe of dust and shit, rubble, ashes, and broken stuff.

CLOTHing and PAPERs

There's a lot of debate about Rachel's wardrobe on some of the boards esp in relation to 13th–15th Towns and the missions that she has at this point and what kind of thing she should wear. There are occasional dudes who say that Ray looks good with a Mohawk or a Bandanna and there are some players that deliberately try to get Ray scarred coz they think it looks cool, but for the rest the dirty bloodstained combats and black T seem to be the only options under discussion except maybe the black leather trench coat and the fur-lined parka for colder climates. But with Rachel, man, that costume shit surely comes with a lot of debate. It's so lawless in 13th Town and there's so much looting there that you can pick up designer clothing at stupid prices if you know where to look.

So dudes were like dressing Rachel in black-market Karl Lagerfield (?) and Versace and Swoon and Virtuality and all stuff like that. I mean, she was straight off the freaking catwalk. Combine that with an AK47 or like a hand-held/shoulder-carried antiaircraft rocket launcher (like the Stinger equipped with that Passive Optical Seeker System or one of the new model SA7 Strellas) and Rachel was sending out like seriously mixed messages.

It's up to you, the choice is yours as always, dudes and girls. I leave aside questions of Feminist interpretation that people raise abt Rachel in a Swimsuit. I am more a realist and I say that it is just a known fact that chiffon and spandex do not work well in a combat situation, that bright colors are not good camouflage and that 95% of the time even IDENTIFYING yourself as a woman round the neighborhood of 13th Town is a bad move. It doesn't make sense. OK. Maybe I react too strongly— even Tory says that Rachel looks good and If You Have Got It Why Not Flaunt It. But then Tory doesn't really think about it one way or the other if Rachel wins the goddamn game or not—she doesn't care.

Personally, I have more time for players like Helium or Astro that cut off Rachel's long brown hair in a basin crop or at least tie it back in the ponytail, and dress her in something 1) nondescript, 2) dark, and 3) hopefully protective and with a hat pulled down low completely over her brown-green eyes. She doesn't cut such a striking figure like that—that is true, bro, for sure—but she DOES tend to live longer and THAT, at least according to me, is the true purpose of the game. Keep it real. Keep it real. Boys, girls, everyone—it's not a fashion parade, OK? I'm still waiting for someone to explain to me why stripper heels or diamanté sandals make any sense at all in a combat bunker or on a freaking mountain trail.

*

OK. When you're over your Fashion Dilemmas plz get on with the Missions concerning the package for that dying friend of McSham. Trouble is you are in the North Side of Town and she is on the South, in the Rue de Jules Verne. What McSham neglected to mention is you cannot easily cross from one part of the town to the other without official papers—identity card, ration books, travel docs, etc—and if you don't have all this stuff with you, you will get shot at the first checkpoint. I'm not joking, it has happened to me in this part so many times, and you then have to go way back to the start of the Level. Dude, you don't want that to happen. It's a long road. So plz GET your papers before crossing the border.

*

Probably goes without saying that things here are still fucked up—partly just coz of Dieter but also unspoken bad vibes with Tory because of the postcard. Plus she is stupidly mad about things that were said in the Spam Conversation at her parents' house at the weekend. O.K., I admit I was more talkative with "Joe" than I normally would be, mainly coz he was constantly pouring me more and more of his best Scotch, just pouring it and pouring it in my glass all the time and asking more and more philosophical brain-testers/computer questions . . . and meanwhile of course I was asking him abt the various offers in the spam archive. What does he think of the Herbal Viagra? Does he like the Canadian Slutcams or the Amstercams the best? It was pretty funny at the time, tho Barbara didn't look too happy and I think Tory was hiding her amusement. Bro—Tory just doesn't seem pleased with the whole world right now. Like she's developed an allergy to humanity in general. Maybe it's also coz Linda hasn't called or mailed 1) to say how and what she is doing these days and all news of Mike the Dentist etc or even 2) to give an idea when she might feel like paying back the cash that she borrowed on that "camping trip" (i.e. motel and bar-crawl blowout) that caused so much trouble. Some things don't change and Linda is one of them. She is an Eternal Pain in the Ass.

Ughh. When Tory came back from spending time with Chelsea (now aka Grieving Chelsea Person) last night she was stone-cold sober. I asked how was it and she said oh y'know great fun if you like three hours of watching a stranger get drunk, talk shit in incomplete sentences, and cry. Jesus. Sorry I asked. I guess Tory's been the main one dealing with Grieving Chelsea Person, who is in post-Dieter meltdown mode. It's not enjoyable what sudden grief can do to a person and pretty freaky when it's someone you're not even that close to. I mean, Tory just knew her from the temp gig really, and no one else had much connection to her, except Dieter of course.

Two days to the funeral and things are ramping up pretty good. And please—Napalm70—as I said before, if you don't like it go read another walkthrough.

*

For papers go to Central Office. That is what anyone in 13th will tell you and it's definitely true. Go early in the morning and don't forget to take supplies incl water, food, and money (for bribes). Pass thru the metal detectors and take a seat in one of the many waiting rooms. It seems they can put anything from two to five hundred plastic chairs in a filthy little room that has no air in it and probably no direct sunlight and call it a "waiting room."

Get used to the waiting tho, it's a specialty of the House. From a window in the Central Offices you can still see smoke from the riots and the burnings and hear gunshots from the skirmishes, but it's like you're in another FREAKING world with its own logic, colors, time, language, and actual rules. Check the marble halls and big wood-panel rooms with 1 tiny desk at the end and the olde paintings on the walls framed in dirty colored gold wood, that show people in togas, uniforms, and crowns in orgies, battles, and Important Occasions etc. On a bathroom window somewhere on the tenth floor you can see that various dudes have scratched their names—other poor fuckers who were trapped here in some incomprehensible semilegal procedure and who maybe escaped or maybe died before their trial ever came to court. L. BRUCE it says in capitals. And then underneath it says Kafka and Jarndyce & Jarndyce— a band maybe? It's impossible to tell where *The Broken World* makers are getting their ideas from.

While you wait check out how Time passes slowly or not at all (that is a lyric from Skeleton). They have weird clocks (in the Central Offices) that don't move for ages and then jump forward five minutes or go back ten. I don't know how they do Time, but it's obviously stretched very thin at some places here. There is also something weird with the space—you ALWAYS get the impression that you are not waiting in the center of the building, but in some abandoned edges, waiting pointlessly, like this system or whatever has even forgotten you are there. They do it all in SUCH good detail I cannot begin to describe—you can practically smell the desperation, corruption, and boredom. When Tory is temping, we say that she is working in the Central Offices today. You don't want to work there. Sometimes it reminds me of high school too.

*

Fuck this. OK. I cannot even concentrate at all on the game at this point coz I'm totally thinking about something else—from last night. No point denying it longer. So with the usual apologies (except to Napalm70 and also DrunkenApe who is another complaining asshole) I'm gonna write about the stuff that's on my mind and get it out the way. Maybe then I can concentrate on this walkthrough. Warning: The next 2–300 words are a downer—so please again ACCEPT THE APOLOGIES.

Round 6pm Me and VEnter and Brainiac went round to Dieter's mom's house to see what was going on. It certainly seemed like a good idea to go there 2 days before the funeral but now I don't know. Just his mom was there and she suddenly looks like a lizard now, smoking all the time, with dry skin and dead eyes behind cracked lids. Look what grief can do to a person. We didn't stay long, just enough time to say that we came and that there was nothing much to say. Fucking Dieter, man. I so didn't think he would be the one to die. There were loads of dudes in high school or in college I expected to be dead long before him.

Strange house they have out there (his mom and his sister, the dad is in Austria)—strange house and certainly too big now. Like the kind of place in some Stalker or Ripper parts of *The Broken World* that I don't like to play. Those kind of big and empty houses that are too big and empty. You just know that bad will come there, or has been there and soaked into the walls. Dieter's ma was watching what looked like the shopping channel on this excessive like Home Cinema setup and talking to herself. I mean—what is she gonna buy? Do they make some unique three-in-one fully retractable battery-operated weatherproof gadget for when your only son has been pulverized? I don't think so. I guess she just had the TV on for company. She told us we could go sit in Dieter's room for a moment if we wanted to think of him, but she wasn't able to go in there herself. I don't think any of us really wanted to go, but it seemed hard to refuse. We went in. Brainiac sat on the bed but didn't say anything. We were all quiet, Then Venter said it's too freaky in here and we'd better get back to the city. When we left we took some stuff, but his mom didn't seem to notice or even care. Just some CDs we all used to listen to and a few other things. I mean, otherwise it will all go in the trash or in a Yard Sale, I guess. Not like his mom is ever gonna need a 6-port router or an ethernet hub or the picture of us all that Tory took at some Heavenplenty gig. Brainiac was quiet the whole trip. I don't think he said a word. A black fucking square.

*

All respect to the coders, programmers, and testers. I mean, mostly *The Broken World* plays fine and doesn't have toooo many bugs or glitches. But there is one thing in the Central Offices that I can complain about which is that it runs fucking slow sometimes. I mean, of course it's meant to run slow in some parts (like I said about time and how they stretch it thin) but then at other times—at random—like when you're FINALLY getting interviewed for the papers you need or whatever, then it sometimes goes slow. Rachel will get up to leave a little cubicle after an interview but it (the game) will stutter and she will take five minutes to get out the door—I only noticed this recently. Or you will be in a whispered conversation with one of the Minor functionaries (of the Central Offices) about how you would like to reward his kindness and efficiency by making a small donation to his holiday funds and you start to speak and the words will come out very very VERY slow.

I don't think this kind of slowness in the Central Offices is deliberate. It may be a bug in this version of *The Broken World* but you never know coz those guys really like to mess with our minds.

*

One thing that annoys me about Brainiac. Even when he turned up the other night to go to Dieter's ma's place, AND HE IS ACTUALLY WEARING THE JACKET THAT HE CLAIMED TO HAVE LOST THAT NIGHT AT DECA-DANCE, even then he doesn't say "Oh yeah, sorry, bro, I found it" or "Sorry, bro, for accusing you of hiding it or leaving it in the bar or like selling it on eBay, yeah, it seems like I had it all along." No. He says nothing and just acts like nothing happened.

*

Did I mentions the time limit? I should have mentioned that. The friend of McSham's is dying, right? And he didn't ask you to go pay a visit to her grave—he wants you to take the freaking gift to her. So get on with it.

Cross to other side of the city (South Side) with papers. Then there's Bridge Puzzle and Backstreets Maze. Apart from the obvious hazards I mentioned already (being murdered at random by soldiers or snipers is the main one) you should watch out for Cholera and mobs.

Irene / The TEAM

You can find Irene laid on a bed in a confusing tenement building, surrounded by dust and memories, and dying from a wide variety of natural causes. There isn't much of that around 13th Town (or around here, bro).

Hint: take fruit for her and say nice things about the room where she's doomed to end her days, sad and alone. Irene looks pretty pale—at first I thought there was something wrong with the monitor. But the monitor is fine, she's just near the end of her time, very close to the end. Give her the gift from McSham. She will unwrap it but because she is weak you might have to help with the paper. The gift is a music box and when she opens up a kind of old and familiar tune starts to play. It's a waltzer or something, slow and sad, and when she hears the tune she cries. I don't know why. You can see the tears when they run down the lines in her face, like rivers or a heavy rain. They really do the tears so good.

When the tune is done Irene talks. She is lucid most of the time—I mean, I guess she makes more sense than most people do in that fucked-up town. The tune, she says, is a code. A call to arms. Her tears were not sadness but Joy (she says), that now the time is come. I mean, definitely nothing is simple in *The Broken World*. A tune is not just a tune. It's a system of signs that decode to mean something (thanks, Clockwork). It cannot be just a tune. I'm not sure if I like that about the game, but whatever. That's how it goes.

*

Brainiac broke his silence after last night's trip. At 9, the first time he called, Tory took it and when he said hi she just held the phone at arm's length away from her and nodded to me like I should take it and deal. I guess she doesn't want any more stuff about Dieter's entrails and who's gonna clean it up and that's understandable, but for me it's like, if he's gonna talk, I want to listen. And today he's talking. He is really talking. I mean, welcome back to the whole big thread concerning how the world sucks and his personality is an experiment gone wrong, how he's still in Beta testing etc and narrating his various adventures doing everyday activities that he somehow makes more complicated than they really need to be. Imagine how tough it can be choosing a shirt when all the colors have some different complicated implication you have to consider. Plus he still won't let go with those Dieter questions. Fuck. It's better (?) that he's talking. So every time, like just now, the phone rings and I answer and I take whatever comes from him. Oh man. It's like suddenly

I'm the guy from fucking Dial-A-Despair. Or 0800 SPEAK FEAR NOW. That's me, that is me. Maybe that's my skill after all. Just call that number like Brainiac—you know you need to. Best to speak it out. I guess. Just call me on the number NOW. (I'm only joking.)

*

They do the scene with Irene all sad and TV-deathbed. No music but you can feel it in the air. She says that far across an ocean, in a place of safe hiding, there's a group of resistance who figured out a way to bring down GARS, Archduke, and GovCorp forever. Plans were underway but at the last minute someone traitored them and they had to flee to that secret location. What they are waiting for now is a signal—a signal telling them when to strike. The tune is the signal and now it has reached Irene she begs Rachel to be the one to take it onward to them in a place called the Far Lands. Sounds like a long way, huh? And inevitably it's out across the freaking lethal Occupied No-Man's-Land that lies around the town.

I guess it's pretty clear you have to say yes to this mission but this is one place in the game where playing hard to get can earn you more informations. Say no to the mission and Irene will really lay it on thick, with all the trembling and tears she can wring out—this is her last wish, the last request of a dying woman etc, and Rachel is the only one with the strength and resources to get through. Say no a second time and Irene pleads that your mission is important and even totally Vital for the prosperities of Mankind. Say no a THIRD time and she will take a long cold look at you, with those 100-year-old eyes and will give you extra Health Points, clues to location of Ammo Dump and some weird Spirit Energy that I never worked out what the fuck to do with it. She will also say that this mission is Rachel's best chance to see Ray again. I mean, if all that is not incentive enough I don't know what is.

Take the Mission. Dying Irene tells you a single code word that will trigger the resistance into action. Then she rambles on about the war (just like McSham), about the fight against GARS, about how GovCorp is computerizing Happiness, about Archduke and some guy called Dindara. I don't know. I can't keep track of it all. Anytime you think you understand it they just make it more complicated.

*

Just now Brainiac showed up on IM again. His icon was still that black square.

I cannot keep patience with the guy.

*

Irene will advise you to take the main Route out of town and use Disguises to get thru the checkpoints, but NOTE: don't listen to her—she hasn't been outside in a long time and her informations is all out of date. The checkpoints are a SURE way to get killed. Instead take my advice that Soldiers at the nearby 13th Town Fortress will help get you thru the wastelands and then on the way to your destination. BACk to the scene: thank Irene for her advice (ha ha) and then ask for more info about Ray and how you can find him, but plz be ready with your hand on your best weapons—you will need them. Just as Irene starts to speech again a whole Freaking Unit of Robot Soldiers from the future come smashing into the room with a fizzle and bang of electrical surges and explosions. I don't know if these guys are looking for the Time Travelers or what the

FUCK, but inevitably there is a huge fight using Claw Grenades and Sentient Rifles, and if you stay lucky to the end the whole room will be covered in pieces of dismembered Robot Brains and smashed polycarbon from their shells. Cool. With robots defeated Irene can tell Rachel some more info and then get her wish to go peacefully from out of that world with Rachel sat at her bedside. If you're not lucky it's GAME OVER, bro, and you face the long and lonely walk back to the startup screen.

*

Tory stood in the hallway just looking at me with an expression. When I looked back at her she just shook her head and walked back to the sofa.

*

Bro. Now is time to think seriously and practically abt getting Rachel out of 13th Town before the whole place implodes.

Head to Fortress as mentioned and show papers once again at the Gate House—they will gain you entry. Plz spend some time in the Fortress canteen. A lot of guys here are regularly running missions across the occupied zones outside the city, but it's really worth using time and effort here now so you get the right team. HINT: You can handpick the people you want to go with you, tho sometimes the game throws in random last-minute changes to yr team. That's how it goes. You have to take the rough with the smooth.

*

Tory stood in the hallway by the door again and indicated with a shrug and a mime of sleeping that she's going to bed. I waited a few minutes then went thru to use the bathroom. She was face down/curled in to the wall but not sleeping. She didn't stir or speak at all.

When I came back to HAL Brainiac had changed his icon one more time and now showed up in the chat with a picture pretending he's Dieter. Yes—right next to Brainiac's name there is Dieter's picture. It is Tasteless. I mean, I'm not even gonna reply to something like that or mention it to anyone or make any kind of comment. It's not worth it. Any comment from me will just make him more selfrightous (I cannot spell it) and maybe worse.

We got some good communications here, bro.

*

Collins is a good fighter, Bent Ron (with the tattoos) is a good navigator, Mad Cyril is a good all-rounder, Chief is a good leader (which kind of suits him with the name, I guess) and there are no prizes for guessing what Chef is really good at. Not like you actually need someone that can make 300 different sushi on a mission like this one. Sherri-Lynne has good skills in Shadow Arts and Destiny. Dvorjac has good navigation too (the same as Bent Ron) but he has a terrible temper. You do not want it. You do not want it. Also avoid at all costs any contact with the guy called Ham & No Eggs. He's no good and that story how he got the name is unrepeatable. After you played this part a few times you can even start to feel sorry for characters like Hillary and Duff and Anthills—no one ever picks them and they're always waiting on the touchline like how me at high school and, Clockwork, Sleeptalk, BugMap (sorry, guys) and all the other nerds here never got picked out for football practices and were just left shivering there. The best approach to these soldiers/guys/ women/whatever you select is to offer (upfront) some cash reward for your safe passage. That language works in every place and army, no offense intented to anyone.

Whosoever you choose in the end Rachel still has to risk her life and jump in the back of a jeep with these soldiers that almost look young enough to be her kids (i.e. compared to her they have lived so little) and who all have words like King of Nothing and Dead Zone and 4.48 Psychosis written on their helmets. Remember to share gum with these kids and tell them news from Home too—whatever home is and whatever news of it might mean. The road is very long. These kids may be human fuckups and like ultimate losers in the world order, but for what it's worth they will be the ones that can save Rachel's (i.e. YOUR) life from time to time if you're lucky and get you thru the wilderness, the no-man's-land, and utterly beyond.

 NO CEASEFire /The VULTURES

Outside of 13th Town whatever halfhearted following to the ceasefire exists in the actual town is rapidly deteriorated to nothing and soon you are subject to all kinds of skirmish, ambush, suicide attack, etc at irregular intervals. The roads are just dirt and there are frequent mountains and difficult terrain. Also frequent "junctions" where the road divides many times and there's dilemmas on which way to go. Just keep your eyes peeled in any directions esp when you go thru the mountain passes. At this point I can't tell if Rachel is fighting with the govt forces to stop the rebel soldiers from ever reaching the capital (?) or if she's now part of an outlaw force of rebels moving slowly toward the capital but in a circuitous direction. She's certainly not one of the peacekeepers that get paid to sit around in the shade with their satellite phones and watch the massacres. It's probably a law of the Geneva Convention that troops must display all proper identification and flags or markings or whatever on uniforms and vehicles but these guys she has handpicked to travel with have none of that stuff at all. They're like shadows that don't belong to anything. They won't answer to their own real names. When you say that you are following orders on a Mission they just laugh and look away.

Outside the town there are Villages—Uzek (?) Irsa, Ash, Thorax, Motely, Bethlehem (not the one in the Bible), Jorina, Dore, and Cuspek. Visit each one for supplies and info about movements of enemy troops esp in the mountain passes. A neat trick is wait til the enemy jeeps come into view/firing range then shoot at the spare fuel canisters they have on the side and watch the motherfuckers burst into flames.

There's a pretty high chance your jeep will get wasted. The route away from 13th is rough and dangerous. Jeep can hit a land mine, it can catch fire from an RPG or even a flare, the axle can break from heavy ground, the fuel can run out at a point where there are no more dumps to pick up. Whatever. If the jeep gets wasted you must continue on foot.

Then there are various assorted places where you can try to steal a new jeep or even a small tank if you are lucky. Encampments of troops loyal to General Dare-to-Execute are near the Ridge Mountains. Also encampments of soldiers loyal to General El Terminator in the valley, by the creek. Check it out. These idiots are probably easiest to steal from—a no-fucking-brainer—since most of them are out of their crazy minds on drugs the whole time and their base gives off a vibe like they are having some like 80s House Rave party with all this techno blasting and sirens and weapons going off all day and all night for no reason. You can certainly sneak in there and get out with a jeep.

*

Warning: Before too long it becomes clear that one of the party you're traveling in is trying to sabotage the mission and get the whole party to die or turn back. Try to keep a track on people—who says what in discussions about what to do and what direction to go in, who is acting suspicious or jumpy, who is pulling their weight in the firefights. It's hard to do this and be fighting full on yourself but you need to keep a close track and find out who it is.

Once you've identified the traitor comes one very big dilemma. Do you make an outright confrontation and try to expose him or her in front of the others? Will they take your word against that of someone they have been Buddies with for some months? Or is it better to engineer the traitor into dangerous positions in hope they get killed in a skirmish or in a fall from a mountain road? Or do you volunteer to keep the first shift of the nightwatch with them and then kill them while the others sleep and claim in the morning that it was a sniper? These are the tricks and choices Rachel faces. But one thing is for sure—the mission cannot be accomplished while the traitor still lives. You know what to do.

Second warning: WHen you finally decide to take decisive action be SURE that you're killing the right one. Once Venter murdered one of the crew (a "captain" called Peanut) but still the Mission kept on getting sabotaged—they got a leak in the fuel tank and then made a 'mistake' with the GPS thing and strayed right into the path of an enemy tracer fire, then they went off route again and ended in sand swamps, etc, etc. So Venter had Rachel kill off a second dude—a Navigator called Nightsights but even then they were still getting in trouble and Venter fucked up so bad he had Rachel kill a THIRD dude. We are talking about an original company of Five—so you can imagine just how jumpy the others were getting, like thinking that the whole Mission was jinxed with guys getting shot by invisible snipers, dying of like "food poison" and inexplicable and undetected cardiac conditions all the time. In the end it was like a freakin disaster area to the Max—Venter had Rachel kill everyone EXCEPT the traitor and then, with both of them almost dead with exhaustion, Rachel got jumped by the bad guy (big motherfucker weapons sergeant called Vertigo) and got her skull caved in and GAME OVER. Game over. Game over. You do not want it.

*

Another warning: I have more stuff here not related to *The Broken World*. Plz think of it like an intermission. Or, dude, if you don't like that idea you know what to do—scroll down, just scroll right on down. Like in that song about Walk On By.

What I have to say is this.

So this afternoon was Dieter's funeral. Tory went to work first after a lot of hassles concerning the arrangements and I guess we agreed to meet her there around noon because the miserable temp assholes would not give her a whole day off for a funeral. Then Brainiac came round and Clockwork, Venter, and me (I mean—I was here already, obviously, they came to pick me up), and there we all were dressed up for somberness and ready to go more or less except Clockwork who was obsessing about the knot in his tie that he couldn't get it how he wanted it (a dark blue tie.) Then for some reason, I cannot exactly remember, we had this difficult last-minute conversation about whether to even go to the funeral or maybe not to go at all. And at the last minute (again I don't remember exactly how it came to this) we decided "let's not go."

I guess it seemed too fake to go there—to go in "good clothes" and stand in the neat lines of the relatives and the friends and sing the songs all together that no one even believes in anyway. I mean, what the fuck what the fuck, what the fuck, like in that other song. What the fuck.

So we didn't go to the funeral and instead went up to the woods above the city—the place I described already where we once went with Dieter and he was climbing so high in the trees. (DO NOT panic, I am not gonna get sentimental here. We just went to the woods is all.) We were all in the funeral clothes already (that bit we couldn't avoid) and crammed in Venter's brother's car, picked up BugMap and Sleeptalk, then went roaring out on the road with a mixtape that Clockwork made and piled out just fooling round there on the hills. We went way off the trails and later spent some time throwing stones at bottles (I was a miss-hit, a total Low Score) and shooting Bob'z air rifle (as borrowed by Venter) and later again lit a fire on the hillside on a kind of grating thing made out of stones but I cannot remember who started the fire, just that there was one and we sat there near to it and sparks were flying upward.

I think it was quite late, and for sure after ten (because I had noticed BugMap's watch sometime up there and I remember thinking "oh it's ten already") and already quite cold when we came down and the sky was all dark and starry and we left the fire burning and Venter was yelling a bit coz he was drunk—I know we didn't have food out there just some bourbon so everyone was kind of drunk and talking shit except Brainiac who was quiet again, in black square/powersave mode. No one talked about Dieter and what happened to him (see—no speeches—it's all under control) but I think it was pretty obvious that that is exactly what we were all thinking about.

Only when we made like an uneven route back thru the nite traffic did Brainiac break his silence to say (in slurred words) that people should turn the radio down (there was no radio playing, anyway, it was a tape). And he went into this big thing about Dieter involving a confused account of some part of *The Broken World* where Ray has a doorway to get thru, and with this combination of potions he has to separate his shadow from his physical body (?) and send the shadow in thru the door (by going under it) and then, from the other side, the shadow itself can unlock the door and so bring Ray himself thru—kind of an obvious solution once you saw someone do it of course, but somehow a hard thing to crack without help. Anyway. No one else (in the car) had any idea what Brainiac was talking about or what point he was making exactly and I think Venter said so (not so smart move) and there was a kind of escalating argument that I don't remember except that it ended with Brainiac getting out the car at a red light and walking off in an ambiguous and unknown neighborhood.

Cool is what BugMap said I think when Brainiac was gone. Cool life. But he was being weird all day esp with me and I don't think he meant it. Cool life can be ended fast enough and all our best achievements get smashed up and washed away. It could be any one of us. No Way in the car crash, Milay with the Drugs OD, Ringo's Brother in Thailand, Katie of that cancer thing. Shit. I said no speeches. And now I'm making speeches. I apologize. I'm not even sure what happened up there on the mountain let alone the stupid journey home. Remember Brainiac walking off and Venter yelling out the window of the car as we moved off but I don't remember what he was yelling, just the sound it made in the car and the tape that was playing. You know, it's late and I'm just trying to keep this shit real.

I think I'm a bit drunk, but I can still walk in straight lines - - - - - - - - - -

----
------------------------------ ---------------- - ha ha.

*

Ugghhh. I have a stiff neck. I've been sleeping at the table. Kind of wonder why I'm here—not why I'm on Earth in general, I mean why I'm writing here alone. Tory is sleeping and instead of lying there next to her I'm here writing words and words and words and words about stupid missed funerals and stupid arguments in stupid cars. Fuck. It goes two ways for me, bro—like I can think I don't like to be here the whole time, writing instead of living. But I also think it's good that there's someone to write down what happened, to write down what life in this World is like. Yeah, like I said, I guess I'm still drunk from the Whiskey.

At a certain place along the River they're building a big motherfucker bridge made from human bones. General Die Die is there a lot of the time and he comes riding in in an Armored Hearse all customized with a gun turret and steel-plate armor that is painted with swirls and spirals in drug-induced color schemes. Crazy. I guess he and his Major Lieutenants are either there to supervise the construction project or to sample the Acid that some of the Kid soldiers are dealing in the game. I mean, it is no way a simple bridge they're making there—more like some kind of massive cantilever or suspension thing (I don't know, I'm not a freakin architect). WHEN YOU LOOK AT IT (capslock) you can only imagine how much horrible slaughter has already taken place to provide the bones to build as much of that thing as they have already, but at the same time, like General Die Die says to anyone that will listen, the River is wide and there is no other way (or place?) for his army to cross. You can see the logic, I guess. So they are killing people all over the area to make bones for building the bridge. Once they are Dead, the corpses are left out on a big old football field and these vultures come down in the sun of noon to pick the bones clean. Enemy saboteurs or infiltrators are constantly feeding a kind of slow sleeping poison to the vultures in hope they can slow down the construction work. I'm not kidding—of all the weird scenes in *The Broken World* this really is one of the weirder ones.

When you get to the bridge plz say goodbye to your jeep buddies if any of them are still alive. Where you are going those guys will only slow you down. Dress Rachel in black and wait for nighttime. Then head slowly across the bridge. Watch out for all the places where it is not completed—use ropes to swing from one part to the next. Watch out for night-snipers also. You can tell where the guards are just because of how the White parts of their eyes are getting closer and closer. Kind of looks like Pac Man or like something from old-school Asteroids. White eyes advancing. The eyes like floating skulls. It's great how they do it. You need lots of stealth in this part—lots of stealth and lots of silence if you don't want to end up floating dead in the cold cold river, or your bones getting repurposed for some part of the bridge. Go careful. You are far from home.

*

Late. Later. Too much later. I don't know why I don't give up and go to bed but there is something addictive with computer problems and HAL has been buggy so I was running various disk-medic apps, plus also I want to be sober before I hit the land of dreams. My head is still running round in circles with Jack Daniel's and remembering stuff we were talking in the car back home and the stuff that no one was really saying out there in the woods. When he got out the car at the red light Brainiac was looking bad, his eyes like the skulls. Shit. Many times when I see him now I think about him and the glitches like I wrote about before. About him and how he sometimes sees thru the wireframe to the nothing that the world is built on. I am wondering if this is a bad thing, Necessarily. I.e. just because you are seeing thru does it have to be morbid depressing? Or could it be a good thing? I think it could be really cool and really good to see that, what is under everything. But when you look at Brainiac and what happens with him in the ups and downs it's not so easy. Dark as hell outside and the stars are fierce bright. Very bright like points of white heat. I don't want to write about Brainiac anymore. It's like maybe I'm one of those vultures come down to pick his bones clean. Just watching and writing stuff. Perhaps I don't like to have that skill—to watch and do nothing. And anyhow, I don't think I can really write—not like a writer in some movie. I just tell what to do in *The Broken World*. The writing is done already—the game. *The rest is BS*, just like Rachel has tattooed on her belly.

HAL is running slow. Not just the Central Offices but also the Bone Bridge. More or less anything in fact and not just *The Broken World*. Even Word will not run straight. Now I'm writing on T's laptop and I have been downloading a bunch of stuff—games and a new version of Word. OK. I still just don't get it that there are people in the world who are actually buying software. It's ridiculous ha ha. My copy of Word was sooooo fucked up and as well as slow kept going into crash mode for no reason whatsoever. So to even write this I had to get a new one. The first copy I downloaded I spent like 3 wasted hours (off of Warezshare) and then it was corrupted in some way so I had to go back and get another one, and then go back online another time to get a serial number from somewhere else coz this one was not Kracked. It takes a lot of effort and stress. And after all that, I'm just ready to start writing again and it's Morning already—can hear the freakin birds start to sing. Here I am and I have to get to sleep.

*

Oh yeah.

The one problem with all that running off to the woods at the last minute in funeral clothes and blowing out the somberness and Funeral etc WHICH IS THAT I forgot to call Tory and warn her that we would not be there and because of that she was left kind of stranded all alone at the funeral with the family on one side and the total meltdown Grieving Chelsea Person at the other.

Oh yeah. She was sooooooo fucking supermad she wouldn't even talk about it. She went to bed right away when I got in and gave me a pretty bad time just by not really looking at me. Dude. I confess at dawn—I'm an idiot sometimes.

 A BaTTLe Coming

Morning = Afternoon. Don't ask how I feel. Tory stomped off to work bright, early, and still not talking to me because of the funeral no-show. After the big fucking Door Slam had retreated I lay in bed as long as possible (which was quuuite long) to sleep some more. Hangover. Pretty well borderline comatose since I woke—dehydrated and crap.

Not much *Broken World* here for you today so just scroll ahead til you find it if you really feel that way. Shrunken Ape, I'm sick of your complaints. I guess I was pretty drunk yesterday. With what we drank in the woods and the Coronas at home. So today I phoned sick to Domenico's, which could so push Miroslav over an edge. Later, to break up my new routine, I slept some more on the couch and ignored the ringing phone. It's a tough life, right? Figured the call was either Branimir (see above) or else Tory's Parents with a harsh new brainteaser and either way (for different reasons) = I didn't want to talk to them.

To make it even more like a superproductive day at the office (ha ha) I had serious computer troubles when I started HAL. Had to go online AGAIN and get yet another copy of Word and serial numbers coz the thing from yesterday was still crashing. Total Crap.

*

11 at night, or thereabouts. Yes—a whole freaking day gone in fastfwd of sweat, sleep, and blatant timewasting. I will never drink again.

Tory came back kind of latish from work having gone out again with Grieving Chelsea (trying to pick up her spirits or her broken fucking pieces or whatever) and when she (Tory) got in she just looked at me real bad again for a moment in silence then went straight to bed. Which, I guess, means she's still not talking to me. At maybe 10 her mom called on the phone about some nothing in particular and thru the closed bedroom door I could hear while T give out a long account of the Funeral and the service and the readings and who was there and how moving it was and which pointedly missed all reference that I was absent. Like I don't even exist—a kind of Ultimate Punishment—confined into a Vacuum Chamber. Tory is a total highscore at that.

Pain pain pain in the head and and no Advil in the apartment. All day I was getting vague memories of more things we did and said in the woods yesterday—a bit embarrassed to think about a conversation I had with Sleeptalk concerning Tory and how we're not getting on so well. And I'm not v pleased at all to remember I ripped my suit trousers in a fool's attempt to climb a tree. I only have one suit, dude, but

BugMap and Venter were up there already and teasing me that I couldn't climb. Buying another suit is not an option. SO at least let's hope for that reason if no other (ha ha) that no one else is going to die around here anytime soon.

*

OK. Over the Bone Bridge you come to a town (no name) that is very heavy under GovCorp crackdown. I mean, since there is a curfew AND a power blackout you will not see much sign of life. Somewhere there is a puzzle with shadows that the moon is throwing. Matching objects to shadows? Kind of creepy/scary puzzle.

Near the market you will come to a doorway and thru the doorway (of a hut or a shanty—I don't know what to call it) you see a room where some kind of shootout most probably took place. There are holes in the wall from bullets and the furniture is smashed. Also you will see there are bodies everywhere—dead people. Somewhere in the room is a child and you need to find her (she's not dead). Look under the bed, in wardrobe, under blankets (?) (or rugs?), in corners. She hides in different places and without finding her you cannot continue the game.

*

The kid is called K-Mart or maybe that is just what it says on the T-shirt she wears. She will be scared and hysterical when you find her but you must save her—get her the fuck out, tell her ANYTHING to make her come with you. Tell her that when the soldiers come back she will be Dead Meat, tell her you are not one of the Soldiers, tell her you will take her to Disneyland—doesn't matter, just get her out of there.

The game runs slowly here also, I never noticed before. The room is full of killed bodies, but don't worry what the kid will think coz she is totally BLIND. Talk about a nightmare. They put you in a War Zone with all the usual dangers, perils, and guns shooting anywhere, and then give you a blind kid to look after. Like BugMap said when he first played this part—they really did it this time.

*

Word just froze up for no reason. But then unfroze again straightaway. I don't know what is going on. Getting bad vibes about HAL.

*

A call from Venter who is wondering where Brainiac is. Venter apparently made arrangements to see him at Bam Zak (I don't know why they've started drinking there all of a sudden) but B didn't show. Now Brainiac is not answering his cell phone and is not at his apt and not on IM. In fact he's not been heard from since heading off at high speed last night. I don't know. I looked for him on IM myself and he wasn't signed in. But a person is allowed to switch off the computer sometimes, no? Venter is making out like he's worried, but there are loads of ways something like this can be explained, like B just slept in late then went back to bed again. That's not unusual for someone in the personality of a Brainiac. Or he got confused about where and/or when he was gonna meet Venter. Or maybe he left town to go see his brother Paul—it could be good for him to take a break for a few days and get out of the city. Whatever. It's not a big drama. I will keep you posted. Like you give a shit.

*

Went thru to look at Tory sleeping. I mean, how is it possible that someone can give a bad vibe even when she's asleep? Does anyone have any thoughts on that because I kind of need to know?

She's a piece of work, Tory. Complicated. I can't figure it out. Even when we first met it was like she was faster than me somehow. Already thinking ahead to something else.

When I came back from staring at her sleeping, Venter IMd again to add the names of some more people that hadn't seen BRainiac since last night—Clockwork didn't see him today and some guy called Thurston didn't, plus he apparently didn't show up for his tech support gig. That can be a long list, bro, when you think about it. I hope Venter knows when to let go of a Topic—he should realize by this point there is no point in freaking out anytime Brainiac doesn't show up for something. Venter acts like the tough guy a lot of the time, but right now he's acting more like an emotional geek.

*

MOTHERFUCKER.
I'm going to say it again.
MOTHERFUCKER
MOITHEAERFUCKER
MOTHSRFUCKERT
Morhterfucker
Amotherfucker
MOTHERFUCKER
MOTHERFUCKER
MOTHERFUCKER MOTHERSFUCIT

MOTHEROTHERFUCKER

MOTHERFUCKER

MOTHERFUCKER

7am. I just did ALL the work on the next part of the game, all in one document offline, and now Word has freaking well crashed and the document is gone. I know I saved it. I know I saved it. I fucking know I did. But when I restarted everything and opened it, there is just total freaking garbage in there. The stuff I wrote is shredded to fuck and mixed up with all incomprehensible symbols and garbage. I don't know what to do. I cannot redo it. It would make me crazy.

MOTHERFUCKER.

MICROSOFT CAN ROT IN HELL.

I'm taking a deep breath. I nearly put my foot right thru the wall.

*

I went out, walked around a bit in the night etc etc etc. The stars are still here—no need to worry, I even counted them. Feeling calmer now and back to business. Here's what I decided to do abt the file I lost.

I'm pasting in the work I did that got corrupted. I cannot rewrite it all. I'm already going insane from the many long nights etc. There may be some parts of what I paste in that make sense if you are a big computer fucking genius or something. Maybe someone knows how to retrieve this file? Clockwork? Brainiac? I don't know where he is. Plz mail me. I already did all the obvious things so please don't suggest that I do all the obvious things again—they don't work.

The stuff that got lost was covering everything from K-Mart (the blind kid) and then to Bridge of Silence, Dave's Cavern, and a possible route through 39th Town. Oh God, this walkthrough is a hard task sometimes.

Here is the FILE. (And yes—now I go to sleep.)

ÄÙ,Ù,Û

  Ù,Ù,Ä˜>˜>Û

  ˜>fl>x(X˘˘˘˘˘˘

Õif˘˘˘˘§

 ¸>#?Û

Ä-?-?Û

ºº-?-?Ä#?#?Û

#?¸>Ä(PX˘˘˘˘˘˘

Õif˘˘˘˘++∏

  òòúúúêúûú≤†††–†

†"†0†2†6˝˝˝˝˝˝˝˝·~˝˝˝˝˝˝˝˝˝˝˝˝˝˝˝˝~·˝˝˝˝˝˝˝˝˝˝˝˝

˝˝˝˝˝˝˝˝˝˝˝˝˝˝˝˝˝Ú˝˝˝˝˝

*BhpJ0J0J0`"e,"5AÏ(x(X˘˘˘˘˘˘¶Ãif˘˘˘˘

  Ì(˘(Û

  Ä˙(˙(Û

  ≥≥˙(˙(Ä˜(˘(Û

  ˜(Ì(Ä(PX˘˘˘˘˘˘¶Ãif˘˘˘˘++∏

  Äå&å&Û

  å&å&Ä˜(˘(Û

  ˜(Ì(x(X˘˘˘˘˘˘¶Ãif˘˘˘˘a˙(˙(Û

  ˙(Z)Û

  Ô°(°(Ä˙(˙(Û

  ˙(˙(Ä(PX˘˘˘˘˘˘¶Ãif˘˘˘˘++∏

  Äå&å&Û

  å&å&Ä˙(˙(Û

  ˙(˙(5511 industry.55Ax(X˘˘˘˘˘˘¶Ãif˘˘˘˘˙(°(Û

  Ä°(°(Û

å&å&Ä))Û

))x(X˘˘˘˘˘˘55

5ßÃif˘˘˘˘˘^)`)Û

^)_)Û

Ã"_)_)Ä`)`)Û

`)^)Ä(PX˘˘˘˘˘˘ßÃif˘˘˘˘++∏

Äå&å&Û

å&å&Ä`)`)Û

`)^)xàf

(n˘˘˘˘˘˘®Ãif˘˘˘˘xÓ

"X: "2

'Û

''Ä°(°(Û

›'¢(Û

›'›'Ä›'›'Û

›'›'Ä(PX˘˘˘˘˘˘©Ãif˘˘˘˘++∏

Äò-ò-Û 45554r345Ä7'7'Û 45554r345Ä7'7'Û

ò-ò-Ä›'›'Û

›'›'x(X˘˘˘˘˘˘©Ãif˘˘˘˘Nhfl'(Û

Ä~'~'Û

KK†4†4 Ä 6 6 6. ".   "®π ∫†∫ ªòª ºàºΩÄΩæxæ¯æpøøh
¿Ë¿`¡ÿ¡X¬—

  ¬P√√»√@ƒ¿ƒ8≈∏≈8Δ∞Δ(«†« »ò» …ê… à ÀÄÀ¯ÀxÃÃpÕËÕh
Œ‡Œ`œÿœX——P—

  »—H"¿"@"∏"8'∞'0'®'(÷†÷ uu~'~' Ä ((Û

  (fl'Ä(PX˘˘˘˘˘˘©˘˘˘++∏

Ä..Û

..Ä((45555RIRachel

K—Mart."45Û

(fl' x (X ˇˇˇˇˇˇˇˇ ((Û

Ä((Û

±±((Ä((Û   because she is blind

because she is blind

((Ä(PXˇˇˇˇˇˇ™Äifˇˇˇˇ++∏

'55A544JE:

": "6666 nightvision and tracer fire.M3Û

M3I3Äã4ã4Û

ã4Ö4x(Xˇˇˇˇˇˇˇˇˇx∂â4˜4Û

Äâ4â4Û

â4â4Ä˜4˜4Û

˜4â4Ä(PXˇˇˇˇˇ≥ˇˇˇ++∏

ÄM3M3Û

M3I3Ä˜4˜4Û

˜4â4x(Xˇˇˇˇˇ¥Äifˇˇˇˇ ã4ã4 ã4ãiib +*∑÷2·2Û

Ä÷2÷2Û

÷2÷2Ä·2·2Û

·2÷2Ä(PXˇˇˇˇˇˇˇˇ++∏

ÄÕ3Õ3Û

Õ36789106666 crawling. craWLING.

·2÷2x(Xˇˇˇˇˇˇ¥ÄifˇˇˇˇŸ2⁄2Û

where it says it is.z"ThHEen<m s not where the
map says it is."66Notsigned. "Notsigned. Go left
in the walkways. Head across the village and
towards a place that looks like a house (old

fashioned house, not modern kind). There is a light
that burns in one window."6…3Ä·2·2Û

·2÷2x(X˅˅˅˅˅˅¥Ãif˅˅˅˅Ÿ2˅2Û

ÄŸ2Ÿ2Û

Ÿ2Ÿ2Ä˅2˅2Û

˅2Ÿ2Ä(PX˅˅˅˅˅˅¥Ãif˅˅˅˅++∏

Äÿ3ÿ3Û

ÿ3ʹ3Ä˅2˅2Û

˅2Ÿ2xàf

(n˅˅˅˅˅˅¥Ãif˅˅˅˅ï4†4Û

Äï4ï4Û rooftop//swimmingpool.a.h.††Û

ï4ï4Ä†4†4Û

†4†4x(X˅˅˅˅˅˅¥Ãif˅˅˅˅∫ü4°4Û

Ä†4†4Û

KK†4†4Ä6 6 6. ". "‾1x^^°4°4Û

°4ü4Ä(PX˅˅˅˅˅˅¥Ãif˅˅˅˅++∏

ÄY3Y3Û

Y3U3Ä°4°4Û

°4ü4x(X˅˅˅˅˅˅¥Ãif˅˅˅˅

6789101156É6É6x(X˅˅˅˅˅˅µÃif˅˅˅˅ê,ê,Û

Œ3 3Äë,ë,Û

ë,ê,55T55€˅ˆÖ˘·Ä‡ʹø¬æΩ¬ʹ·∫πΩ«Ã'˂˅ÿˆÖ˘‡fl,·œøæΩπf

·˅µ••Ø¥Ω≈Ÿ◊ˆÖ˘ïÅ˚Å˘ïÖ˘˅Ÿ˅ÇŸÿ"ÃÿŸÖ˅‾Ö˘˅Ÿ˅ÇŸ¬àMsŸŸ˅˅

ŸÅ˅‾Ö˘˅Ÿ˅˅ŸŸ˅≈©|ZN«Ÿ€€˅€˅Ÿ€‾Ö˘€ŸÄ˅ŸŸ°ìê{s¥Ÿ˅˅Ÿ€€Ÿ˅

‾Ö˘€Ÿ˅˅Ÿ˅Ÿ▯âîïï¢˅€˅˅Ä€˅‾Ö˘

˅Ÿ€€˅˅€°ëwâÑ∏É€˅˅‾Ö˘

€Ÿ˂€˅€€èïñëô—É€˅€‾Ö˘€ŸÄ€ ˅€ûçÉÉòΩÉ€Ÿ˅‾Ö˘

€Ÿ˂€ʹ∑ùàlÜâ«µÇ€Ä˅‾Ö˘

€Ÿ›⁄§ùoKq{|ü≥Ä‹\€⁄⁄ŸŸ˜Ö˘‹Ÿ›∞öçw;Wxáâeì÷€€⁄ŸÿŸ˜Ö
˘›Ÿÿîèxā\4XÉéyf∫€€Åÿ˜Ö˘›⁄»éÉ[óJ%%7à{?S€⁄Åÿ˜Ö˘‹€≥Üh
sì-

9[H,‹Ÿÿ◊◊ÿ˜Ö˘›‹ö{}†;$F⁄Ÿÿ◊÷ÿ˜Ö˘›'àd∫Ã3E]OaíâCöŸÿ◊◊'
Ä‰,‰,Û

‰,‰,ÄÊ,Ê,Û

set; selet. select a appropriate device from
itemens. rom its. From items emu. From items menu.
Ê,‰,Ä(PX˘˘˘˘˘˘µÃif˘˘˘˘++∏

ÄΔ3Δ3Û

Δ3¬3ÄÊ,Ê,Û

∂Ãif˘˘˘˘+,Û
Ä++Û
++Ä,,Û
,,x(X˘˘˘˘˘˘˘∂Ãif˘˘˘˘

Û

Ä   "le"5

23456

1Åÿ ˜ Â˘ ‹€≥Ühsì-

9 [H,‹Ÿÿ◊◊ÿ˜ Â˘ ›‹ö{}† ;$ F⁄Ÿÿ◊÷ÿ˜ Â˘ ›'àd∫Ã3E]
OaíâCöŸÿ◊◊'ÿ˜ Â˘ ›≈Åg›‹©±™†úôïì⁄Ÿ◊÷÷ÿ˜ Â˘ ›Õàk≈‹
∏´¨¶úúöû≠ŸŸ◊+'ÿ^ Â˘ ›‹€¨☐x‹ ûùòïúõôü"ÿ◊'‹+^ Â˘
›advice€€ôz¢‹£îêèóóëmqª◊+'+˜ Â˘
›‹€›Ÿôy≥¥ïãçêåä{dªÿ+'◊˜ Â˘ ›€‹€⁄ôwÜìãâêÖÖtü'ÿ◊'+˜
Â˘ ›⁄‹€‹€ëÄ}âÑà|Éh∂Ÿÿÿ'+˜ Â˘ ›Ä€
‹‹Åuaw}yumaᵀᴹŸÿÿ◊◊˜ Â˘   turn left and look ›‹Ä€
Õà~☐CWmY5yëÿŸÿ◊' downwards ˜ Â˘ ‹‹Ä€ ª~|tp$
=râΩŸÿ◊'˜ Â˘ Å€

⁄ô~⏢ypI I│ãûÿ◊′′^ Â˘ Ä€

⁄′⏢}run│yt}xBm│àäŒ◊′′^ Â˘ €⁄€⁄¿││vuy¿⁄{quÅã∑◊′″^

Â˘ €⁄€⁄Æ{trpá€÷údenyï¿″—^ Â˘ï ˇˇˇˇˇˇˇˇˇˇˇˇˇˇ

  ø998ø6⁄Ÿÿ◊˘‹€≥Üh˜Âsì +ÿ   Ä

  ¥¨ƒ©¨˘^¨¨©uip7ø6ø6

Û   ∞§•∂†^¥†¨¥˘¨¥¥¥√vv¥çç∫√ç√

     Ä(PX˘˘˘˘˘˘∂Ãif˘˘˘˘++∏

  ÄÀ3À3Û

  À3«3Ä

Û

  TFGYU¨¥†ƒ¨√√√∫^¨¨˘¥¨¨¥†ƒDFCFF©√ππø¬°^μ^¨Δ^¨Δ¨ΔΔΔ

ΔΔΔΔ

     x(X˘˘˘˘˘˘∂Ãif˘˘˘˘∏πÛ

  Ä∏∏Û

  ∏∏Äππû

  1112345614545656õ5Äõ5õ5Û11123454545656õ5Äõ5õ5Û

  ë,ê,55T55€⁄^Ö˘•Ä‡′ø¬æΩ¬′•∫πΩ«Ã′‹⁄ÿ^Ö˘‡fl,•œøæΩπƒ

  •⁄μ••Ø¥Ω≈Ÿ◊^Ö˘ïÅ˘Å˘ïÖ˘⁄Ÿ⁄ÇŸÿ"ÃÿŸÖ⁄¨Ö˘⁄Ÿ⁄ÇŸ¬àMsŸŸ⁄⁄

  ŸÅ⁄¨Ö˘⁄Ÿ⁄⁄ŸŸ⁄≈©│ZN«Ÿ€€⁄€⁄Ÿ€¯Ö˘€ŸÄ⁄ŸŸ°ìê{s¥Ÿ⁄⁄Ÿ€€Ÿ⁄

  ¯Ö˘€Ÿ⁄⁄Ÿ⁄Ÿ⏢äî ï¢⁄€⁄Ä€⁄¯Ö˘

  ⁄Ÿ€€⁄⁄€°ëwâÑ∏É€⁄⁄¯Ö˘

  €Ÿ‹€⁄€€èïñëô—É€⁄€¯Ö˘€ŸÄ€ ⁄€ûçÉÉòΩÉ€Ÿ⁄¯Ö˘

  €Ÿ‹€′∑ùàlÜâ«μÇ€Ä⁄¯Ö˘

  €Ÿ›⁄§ùoKq{│ü≥Ä‹\€⁄⁄ŸŸ¯Ö˘‹Ÿ›∞öçw;Wxáâeì÷€€⁄ŸÿŸ˜Ö

  ˘›Ÿÿîèxã\4XÉéyƒ∫€€Åÿ¯Ö˘›⁄»éÉ[óJ%%7à{?S€⁄Åÿ¯Ö˘‹€≥Üh

  sì-

  9[H,‹Ÿÿ◊◊ÿ˜Ö˘›‹ö{}†;$F⁄Ÿÿ◊÷ÿ˜Ö˘›′àd∫Ã3E]OaíâCöŸÿ◊◊′

ÿˇÖˇ›≈Åg› ‹©±™†úôïì ì ⁄ˇŸ◊÷÷ÿˇx(XˇˇˇˇˇˇµÃif ˇˇˇ¶,¶,Û

¶,™,Û

3K¶,¶,Ä¶,¶,Û

¶,¶,Ä(PXˇˇˇˇˇˇµÃifˇˇˇˇ++∏

ÄK3K3Û

K3G3Ä¶,¶,Û

¶,¶,x(XˇˇˇˇˇˇµÃifˇˇˇˇ»≈,Œ,Û

≈,◊,Û

≈,≈,ÄŒ,Œ,Û

Œ,≈,Ä(PXˇˇˇˇˇˇµÃifˇˇˇˇ++∏

Ä∫3∫3Û

∫3∂3ÄŒ,Œ,Û

Œ,≈,x(Xˇˇˇˇˇ513th Town"513th Town"5556has often been ston before.

56:has often been stonE before. Use the third door (blue door) and exit window (use drop and roll) — will lead towards Gardens. Watch out for statues (come to life when you are not looking at them). (Also - cherubs with ARROW things that are cold poison — made of stone).

"µÃifˇˇˇˇr» ,Ô,Û

",′,Û

",",ÄÔ,Ô,Û

Ô,",Ä(PXˇˇˇˇˇˇµÃifˇˇˇˇ++∏

Äi3i3Û

i3Ω3 Ä Ô, Ô, Û

Ô,",xåf

(XˇˇˇˇˇˇµÃifˇˇˇˇÔ,Ô,Û

ô,\-Û

ô,ô,ÄÔ,ô,Û

ô,ô,x(X˘˘˘˘˘˘µÃif˘˘˘˘Ó,ó,Û

ÄÔ,ô,Û

ô,ô,ÄÓ,ó,Û

ó,ó,Ä(PX˘˘˘˘˘˘µÃif˘˘˘˘+5655le+"

Ä∆3∆3Û

∆3¬3ÄÓ,ó,Û

ó,ó,x(X˘˘˘˘˘˘µÃif˘˘˘˘—‰,Ê,Û

Ä‰,‰,Û

‰,‰,ÄÊ,Ê,Û

Ê,‰,Ä(PXYOU˘˘˘˘˘˘µÃif˘˘˘˘++∏

Ä∆3∆3Û

∆3¬3ÄÊ,Ê,Û

∂Ãif˘˘˘˘+,Û

Ä++Û

++Ä,,Û

,,x(X˘˘˘˘˘˘∂Ãif˘˘˘˘

Û

23456

1Åÿ ˜ Â˘ ‹€≥Ûhsì-9 [H ,‹Ÿÿ◊◊ÿ˜ Â˘ ›‹ö{}† ;$
F∕Ÿÿ◊÷ÿ˜ Â˘ ›'àd∫Ã3E]OaíâCöŸÿ◊◊'ÿ˜ Â˘ ›≈Åg›‹©±™†
úôïì¦∕Ÿ◊++ÿ˜ Â˘ ›Õàk≈‹∏´¨¶úúöû≠ŸŸ◊+'ÿˆ Â˘ ›€¨x‹
ûùòïúõôü"ÿ◊''÷ˆ Â˘ ›€€ôz¢‹£îêèóóëmqª◊÷'÷˜ Â˘
›€›Ÿôy≥¥ïãçêåä{dªÿ+'◊˜ Â˘ ›€‹€∕ôwÜìãâêÖÖtü'ÿ◊'÷˜
Â˘ ›∕‹€‹€ëÄ}âÑà|Éh∂Ÿÿÿ'÷˜ Â˘ ›Ä€
‹‹Åuaw}yumaᵐŸÿÿ◊◊˜ Â˘ ›‹Ä€ Õà~⬚CWmY5yëÿŸÿ◊'˜ Â˘
‹‹Ä€ ª~|tp$ =râ∆Ÿÿ◊'˜ Â˘ Å€ ∕ô~ ypI I|āûÿ◊''ˆ Â˘
Ä€ ∕' }|yt}xBm|àäŒ◊''ˆ Â˘ €∕€

}|yt}xBm|àäŒ◊''ˆÂˇ€ˇ€ˇ¿||vuy¿-{quÅā∑◊'"ˆÂˇ I   do
not know. €ˇ€ˇÆ{trpá€÷údenyï¿"—ˆÂˇïˇˇˇˇˇˇˇˇˇˇˇˇˇ

           Û

                   Ä

Û

           Ä(PXˇˇˇˇˇˇ∂Ãifˇˇˇˇ++∏
      ÄÀ3À3Û
      À3«3Ä

Û

           x(Xˇˇˇˇˇˇ∂Ãifˇˇˇ∏πÛ
      Ä∏∏Û

      ∏∏Äππû

      π∏Ä(PXvlˇˇˇˇˇˇ∂atÃifˇˇˇˇ++ka∏

      *

Morning again.

Tory woke and breakfasted in silence. I tried. I tried to talk to her—
abt the funeral no-show thing, about the small saga of yesterday with
Venter and the supposed disappearance of Brainiac, about the weather,
and about the state of the Union. Bro, I basically tried to talk to her about
anything, but she wasn't really willing to talk. I'm still apparently confined
to Vacuum Chambers. I'm starting to think there's something more
wrong with her than she's willing to say. Like she's logged out or maybe
logged in elsewhere. I don't know. Probably it's all OK. She had her phone
in the Kitchen and I thought she was checking texts, but when I asked
her like "Who's that?" she said "No one" and just kind of grunted.

Just before she left for work she sat for a moment with her laptop and I was watching her fingers move on the keyboard and her eyes flicker on the screen. I was thinking about that time she was IMing someone—the guy before, that she had a thing with. And I was wondering how would I possibly know, now, one way or another, just what she was typing and who she was typing it to.

*

After blind kid K-Mart, and all the stuff I lost in the night—I'm sorry there's nothing I can do, I cannot write it again. I'll try to come back sometime. You just need to know one final thing about the next part of the game, dude—there is one Big Badass battle coming. If you can learn what I've noted below it might just help you survive.

Try to remember:

1. Soldiers are strong against Spearmen, average against Centaurs and Mermen, but weak against Horsemen and Griffins.

2. Spearmen are strong against Horsemen, but weak against Soldiers, Centaurs, and Mermen.

3. Horsemen are strong against Soldiers, average against Griffins, but weak against Spearmen.

4. Griffins are strong against Soldiers, average against Horsemen, weak against Spearmen.

5. Centaurs are strong against Spearmen, average against Soldiers and Merman, weak against Horsemen and Griffins.

6. Mermen are strong against Spearmen, average against Soldiers and weak against Horsemen and Griffins.

7. Holy Armies are strong against all Spirits (you will see but not have these), weak against Horsemen, Mermen, and Griffins.

8. Armored Cavalries are strong against Soldiers, Mermen, Horsemen, and Griffins, average against Spearmen, weak against Pikemen.

The BATTLe

Slaughters. Evil. Inhumanity. Tortures. Excess. Barbarian and Killing Zone. The true freaking horror of Man.

Those are just *words*.

Massacre. Bloodlust. Atrocity.

Those are just more words but none of them will really describe what happens in the next town and those near it which are called together Blood Corridor—I think the reason is clear as soon as you start this part. It's not so much what Rachel has to do—she is used to killing and stuff—it's more about everything she has to SEE.

I mean, there are just two groups of people left in that part of *The Broken World*—the dead and those ready to die. As far as action is concerned there are raids by units of advancing or even retreating soldiers and the partisans, also rearguard actions or "defensive" actions by the forces for freedom and liberation and Rebels and mobs of justice and vengeance and also various crowds run out of control as well neighbors that are just settling grudges. All that and more is what Rachel will see. It's a splatterfest, dude, a freakin Gorenival, the TSZ x 20. Also, check the lines of starving losers that you find in random fields, who are digging their own graves and then getting shot in the back down into them, buried with their sadfuck improvised spades. The rapes and gang rapes. The mass lynchings and stonings, the various tortures—some spectacular and others kind of less so (i.e. lame)—the bulldozing of civilian encampments, firebombing of refugee or prisoner camps, poisoning of water supplies in villages, towns (and also suburbs). The packs of vagabond soldiers on drugs—weed, cocaine, and even that Acid—and resulting massacres that get "kind of weird." (Stay near the back, Sister, don't try to be no heroine—just stay back and pick up what little points you can.) The graveyards that get dug in football pitches at midnight, the swimming pools stuffed full of the dead, the streets littered with rotted bodies that are lying next to children who will also soon be dead. The aerial bombardment of civilian population, the swooping attacks on sad/pathetic columns of like would-be escaping refugees, with their dismal and repetitive carts carrying mattresses, furniture, grandfather clocks, and yet more crying children. Why the fuck are they taking the furniture, bro? I don't get it—even an idiot can see that you don't need a wardrobe where these guys are headed. Or the casual killing of one or two individuals in a crowd for no comprehensible reason with random sniper fire, the detonation of passenger boats to sink in a harbor, the execution of hostages, one an hour, on the hour and every hour until ransom demands are met, which is like never so the executions never stop and just go on and on day and night thru the whole section like a terrible fucking metronome. Also attacks using napalm, defoliants, and portable nukes. Rachel running, watching, and waiting. Rachel standing doing nothing at the fence they put up real quick and that looks like it will not hold, stood there with the peacekeepers, no peace at all and certainly no peace to keep. The armed searches and hostages taken in hospitals and nurseries, the executions on the steps of Mosques, Town Halls, Public Libraries, or any other location you can think of, or of any location which the makers of *The Broken World* ever had like the crazy vanity or misfortune to build, maybe hoping that better events than these would take place in their creations. I don't know. I cannot fucking tell it to you in WORDS.

*

I am getting stirred crazy. Twice this afternoon the phone in the apartment rang, and when I went to answer there was just a hang-up, the number labeled "untraceable." Must be a stupid mistake caller. I mean, even "Lorraine guy" has a traceable number and in any case he hasn't called for so long now I guess he found her somewhere. I can still hear that guy's voice saying "Lorraine. Lorraine?" He wanted her so bad! I can picture him calling all the combinations of numbers like the one for this apartment, making his way through a precise mathematical permutation of all 11 freakin digits, switching them round and switching them round again (I cannot work out how many that will be in total. I have to ask Clockwork) until he finally found her. Who knows. Maybe he just got wise to the true truth—that there is no Lorraine—and then jumped off some landmark tall structure and into the night. I do not know and I do not know who is calling me now.

*

It's maybe no coincidence that Rachel not Ray must get through this Blood Corridor bearing the one-word message from Irene. I mean, there's a lot of crap talked on the boards and other places about how women are weaker and cannot stand pain or deal with violence but it isn't true (just look at MissOctober, she is not a pacifist player by any realistic definition) and this Mission will prove that, dude, if nothing else. Motherfucker. Fatherfucker.

I guess the only advice for this whole section is TRY AND STAY ALIVE or, as Sleeptalk said once, hang on, at least until the forthcoming weapons amnesty. That's all you can do. You have to get to Far Lands. This Route is the only Route I know.

Climax of the Blood Corridor is six Battles, each one worse/harder than the one that went before it, or better if you want to look at it that way. In each battle there are parts you must play, tasks to accomplish, slaughters to perpetrate. You cannot get thru this without blood all over your hands, I don't care what anyone says. Where did the people that made and coded the game even get their ideas? This part is like they downloaded the whole thing directly from the head of a guy that is locked up in an insane asylum. Here are some notes. I cannot do it all right now.

Bickers Field. (Trench Warfare. Machine-gun advance.)

High Ridge. (Altitude Puzzle.)

The Westway. (Guerrilla Skirmish. Petrol Bombs. Bayonets at Dawn.)

Uzek (sometimes written as Useck). (Massacre.)

Atrocity Puzzle. Use Horsemen and KOBALDS but do not use the Spears.

Sheffield (15th Town). (Firebombers. Minefields. Slow Advances.
Halloween. Ceasefire Trap. Hotel Improbable. Disco Inferno.
Execution Squads. Taking the Towers. Cut and Run Puzzle. Siege
Puzzle. Total War. Where Have All the Flowers Gone. No
Surrender. Never Surrender.)
Michigan. (Blue Phase, Red Phase.)

The battles are awesome but I don't want to talk about it much. I
mean, after a part like all this with all the slaughtering I think it's pretty
easy to see why GC and Yoko898 want to find a total pacifist solution
to the game, even tho it's truly fucking impossible to see how that could
ever work. Rachel's health and morale levels will be low at ths point,
dude. I mean, afterward you won't want to see another bayonet or
another stomach and I guess you'll never see one without immediately
thinking of the other. I'm sick of it. I don't mean just in the game but in
the world, bro, the RW—I'm thinking about pics that Jo Bo's brother sent
back from the war and those that Brainiac was using for a icon til he
found Dieter's pic to play with instead and that video Clockwork
downloaded from the Internet somewhere, of a guy that got his head
cut off using scissors, in Beijing. Or *Face of Death* on cable TV. Sick of
that look on guys' faces. Dazed glint in the eyes. I mean, even like the
gameshow dudes eating live bugs or whatever and vomiting the largest
amounts in a bucket to win big cash prizes. More than anything else I just
see the freaking glint in the eyes of that presenter who is stood there
with the measuring stick. Sick of it (no joke intented), sick of all that. I
mean, some of the stuff in this part can even turn the stomachs of the
real shoot-em-up guys and girls like Helium and Scat or Vengeance or
Miss Kittin.

*

The phone went again. Who the fuck is calling me? Everytime I answer they hang up. I cannot figure it out. Maybe it is Brainiac. Maybe it's the guy Tory met on the Motel expedition and he's somehow confusing her home number and her cell number? I don't know. Tory says it was all "nothing" anyhow so I guess I don't need to think about it. His postcard has certainly gone from where it was left there on the table in the hallway. Who the fuck is calling with a unlisted number?

Venter heard from some guy (I don't know) that Brainiac again didn't show up for work today or yesterday. Jesus, so now Venter (i.e. Mr Overreactions) has got it in his head it might be a good plan to call in the cops and declare Brainiac as a missing person. I say, 1) it's only 36 hours (?) and 2) B is impulsive at the best of times let alone when he's distressed. There's no need to start a nationwide dragnet manhunt just yet. Enough about it already.

The other thing that bothers me is abt the people in 13th, 14th, and 15th Towns (i.e. Blood Corridor). I mean, do the guys making the game really put as much effort in at this point when they know very well that all the people they create for those towns will inevitably die of starvation or get napalmed or machine-gunned by the truck and bus load? I wonder how that works. I mean, for sure in the Crowded Earth they do everyone with the permanent integrity (thanks, Clockwork) and all persons in the crowds have lives, futures and pasts. But I don't think it can be the same around 13th Town. People that live there are just cannon fodder, food for the War. They are just Shapes, "truly truly just born to die" (again, like the words from the Skeleton lyrics). I'm not saying this as a technical expert (that much is clear already, I think), but here in Blood Corridor the programmers etc must just cut corners and make population in batches—using a crowd generator, or more like a victims or corpses generator. Ughh. Bro, I would not like to live there or be made in that way—with just enough Life, just enough detail, just enough Energy to like "be" there in one dumb village or another, living half a life like a sleepwalker and just enough impulse to like stand when advancing armies come all marching in, or just enough instinct to look startled in the eyes and scream when that shrapnel is sticking thru in your stomach. It's harsh to even think about it. Like the guys that made the game probably put more details in the guts, blood, and screams of these poor motherfuckers than they did in the rest of their lives. I never really stuck around long enough to look. But now I think about it I can imagine that in those towns and villages many people are just looped on simple activities. Old guys sat on porches, kids playing hopscotch, women drawing water from the well, farmers leading cattle thru the streets. And that's all they do by day (sleeping in loops by night). There's no depth—they are doing those things and those things only, like that's all their life. They are just waiting for the battles or biding time for the army and the mass executions. They are just so much fucking scenery. I know I'm not the Life and Soul of any party but now even I'm getting depressed. I apologize. We are so fragile. Even Tory's parents cocooned out there in the Burbs protecting themselves with alarms and questions and a circle of ridiculous spams—like ANYTHING they want there they can probably buy it, but still their house is an encampment of anxiousness (I don't know how to spell it). Ughhh. I only wanted to write a walkthrough.

*

Motherfucker. One bit of very concrete news. This shit is 100% too near the bone or the knucklehead (or whatever they say) and I would appreciate it if people did NOT immediately send me smartass emails or make sarcastic comments on *The BW* board. I am totally confused.

When I got back from Domenico's tonight Tory had been back to the apt after her work, packed a bag, wrote a kind of note for me, and left again. She basically moved out.

The short note she wrote me is private, so I guess I won't type it all in here, but mainly she was saying that this exit is just for a while, that she's moving out probably, just while she gets her shit together and also criticizing me for various stuff (esp the thing with Dieter's funeral, but also attitude to her family members and the fact that she's sick of how the vibe is between us all the time). It made me scared quite a bit. Fuck it. Then I wondered if the hang-up phone calls today were maybe Tory— calling in to check if I had left the apt yet just so she could come along all sneaky when I wasn't here and grab her stuff without confrontations.

What the fuck. People are getting out of my life like they think it's a matter of Urgency or like that part when they exit the thermonuclear submarine when it's sinking in the Bay of Dreams.

The Laughing GENERal

You can call it a kind of escapism if you like, bro, but right now I'm just getting on with the walkthrough. I'm not gonna sit around and wait for any more negative developments in my so-called personal life. I have beer and the computer is working—for now that will have to be enough.

One of the best fights in the whole of *The Broken World* comes at the end of the Blood Corridor, where to complete her journey to the Far Lands Rachel has to track down and defeat General Die Die in the heart of the War Zone (which is pretty much his creation and in any case his favored hangout). First you must follow rumors on his whereabouts that will slowly lead you to the precise location of a Wrecking Yard near what they are calling 135th town.

OK. Once again I will not even talk about the numbering of the towns which by this point seems to have a life all of its own. One time there was even some university Freak showed up on the Board and said he was writing a PhD Thesis on the Numbering of Towns in *The Broken World* and its significance in the Universe and he was asking people to spout off their theories and opinions about it. Scat certainly posted him a lot of his opinions but it wasn't really about the topic he mentioned. More just like he should keep away from the board with these questions under threat of having something vicious happen involving the modem cable and a part of his anatomy. Afterward there was like a really violent flame war going for a month at the end of which the Thesis dude had his IP address logged forever and was banned from the board.

But I'm getting distracted. I want to write about Rachel v GEneral Die Die, which is one of the coolest fights in the game.

The scene starts when Gen Die Die's multicolored armored hearse pulls up. Get inside and you see him close up and face to face for the first time with his green-and-black camouflage dinner suit all patterned with an overlay of these cool-looking golden skulls. Scary. Die Die laughs when he sees you and you get to see all like gold teeth in his mouth and then takes yr hand to kiss it. PLease to meet you, my child, is what he will say and then he will laugh to himself again ha ha ha as the door (to the car) shuts and the only light in there is tinted all yellow from the tinted windows and the world outside looks so distant and kind of strange.

There follows a conversation. First of all Die Die will offer you a chance to be his friend—making an offer to join him on the side of the Zorda and GARS. Say no to this offer. I guess it's obvious why. While you're talking Die Die will softly touch the gold rings on his fingers and as time goes by he will talk quieter and quieter and pull you closer and closer to him so that he can whisper in your ear. HINT: Plz DO NOT GET

TOO CLOSe because he is trying to hypnotize you. Use a Shield Charm if you have one, otherwise a Blanking Potion.

Wait til Die Die has finished all his talking then strike immediately using the Dagger of Tormana (that can be rescued from River in previous part—if not you have to go back. I apologize). When the Dagger hits home Die Die will roar in Anger and in the struggle that follows he will pull out a Needle Gun. The main thing is to get the fuck out of his car—kick open door and roll to safety as he fires.

The fight with General Die Die will then continue outside the armored hearse. You will have to fight hard to get thru this in once piece, bro. It's rare to come out of it alive. You can feel your heart racing. All around the place are his various soldiers. When he gets weak from your attacks he will just randomly kill one of his followers—the Kill will increase his Health and Vitality levels so that he can stay strong in the fight with you, and you will hear his terrible laugh and see the golden skulls reflected in his eyes. HINT: If you take time to kill the acolytes of Die Die then he will have no further victims to feed off as easy food to replenish his energy.

Just when you think the fight might be over—Die Die is wounded from your kick and knife attacks and his Evil blood is oozing thru his camouflage trousers etc—just at that point they pull this weird/ spectacular thing and he changes to become a kind of giant demon "thing." They do the transformation really freaky—with lightning that kind of comes from inside him and his eyes burst white and red like petals of exploding fire and suddenly the new version of Die Die erupts from the body of the old one. His human form is discarded—smashed and exploded—as the demon thing emerges at high speed, tongue lashing and claws extended.

*

Venter turned detective and went round to B's to ask the neighbors if they have seen him. Then he called here to relay the news. Seems the neighbors in one apt are two dudes apparently in a punk/skater band and there are two "nice college girls" downstairs who just moved here from Bumfuck, Texas, whose main interest was asking V if he knew where they could buy some dope. The old neighborhood hasn't changed. Venter didn't bother with the ground-floor apt where they have the unpredictable Rottweilers and a teenage son with some sort of learning difficulties. The long and the short is no sign of Brainiac. When he got here, Venter was working his way in a panic again, starting to rant about calling the cops or making a trip through the rain to nearby Emergency Rooms in the area just in case B did anything stupid. Bro, it's ridiculous—the next thing Venter will be hand-painting Brainiac's picture onto Milk Cartons.

While we talked I was constantly on the edge of telling Venter that Tory moved out. But somehow I couldn't find any good way to introduce it into the conversation and in the end I gave up. I guess it didn't seem like the right time to be putting my private troubles on any1's agenda. I mean, Tory (like Brainiac) only just left really—there's still time for her to change her mind and no need for me to start announcing more stupid bad news to everyone yet.

*

The Demon Die Die (I don't really know what to call it but it's pretty disgusting) cannot be wounded using ordinary bullets—they just bounce right off. You need to use the Needle Gun (from before) or maybe Spear Weapons. The lower part of the Demon is heavily armored but near the top there are some unprotected places.

Many times the Demon Die Die will attack you with flames and a kind of spinning attack using Claws. As darkness falls you'll need to switch from ordinary vision to Thermal—lets you see heat and tell where Die Die is. Of course "he" also has Thermal and can anyhow tell where you are just the same. Man, it's cool how the colors look—you can see the Demon in all pulsating and shimmering orange, red, yellow, and blue. In Thermal mode blue is the color of cold, and in the center of the Demon Die Die there is a beating blue heart—cold as stone.

Near the Wrecking Yard is a kind of Food Refrigeration Plant and you must try to lead the fight in that direction. Once there, trick the Demon into throwing fireballs at you then DUCK the fireballs (obvious!) but make sure they hit and burn holes in the Refrigeration Units. These Freezers are your chance and once one has opened have Rachel run inside and hide. Now here's the trick. If you can spend twelve minutes in there hiding your body temperature will drop so far that when you exit the Freezer Die Die/Demon will not see you at all. (NOTE: This state doesn't last forever coz soon the body heat returns. Anytime you go back in the Freezers and wait long enough to cool down you can get five minutes' invisibility.)

In the Wrecking Yard itself is a set of machines and contraptions for breaking up and crushing the cars. Try to steer the fight in this direction. Maybe there should be like a skill of "fight steering." Hint: At first Rachel cannot jump high enough to use the kick attacks on Demon's head but by jumping on the roofs of the cars waiting to be crushed she can get a kind of high-speed bounce that will let you go higher. Your kicks will not kill Die Die—he is technically dead anyway, dude—how can you kill what is not even alive? But they will weaken him further and that is what you want. When the Demon's weakness gets low enough it will be forced to transform back to Die Die himself—he cannot maintain transformation if he doesn't have enough energy. When the levels drop you will see the gigantic Demon wither and instead become the figure of a tall man all in reds, yellows, and oranges except in the center a slow-beating heart of stone-cold blue. Cool. But Die Die will not be afraid. He will walk toward you.

Down near the Crushing Machinery there is a switch for the Halogen Lighting and a switch for the Electrical Generator which is good news coz what comes next is too complex for Thermal—you need to see properly. Enter the code for the lighting (you should have collected it in the previous town) and then pull the switch. There will be deep vibrations and the generator kicks in and suddenly the Wrecking Yard is lit up and the battle can truly commence. (Don't pull the other switch. It will only bring DEMONS.)

*

I logged on various *BW* chat rooms/message boards but no sign of Brainiac there. On a General part of one obscure *BW* board I did find where he wrote a long post with the subject line "Pissed with life etc" and I was reading it, sure there might be clues until I noticed the date and saw it was up there a year ago. I.e. not really news and not really relevant.

Later there was an email from Tory. Total 3 lines. Great. Just to tell me in line 1 that if I need to find her "for now" she is staying at Grieving Chelsea Person's and then in line 2 "that here is the phone number" if I need to get in touch with her there for any reason. Like suddenly those two are good friends. Line 3 just says "hope you understand and hope to see you soon" but after this I'm even more puzzled. What am I supposed to Understand? And why the fuck would I want to see her after all this? I read the mail maybe six or eight times. It doesn't add anything to the note she left before. That note was private but I will say it featured the three most popular breakup words—NEED, SOME, and TIME—in that exact sequence. I'm dealing with someone that suddenly decides to take off for no reason. OK, the funeral thing. And I am a lameass sometimes. But I don't get how any of that is really "needing time" or "packing a bag" territory.

I thought hard about replying. But really, when I read Tory's mail again it didn't seem like it's waiting for a reply. More like it says what IT wants to say and the rest can GO TO HELL.

*

Back to the job of kicking ass and if you don't like VIOLENCE then just go play *Purple Cartoon Racer* or *The Masked Blondes and Brunettes of World Wrestling Sumo Tag-Team Submarine Adventure*. They do it so good there in the Wrecking Yard with Rachel and Die Die fighting each other under the floodlights—whirling and crashing and jumping. Somehow Rachel can seem more at home here in the center of this terrible fight than in any other place or time, even better than when she was in that trailer with the fridge magnets, pictures, and everything. Soon her clothes burn in some places and there is a mix of sweat and blood on her face, and a soft rain begins to fall. Die Die is pure Evil, his camouflage and gold-skulls outfit all charred, torn up, and splattered with his own blood and that of his opponent (i.e. YOU, dude).

Now comes the tricky part. Jump and then use stun to drive Die Die down to the ground—when he falls keep jumping to keep him knocked down for longer. (You can stun him this way but you cannot kill him—there is no point in jumping and jumping beyond a reasonable point. Venter I am talking to you.) Once Die Die is properly stunned Rachel must immediately begin to climb the tall yellow crane that stands just above the Crusher Machinery. NOTE: If there are any of Die Die's followers left you must kill them NOW—you don't want any Acolytes left who can spoil yr plans to kill their Master. At the yellow crane climb quickly up the metal rungs and don't forget to look down coz Die Die will be after you. At the top there is a ledge (or platform?) outside the cabin which has the Crusher and grabber controls. Wait there for General Die Die—he will not be long.

From the top you can see in all directions over this whole part of *The Broken World*. Man, it looks like those pictures in magazines where you kind of want to look at it but at the same time you don't, coz it is waaay too GRAPHIC and when I say that I'm not talking about those hardcore pics of four Scandinavian chicks and two black guys and a white guy with a lot of tattoos all over—I'm talking about those award-winning pictures with people that have got their fucking heads hanging off or like a stump full of shrapnel and maggots where their legs used to stick out and the smoke rising in a distance and behind them a big confusion of mud, sand, bodies, and burned-out buildings everywhere. Anyway. Whatever.

As Die Die climbs up the ladder you can see him truly pathetic now. Just a wounded raving lunatic with desperation in his eyes and a lot of gold teeth in his mouth. When Die Die reaches the very top give him space to climb onto the platform—it's all part of the plan. Once he's on the platform then you can launch back into battle. You need to chop and kick and hack but also move slowly round (anticlockwise?) so that Die Die follows you further and further round on the platform—more fight steering. When you get to the place where your back is right up against the DOOR to the control cabin STOP and hold yr ground. Stay there and try to bring Die Die closer and closer to you, use short punches and basically wait for him to come. Do not kick him back—you need him REAL close. When he is close enough choose the 12-Bore Shotgun from your Items and blast him fully in the chest with both chambers. The gun will do damage but it won't kill him. The important thing is how the force of the shots he takes is pushing him backward. After both shots have caught him right in the chest he will be 1) off balance and 2) dangerously close at the EDGE OF THE PLATFORM. This is a cool combo, bro. It's exactly what you want.

The moment Die Die is there—right on the edge of the platform, knocked back by the force of shotgun blasts—that's the time to run and jump. Use a both-feet attack and hit him hard. Die Die will stagger backward, confused. Like he didn't expect a run-and-jump—he was expecting the needle gun or the rocket launcher. Ha ha. As he staggers kick again, aiming high and to the top of his chest. This last kick is the Death Blow. Die Die will go back, overbalanced, and at first he just laughs like what a puny kick how can you expect to defeat a great Evil like me—the commander of a Rag Tag Army—using just a kick—and he laughs ha ha ha. But then he will realize that he's unbalanced and the 2000-feet drop from the top of the crane is below him. And then he will start to fall, arms making a windmill of spinning gold skulls as he goes down, and his laugh will turn into a scream that they make like a cool echo all over the landscape you see down below with the half-wrecked multicolored hearse, the burning cars, the mud, dead bodies, and blowing sand.

If you got all the positions right Die Die will fall perfectly positioned and right into the Crusher. Cool. Go into the cabin and activate the controls. Put the Crusher on supercharge and you can watch as the claws and shredders mash that motherfucker til his bones are dust. At this point GEneral Die Die is officially defeated. You might want to go out there and blast the Rocket Launcher into the Crusher a few times just for olde times' sake. I mean—it might seem like overkill, but Die Die is a nasty mfkr and you should make double, triple, and superfucking sure that he's not gonna make any last-minute comebacks.

*

Man, the first time I defeated Die Die I probably used nearly all of the potions, force fields, and other stuff I'd been collecting over the course of the ENTIRE GAME. I mean just to stay alive. The fight lasted the most part of a day, and Die Die almost killed Rachel on 5 separate occasions. Tory was in the apartment when I started the fight and then she went out to work and when she came back I was still sitting there in the same place, just some pretzel packets thrown around the couch and me staring at the screen. I beat Die Die pretty well, I guess, but I can do it better now. In the end, I just barely outlasted him, and when I cut him down for the final time. I watched the Crusher go into action and heard the horrible screams and the splatters of blood and electric lightning that splits the sky when he's dead, and then danced around the apartment, making an utter fool of myself. Tory thought that was so so so fucking funny then. A lot of good that does me now she's gone.

The E. L.

For some reason I have ended up tonight in that Gray Zone that lies between beer number 4 and beer number 6—i.e. a place where a DOWN feeling can definitely take hold. I think it's maybe safest to keep drinking myself to the other side of the safety margin. You will have to bear with me on this. I'll do some very quick updates on the Frequently Asked Questions:

1. Venter called to say he still hasn't found news of Brainiac (or Brainiac himself for that matters) in any way, shape, or place.

2. Tory didn't call. I thought she might but she didn't and she didn't IM and she didn't email again and she didn't come round and I

didn't call her or email or IM her or go around to see her, which would be difficult anyway coz I don't know where the Chelsea Person lives.

3. Brainiac also didn't call or IM or email or send a message by a carrier pigeon or communicate by any means of sending a message that has yet to be invented either now or in the future.

4. Dieter also didn't get in touch. But I guess we can take that for granted at least given that I am an atheistic almost-drunk dude and I don't believe in ghosts, and not Santa Claus and not fairies. I miss Dieter.

We're talking about a situation of total stasis. Clockwork says it doesn't even EXIST in nature but I think he has to look at the evidence above and agree with my findings. Total Fucking Stasis.

*

After sending Die Die to the Crusher by Special Deliveries you must leave the Wrecking Yard but don't forget as you exit to plz loot whatever you can concerning health upgrades, weapons, cash, Items, medicals, food, and etc. You know the routine.

The next level (called the EL) must be accessed by a secret door located in a small supermarket maybe 10 miles N by NW down by 1 of the dirt tracks that passes for a road in this part of *The Broken World*. I know—it's a STRANGE place to put the entrance, and when you get there it's hard to believe that you came all the way thru the DMZ and the battle and defeated the monstrous freak Die Die just to find yrself at a supermarket with a faded LOTTERY sign and a fat dude sat outside on a beer crate and a kind of unimpressive selection of supposedly fresh produce in the right-hand aisle. I mean, what kind of message are they trying to portray by putting the doorway to the next level in this location, right next to the shelf of Hot Sauce? I give up. Not everything means something—remember that and you can save yrself a lot of heart attacks. I got that advice from Joe. Hi, Joe. I guess he's not reading this walkthrough. Another example—just coz Brainiac said "you guys will be sorry" sometime when he was drunk that night in the car coming back from the woods etc does not have to mean he was gonna do something stupid. I don't think there's enough reason to start freaking out.

Anyway. You don't need a code to open the secret door but since you cannot get to this place without defeating Die Die I think that killing him must be the method of opening it.

Open the door. Step thru. Then close it behind you—it pays to be neat and tidy.

There will be a kind of shimmering (I don't know how else to describe it) and then you will be in the Fourth Level—the EL, which is maybe time for a recap. First Level is from start to roughly Fifth Town. Second is all the offworld (including time in the Crowded Earth which some people call a level in its own right, but not according to me). Third Level is from Rachel at the Motel thru the War Zone and up to and including Die Die. Again some people divide this up into two levels but not me. Then comes this one. Fourth Level. EL. The whole game has seven or eleven (or fifteen) levels, depending how you look at it. Of course there are always more levels that appear as options plus sublevels, bonus and hidden levels. It's hard to keep track. The various complainers know what they can do if they aren't happy, i.e. write your own walkthrough, guys or girls—I'm doing all this work as a free community service and you have no right to bug me the whole time. I wish that some people (e.g. DrunkenApe and Strontium) would hear that good. You are getting BORING, with your wiseass abusive remarks. Guys—I'm sick of the stuff you write. I say no more. This is the EL = Level Four.

You walk and you look around. There's just a small town you come to at first, with a series of wide streets and maybe thousands of buildings with many deserted rooms. Then there are forests, train stations, suburbs, big roads, small roads, a desert on the outskirts, and beyond that you find smaller towns and several larger cities. There is even an ocean. It is freaky and after a time—pretty soon perhaps, but it can take longer than you'd expect—pretty soon *you realize* what it is that's *so* freaky. *There is no one there and nothing to do.* Nothing. No one. Nothing at all.

There are no other people and no creatures and no monsters or anything whatsoever to fight. Nothing to do. There are no agents, no assassins, no zombies or Zorda, thugs or marauders, no Generals or rebel forces, no thugs or joyriders, no rippers, killers, no crowds, no cannon fodder, no friends, lovers, allies, enemies, or like mortal enemies, in fact no people at all. Just a freaking landscape. A world inside the world. But empty. The EL. Deserted. EL—i.e. Empty Level. Riverbanks. Office blocks, houses. Huts, gardens. Airports and ferry terminals. Parks. All empty.

*

Fucking empty apartment also.

The answer to my FAQs are the same as before. Now, I thought maybe I could go over to Brainiac's to see what I can discover but what's the point? I'm not a Detective Investigator.

Maybe it's not the best thing to be writing about The EL at this point. I mean, I love it—it is truly one of the best parts of *The Broken World*. But the Emptiness thing rings a bit harsh in this current apartment/place I am in life. Something about those miles and miles of nobody home that makes me feel cold in my bones.

*

The more you look around the EL the more you can start to think that maybe here the ppl that wrote and coded *The Broken World* must have somehow lost interest in what they first set out to do. Like maybe they got bored of the chasing and the killing and the fighting and all that endless struggle with GARS. I mean, dude—is that possible? They got bored of the crush of people and all the chattering voices in all those languages that no one can hardly understand them at all just like when you spend too long in a mall and you just end up wanting to kill everyone or close yr eyes in the elevator as it sinks on down thru different floors or like they just no longer wanted to make any more of those hidden levers to pull, or those secret compartments to open, or complicated codes to crack.

Like they didn't want to make anymore weapons to upgrade from Dagger to Sword and Sword to Axe and Axe to Crossbow and Crossbow to Musket and Musket to Rifle and so on up the inevitable ladder to RPGs and Cruise Missiles, or they didn't want to make any more routes to trace, slides or chutes to slide down, mazes to navigate and hidden trapdoors to fall thru, or more fucking items to collect or store or barter or lose or find or potions to drink and mystery tablets to take, and instead concentrated only on the landscape. And so they just made buildings, houses, hills, roads, streets, plains, wilderness, construction sites, stairwells, housing projects, hotels, schools, factories, waste-lands. All empty. Empty. Just empty and blown by the "gentle breezes" of the Empty Level.

Or maybe they just didn't want to make more strange races of aliens, or lots and lots of hidden and anonymous conspirators to track down or an army of deviant Robots with dangerously damaged memory chips, or paraplegic Nazis or Hypnotized Surfer Chicks in those tiny bikinis that are too small and made of string or whatever or a town full of freaking hillbillies, or a city full of glamorous fools, or an army of conscripts or religious fundamental zealot maniacs, or just like lots and lots and lots of *people* or whatever. No. Not at all. Nothing like that in fact. Fuck it. They just wanted to make *space*.

And, bro. They succeeded. It's cool beyond a doubt even tho, as I said before, in the place that I am in right now—i.e. an empty and deserted apartment—maybe it's all a bit too close to the bone. Just the landscapes they made here are amazing—it puts so much other stuff to shame. All the Textures, all the Surfaces of things, all the ways that light moves, all the ways that shadows fall, all the ways that darkness comes and goes, all the kinds of reflections of light, the refractions of lights, the ways that light will pass through water, or the way that it will strike against glass or chrome or sand or concrete, or hit the top leaves on a tree, and flicker in the breeze. I mean, maybe they decided that here, just this once, they could just make a perfect empty space and leave it for Rachel to find.

*

I did a bad thing and went thru a bunch of Tory's stuff she left behind. I wasn't planning on doing it, and I'm not making out like it's really an OK thing to go looking thru someone's private notebooks, letters, papers, and closets. I hardly found anything anyway. I don't know what I was looking for—I guess evidence that she is fooling around or more things/items related to Postcard Guy. The only thing I discovered was like a half-written letter to Paul (Brainiac's brother) that was shoved in a box with some old letters of hers but I couldn't even tell when she wrote it and the content was pretty vague. Then there was also a postcard sent to her that just had a cross written on it (like a kiss—not like a crucifiction-type cross) but again I cannot tell when that was sent. It was a postcard of a waterfall. I mean, maybe I sent it. It could be my writing, maybe three years ago. She could have taken any real incriminating stuff with her anyhow. I'm feeling basically reassured with what I found. I know it's not good to make a habit of reading other people's stuff but in the circumstances, I don't have a guilty conscience. I keep looking at that X and wondering if it's from me. Whatever. It's only an X. What does that matter? X can stand for anything—that is what Clockwork says, at least in mathematics.

*

Long days at work with not many customers. And, bro, the hippocrasy (I cannot spell it) of Ants-up-the-Ass and his Brother is off the scale. Those guys were so full of speeches when they fired the Stentson 1.0 and full of more speeches to me when I was skipping shifts— concerning Improve Your Attitude, Mouthfucker, or get another Employment etc. But it's those guys who totally skip out the whole time on any excuse "to do important stuff" or "get important stuff" (which means i.e. sit in a Ukrainian bar). There are whole shifts where they leave me, Ashton, and the Stentson 2.0 to go it alone. "I will be back," says Branimir like he thinks he's Arnold Schwarzenegger going out to save the Universe or get elected to Office or something. The ovens are into ThermoNuclear again but Mr Miroslav is too freaking busy to call Metal Micky or whatever his name is to come fix it. There is only so much the three blind mice (me, Ashton, and the 2.0) can talk about before boredom, repetition, and the heat of those malfunctioning ovens leads to inevitable mischief.

Today for example there was a childish fight with food items causing a huge mess after which we all retired (bloody but unbeaten) to our own sphere of interest. Fuck—I can only keep focused on that kind of trivial shit for a short time before I slump and start dwelling on Tory again. Maybe you can picture it—me making notes on *The Broken World*, Ashton calling his boyfriend on the Domenico's phone line, and the Stentson 2.0 just sulking, all of us dusted in a faint layer of flour. There was even a trail of food debris leading to the Stentson 2.0, sat on the sidewalk in what is now known as his Spot—i.e. with his back to the storefront, his helmet beside him, fingers playing with the bits of gravel that are out on the ground down there.

The fact that Ashton was calling his boyfriend for 50 minutes explains why we're not busy—I mean, if anyone wanted to order CCF it wouldn't be possible to get thru, it doesn't take Stephen Hawking with the voice-inducer-thing to work that one out.

And of course when Branimir did finally get back to Domenico's he was madder than hell coz HE HAD BEEN TRYING TO CALL THE STORE FOR MORE THAN ONE HOUR (he said), not to order a pizza—which he doesn't even like—but just to talk to the Stentson 2.0 about something apparently absolutely URGENT, and all the while he could NOT get thru—

because of Ashton and how he was on the phone to Cliff all that time, like I said.

(Just a side note. It's hard to believe that Ashton's boyfriend is really called Cliff coz it sounds like such a fake name. But Ashton insists that that IS his real name and says I'm narrow-minded about names. Ashton is a freak. Hi, Ashton.)

Anyway Branimir was madder than hell about the phone being engaged and he said he wasn't gonna take it anymore and he kept saying that over and over again. He was madder than hell and not gonna take it anymore. He was madder than hell and not gonna take it anymore. He was madder than hell and not gonna take it anymore. Etc etc etc and he was even more madder than hell when he saw the remainder of the mess from the food fight in the kitchen area and the half-assed attempts we'd made to clean it up. By the time he left "to go get more important stuff," he was yelling in Ballistic Mode that we would all SEE what HAPPENED etc and MOUTHFUCKER etc and it was only afterward—like waking from a weird dream—that I was thinking what deep fucking shit this all could easily be if I lost the cooked circular job at this particular not so convenient point in my time and life.

(Beer number 5 is all gone. Like Tory, I guess, and Dieter in their different ways. And maybe B. I'm still in that Gray Zone, moving way too slowly thru the numbness to the Comfort Zone and inevitable sleep.) Beer number 6 is waiting for me.

*

Of course there are plenty of quite different "explanations" of the EL put out for heated discussion on the boards. The Grinning Cat school of thinking has a theory (now there's a surprise) that says EL is like the ultimate level and the very heart of the game coz it's the one where Rachel is "closest to her own true self." I just repeat the words from GCs postings plz do NOT start to flame against ME. Of course EL is also the only level where the Total Pacifist Solution that GC and others dream abt has ANY chance of working (ha ha) and with all its natural beauty it's certainly a gd place for contemplation of harmony etc. Ha ha again. I cannot write all the stuff that the GC/Y898 crew are coming up with. Check it on their website, if that's what you're interested in. But check your AKs at the door. And be nice to the girls.

Another theory advanced about the EL by some people (Jo Bo, that kid I mentioned, for one example) is that maybe this part of the game is not even completed. According to his big idea they built the EL this way and were just gonna go thru later and fill in all the people, puzzles, and problems. But for some reason they never quite got around to it—I don't know why.

I agree this *could* be true but then again a whole level seems like a Big thing to have dropped off the To-Do List—I mean, they do sometimes forget small stuff. Kind of like glitches. There is one guy in 56th Town that has no shadow—that kind of mistake is possible. But the idea that they somehow forgot to populate an entire level seems like stretching the bonds of reality.

Also. My other problem with this idea—that they built the landscape first and were then gonna "come back later" to put in puzzles and a population—is that I don't think they build games in that order. It sounds a bit more like God's sequence for building the world. I know, I'm not a technical expert. But when it comes to computer games do they really build the world first and then put the problems in? Not in my best guess. I think *The Broken World* is more or less inseparable from the sum of its problems or whatever CW says. You can't really have one without the other. My money is on the fact that the EL was meant to be just exactly like it is. Just landscape. Empty.

It's lonely. Not unlike some parts of the RW. You can walk in the mountains. You can walk in the center of the empty city streets. You can walk on the beach. Watch your footprints. You can even dream of what it would mean to meet another person here, in this abandoned place. Yeah, like some parts of the RW. Sorry. And fuck off BadApe and Rhomboid—I will stop feeling sorry for myself when I get a good reason to do so.

But in another way, I mean this is weird—in fact you cannot even call the EL *abandoned*. Abandoned means that once there were some people and objects and items and creatures and Perils here and *then* they vanished or were spirited away or moved to another level coz they heard the weather was better there or the crime-rate figure was lower. And that's not the case. There NEVER was anything. Just all this space and these like endless landscapes of impossibility. (I think I maybe got that phrase from the GC site. I'm sorry. Hi, girls.)

*

Getting hungry. No stars in the sky tonight—there is way too much cloud.

I need a break, but work is good coz at least when I'm busy writing I don't keep thinking about Dieter and Tory and Brainiac. I hate it when I have all these topics going round in a circle, like I have iTunes on constant random shuffle but the same 3 songs come up too often. Like what the fuck is happening. No word from Tory. I have music on the speakers and beer number 6 is really going down OK—I think I can finally see some light at the end of the bottle.

Venter called my cell WITH THE LATEST (CAPSLOCK fucking stupid random capslock I apologize). I was trying to say that he called with the latest facts (i.e. rumors) concerning Brainiac. Apparently Paul (Brainiac's brother) got a phone message from a friend of his (and Brainiac's) saying that Brainiac was with him (Michael) (the friend), about 900 miles away, but safe anyway. If you are confused about this just think how I'm feeling, bro. Venter is gonna call and check out the story with Paul. Feels like I'm in the center of a machine that can produce any kind of useless and uncertain info in no time at all. We're too jumpy. I told Ashton the "Brainiac story" and I was shocked stupid to find the words "missing person" come out my mouth.

Breakfast cereals and outdated milk at nighttime again. I'm back to that old sad Loner Routine. I took some time out from the walkthrough and wrote a long email to Tory. Hi, Tory. There was some ranting stuff and some apologizing stuff and some questions and some wondering where we've been, where we got to and where we're headed next. I kind of read it thru then deleted it. Now is not the time, I guess—and words just seem to make it all feel worse.

The same 3 songs on shuffle—Dieter, Brainiac, Tory and, man, the Tory song comes up way more than it should do statistically. I think I'll take a break for a while. 0:00:00 is what the clock says as usual. Fuck. The night's done that same old dirty trick that it likes to do and my mind has turned onto Depressing Topics and cannot let go. I spoke to Venter again. He came by at Domenico's and in a quiet moment again I wanted to tell him about Tory and how she moved out but there was nothing I could do, he was already moving on. I apologize, dude. I'm trying to keep it real but it's hard here, living on ice cream, ramen noodles, and takeouts (plus the cereal).

Venter came round a bit drunk to relay that he has spoken to Paul, who said that Brainiac was not with Michael (the friend of B and P) and that in fact he (the friend) had not heard from Brainiac in months. OK, I said, and Venter said Well, I thought, you know, we should pool information, then I said I don't have any information to pool and then I considered again telling him about Tory but decided it's better not to. I don't know how the wires got so crossed with rumors of B. News turns into evaporated news, which is basically no news at all.

I admit it tho, I'm getting too distracted now. Jesus. It's not like a walkthrough anymore—more like a forum for some guy with Attention Deficit Disorder. There are certainly some "customers" that really do NOT like the amount of off-topic stuff I'm writing here. Seems like anytime I check mail there is something new from some abusive bigmouth Doood calling me a FOOL and telling me how my walkthrough cannot navigate a way out of a paper bag or who thinks I'm an asshole and that I will rot in Hell because I didn't give the solution to some obscure Puzzle or Task and/or (descending into all kinds of inevitable/ predictable attacks) trumpeting that my genitals are too small and that's why Tory left etc. Ha ha.

It's not all funny tho. Yes. I'm talking directly to you DrunkenApe, Naplam50, Flamer, Scud99, HomeBrew, Bovine, Jihaad, Big Balls, etc, since you are all obviously the same person with a grudge to grind against me. Don't think you can hide your identity for long or that I don't know what is going on. Dude, why not give it a break and get on with your own life instead of picking mine to pieces with all yr abuse and "wit"? Assuming you actually have one. I'm not gonna say anymore about it, and plz—don't hurry to respond, I won't be reading anymore of your dumbass mails.

I thought beer number 6 was supposed to definitely be a good one— the kind of push on thru to the Other Side. But it doesn't seem to be working that way.

MORE about the E. L.

Another theory that some people like is that the EL was MADE as a sanctuary. I admit that in theory it could be a cool place for Rachel and Ray to meet and hide together, a place for happiness. Imagine them enjoying long walks, sunshine, and the empty ocean like some perfume ad at a multiplex. Walking the deserted freeways and scaling the mountains, which have no hazards, lazing round in empty suburban houses and hilltop mansions. Safe forever. I can see the appeal. GC and Yoko898 even proposed that uniting Ray and Rachel together in the EL could be an ending/solution to the game—not that anyone ever did it, at least as far as I know. More like a fantasy.

Also. AnyTIME PPL TALK ABT the EL on *The BW* boards it leads inevitably to Debates concerning how *long* is it useful for Rachel to be there. Everyone knows you have to pass thru there, that is clear, but everyone has his or her own theory on why and how long it makes sense to stick around. Man. Of all possible rumors in the whole freaking world if you listen long enough in places where the game is discussed you can hear most of them said about the EL—that there are invisible creatures there, that it will give Rachel cancer, that it is based on a 15th-century prophecy, or whatever. I think all that talk just happens coz that place is such a perfect freakin mystery. Wherever there is a question or an emptiness then people start to speculate like who shot Kennedy and did people really land on the moon.

*

More ravings from Branimir who, after Ashton's long phone calls and the out-of-control food fights of recent days, is now obsessed with imposing discipline. Thursday afternoon he called us all for a meeting at the end of the shift. Cue the melodrama music. While we waited Ashton whispered to me and the 2.0 that this was gonna be "hand over the apron forever" or "kiss the cooked circular job goodbye." Ha ha. Not funny. It turned out to be just another early warning/ announcement, i.e. soon it's going to get tough and there will be Rules and Hoops to jump through and Staff Assessment and Promotional Structures. I don't think he means the Hoops thing for real—more like a metaphor?—but in the back of my mind I was picturing that maybe he'd already been to a Sporting Goods supplier and picked up loads of brightly colored discounted hoops.

Apart from these mental diversions I was 1) trying to nod super-attentively when Branimir and Miroslav explained the whole forthcoming Staff Assessment deal and 2) trying not to look down into the precipice that I'm standing on if the CFF employment suddenly disappears.

OK. They are high on enthusiasm and low on the detail right now but what Branimir proposed in his "staff assessment and promotional structures" speech is the Introduction of what he proudly and without irony called a D Star Assessment System—the D stands for Domenico's. D Star will be for all staff (i.e. me, Ashton, Stentson 2.0, plus Larry, Ted, Dione, and that Cookie who does the Early shifts so I never really see her.) It also involves setting up "monthly staff star meetings" and "discussion sessions to develop the potential". Confused? You will be.

*

I have to take a break and watch some TV. The screen on HAL is hurting my eyes. I will be back.

Now I got a direct call from Brainiac's brother—Paul. A crisis brings them all out the woodwork. There was even a "concerned call" yesterday from Brainiac's ex-ex-girlfriend Pixels. Anyway. Paul asked can I tell him anything that might help the family find B? Sounded like he was stressing but clearly I don't know a freaking thing.

Pretty strange atmosphere to talk to Paul at all—cos of the whole thing with him and Tory in the past and then finding the letter she half wrote to him. Maybe she wrote a different letter and did send that one. Maybe she wrote him a 110 times. I don't think so and I don't think he sent that X. And now anyway he calls at the same time as this weird meltdown/moving-out disaster thing between Tory and me. I got the impression he didn't know about that and that he only called from desperation or "for completeness" (whatever that means) in tracing B. Me and Paul don't exactly get on. Probably natural when there are mutual ex-girlfriends involved.

*

Back to Domenico's topic. O my God—like Ashton said afterward—it's like Branimir was talking to someone at McDonald's. Or like he was talking to someone from a smaller and even more depressing franchise that copied their team-building BS from McDonald's. Only Branimir doesn't seem to realize that you cannot run a single seven-employee pizza-delivery place—in a "not-yet-up-and-coming" neighborhood —as if it were a franchise arm of a great and faceless Multinational Empire. I mean, for one nobody at Domenico's will take the stupid D Star System seriously. O spare us. He is organizing the "paper work." I am sooooo not looking forward to it. Since I haven't even spoken to Tory since she left, I don't know what the deal is with her and the rent. This month is paid but shit will hit the fan and blow all over the apartment and out the door and down the street (taking me with it) if we're not sorted out before next month, because I cannot pay it on my own on the shifts I'm currently working, even counting Rolo's share.

Another FAQ. I finally told CW and Venter about Tory moving out which I guess means everyone will know pretty soon. It's OK. I don't want a situation where everyone I meet I have to tell the whole fucking story to, because that makes it worse, as if every time I tell it it kind of happens all over again. With Venter and CW I worried they might think I was hiding something by not telling them before now. Sometimes they check in on this walkthrough, so I guess they could have read it here. Anyway. Doesn't matter. They both know everything now. It's good not to have secrets.

*

About the EL again. My advice is that you take time for Rachel to be alone, get rest, and set her mind straight after all the killing and madness of the Blood Corridor. Try to wander, explore. Just remember nothing there can hurt you. In case you cannot face the idea of travel without a detailed itinerary (Tory's dad Joe says: "We get so nervous that we'll miss the important stuff") I present you HERE an official guide of 3 things you must see in the EL if you only have a short visit.

1. Airport. Definitely unmissable. A huge international airport i.e. think LAX only here there are no passengers and no crowds of people showing up to welcome or wave goodbye, also no cleaners, flight crews, security guys, baggage handlers, etc—you get the idea, i.e. no people at all. I guess I don't have to name all of the different people that are not there—I can fill the whole Internet that way. It's empty. As you wander you feel like the last security guard—the last one with the keys whose job it is to lock up at the end of some longass shift. Strange. Only as I'm writing this do I get that *that* is a feeling you have quite a lot in the EL. That you are the last one on the planet. Ready to shut things down. Kind of freaky. Like they say—the last one out plz remember to switch off the lights.

2. The Funfair. OK. It's a bit like Elvis (or Jacko) or something to be wandering abt an empty funfair. But it is without a doubt cool. One time me and Tory went to a funfair (in the real world, not in *BW*. Obviously) and did this cheesy Tunnel of Love maybe three or four times.

I just got up and walked into the other room to check in with Tory but of course she's not there. I still sometimes think about her like everything is totally OK and that she's there in the next room on the couch reading or whatever and then it all comes back in a flash that she's not in the next room lain on the couch reading or whatever at all. I'm wondering if I should really call her in this case or am I like trying to tough it out and say the Ball is in her court and she should call me. It's tempting to call or write but I think she should make the next move.

3. The Desert. I know we have deserts all of our own on the actual Earth and what is so special about one in *The Broken World* where all the grains of sand are made out of pixels? I guess I'd say you just have to go there. I mean—the EL is one kind of emptiness and then in the middle of that they put another different emptiness that is the desert. It's a good place to think and feel small. Just take a look at the dunes forming and unforming (?)—I love it how the wind blows the sand (just an algorithm according to Clockwork but it's still beautiful). Don't stay there too long. It can totally make you feel small.

*

Pretty much the last thing Paul asked in the phone call was "Can I talk to Tory?" Apparently he might come to see if he can find Brainiac (what is he, a detective now?) and he would like to catch up with T when/if he's here in town. The question kind of freaked me and when I answered I started to think he could see down the phone and tell that I was hiding something. Just feeling paranoid about it all I guess like in the Skeleton song "Mission to Remember," where he says that people that he meets are plotting against him. I mean, I didn't lie but I was definitely giving an ambiguous reply when I said that Tory was out (true) and that I wasn't sure when she was gonna come back (also true). The whole conversation felt less than good tho. What I don't want right now is Paul in town and hooking up with Tory to relive the freakin good old days.

(In fact the VERY last thing that Paul said in the phone call was that he was gonna call the COPS about Brainiac. What is his problem, overreacting again? He was always like that. Doesn't make sense.)

*

When you have done with the sightseeing it's finally time to quit the EL.
You need to get Rachel back to someplace (anyplace) where there are
people to fight and tasks and missions and enemies. Strange to think it,
but even enemies can be missed. It may be sad to take Rachel back to
the fighting but remember no holiday can last forever, at least unless
you are Linda. She's made a good job of it since leaving home, getting
married and divorced a few times, and going generally AWOL. Her latest
postcard arrived yesterday from Hawaii or somewhere else all sunshine
and bad taste—a place where she is, according to the all-caps, STILL
HAVING A BALL WITH DENTIST MIKE who has apparently OFFERED TO
FIX HER CROWNS. I guess we can just thank some great benign force
field of the Universe that she didn't bump into/hook up with a plastic
surgeon. I put the card on a pile of Tory's accumulating mail. That's how
it goes.

There are quite a few exits from the EL different players have
discovered, but the only one I ever use is right at the coast—a small
beach town at about 20 17 S, 57 33 E if you can figure THAT out using
GPS. The exit itself is located underwater, maybe one mile out from the
shore. Leave your clothes on the beach—yes, this is one time where
you CAN get Rachel naked, but by this point I guess they figure no one
is gonna be stupid enough to think about it like that anymore. I mean, it
may seem strange but by now being Rachel feels just like it does being
Ray—it is your body, it is you, you are not gonna be staring at yourself
in that way (unless you have some Vanity problems). You *are* her, bro,
and there is no way you'd be looking at yourself the same way as some
hot chick you saw wearing waaaaay too little one afternoon on a platform
of the subway or at a crossing in midtown or behind the counter taking

drinks orders at BamZak. Suddenly I'm thinking too much about girls. Sorry. Maybe I'm starting to get serious about what it might be like to be single again, now that T has apparently gone.

Swim out near mid-afternoon when the tide is just turning. Head toward the 2 distant islands and the tide will work with you. When you've gone about a mile just hold your breath and dive. Go down past galleon wreck and kind of corny waving seaweed—into coral cave with doorway at the end. ("Airlock to the future" as GC said). Say goodbye to all the great serenity, scariness, mystery, and emptiness that is the EL. I guess no one can ever know for sure what it's all about. If you have some ideas please mail me.

WEATHER, TRANspoRT
AND Tears

Ashton hit a nail on the head when he said work today was pure boredom in cooked circular form. Ha ha.

The only thing of interest was that Clockwork came round briefly. Then he pissed me off by dropping into the conversation that he saw Tory last night, apparently with Chelsea Person in a bar. They were at No Slime. Clockwork was just leaving and didn't speak to Tory, but he said they exchanged a look and kind of nodded. At least that's what he told me, but at that point I pretty much bailed out from the conversation. It was too weird to hear about her when we still haven't really communicated. I mean, I wrote an email for her again two nights ago and then deleted it again without sending (again) but that doesn't count as communication—I think she has to be the one that makes the first real move, since she was the one that moved out.

When CW told me he saw her I changed the subject matter and then a few minutes later when he asked me how I was feeling about it all, I guess he was expecting me to totally blow up about it, I pretended that I didn't really hear him and said I had to go to the bathroom and when I came back I made like I immediately had to go get some bases for the circular food (from the Deep Freeze in the storeroom). I mean, it's OK for me to talk about it, sure—I don't have a problem—but I know that other people don't really want to talk about this kind of stuff. I was just making it easy for him.

*

When Rachel comes out of the EL to discover the next level the sky she finds herself under is so thick with snow and dark already. Everywhere you look there are men blundering about wearing parkas and yelling a lot. Welcome to the Antarctic Research Station. Trust me tho, even here, despite the fact that you're like several thousand miles in the wrong direction, you are also one big step closer to the Far Lands and the purpose of yr Mission. Sounds like a contradiction? Don't worry—all will become clear. Guys run this way and that, some of them apparently taking orders over their radios. One thing is for sure—you don't want these agents of Chang or GovCorp to catch you, so please, RUN & HIDE as quick as you can. Use stealth and GET OUT OF THEIR IMMEDIATE VICINITIES.

NOTE: I don't think you need me to explain that the right clothes for diving off a beach on a semitropical island (i.e. full-frontal nudity) are not the same clothes that are good for facing snowfall in subzero blizzard conditions. Yes—it's a really good idea to find clothes and get dressed at this point. Bro, you can watch yr temperature levels and health go dropping way down and very fast if you don't take care of business right away.

All around in the blizzards are dogs barking, guns shooting, and the men I mentioned yelling into the walkie-talkies they all seem to have, using several languages that you cannot understand.

Duibbyoahah, they say (or something like that, I'm not a Lingusitc Expert). *Esana a ikothra, duibbyoahah?*

Does anyone know what they are talking about?

This part always makes me think about all the different languages in *The BW*. I mean, stuff that people say to Ray or Rachel that you don't understand but also like stuff that you just hear in the background; things shouted by dudes on street corners or words that get yelled between combatants in a terrible firefight or things that some guys are yelling at Rachel from passing vehicles etc. I guess I don't know if half these things are even real words.

Also in one part—Rainforest Bonus—Rachel has to learn a whole new language so that she can escape from some far-off jungle village where she gets stranded following on from the part when she gets pushed out of a light aircraft by representatives of Zorda who have apparently made their way to Earth. Cool.

Some words she learns there I can still remember quite an achievement, since I can only remember 3 words of German that Dieter taught me. Here is the evidence:

German Words:

Kaput	Broken
Ja	Yes
Dumbkopf	Stupid

Words from the Jungle in *The Broken World*:

Swanitti	Thank you
Forgusia	Tomorrow
Gochin navada	I am sorry
Gytada	Moon
Eussu	Possible
Eussuna	Impossible
Winsu	Rive
Borjuh	Perimeter
Dioscz	Flowers
Fihjajoh	Sniper
Firouidus-eb-yuhuicio	Particle accelerator
Yasana ichtoya	Please come back

Those words all work in the game but I still don't know if they're real.

*

Once you get clothes head thru the research station (or whatever it is exactly) and find the GREEN HUT. When it comes to the door either use the lockpick from Items or the baseball bat in non-standard mode—that will also do the job. Go to work, bro, as Venter says, go to work. Get the door open.

Inside the hut you find there is no light except the pulsing glow of a complicated-looking piece of portable super-hi-tech-looking equipment that has got a harness, wires, dials, and plenty of flashing lights. Congratulations! Your travel mode just got a serious upgrade to Executive Class and the Far Lands are not so far anymore. It's a teleporter.

*

I wrote a one-line email to Tory saying *Gochin navada. Yasana ichtoya.* But then I deleted it. I don't know if now is a good time to be making contact by references to obscure parts of the game, esp as she doesn't care about it that much. I don't know if she really wants me to be talking to her. Maybe it's better that there is some silence. I mean, people talk too much a lot of the time—she said that to me once. Or maybe I should have written something more poetic. I could have sent her a message like *Uresa na edan richio,* which means *Outside the snow still falls.* But I didn't send her any message, nothing at all. Among the papers I went thru nites ago was a photo I gave her once, way back, with a message written on it, the ink stained into the picture. The photo was her in front of a parking lot. It didn't have a special significance except I guess that she liked the picture which didn't happen often. If I showed her pictures she would always say why do you take such nasty pictures when they are of me? Can you plz take a picture where I don't look tired? Or that she looked overweight in some pictures, or why was I taking a picture when she was just wearing the kind of clothes that are used for bumming around the house? Why did I not take pictures when she was wearing something nice for once? I don't know.

Man, I love these places like the Arctic Base where the weather is totally identical day or night, and all year round—something you can always rely on even when the rest of the world is full of freaky change. Example: check the way there is always dense fog in the Border Towns, or check those gloomy towns where it rains all the time or those places where sunlight is always coming thru the trees in long shafts like late afternoon etc. I wrote already how it's always snowing on the edge of First Town, and how the snow there can slowly cover your footsteps and how Tory so loved it. Fuck. Now I'm writing about her like in the past tense. This is stupid. I will mail her later, or maybe try and retrieve/salvage some bits of the mails that I already wrote her and then trashed.

There are even some places in the game—more than enough of them, at least according to me—where it is ALWAYS night. Night is not strictly considered weather but you see why I mention it now. Hear me, bro: Do not hang around in 89th Town waiting for morning to bring safety coz it will NEVER come. I mean, it's surprising that the residents are brave enough to stay there so long. Maybe they don't know that it's different anywhere else on the planet or they just got used to it somehow and think that going for a walk with a flashlight and a set of spare batteries is normal. I couldn't live in darkness like that—there would be no edges between things (?), no passing of time and anyway the dark makes it so easy for the Monsters that prey on that town. Ughh. I'm getting shivers. I think it's important how the alternations of day and night make a shape out of time—it would just be too confusing if they weren't there.

*

After work I met Venter in a bar near Union Hall and we walked over to Brainiac's place, with no real agenda but to finally check things out. There was no sign of the skater/band kids Venter already talked to and no sign of the nice college girls (probably too stoned or just too busy performing on their webcams) and in the downstairs apartment the shutters were closed. I'm not sure if the shutters are to keep people OUT or if it's to keep the dogs IN but either way is fine with me. From inside came sound of that defective kid's music—I guess he also has some defect in the musical-taste department, coz he was playing Sine

Invaders "Maelstrom" at full volume, repeatedly, like two chords were trapped inside the apartment and just wanted to beat themselves to death against the walls.

I went past the noise, up the stairs, and knocked on Brainiac's door, but that approach was never gonna work. No answer. No surprise. When I came back down to street level Venter laughed at me and bombarded me with a small amount of gravel that he'd been saving to do just that. Then we went around to the back of the building where Venter kicked off from the trash that's piled up there and made a huge fucking jump for the bottom of the fire-escape ladder where it's tucked up and then he pulled himself up with the strength of his arms while I waited around and looked at the floor and tried not to seem like I was part of some tag-team breaking-and-entering outfit. When Venter opened up the door to the apt for me a minute or two later his stomach and his DON'T ASK ME I JUST GOT HERE T-shirt was kind of stained in blood from where he had scraped it on the metal ladders with the rust and everything but he was looking OK about it. I mean, as I said before Venter actually likes the Action lifestyle.

And for the rest, not much to report. B's apartment is deserted. Yes, OK, it still looks like it did when I was round there last time—i.e. like an experimental bomb was exploded just above it or like it is rented as a test station for growing strange biological cultures in human spaces. We are talking about mess, clutter, and disorganized chaos on a scale not ever seen before in the whole history of untidy apartments. It stinks too. But no big clues to be sniffed out, i.e. Brainiac was not rotting in the bathtub (not a good place to lie down, bro, I don't recommend it) and he wasn't swinging from a belt or bed linen or an electrical flex or anything like that and there were no notes about sudden unexpected trips to Mexico or bad debts or alien abductions or notes abt trips to meet

Intriguing strangers that he met online or any mysterious unfinished letters about last-minute and hasty decisions to go jump from some very tall structure in the city. Nothing. Nothing much. Nothing useful. Just an untidy empty apartment.

Dude. For my tastes it was just a little bit too much like the visit we already made recently to Dieter's place. Only looking in Dieter's room—with the stacks of music CDs that will be coming soon to a garage sale nearby and his workout clothes still on the radiators—you knew for a fact already that this was a kind of closed case—a story that was not going anywhere anymore. But in Brainiac's apartment you really cannot tell one way or another—I mean, maybe it's the end of a story and maybe it's the start of one. After a time I sat on the sofa hardly moving, partly freaked and partly just so fucking tired. Even Venter seemed faded and for a while we existed in a kind of Temporary Underwater Silence. Later I switched on B's computer and skimmed thru the emails—nothing that could surprise me and nothing that might "explain" his absence. While I was clicking down the inbox Venter went thru the whole apartment again, opening cabinets and doors, flipping thru papers where they lay on the floor. It wasn't *Forensic Detectives of Woodstock* (or even Altamont) but what the fuck—there was nothing there of any use at all.

I could get frightened of empty spaces. I don't know if there's a special word for that, like some people are frightened of small spaces, and some people are frightened of crowds—there are words for that. But what's the word for people that are frightened of emptiness? Like this apartment minus Tory and the key Items of her life. Or Brainiac's place. Or Dieter's room. Just wreckage left behind, and traces and that Emptiness. Motherfucker. I am getting to sound like Tory's parents calling in with their crazed questions from the suburbs. Maybe next time

Joe calls I can ask him something in return. Hey, yeah, Joe, I will help you with that question concerning your Magnetic Travel Chess Kit and how come it's not so Magnetic anymore, but maybe first you can tell me what the word is to describe people who are frightened of emptiness? Can you help me with that? Joe, can you hear me? No answer? And oh yeah, yeah, by the way Tory packed a bag and walked out on me for no real reason at all. I think that would go down pretty well.

*

The short version about the teleporter is that it has lots of buttons and you need to press some of them FAST. It's not technical genius what I'm suggesting here, but it's better than a rifle butt in the face followed by a lifetime of interrogations in an underground NESTADO prison at Mercy of Dindara which is what awaits you if you don't get out of the Arctic Research Station on the next available teleporter. NOTE: That sound you can hear from outside is the sound of agents getting closer by the second, so plz DO NOT stand around wondering how these guys figured out that Rachel would show up in the Arctic. Hook yrself up to the harness/backpack (?) then hit the red button, followed by the green button simultaneous with the mauve button. I think that's the color. At least it kind of looks like the same color as some pants that Tory once had and I think she said the color was mauve. The dogs will be barking outside by now so plz plz (like I said before) press the buttons.

The teleporter is way cool even if by Clockwork's analysis the science is "kind of dubious." Teleporting into a new place is just like the experience of being blindfolded in a car, driven to a new location, pushed out in a strange street at random, and only THEN being allowed to take off your blindfold. Yes. Cool cool cool. I mean, light will spin out of the machinery in all directions as you fly thru nothingness to some other place maybe hundreds or even thousands of miles away. Q: What can be dubious about that? A: Nothing.

Q2: Where are you headed now? A2: You are getting the fuck out of there.

GET THE FUCK OUT OF THERE. I can still hear Dieter saying that, about Minnesota, and I still laugh when I think about his scary voice that he used in the prank phone calls he made last summer. I guess in some ways any place is better than a small town that you grew up in, except maybe a blizzard full of dog-handling NESTADO Operatives in white camo gear.

*

It's way late night, and just for the record I did some things I said I wouldn't do.

First—I called Tory. I called her cell, late (i.e. not that long ago), and then before she even answered or had time to not answer I quickly hung up. I know that's a bad thing to do and irresponsible, esp since she can very easy look to find out who it was and see my number in her recently missed calls. I don't know what I was thinking.

Second—I looked at the badmouthing emails from DrunkenApe/ HomeBrew/Scud Something etc (or whatever), which are still arriving every day and going straight in a folder called Junk. Even tho I only opened the folder and not any mails, it was not so smart coz then I could see very well how he's writing three, four, or even nine times a day, and that the names he's using get stranger all the time and the subject lines get more and more crazy and aggressive.

From: Marvel F. Killer Rifle
Subject: YOU ARE GONNA GET IT

From: DrunkenApe
Subject: Bro, how come your description of 40th Town leaves out the Helicopters?

From: halimat fahd
Subject: No solution to the Gridlock Puzzle? Ha Ha

From: Even Bigger Balls
Subject: No Good is No Good is No Good

Etc etc etc.

In some ways it's worse now that I didn't read the recent freaking mails, because I'm just sat here imagining all the crap he's written, and that takes up so much more room in my head.

The TEar MaP

When you come spinning out of darkness you can end up in some pretty neat and freaky locations but PLZ stay on Mission—you need to consult the teleporter manual, it's like 300 pages long and not exactly a beach read unless your name is Clockwork ha ha but you *do* kind of need it to navigate.

*

With help from the manual you need to locate teleporter batteries/power packs that have been hidden all over *The Broken World*. TEN of these packs together give enough energy to reach the Far Lands where you're heading with the one-word message from Dying Irene that she wants you to take to the resistance in hiding. Remember? You have to pay attention. It's a pain in the ass with the power packs, I know—it should all be batteries included but instead they like to make life hard.

HINT: Don't panic. Don't get stressed. To find batteries use the blank pages in Rachel's diary from Items. HINT: Cry on a blank page and a clue (Map) will appear on the paper—brought out by the tears. NOTE: Use the Think menu. It doesn't really seem to matter what you cry about. Make Rachel think about Ray. Or about all that stuff back in 13th Town. Or about what happened to K-Mart or about whatever. Doesn't matter. You just have to cry. Venter sent an IM to say that you can even chop an onion like they do in movies to make the actors cry. (NOTE: I don't think there are any onions, bro—apologies to Venter—I checked and I didn't see any in the long appendix of poss items for the game. Strange to think about it like that—it's a whole world without onions. Don't waste time searching for them or wondering what this means. It's just a detail. Make Rachel cry another way.) Each tear that falls brings out more of the Map containing the locations of the power packs. There are ten locations (ten power packs), and you have to visit them in sequence.

*

When Tory was here she always had issues with the crying, like asking how come it's Rachel who gets these girl things to do—like look after a blind kid (K-Mart) or rescue a baby pigeon from the rain after it has fallen from its nest under a railroad bridge etc. Also, why is it that Rachel has to *cry* to get the maps she really needs? Can't she get what she wants any other way? What the fuck? "Women are not just a bunch of cooks, hookers, hormonal cripples, and emotional hysterics" is what Tory said and even now after all that has happened I'm not going to argue with that. Hi, Tory, I guess you're not reading this, but Hi in any case. For me her thing about how come Rachel gets all the so-called girl stuff is (was?) kind of unfair anyway—I mean, is it a definition of "girl stuff" to be fist-crunching evil monsters like Gen Die Die into the crusher and then mashing them to death like that? I don't think so.

*

One other thing—I don't want to see another cooked circular food item for at least 12 hours (or longer if possible). I have been working Hard Labor levels at yr friendly neighborhood Domenico's with a consecutive sequence of three days morning, afternoon, and evening shifts. Yes I'm beat and I stink and I'm trying to make Dollars and I'm sick of it and I'm trying to act like a hardworking essential Cog in the Wheel but I don't know if I can hack it anymore. Trying to get a good atmosphere going with Larry and Dione and that Cookie on the day shift is impossible (Larry watches *Rat Run*—I cannot get down to that level) PLUS it doesn't get any easier when you also have to deal with the Brothers and their constant gloating about so-called Improvements to the D Star System.

When Miroslav shows up he makes a big show of watching everything tightly these days—like today he was looking (i.e. staring) at how people are using the register and how they're using the oven and how they're using the fucking circular fucking slicer (used to cut the circular food). The real highlight tho came yesterday when Branimir was bragging to some customer guy (Al, I think he's called) and talking all about D Star but somehow getting confused and calling it Staff Reprisals System, which to me sounds more interesting. I was laughing so much, but trying not to let it show. I don't think my co-worker (hi, Larry) even noticed the word meant anything different. Staff reprisals. Ha ha ha. It gets my vote anytime. Ashton, just say the word and I'm behind you.

Also. Does Rolo still live here in this apartment? I think maybe he does because I see that his crap moves slowly around from location to location over the days and nights when I get back. Like one day his boots are by the door and the next they are just in front of the couch, facing the TV. Or like one morning his jacket is thrown on the kitchen table and that night it is on the floor by the bathtub. Or the bag where he keeps his grass and rolling papers is slowly moving around from one armchair to the other like time-lapse over the days. I never see him though.

I don't know why I'm suddenly writing so much about all this—I apologize. Tory says (or used to say? I'm not sure what tense to put her in) I have a kind of problem with DETAIL. Like I cannot figure out which details really matter and which it's better to ignore.

*

Get the power packs and don't delay. The big clock is still ticking. Please don't ask me again why they're all distributed in random crazy locations like crowded train stations, major sporting events, shopping malls, lap-dancing clubs, national monuments, aquariums or zoos, as well as abattoirs, firing ranges, nuclear research facilities, golf courses and Inca temples, etc etc. You get the idea. I guess that the henchmen of the Archduke must have hidden them in places like that so that no one would ever gain enough teleporter energy to get to the Far Lands? Or maybe Dindara himself (some big shot in GARS) flew above The Broken World in an airplane and scattered them down at random, just to be a SmartAss? I don't know. And don't ask me why there always seem to be operatives or GovCorp cops in the neighborhood when Rachel turns up to collect the prize. That is how it goes sometimes then fighting cannot be avoided.

*

One place you can go with the teleporter is Switzerland. It's very clean there and they make the mountains tall and beautiful. Sometimes I think I would like to go there. Not in the game, but in real life. It would be good to escape from what they call reality here.

*

While I was at Domenico's I got a call from Tory. When the phone rang I checked it before answering and there was her name on the screen— just like it always used to be except it hasn't been there for so long. I was staring at her name, paralyzed and then on instinct I nearly picked up. Then it kinda went thru my mind that I was in Domenico's and Branimir was there at the ovens and Ashton there at the register and no I don't really want to be having a private emotional conversation with these two listening in, no matter how much the radio might cover it up.

So I flipped her into voicemail. There was a text shortly after from the Messages thing (or whatever. I don't know what to call it), but I didn't call to play it back. I just kept looking at the phone from time to time, busy all afternoon, thinking what Tory might have said there and what the fuck was going on.

*

Note to Halogen and some other players that seem to get confused: Like I said already if u bothered to read properly, the new energy packs for the teleporter must also be collected IN SEQUENCE (i.e. 1, 2, 3, 4, 5, 6, 7, 8—do I need to continue with the remaining numbers or can you figure that out?). If you go to the second destination without going to the first one first then the right things will not be there. Simple as that. OK? It works the same with ALL locations/destinations on the Map—only by visiting one place do you unlock items in the next.

One thing leads to another, to another to another. So much of *The Broken World* works in that way—where one thing must get done first just so the next can even exist. *Everything is all the time connected. Get Well Soon* and *HEltker Skelter Soon Come Soon.* That is some graffiti you see in different parts of *The Broken World.*

It's like each action you make is actually unlocking the future but it's not just items, dude. It's people too. No one will meet you at the Helipad in 122nd Town if you didn't make a drop-off in the Desert. Claudio will not come with the diamonds in the suitcase if you didn't speak to Greg Nolan in the Park and collect the butterflies (?) from him the weekend before. Jose will not be born if you don't assassinate Siso, cut his head off, and bury it under the bridge (in the missing part, where I lost the file. Apologies.).

And places also work the same way. No 19th Town without 18th. No Saloon without the Hotel Lobby. In the House on Wounded Hill it's even the rooms of the house that only come into EXISTENCE when you find clues elsewhere in the town. So locate the toy/doll and then go back to find the nursery appeared.

The whole freaking *Broken World* is full of Items that are only there if the right people have been spoken to, or locations that only come to life if certain places have been visited or objects collected. And plz be warned—the past and the future are connected in ways that are not always totally obvious. If Rachel doesn't answer the phone that rings in a dark empty street (19th Town) then 3,000 miles down the road there will be no consignment waiting for her in the Stardust Motel.

It pretty well makes sense to me. I would never have met Venter in the first place if we didn't both like Skeleton coz Venter had some lyrics from them written on his skateboard when I first saw him when a bunch of people were hanging out on the steps in the park and I said "Skeleton, huh?" and Venter said back something like "Uh-huh" and that was the first conversation we had and how I first got friendly with V and therefore later with Brainiac and so on and even how I met Tory, in a convoluted kind of way (for all the trouble that has brought). And then I start wondering how I'd even heard of Skeleton at that point (this was all like waay before they were as popular as now), i.e. whatever got me into them in the first place kind of unlocked the friendship with Venter—like you can trace it back and then keep tracing it back to fuck knows where. One thing causes another, then another, and also another, following a strange trail.

*

I know. I was gonna write about the final teleport and what you need to expect but I lost track. Please forgive these distractions.

*

Right after work was over I sat outside on the curb at Domenico's and played Tory's message. I heard her voice in a strange way, kind of familiar and totally like a stranger's, like a wrong-number voice. I cannot describe it but it was also a shock how much I recognized the details of that stranger voice. Her way of stressing words. Her punctuating. Shit. When the message was done I played it again to make sure I didn't miss something, some clue. She was just saying hi, very low-key, and then kind of suggesting we meet—I don't know why. From the 37 words she said I couldn't figure out a reason. To be nice? To say something? To give back the keys to the apartment? It wasn't clear.

Later T's parents also called. Strange, coz I'm not really sure if they know Tory moved out. I mean—I guess she told them, but then I'm not sure she did and I don't feel like it's my job to keep them informed. So when we spoke I kind of hedged around it whenever she was mentioned, keeping things vague like I did before with Paul, not saying much except fine fine, things are fine. Stupid I know and afterward I felt like a dumb conspirator. Anyway T's parents had a big brainteaser Question for me about their driveway and the gravel on it. This was for sure one of the best yet, so here goes: Do I think that it's possible that someone is stealing gravel from their driveway? Somehow even Joe sounded skeptical as he asked me this, like he couldn't believe he just said it, or he starts to think that the fabric of reality out there in the Burbs is somehow bending underneath him. Do I think that's possible? That someone would be stealing that kind of thing in small-but-increasingly-noticeable amounts? Joe has been thinking, lately, it seems, that there is less and less gravel on the drive than there used to be—"markedly less" is what he actually said—and he wondered if someone might be stealing it.

Bro, I can tell you. There are some questions in the world that even I cannot find a way to answer.

THE Far LANDS

The final teleporter takes you to the ultimate coordinates—the Far Lands which at first seems kind of deserted except for strange bat-creatures that fly by day and attack on impulse.

You find yrself in a barren landscape. Like desert but with no heat. Just that nothing grows. Miles and miles of dead stone. No water. In some ways it's a bit like the window box that Tory and I tried to keep up last summer—a kind of eco-disaster zone. I'm certainly not claiming to be a talented gardener.

NOTE: You can leave the teleporter where you landed—with the batteries all spent it's just one more piece of soon-to-be-rusted techno-junk in *The Broken World*. You will see the "desert" (not really a desert) is divided in areas—red stone, yellow stone, black stone, brown stone (each area more difficult than the last)—and there's a series of rough pathways and tracks. Head North.

Thru the desert you must locate the rock circles (?)—"Stone Age" structures that are carved with things like pictograms (or bits of ancient computer code?). Make a note of these markings because YOU—fucking capslock—you will possibly need them later.

*

Not at work for the first time in 100 million years, this morning my only ambition was a long lie-in but oh—no freaking chance. Maybe 8am instead there was an endless buzzing on the door buzzer that I ignored for ages but it just wouldn't go away. So I got out of bed, not really awake enough, went to the buzzer and buzzed to say OK, OK, who the fuck and this voice says it's the COPS on the intercom, can they come in. And I was like OK.

I guess I was thinking maybe it could be something to do with Tory, or with her dad maybe, and my heart pounded in my chest and I pulled on some things to look presentable (i.e. CLOTHES) and opened the door. There were two cops, a man and woman in uniform, the guy out of breath from the stairs. Only they didn't say sit down we have something to tell you or any BS like that so I was relieved. Instead the woman cop asked was it OK for THEM to SIT DOWN and it was like she was talking to a retard or something. I just said fine, the guy certainly looked like he needed it. That's OK. SO we all sat down and it seemed more awkward than it needed to be until the guy cop finally said they wanted me to help them by answering some questions about Brainiac and I said did something happen? And he said no and she said that since he's missing officially now they have to try and build up a PICTURE of what his MOVEMENTS might have been, again like I was a retard who hadn't seen any cop shows so I didn't know how things get done or what they might be there for.

All while they were talking I was heading in a wrong direction thinking about Brainiac's movements—like the way he would rub at his forehead with the flat of his fingers, or the way he would shift weight from one foot to another and then bend slightly at his knees if he was stressed or preoccupied and even tho I knew this wasn't the kind of movements they were talking about at all I couldn't help but kind of play them in my mind like little videoclips. But despite all that, or like at the same time as it, I was still answering the questions they needed me to answer and filling them in on when I last saw Brainiac and his POSSIBLE STATE OF MIND, as the lady cop spelled it out for me like I was stoned or in a coma and they were talking down to me at the bottom of a well.

Only afterward, when they were done and gone and I was drinking coffee, did I get a feeling that didn't go away. Like what if something has happened with B? It's so inadequate thse cops wandering in so long after the event, like underwater divers, so slow. Like if he was some rich guy or a celebrity they would have found him by now. Maybe this time I won't be able to talk together with him afterward and laugh with him about how down and dark and very weird he got and how he "really scared us this time." This time it might not be that kind of story. There's no rule or law that says it's going turn out bad but there's no rule or law that says it's gonna be OK either. Just knowing that it's all up for grabs is a shock sometimes.

*

Oh yeah.

There was just A MOMent as the cops were leaving when I thought abt telling them the whole story with DrunkenApe and all those abusive mails which are definitely harassment but then before I really had a chance they were out the door and somehow I thought better of it. Bro, it's sad but maybe I really have seen just too too many cop shows or movies and I have played *Precinct 191* and also *Rogue Rookie* too much so I know how it goes down when a member of the public tells the cops that some random stranger is sending weird disturbing and repeated emails to them and the cops will say "Sir, Did he do physical harm to your person or your property or family pets?" and the person says "No" and the cops say "OK. We're busy catching the real criminals—the ones that actually do things." Or "Sorry, madam. You have to let us know when there's something more concrete to go on." That's the problem, I guess—I knew it when they walked out and down the stairs and their walkie-talkies were crackling with that sound they make—I've seen too many cops shows, played too many cop games to take it seriously.

*

At the edge of Brown Stone area—after the Valley of Death Puzzle and Laserquest—the landscape changes and you come to the edge of a large lake where there's always lots of mist. Not many people around, just some stupid farmers that don't seem to know anything about stuff that's going on in the rest of the game. Find the boat that's tied up on a small jetty (east edge of lake), answer riddles from boatman and then set sail into that lake. The boatman is dead (I think) but still keeps on hanging around there by the water with his miserable boat, waiting for stray travelers like you, seems kind of forlorn. I always thought that death was meant to be the way out—you know like the end of all that hard labor.

Fuck. Maybe there's more beyond the grave after all—more work, more of the D Star System, more Branimir, more Miroslav. Ughhh.

Sail thru the mists. N by NW. They do it real creepy and it's hard not to be scared but don't be scared coz Rachel can tell it just the same as Ray. The last time BugMap's uncle had cancer he was convinced from day one that he was gonna die. (I'm sorry for the downer attitude here— I think you know where it comes from.) There were guys in his ward that had it much worse than him but they survived and they carried BM's uncle out of there in a box. It's a question of mental attitude.

After all the high speed of the teleporting and fighting and stuff it's cool to go slower on the boat, solving clues and navigating yr way thru the mist. As you get closer to the islands the boat will talk to you in a kind of spooky whisper. Mostly it's grumbling and muttering to itself about how cold the water is and passing comment on the freaky creatures and skull faces that are passing by below and scraping along its hull. Uggggghhh again.

*

Since this morning I've been thinking more about those rooms I mentioned in House on Wounded Hill—the rooms that only appear after you've found certain objects by exploring the town. And I started to wonder where those rooms are when they're not there in the house. Or like where is 29th Town if you arrive there at its location without first being told about it by a certain Traveler in a Bar? OK—I know it's not where it should be, not where it will be later. But where is it then? Where are things when they are not used/needed in the game? In some ways you could think that it's like the same kind of Question such as where is Tory now? I can't imagine, even tho she didn't vanish in the same way as Brainiac. I mean—where is she now she's not in my life? From the message she left it was hard to tell where she was when she called—there wasn't like any significant or noticeable background noise. She might be in the lobby of some temp gig I didn't hear about, or over at Chelsea Person's place. I don't even know what part of town she's in etc.

I guess it's probably the kind of Question that only Clockwork can answer for me (related to the game—he doesn't know any more than I do concerning the whereabouts etc of Tory). Hi, Clockwork. But the more I think about it the more I imagine a storehouse somewhere—outside the game—a place in which things that aren't needed are kept until they are needed. Store of possibilities. And the more I think about it the more I wonder what that place is like. I mean, it must be a storeroom, or something like that, but it would have to contain an insane mixture of stuff in lots of different sizes—from a microscopic blood sample that is sometimes in the GARS Labs, to the whole of several towns that are appearing and disappearing at various points there in the game. It must be a strange place that storeroom, and very big to accommodate all that stuff. I apologize again. I'm getting distracted.

*

Solve Puzzle of the Lake. Hint: Use Potions, don't use Charm.

*

Miroslav and Branimir are driving everyone INSANE with the stupid duties they are inventing for everyone. Seems like any moment we're not directly busy with the preparation and heating of cooked circular food items we have to fill out various bits of paperwork or have what Miroslav calls microtraining sessions, or else we're checking boxes to say that "the facilities" have been cleaned and inspected and later (just before the shift ends) getting a ten-question Quiz involving facts from the manual on the ovens or the ventilation systems or whatever, which is a "KEY" part of the so-called D Star System. Like I said to Ashton—the bottom line is I don't care what voltage the oven is working at, or how to reflow the ducts for Optimum fan assistance—I know how to turn it on and that's what counts. If the oven needs more attention than that they can get some guy like Goran or "Micky" down there to fix it.

*

After work I came back home via the groceries store and tried to stock up on food Items, ate Noodles in a kind of Sauce. I was still eating when Venter, BugMap, and Sleeptalk came round and we had a kind of mini-conference about Brainiac. As an event it was confusing. BugMap was in a weird mood, like his brain was busy with something else. Venter talked and talked but still found time to help himself to half my noodles. As expected it seems like the cops were called in, by Paul, tho mainly after requests from other family members. I cannot blame them for taking action, however useless it seems.

It was already pretty late when the slightly stoned crew left (thanks, Rolo—I will replace the grass or pay back somehow). Afterward I spaced out on the sofa and later played T's voicemail message from yesterday again, like it was an artifact of another world and life. Her voice so familiar it makes me smile as soon as I hear it, but then I remember she's a stranger now. I'm still wondering what's going on. Maybe that will never change and I will never understand what happened—it's not like she's legally obliged to explain anything at all. But now that I'm writing this I realize (?) that by flipping her into voicemail I have put the pressure back on me—it's my move. She made a step and left that message. Now I have to do something. I cannot just wait and watch it all. I have to do something, make the move.

*

Solve Ghost Ship (Puzzle). Hint: Use Rifle.

*

I think my favorite training was Thursday when Miroslav and Branimir staged a fire with pizza cartons out back and then supposedly demonstrated several safe ways to put it out. Man, it was hilarious. Miroslav was sitting on his fat ass as usual squirting out jets of lighter fluid and flicking matches at the pile of boxes his sappy brother had constructed (getting increasingly breathless in the process). Then when the fire went swoosh with a large flash (that was waaaay too much lighter fluid) Miroslav had to get up fast before his shoes, trousers, eyebrows, hair, etc etc all got like third-degree burns.

After that Branimir attacked the blaze with a fire extinguisher (definitely the wrong kind) like he was Red Adair on TV or something, an old pair of what I really think was *boxer shorts* wrapped over his face to protect from the smoke. Fucking top-level clearance, weapons-grade highly enriched hilarious. I'm really looking fwd to when there's a real fire. I can just see me, Ashton, and Stentson (2.0) all struggling out of our jeans and shorts like crazy to get something to put over our faces while an inferno blazes and we will all be burned to death and the Brothers will come in next day to inspect the charred ruins with the Fire

Department who will inform them that a bunch of seminaked fags were having a pant-sniffing orgy while it got consumed by the flames and Branimir will shake his head to Miroslav in that biblical disgusted and weary way like it was NEVER EVER EVER like this in the old country.

This kind of confusion aside, I think the chances of my losing the freakin job by the end of week two in the so-called D Star System are really pretty high. If I'm not laughing I'm totally depressed. Also unlucky. At one point I thought I can grab a chance to call Tory back on Domenico's phone line, but just when I'm dialing the numbers in walks Branimir giving me Bad Looks and a long lecture about what he calls waste-of-phone-crime. Heads up—if anyone knows about any low-effort high-pay openings in the neighborhood please feel free to IM me. I swear it to the D Stars (and the real ones you can just see past the light pollution) I'm going to be desperate soon.

*

Solve Storm of the Lake (Puzzle). Hint: Use Charm, don't use Potions.

*

I made the mistake of opening some of the recent mails from "DrunkenApe." I know I said I wouldn't do that, but then I started thinking that 1) it's kind of absolutely fucking chickenshit not to open mails on your own computer and 2) this Asshole has got to run out of ideas sometime—there are only so many variables to "You are An Idiot and I Do Not like your walkthrough" or "It's no surprise to anyone that your friend died and another went missing and your Bitch girlfriend walked out Loser."

For sure in the five or six mails that I read tonight it's mainly the same dumbass crap as usual. Go back to Insults High, you asshole. But then in ONE MAIL (THE MOST RECENT) I DID FIND SOMETHING (fucking capslock comes at the most inappropriate moments) different that adds a whole new Dimension. In this particular mail with a very inventive subject line "Pussy" the DrunkenApe or Geronimo (as he's calling himself this time) claimed that he came by Domenico's yesterday to "see me personally and sort out some things" and adding that I "wasn't there" but he will "for sure come round another time; and bring a baseball bat."

NOTE: I don't really believe that Geronimo, Duke Nuke, Jihaad, or Big Balls came around to Domenico's. No way. He's just some loser. But then for the longest time after I read that mail I was remembering that at D's this afternoon there WAS a car parked just over the road for ages with the same guy sitting in it with no facial expressions. A coincidence, I'm sure.

You're not scaring me, asshole, no matter how Crazy your names are. Your mails are going straight to the trash from now on and out into cybervacuum just like the spams, special offers, and mails from my ex-landlord and his legalistic representatives. Save your breath or your finger muscles from typing, bro, or more likely save your neck muscles from controlling the keyboard with that stick you hold between your teeth to peck at the keyboard like a demented bird. If you don't like my walkthrough please find another one to read. GO find another corner of the Internet to hide under. Or even better—write your own walkthrough— I REALLY can't WAIT to read that ha ha. You don't know shit about *The Broken World*. Stick to *Dungeon Queens of the Hollywood Hills* or *Arrowhead Destiny IX* or *Silent Whimper* or other lameass crap games like that. Write what you like to me, asshole. I'm not hearing you. You are moving your lips but no sound is reaching me, like you are an astronaut on a doomed mission, floating away from the capsule with the lifeline snapped and mouthing words that the suit-radio cannot transmit because it's broken.

 WhisPERS

I try to get on with the job.

The lake has 4 small islands plus a larger one. The center of each island has a shrine under the branches of an old tree that is wizened and the branches all knotted. The shrines are spooky (too much mist, and too much Atmosphere). There are monsters on each island. You know what to do.

Somehow with the fog and cobwebs and the old trees and the isolated beaches made largely of broken skulls (I guess I didn't mention that before) they succeed in creating a real atmosphere of doom and gloom. OK—a place called "Far Lands" might *seem* like a good place to base the resistance but I think maybe they could have gone for somewhere just slightly less far and still have been safe from the Henchmen of Octagono or GovCorp, NESTADO, Dindara, and Chang. The atmosphere there is really strange—like no one says anything, but you know right away as you get there that the world is heavier. Like if there's a break-in at a certain apartment and stuff gets stolen, afterward for weeks the whole place is stained with an atmosphere of distress and invasion and something very wrong. That is how it is on those islands. Only stronger—like in this case you get the feeling there are more bad things to come. I won't say any more than that—it's not a spoiler for anything—I'm just saying that the atmosphere is very bad in there on those islands in the mist that makes it really hard to see.

When you get to the final island you will notice: 1) Rachel is moving much more slowly and vision is blurred, 2) many of the controls that control her moves don't work anymore, and 3) the real bad news—magical objects don't keep their properties and mechanical weapons don't really function properly. Logical deduction: When you come to the Demons that guard that island you have to defeat them using swords, dagger, and pure wits alone. Go to work. Once again, you know what to do.

*

Going back to Domenico's. There were some hang-up calls there yesterday, probably not linked to the guy in the car and the email message. People are always calling there and hanging up. We're like a prime target for idiots and timewasters.

Maybe I SHOULD have told the goddamn cops yesterday about the whole thing with the hate mails and SatansHead80, which is another very original name he apparently likes to use. I mean, basically this is the situation—the fact that it has to be SatansHead80 tells you that he only came on the scene after 79 other assholes from Bumfuck Nowhere already had the same great idea for a scary name. I shouldn't worry so much about it.

And then just now—I was looking for online news about the Skeleton tour and started to think maybe this SatansHead/Jihaad/DrunkenApe could even be Brainiac. Like he's tormenting me as a part of joke (?) but then in his depressions it turned a corner and he got obsessed, serious (?), and now he's maybe hiding in a cellar with Internet connection and sending me psychotic emails every day and night. I mean, now OK, I'm laughing about it, I know Brainiac isn't a dangerous crazy that needs to be locked up behind bars, but, bro the fact it even WENT THRU MY MIND for a moment proves just how much this whole stupid thing is getting under my skin.

This is the part of the movie where someone has to slap me or throw cold water at me to snap me back to reality. But it's not a movie. It's already reality—I don't need to be snapped into it. It is reality. Man. There's nobody here in the apartment or in the nearby vicinity that could help out. It's just me sat here all alone in the untidy mess of two weeks living alone. Total isolation. (No, I don't want volunteers to come round and hit me—I'm just pointing out that I was freaking out there and that I need to calm down.)

*

Once the Demons are defeated head to the center of the island, where there is the biggest of the craggy trees.

All the while you're walking Rachel gets slower and slower. And then when you reach the tree the whole game kind of grinds to a halt and nothing happens, which is frustrating. You cannot play while Rachel is immobile like that but it doesn't seem like a movie. I mean, who wants to see a movie of Rachel lying under a tree looking pale with twitchy uncoordinated movements like she's fucked up on drugs? It's hard work to work out what has happened and many questions arise—is Rachel dead maybe? Is she in a coma or a trance or something? The freakin game is messed up? Like I said before DO NOT PANIC. You know what happens if you panic and DO NOT turn off the machine or try to force quit. You have to let this play out, in whatever way it's playing out.

*

After some time Rachel will stir and you can get control again. As she wakes there are some strange things, almost hallucinations—the sky blisters and the sand moves at her feet. Words appear in the sand— they say FOLLOW THE SOUND. It doesn't make sense at this point, maybe later. FOLLOW THE SOUND, yeah. But there is no sound. Move toward the tree and various shapes and patterns will flicker in the air. Among the flickering there start to come various "people"—in fact shimmering and ghostly faces. Don't try to shoot them—bullets won't work and anyhow THESE are the dudes you are looking for. The faces swim and shimmer a bit more then they explain they are Leaders/Elders of the resistance. Following their escape to the Far Lands they apparently took the added precaution of fleeing to totally another plane of existence. No surprise that these elders look kind of demented. I counted six of them. Two guys, two women, and two I'm not sure what—kind of ambiguous personalities like from some band that Sleeptalk thinks are cool. Hi, Sleeptalk.

*

Another hang-up, only now here in the apartment. This time I thought there was breathing at the other end. I don't care anymore. Then afterward the phone rang again and I let it ring. It's kind of stupid to get to a point where you are too frightened to even answer the phone in your own home.

*

These leaders or whatever do a lot of flickering in-and-out appearances etc etc and when they talk it's mainly in convoluted circles abt weighty "philosophical problems." Example:

"What about Energy?"

"Mm. Yes, what about Energy."

BugMap is always making fun of these guys. I guess he always makes fun of the game if anyone takes it too serious. I'm relaxed about that. It's good to have a sense of humor. Dude, these elders make even less sense than Miroslav when he's drunk, like the act of leaving their bodies to chill together in another astral plane or whatever has left behind some brain circuits. It's pretty hard to believe they're the heart of any big plan to overthrow GARS or fight against Chang etc. I mean, like Venter said if they are the best the resistance can offer there's not much hope for the ppl of Earth—GovCorp will reign for a Million Years.

DO NOT give up hope though, there's no need to let the general atmosphere of weirdness and incompetence get you down. Pass on the one-word message from Irene—on that one word hangs the Fate of a world. Just that word (I cannot tell you what it is—they randomized this for each copy of the game) is all it takes to shake things up a bit and when they hear it the elders are instantly more alert and activated. They thank you for your trouble getting there—I mean, considering how many times you came close to death and mutilation to get this far I think thanks is the least they can say. After this tho they proclaim that despite all urgencies they need some time to think about what comes next. (Again you can really wonder WTF—endless meetings in another dimension doesn't seem like a very good strategy. Didn't they learn anything after Seattle? is what Sleeptalk said. Any fool can see that what will bring down GARS and GovCorp is Kicking Some Ass.)

*

I went over to BugMap's place just to get out of the apartment, but he wasn't there so I just came back.

*

There are some neat puzzles you can do in the wasteground—no big deal, just picking up on Health Points or Desert Skills to kill time. Eventually one of the leaders/elders or whatever, a woman called Five (I think) takes physical form and meets Rachel in the cave (near the tree). There is a complicated interrogation. You have to convince her that you are for real and not an imposter etc. Assuming you pass the interrogations, Five takes you deeper into the cave. She moves kind of weird coz she has been so long hiding in another dimension and isn't used to having a body at all.

Five talks in whispers. The more important the subject, the quieter she talks. At this point in the scene she's practically inaudible. She says she wants to give you a weapon that needs to go BACK to the other side (i.e. to the real world, to the resistance in 73rd (?) Town). Jesus. I know what you're thinking—another thing to fetch and carry, no doubt with more perils on the way. I guess, if nothing else, once the whole war against GARS is over and GovCorp is extinguished Rachel and Ray can open an Inter Dimensional courier service.

Strange thing is that this weapon they want you to take back is not a gun or a Kickass Laser or a bomb. It's just something they call the Replicant Code and it's apparently so important that Five will not really tell you what it is. Great. After a lot of barely audible blah blah Five whispers directions on how you have to meet her LATER at some special place—a lab right at the Northmost point of the island. To get to it there are a bunch of Perils you have to encounter etc. When she has finished talking she dematerializes and you are left alone in the cave. The walls are covered in graffiti—mainly the names of soccer teams and abusive messages for people that don't exist anymore. Don't waste time reading it all.

*

The whole afternoon in the apt the phone didn't ring for a long time and when it did I was all rehearsed with a big speech about fuck you coz you aren't scaring me, you twisted freak, but when I answered it was just some call-center fool in Nebraska or Yangtse Province trying to sell me a deal on cell phones for my whole family. Oh yes, I can pretty much guarantee that I was NOT her favorite customer of the day.

Maybe inspired by that (ha ha) I finally called Tory back and tried to fix a date and time for coffee with her. It was that kind of stumbling but totally basic and stupid conversation that you don't really want to have with a person you lived with for four years. I don't know how to do stuff like that and would gladly skip the chance to practice. Some Skills you don't want as a high-score. But meanwhile I'm feeling more and more ridiculous in the apt without her, not knowing clearly what her absence is about, and I think I've written then deleted more than twenty emails to her since she walked out two weeks ago etc. We made plans for Friday at a neutral location (Starbucks at Borders—it doesn't get more triple thickness Insulated Neutral than that). She said yeah it was probably good to talk. There's always something so unreadable about her. I don't know. Maybe she really is seeing the Postcard Guy and she wants to talk to me now coz it's serious, or coz she has been seeing him but now she has doubts. Or maybe it's not that at all and she's just tired of how it is with me and her the whole time. Or maybe she's had a total freakout and it's Tory sending me the constant barrage of abuse under fake names like Digital Warlock, King Corpse or whatever etc. I don't really think so but weird things can happen. I saw it on an E-special—*When Love Goes Wrong*—that was the title, and there were ex-lovers stalking and mailing each other like 300 times a day.

 **MURDER / CrOSS-Connected**

(Follow Five's directions to the North Lab. JUST DEAL WITH THE PERILS YOU ENCOUNTER ON ROUTE—I CANNOT WRITE ABOUT IT NOW.)

At the Lab. Go to the basement. (SOME STUFF WITH DOOR CODES, and a REMOTE CONTROL DRONE THING THAT YOU HAVE TO DESTROY. I WILL WRITE ABOUT IT LATER.)

Lab. Once you get there they strap you in some nasty-looking chair and the elders play a film that is somehow everywhere—in your (Rachel's) head and all around the room at the same freaking time. ALSO SOME STUFF WITH A TRAITOR—ONE OF THE LEADERS, IN ANOTHER DIMENSION—YOU HAVE TO FIGHT. USE PSYCHIC ABILITY. I WILL COME BACK TO IT. The film works like a mad old-school rave club projection with all numbers, words, and images rushing by at high speed and which you have to remember. THIS IS THE WEAPON—THE REPLICANT CODE. WEIRD. IF IT WAS JUST A QUESTION OF SHOWING A MOVIE THEY COULD HAVE DONE IT AT A REGIONAL MULTIPLEX—THAT'S WHAT BUGMAP SAID. It's like they're tearing the world apart (?) and feeding it back into Rachel thru the pictures, all distorted like the wrecked file I pasted in here way back (and making just about as much sense). Controls on Rachel function intermittent and sometimes you are basically just left watching her twisting and turning in agonies like she's wrapped in that coma again. SOMETIMES THERE IS NOTHING TO DO BUT WAIT. AND WATCH THE HEALTH BAR DRIP STEADILY DOWNWARD.

A lot of people have a big theory about what the Replicant Code is. I mean—yes, OBVIOUSLY (capslock), Snake Eyes—it's apparently a weapon that can bring down GovCorp forever. And yes, BBoy or GhettoSytle83 or whatever you're calling yourself—it's just a very extended and hyperfreaking complicated list of numbers, words, and images. What I mean is, apart from all that, WHAT is it? Code for a virus? Mutated codes of Human DNA? Access codes for something? The formulas for a chemical attack? The script for a summer blockbuster movie that is somehow gonna destabilize the mentality of all the bad guys in The Broken World? Impossible to tell.

Once the projection has started Five comes close to the chair thing where you're strapped in and whispers THAT IN ORDER TO TRANSPORT THE WEAPON (REPLICANT CODE) YOU FIRST HAVE TO MEMORIZE IT ALL— we're talking about maybe 2 thousand lines of text and pictures. MAN, SHE TALKS SO QUIETLY AT THIS POINT. IT CAN DRIVE YOU NUTS. Five stands close while you lie there, she holds your hand very briefly and as she looks at you, you can see that HER SKIN HAS THE CLOSE-UP TEXTURE OF BADLY LAID ASPHALT. That is an irrelevant detail—I apologize.

Hint: Keep your eyes open at all times and pay attention. Learn the Code. Here's just some of the images and numbers and words that I have seen inside the Replicant Code:

A yacht on a sea that has no horizon coz the sea is the same color as the sky.
Grinning corpses.
Iris flowers (T said look, look, those are iris flowers—so beautiful).
Rusted metal.
74885909999999923
237534
34798354024303
80570845
85900
85000095
"END ALL."
Cyprus.
Metal Distortion.
Infants.
"LOSS ADJUSTMENT."
84824084756149786
347
53799333

I will add more later, when I can.

*

There was a car wreck just outside the window. Some guy ran a red light and then this truck couldn't stop for him. The car was totaled and the truck spilled its load (of sugar). I saw it all and was kind of expecting to go out there and find blood all over, but before I even got out of my seat the driver was getting out of the car totally unhurt and yelling at the truck guy (also uninjured) like it was all his fault. And soon they were surrounded by other people all with an opinion and gesticulation, also various people starting to loot the sugar—carrying off these bags of it in their shopping carts and stuff. Sorry. I get distracted when stuff happens just outside the window.

*

When the playback of the Replicant Code is over the control of Rachel will come back to you slowly. The figures of the elders disappear and you find yourself alone and back on what a lot of players call the Grim Island or Death Island. Sounds good, huh? I won't go into the names just now.

Make your way back to the boat (you know where you left it, dude— I'm not going to tell you). There are various puzzles to solve. A secret track to follow. There's a bird that will lead you the way if you feed it birdseed from Items. Even the birds look freaky and scared in this place.

When you get to the shore there are dark clouds and a storm suddenly starts and rain pours down. Plz take the flare gun and launch the blue flare (distress signal) and the yellow flare twice (danger), they are both in Items somewhere. I know what you're thinking—like what exactly is the distress? what is the danger already?—she's on the shore, that's not a danger, she has the Replicant CODE, she's not carrying an Improvised Explosive Device across a ridiculous unstable footbridge— what is all the fuss about? She should just get out of there somehow or stay put until this part of the game (with the storm) is over. But that's not how the game works, not how *The Broken World* works.

Bird leads you to a small low dirty concrete building—some kind of bunker—and the rain continues to fall. When you arrive at the building you hear the sound of crying from within. FOLLOW THE SOUND. I guess this isn't what the writing in the sand meant before—too obvious. Head up to the door of the concrete building and as you do so the bird will flee, upward into the darkening wet skies where the blue and yellow signals still hang heavy right above the beach, and the cries will get louder inside. (I copied the description.) FOLLOW THE SOUND, well, maybe. Open the door.

Now the bad news. You will lose control of the game again here, as Rachel enters and the storm continues outside. Do not fight it—there's no other way forward than this. Inside the small single room there is a flickering fluorescent light and they do weird shit with the sound again filling the air in a kind of retarded white noise. The crying continues from the shadows— a child. Maybe that's the sound that was mentioned before. Even without knowing for sure what comes next, it's already clear THIS is a bad place.

*

Rolo came in and went out again but he didn't come to my door. He just left a note in the kitchen saying plz can I at least PAY for the grass that everyone helped themselves to and that it's not cool to be taking it without asking.

*

Somewhere in the flickering dark of the room (chamber?) you will hear the crying again but Rachel will never discover who that child is coz there, also hidden in the shadows, is SOMEONE ELSE who has a very different agenda.

This second figure steps suddenly fwd and out of the dark. Rachel sees at once who it is and gasps uncontrollably. Confusion and terror. But the way they do the movie your view to the person is blocked by Rachel's hands as they come up to defend her face against the gun that the person is carrying. Too late and too little.

You hear gunfire. Bang. It all goes so fast, but after the gunshot the child crying that was there very suddenly stops. A kind of terrible silence. And then you hear more shots, another bang, bang. The camera moves up slowly and away like it's clinging and crawling precariously to the ceiling to escape from this terrible scene. Down below you see that random kid dead and you see yourself—Rachel. She's bleeding now and her hunched assassin, wrapped in shadows, is running away and into the rain. There on the concrete floor Rachel dies. There is no other way to describe it. The blood comes gurgling up from out her throat like when drains are blocked and the bathwater won't run away. She says "Life is so precious . . . even now" but the rest is inaudible. I turned the volume up like a million times but you cannot hear it—nothing audible at all. A sick sick world, where your last words don't count or even get heard. Then those green/gray pixels lose their sparkle and Rachel's eyes finally flutter and close.

*

Perhaps the most freaky glitches in *The Broken World* are where things get cross-connected so that making one action also makes something else happen that isn't really connected. Weird. Happens in the real world too.

For example: At Domenico's for some reason, the action of turning on the light in the storeroom causes the ventilation and lights to go off instantly in the toilet. Yesterday Miroslav finally called in the handyman

(Micky) and asked him to sort it out. Ha ha. Micky spent hours tracing wires all over the place, looking for clues to the cause. He even rewired various things, but didn't succeed in solving the problem, only managed to stop the pilot light on the ovens from igniting for about three hours. That produced a lot of happiness. Every time this thing happens (with the light in the storeroom and the ventilation in the toilet) it can cause a big stink in the toilet. I say no more than that—there's no window in there, so you can imagine. All afternoon while Micky was working, there were moments when suddenly the hum and rattle of the ventilation stopped and the Brothers Grim (another name for them courtesy of Ashton) would look up at the ceiling, with open eyes like dudes in a Frankenstein movie, like there was some kind of spooky and ominous fate in operation.

In *The Broken World* I guess the cross-connections are programming errors of some kind. Like when Ray is on the Colony—anytime when he lies on the Medi-bed a cat appears and then his Phaser sparks into action. I don't think they planned it that way.

There's even a tiny cross-connection there at the scene where Rachel dies. (Apologies for reminding you of that—but there's no point pretending it didn't happen). So while she's scraping and groaning in the rubble and trash on the floor, with blood going out everywhere, try making Rachel reach for a stick that lies just ahead of her on the ground. As she reaches, a music box hidden on the floor among the junk will start to play an old but familiar tune. Maybe it's just a musical windup toy belonging to the kid that was crying—a toy that at this point just randomly starts to wind down a last bit. Or maybe it's a music box left here from some previous desolate occupant. You cannot know for sure. But to me it seems like a glitch—makes no sense at all that those things are connected forever.

It reminds me what Venter once said about the night his dad said that his mom had gone—they were all at home eating beetroot salad for dinner and he tried not to cry. Then from that time on whenever he tastes beetroot he thinks of that night and his mom. Sometimes I even think *The BW* is like a brain—I mean yes, a world just like Venter always says, but also like a brain. And the people are like its thoughts, and there are many many connections between things, like beetroot and a departing mother, I don't know. I guess some things get linked together like that, randomly but forever.

*

Tory called again. Same flash of something when I see her name on the screen of the phone. Apparently Starbucks at Borders is closed for some refurbishment reason. She was there today somehow. I didn't ask. So now we will have to meet at Starbucks in Barnes & Noble.

Later Tory's parents called again and I was again wondering if they really know by now that Tory's moved out. I mean, I think they must know for certain, but if they aren't gonna mention it then neither am I. The whole conversation felt like it was really about something else. Me being vague and using "we" in a meaningless way, saying "mmm" sometimes instead of "no" or "yes." I don't know who I'm protecting, but it's mainly Tory I guess. I wish life wasn't so complicated.

Nothing seems to affect my basic role as far as Tory's parental units go—i.e. it doesn't matter if I'm living with their daughter or not, I still get to answer all the Big Questions they can throw at me. Here's an update on the latest arrivals. Do I believe that polar ice caps are melting? Do I believe that their house is in a good position in that event that the global water levels are rising? What was the name of that song Dean Martin used to sing at the start (or maybe the end) of all his concerts? I mean—

WHY for ONE SECOND do they think I might know the answer to that? What's the most reliable brand name of burglar alarm? And—my favorite of all recent ones—do I know a solution to get pollen stains off a white blouse Tory's mom has somehow managed to get covered in pollen???? I think maybe Barbara was hiding in the bushes to keep watch on the drive to see if anyone was really trying to steal the gravel from under their very noses. I'm telling you AGAIN, bro. They are going crazy out there in the Burbs. It's freaky to think of them out there, what the world they revolve in actually is. Pollen stains and the dangers of ice caps slowly melting.

*

Rachel is beautiful. Someone like her doesn't exist anywhere in the world. To me that's true beauty, i.e. that cannot exist. Not like some movie star sitting in a trailer. But something beyond. I don't want to write about it much because someone (i.e. Tory) might take it wrong, even now, I wouldn't want that. Hi, Tory. See you for coffee. I keep trying to persuade myself that it wasn't right with us, that she's not right for me, but that doesn't feel right either.

Rachel's brown eyes with the flecks and pixels of green are closed now. You can only watch her life-status bar trickle down to the absolute zero. There's nothing else to do.

I cannot write about it anymore right now.

There are times when I hate how the game makes me feel. I don't know. Yes, OK they can write that on my gravestone—"I don't know" or "He didn't know" or "He didn't have a fucking clue." We make these people out of codes and pixels and we give them names—like Ray or Rachel or Dr Myzatium or Whatever—and we put in hours playing them—hours of surviving, building skills, and everything—and then, when it comes to it, dude, we can only watch the blood spilling over the concrete, no one there to clean up, and no one there to hold her as she goes. *The BW* is harsh sometimes and sad and relentless. That's all I can say.

Earth AGAIN

Next level starts with a movie—you're not in control of the game yet. You will see the deep spaceship (that Ray was in before), only now you see it from the outside moving slowly in toward Earth against a backdrop of stars. Then you get a long track of all the sleeping corridors with automated lights and stuff. Eventually the shot comes along to RAY in the Cryonics Bay, lying curled in his freeze pod (I don't know the word for what they call it) where he's sleeping a deep, frozen sleep.

With Rachel gone you must be Ray again. They keep you shifting and changing. They throw you from pillar to post.

*

You get control of the game and you are Ray, but somehow you're not on the ship. Instead you're in a large dark house, all shadows and cold. Don't panic. All thru the house there are scattered "artefacts" of Ray himself—a photo of him and Rachel, the first gun he ever gets in the game, a pair of moon boots, Amulet of Hope, etc. You have to move around the house and collect ALL these items but it's not like you're in the real world coz the moves are slow and dreamy and the rooms of the house don't join together how you expect them to. Be warned there are also Perils in the house—ghost figures that represent what you (Ray) are most afraid of—a laughing ghost of Chang, Operatives, several versions of Archduke, etc etc. You must defeat these phantoms (also with a Time Bonus).

All the time in the shadow house the "ping ping ping" of the spaceship's alarm sounds louder and louder—summoning you to be awake and get on with the mission. As you continue and collect things there will be an important clue: go to the upstairs window of the ghost house. At one moment there will be a sound outside—white noise, the crash of rain like in a storm but there is no storm—and outside in the sky the light of blue and yellow flares will explode and Rachel's voice will whisper *"Find me, Ray. Find the flare, Ray, and you will find me. Life is so precious even right now."*

Finally near the end of this part the alarm gets very loud and you come to a room with a mirror (not Mirrors of Truth and Mirrors of Untruth. That's later). You see yourself (Ray). Walk toward the mirror—reach out and then step into it. You will merge with the Ray that was waiting there.

Then the game continues. Fate will twist and twist again.

*

I went out to shoot some random pool with Venter, BugMap, and also Dieter's sister (invited by BugMap). As we went up the big stairs I asked her how things were and she said she was "doing OK," "kind of," and then I said "yeah" and there was a small silence and I went into a kind of monologue that was trying to make work at Domenico's sound like it was funny, but which was really just filling the air with words so we didn't have to sit in silence all the time. Later, when we were ordering drinks she looked at me and did that kind of small laugh and shrug combination, the thing that people do when they're thinking about something that can't be explained.

To tell it straight we weren't exactly the most talkative or Hilarious group playing pool. But we sank a few beers and got on with the game/s. At first we played doubles, Venter and Me versus BugMap and Dieter's Sister—Angela (yes, she has a name). Then we swopped the teams—Venter and BugMap versus Me and Angela, which was an absurdly unfair contest, although Angela can play better than me so our team wasn't a total disgrace. Then Venter felt like a big need to beat BugMap all on his own (it can get like that with the competitive types) so me and Angela sat it out and talked. No big deals.

A said her mom was pretty bad still after what happened and I had rerun mental pictures of her sat in front of that excessive kickass Home Cinema setup and soaking in all the voices and pictures of the Shopping Channel, which kind of sent shivers into my spine.

At maybe ten or eleven Angela went outside for a cigarette and I went to keep her company. I guess at that point I had already told her the whole story of the Funeral no-show (which she'd already heard from BugMap and Venter) and she said fine, fine like she knew that that wasn't what it was all about anyhow and she was asking about Tory and I told her a kind of limited version, and I guess I was starting to think or realize that Angela might be cute and at that point I decided to say my goodbyes and head home. See you around, yeah, see you around. See you. See you around. Yeah. See you.

Coming back I walked past B's place, not an essential part of the route but not a huge detour. No lights on in the whole building, not even in the whole block, and nobody home, just the fucking dogs barking mad and out loud, all locked behind the shutters in the apartment downstairs, and soon after the rain began to fall.

*

It's hard to imagine Brainiac. Where he could be now. I mean, the fact that he stopped showing up for the Phone Support gig doesn't really prove a thing. I mean, he could still be here, just living in some part of the city that none of us goes to—it would be so easy. The city is so so big enough if he wants to disappear. Or he could have gone out of town. Brainiac liked rural areas. (Again, bro. I'm having an issue with the tense.) Or I guess he could be dead, but I don't think so. I get the instinct he's alive and just dealing with what goes on in his head. Time will tell. Like how long has he been gone? Two weeks, maybe three?

WHen I think abt him NOW I STILL SEE HIM SAT AT HIS DESK (capslock—I will hunt down and murder the guys that designed this keyboard). I still think of him sat at his desk and working on that office/prison-room puzzle and arranging objects to help make the perfect escape for Ray. I mean—the Brainiac is a total genius like that. A freaky permutations or persistence king. But in real life it's not clear if he can get out of the place he is in his mind. I don't know if he can put the pieces in the right place to do that. I hardly know what the things are that he's arranging in his own head. It's fucked up. I admit I cannot

publish a solution to that part concerning Brainiac no matter how I want
to. It's not really in the game.

*

Fuck it again. Now I'm kind of wishing I didn't start on this stuff about
Brainiac because it's getting me down just like the death of Rachel
always gets me when I have to think about it. FOLLOW THE SOUND,
yeah. FOLLOW THE SOUND. Who knows where the Brainiac has gone? I
mean, he could have gone like anyplace by now. And Rachel—being
dead—she will not go anyplace at all.

*

Next time Ray's eyes open you are behind them and you are in the real
Broken World now—not in that freaky dream house. You are Ray and it's
hard not to get cold shivers when you see your face reflected in the steel
doors of the cabin—home again, home again. Not Rachel, not auburn
hair, not brown with so-green eyes—just your old face (Ray's) again, the
face with the scars and the barcode tattoo. When you move Ray thru
the ship and walk him down to the equipment stores and into the airlocks
etc it's like walking in boots you haven't worn since last winter.

(The start of this level can feel like it runs a little slow. I didn't notice
that before. But the spaceship seems kind of clunky and the stars do this
stuttering thing sometimes. Can anyone give good advice?)

Switch off autopilot and land the ship. A voice announcement with an
East European accent says repeatedly *Welcome to Earth, Welcome to
Earth, Welcome to Earth* in a way that doesn't make you feel welcome
at all.

NOTE: You may be back on Earth but it's not the Earth that Ray left behind and not the Crowded Earth he went to. No. Things have certainly changed around here. Even the Space Port itself looks like it's seen better days with obvious marks of gunfire all over the place, as well as some areas cordoned off for security (nothing too interesting down those hallways—don't waste time investigating). And from what it looks like out the windows and the chatter of conversation from the various evil-looking dudes hanging around in the loading bays, there has apparently been some sort of world war or atomic catastrophe. I've never figured out exactly what's happened—just too many rumors in too many languages. I mean, you cannot work out whose fault it was or what the "sides" were in the war or anything like that. Lots of ppl speculate but it doesn't really matter. Facts are simple: 1) the Geiger counters are working overtime, 2) the city beyond is tense and BURNING, and 3) the sky outside looks angry like a bruise.

The real Bad News is that Robots have apparently taken over the Earth and they are working along with some bad guys that used to be GovCorp Operatives but have now switched allegiance to the new Enemy (NESTADO) and all the towns are in ruins and what is left of humanity is kind of huddled in the wreckage of once great buildings. When he hears this (in some briefing with a fat guy) Ray looks pissed off—leave the planet alone for any length of time and THIS is what happens. Your mission, as the fat guy explains, is to fight against the bad guys that used to be Operatives and also the Robots. Ray says, "Whatever. Bring it on." I guess he doesn't listen to these briefings much anymore. He just wants to find Rachel again.

They don't waste much time throwing you back in deep water. Before the briefing even comes to an end the Space Port comes under Robot attack. Top-of-the-range Strafer Missiles come punching thru the Teflon wall surfaces, puncturating the fat guy in the head and spurting his guts all over everything in the nearby vicinity. GRAB ANY WEAPONS YOU CAN AND START SHOOTING. Just remember this simple advice (thanks, Venter)—if it's a Robot you want to get rid of it. Most of the other ppl or creatures you encounter will be your friends.

Halfway thru the Space Port fight (just past the Airlock bridgehead) you will be joined by a new ally. Press a red button that controls the Airlock door and it opens to reveal Lao Pi (from before)—grinning and carrying a total shitload of extreme heavy-duty weapons. Cool. Level Up and start using the Sonic Blaster. If things work out according to "plan" the only Robots left in the Space Port will be the good old Soda Vending Machines and a few Semiretarded Baggage Drones. Anything else with so much as one single microchip will be heaps of scrap metal, charred wire, and slowly dying flames.

*

When I talked to Stentson 2.0 he was spilling gossip on Domenico's like otherwise he was gonna burst his large ass. (OK. He doesn't have a large ass.) Ashton got in a big row with Miroslav coz he (Ashton) showed up wearing Eyeliner on Wednesday. Branimir stopped the van just out front of the store for like five minutes and then got a parking ticket and went into some kind of Rage Mode. Cookie that mainly does the morning shift burst into spontaneous tears last week sometime during a confrontation with Miroslav about the rules of the freakin D Star System. Crazy. Like suddenly The Big D is turning into the stress capital of the entire world. Then he said almost overnight a few posters appeared in the Kitchen with various instructions and safety warnings. I haven't seen so much action in that place since the Dept of Public Healths paid a special visit.

When I got in yesterday Ashton shot me a glance that said Welcome To Hell and I wasn't laughing. First, it was hot and busy—a VERY bad combination. 2nd, Miroslav is supposedly sick so the King of badly repressed Rage, Branimir, comes in alone to join me, Stentson (2.0), Ashton, and Micky who is apparently just there to try and fix (again) the cross-wiring between the light in the storeroom and the ventilation in the toilet which has now gotten more complicated and involves the outdoor emergency lighting. Anytime you switch OFF the light in the toilet now the bigass 1000kw electrical floods come on outside illuminating the neighborhood like a chopper squad SWAT team are just touching down.

Anyhow. All through this morning Branimir sat at the counter in Bad Mood mode looking thru various multiple-choice assessment papers we'd done, breaking the silence only occasionally with snorts of derision and muttering words like NO or NO. WRONG. IDIOT. When that was done he conscripted me to leave the rest of the freak circus behind and we set off in the "van" together to visit the wholesalers where we are supposed to pick up more pizza bases. Maybe sales are better than expected this month (I don't think so) or maybe they're stocking up on supplies in the case of Armaegedon (I cannot spell it). All I know is that the whole afternoon I'm on strict best behavior trying to be like a sensible employee, and that halfway across town we get in terrible traffic and pretty soon we're at a standstill in unnatural degrees of heat. What's weird is that as I start to sweat in there I realize that I've more or less NEVER spent anytime alone with Branimir (why would I? he's an objectionable loudmouth). Once we get stuck he exhibits classic symptoms of asshole behavior. At first he puts the radio on. It's a well-known fact that only assholes listen to the radio. Then, of course, he's not happy with the channel. Then he skims thru half the dial at such high speed you can't even figure out what is music and what is noise, and (surprise) he still cannot find anything that he's happy with. Then he tells me to find good music. "Good music" he says and makes a jabbing gesture towards the radio. I'm twisting the dial all over the place—I never even owned a radio. And he's shaking his head in a way that makes out like this is all my freaking problem. In the end I do find some music that Branimir is apparently happy with—Country & Western. Oh no. I cannot believe it even now.

Man. We spent like two and half hours in that traffic. And the whole time it was a diet of songs concerning men that killed other men, or hearts that got broke, or brothers that turned bad, or women that walked (hi, Tory—I was thinking of you today), or girls that held a rose. Country & Western. It just doesn't make an obvious connection with Branimir for me. Except maybe coz he's far away from home—I mean, who knows what he left behind, but I don't think it's a cattle farm. Don't worry, I'm not going to get carried away. Branimir is still percentagewise mainly asshole as far as I'm concerned. I'm just trying to make up my mind about him crying at a song by Steve Earle.

When the song was over Branimir said something. It sounded like "You?"

And I said "What?"

And he said "What about you—girlfriend?"

And I was like "Huh?"

We were stuck there in the traffic at this point.

He said "You have a picture of your girl?"

And I was feeling invaded somehow but still answered—no.

And Branimir was like matter-of-fact. Almost like making a joke: "What no girl, or no picture?"

And I was thinking well in fact in my wallet I do have a picture of Tory, but I don't have a girl. So I said—"No girl now. Not at the moment."

And then neither of us said a thing for a while until the traffic started moving again and another song came along to change to mood.

SUBTERRANEANS

Even once all the robots in the spaceport area are destroyed, this is really not one of those situations where you can just pick up a bus to the city or ride the subway. At a time like this the ONLY safe way to the city is to take a route thru the sewer system. (I'm NOT joking, bro. You can take another route if you want to become Robot meat, but don't hold me responsible for what happens.) The sewers, man. What the fuck is it with Ray and these kinds of subterranean tunnel systems? They are always sending him down into places like that, all twisting and turning in dark passageways where anything can jump out on you at any point. Plus this one also kind of runs slow. It's starting to drive me nuts.

Ray and Lao Pi have maps of the sewer system—the trouble is those maps are somehow time-sensitive and the info on them fades more and more with each passing minute. You must make your way thru the sewers together as fast as possible—running thru the map as the info on it dissolves and the map itself blisters and fades.

*

Watch out for the Sewer Hazards:

Jelly Fish (radioactive).
Homeless Psychos.
Alligators (I'm not joking).
Tunnel Floods.
Tunnel Blockages.
Tunnel Collapses.
Amebas (also radioactive).
Robots "*Search and Destroy Series*" (I'm saving the nasty
    mfkrs for last).

Also collect Sewer Items:

Breathing Mask.
Skewer Pole.
Flashlight.
There are more. I will come back to it.

*

Looking out the window. No signs of life. All quiet. It's all quiet out there. And all quiet in this room, sitting at the computer. I'm getting distracted again.

Once I got back off the epic "van" trip to find CF bases, it was just me and Ashton left alone holding the fort together at the Big D's. We spent the small ration of available downtime making up new names for Branimir and Miroslav (already aka Brothers Grim), including The Chemical Brothers, The Barrel Brothers, The Brothers from Beyond Time, The Band of Brothers, The Banana Brothers, Doobie Brothers, The Brothers Karamazov or something. Right now I think The Barrel Brothers fits the best, because they could both REALLY do with some time in the Weight Loss clinic. I'm still laughing at that. I guess I can say anything I like about those fatass idiots B&M coz they don't have Internet and will NEVER read this walkthru.

*

When you get to the town itself be careful coz the navigation is a tough one and after months in the freeze pod Ray isn't exactly at the height of his powers—i.e. please be careful. The whole town was originally laid out on a 3D interlocking grid system but in the war with all the A-bomb explosion(s) it got bent, overlapped, and twisted out of shape. Here and there are pockets of survivors—mostly lost, aggressive, and paranoid. Try not to get close—there are few points to be gained by murdering these losers and frankly, there is bigger work to do.

Tip: In combat mode you can still communicate with Lao Pi using the code you made with him from before. Try banging the rifle butt to tap out a message—helps coordinate attacks.

*

Chief Mutants (in ascending orders of difficulty):

Biker Mutant
Cop Mutant
Cheerleader Mutant
Mutant Dogs

B-Boy Mutant
Electro Mutant
Goth Mutant

Yuppie Mutant
Nun Mutant
Pregnant Mutant
Crack Hooker Mutant
Rollerblade Mutant

Town Hazards:

Firestorms
Nuclear Firestorms
Rain
Radioactive rain

There are more. I will come back to it. I never figured out how to beat the Rain in this part. Does anyone know how that works?

*

Find a part of town where there is a large train station, in front of which there is a public square with fountains and "abstract" statues. In the center of the square is a line of benches where various tough guys from the area gather, drinking Surgical Alcohol to improve their strength and sense of humor, reminiscing on what life was like before the Robots spoiled everything. You know the scene—I guess every town has a square or park like this one.

One of the guys that hangs around here is vital to your missions i.e. can guide you and Lao Pi out of here. You have to work out which one and a wrong decision can cost your life. HINT: It's NOT the guy with A SPIDERWEB tattooed on his face and it's not the woman wearing dirty flesh-pink pantyhose that looks like a human donut.

Wait a minute.

*

Shit.

Turns out all those crashes I was having, where I thought my copy of Word was buggy and I was downloading a new one and that didn't work either and when I thought that even parts of The Broken World had some kind of problem like the Bone Bridge and Sewers System etc were running very slow and stuttering etc—I can spare you the full fucking recount—but it turns out that none of this was a problem with Word or The Broken World at all. I apologize to the programmers and coders.

Man, it turns out that the hard drive on HAL is ALL FULL to bursting and because of that completely fragmented. I found out earlier coz I was looking for an autosave of the stuff I lost, but couldn't find it—no freaking autosave. Then I tried to open up the iTunes and it started to open but then it choked and froze and then there was a well-known and unpopular error message to say Not Enough Space On Disk.

Not enough memory. Sorry there is not enough memory to complete the action requested. Please try clearing some space on the hard drive by compressing or deleting unwanted items. # Error 454.

I was like what the fuck? I don't believe it, what are you talking about not enough space, that is horseshit, man, it's a 20gb drive? And then I did some investigations. Turns out that from a 20-gig drive there is only 563k left free! Ha ha ha. Not enough memory. I'm a freaking idiot. It's suprising that HAL works at all.

Time for a big spring-clean of HAL now. Gotta take some time and throw some crap AWAY otherwise this walkthrough will be sinking under itself and into the oblivion of silence.

*

OK. OK. I know it's late and everything and with work and all I REALLY (CAPSLOCK) need to sleep so I don't fall asleep at the counter, but anyhow I just looked right through the C drive. This is what happened:

Man, what a mess. I mean, first off the drive is so totally disorganized with only myself to blame so that at first I can't even tell where things are. I mean, I accept that the drive is full but my question is *where* are all the big files so that I can throw them out? I can empty the cache from IE. Which saves like 20mb. Nothing. Then I'm like clearing the desktop. Files everywhere. To-do lists. Letters. IRS stuff and loan stuff from last year. Notes on *The Broken World*. Amusing texts or whatever that people sent me. Pictures. I don't know—files, ZIP files, jpgs. A big stack of MP3s that some cousin of Venter's copied on there when he wanted to burn a CD. PDF manuals for programs that I don't even have anymore. In fact a lot of it is stuff that I don't even recognize from the names so I end up opening files at random, esp big files. Basically looking for stuff to delete/erase/move to Trash. At the same time I'm kind of sifting stuff. Putting things in places. Clearing the desktop. Clearing the mess.

I find a folder more or less full of movie files and also there are some movie files all over the desktop—mostly from the time when Clockwork had a handycam. These are pretty big files and they are mixed in with a lot of Word docs—this is no filing system, dude, I warn you. One file called Fairground. Me and Tory stood in front of the dodgem cars. Laughing and fooling around with clothes I almost forgot. Haircuts we don't have anymore. Maybe 50 seconds. And gone now, in more ways than one. Motherfucker. I don't know. Filmed by Venter. I drag this one to a new folder that I make called Movies to Keep. I have a briefest thought about this Neutral Coffee meeting we have planned for Friday, but I don't like to think about it really. Too weird. Too much packed around it (mentally speaking) so I let it go. Another movie file called August. I have no Idea what it is when I open it. And then I get a big surprise. The first frame is a patch of green grass, the video camera pointed at the ground. When I press play it's just this same shot of the grass looking down. About three minutes. I didn't watch all of it—I'm not crazy—instead I fast-forward. Sometimes you can see my (?) feet entering the shot and at other moments you can see my shadow bobbing into shot. There's the sound of birds and distant traffic. That's all. At times the camera, or me holding it, is moving so fast that the compression on the mpeg cannot keep up and the image is pixelating. Green pixels. Dancing. I drag this one to the Trash. Another movie file called Lakeview1. Me and Tory again. A distant shot. We're trying skis on in the back of her parents' place but there's no snow. 4 other files called Lakeview2, Lakeview3, Lakeview4, Lakeview5—all more of the same scene. By the end—in the last one—we are pretending to ski, right there on the gravel. 90 seconds of foolishness from way back when. I place this last one in the folder called Movies to Keep. The others I drag to the Trash. Another mpeg file called Mountain I don't open, just drag it to the Trash. Another file called Martin I also Trashed without opening. Sorry, dude. I need the space. Another file called Miles&Seth. I put this one in the folder called Movies to Keep.

There are movies from some party, movies of me and Tory at some Wilderness Trail, movies of the old apartment where I lived before this one, movies of friends, people that can hardly be remembered, movies of like family people. There are also like files from the Internet or that people gave me. Gross stuff and stupid stuff mixed together. A guy with like a huge penis penetrating a woman that looks in pain. An animation of household items that are singing a song about a president that isn't even alive anymore. A shot from NASA off some Mars mission flyby to an asteroid. Then more personal stuff. A file called Wendy that goes straight in the Trash. Another one called Discotheque also straight in the Trash.

Then a file called Saturday. I cannot think what the fuck that is. I open it. And it's Dieter of course. From the day in the woods, like wayback. A shot of him climbing a tree. Going upward. Clockwork, Tory, Brainiac at the bottom. I don't know who's filming it, could be me, could be Venter. You can hear some laughing or mumbling even right near the camera microphone. I guess that's me or maybe Sleeptalk. Dieter climbs. I mean, the clip is maybe 40 seconds long. A stupid movie. Like Dieter has been caught here always. Climbing. And will be forever, I guess. Frozen in a loop of time from that day in the woods. The sunlight looks real good. I put this file in the folder called Movies to Keep. Two files called Freeway. Just headlights from cars and taillights and stuff.

I don't know. Like something from a pop promo. Stupid to keep that. I drag these files to the folder called Trash. Another on the forecourt of a McDonald's. Me and Venter laughing abt something but no sound on the file. No way to tell what it is. It goes in the Trash. I keep going. I'm saving lots of space by deleting these movie files. Another Fairground file—but spelled wrong—Fairgrund. Not near those dodgems this time, and no people as such. This one is just shot from what is maybe the front part of the Ghost Train—you just see a lot of darkness at first but then the whole thing moving with swirls and blurs and those superbright flashes of light plus all the sound of music and that excited screaming in the background. I put this one in the Trash. And then I take it out again. I open it, go to full-screen mode, and let it play.

Swirls and high-speed blurs. The darkness thunders and the flashes come and go as that train goes round its corners, screeching brakes, and there is screaming and music that thumps from HAL's speakers. You can imagine what it would be like to be on that train when it's thundering like that, going round on its tracks, in its endless circles. Or what it would be like to be stood in front of that train and just hoping that it'll maybe stop in time. I don't know. One day we will all be free. But until then, dude, it is struggle and fire.

*

I'm sitting here in the daytime that's starting to feel like nighttime the whole time. I'm disoriented. I look out the window. Nothing happening. The phone isn't ringing.

*

Three weeks to the day since Brainiac disappeared.

Nearly four since Dieter died.

And two and a half since Tory left.

I'm loving these anniversaries so freaking much. I'm sitting here with a clock and a calendar.

FrozeN TIME

When I finished with the mpeg (Movie) files I thought I maybe cleared half a gig of space. I mean—that's good, but not nearly enough to sort the problem. No way. Should be running with like a third of the C drive clear. (Sounds like I got a job in phone-tech support. I apologize. But when problems come you got to sort it out.) So I started looking around for something more—I had this feeling like what the fuck? I mean, what the fuck IS all the stuff on this drive. I didn't know I had so much Junk. There was so much crap on there. I mean, years and years and years of it, like I said—HAL is more or less an antique of former days of computer revolution—there's an inevitable buildup of useless data. But all the stuff I was finding was just folders of documents. Old mail folders, sure, that takes a few MB. Some pictures. Just not big enough. I was searching, looking around.

And then it happened. Revelation.

Down there, deep down there somewhere in the kind of folder in a folder in a folder in a folder etc kingdom of No Freakin Return is a folder called BWGSVOLD. And as soon as I saw and read the name I knew instantly that this must have been what I was looking for—that this was it, that this was where the best part of those 20 fucking gigs of memory got used. Right there. I'm looking at it now. Typing this on T's laptop. And staring at HAL.

Right-click the folder BWGSVOLD and straightaway it opens. What I can see inside is something like 30 or 40 files—no more than that—and each file starting with the same two letters and then just numbers, only numbers to name and tell the difference between them.

BW239000887936.gsv
BW320065196462.gsv
BW333390945896.gsv
BW333876790980.gsv
BW344287111222.gsv
BW350006519311.gsv
BW353367653540.gsv
BW364987792102.gsv
BW366087623148.gsv
BW399988648790.gsv
BW399990356788.gsv
BW400067909841.gsv
BW400073498744.gsv
BW529642908786.gsv

BW529899076256.gsv
BW534348626361.gsv
BW544000709152.gsv
BW556929072093.gsv
BW560007866897.gsv
BW578609810220.gsv
BW590920087412.gsv
BW593125637088.gsv
BW652389749912.gsv
BW677897490909.gsv
BW778778974939.gsv
BW647928074642.gsv
BW735468923678.gsv
BW835626677890.gsv
BW847364687877.gsv
BW860078537900.gsv
BW863087366211.gsv
BW867790762454.gsv
BW881212732622.gsv
BW899930910842.gsv
BW899980097394.gsv
BW954443683329.gsv
BW986087913981.gsv
BW998764543450.gsv
Etc.

Oh bro, it's a Museum of the failures and fates and dead ends and blunders. A folder of almost-tragedies. The end of time. The deep freeze of history.

I need to make it clearer—I know, man, I'm getting there, I'm getting there, just thinking it thru. Each of those files is a saved version of *The Broken World*. A version I stopped and saved at someplace where things had gone bad—a dead-end place, a near-death place, a point of total stuckness or stillness or whatever.

There is the version where, after like months and months of playing, I took Ray on a shortcut thru the Arcan Swamps and he stumbled in the quicksand and no matter how hard he was struggling and hollering for Rachel or Lao Pi and throwing the rope for the tree and everything, I couldn't get him out. He was sinking and sinking. Getting shorter of breath and I couldn't let him die. So I saved the game with him stuck there and stopped Time. And I know that if I open it, bro, time will start again and he will die. So Ray is like that forever now. In the swamp, with the birds waiting to start singing again, the insects waiting to start up with their terrible clicking and churping.

There's the version where I was fooling around and Rachel took off from 12th Town and didn't go on her Mission. She was like heading to the airport and I had her getting on the first flight at random more or less. And Rachel was on the plane and somewhere over Houston it hit very very bad turbulence and a crack appeared in the wing and it started to tear free. And I was like holy shit. And It was clear, I mean OBvIOUS, that nothing could be done. And people were clinging to each other and screaming and lightning was "splitting the sky" and as the plane fell I just had time to save the game. Rachel was on her cell phone to Ray and I saved her there. So that they would always be together. The plane is falling very very fast so I know I cannot ever like, open it again, not for even a second.

There's the version there where I had Ray go off in the mountains and he was studying karate and stuff but the teachers were weird and they wouldn't teach him to fight—they would only teach him how to draw perfect circles in one stroke of a brush using paint and stuff like that and he stayed there nearly a year. And in the end he kind of wouldn't leave. I mean—I could make him leave but then he'd get sick and Health would drop and he would mutter in a delirious way that he had to be back with the Monks. So I'd take him back and do all the tasks to train him and stuff and to recover but he still never wanted to leave. I mean. I like it there. Something so cool about it, but at the same time it was kind of crazy to be spending so much time on the game and all of it was like these Buddhist jokes and things—Ray didn't want to hear a thing about GARS, just about perfecting himself in the highest possible inner way. So in the end I saved the game and left him there in the forest in the mountains, started again from the very start. Stopped time and took it back to the top.

There's the version where in a fight with Archduke Rachel got flung from a window of a speeding train and, I don't know how I managed it, I somehow succeeded in saving her before she hit the ground.

There's the version where in a complicated fight with an agent of GovCorp Rachel is flung from a top of a cliff and I somehow saved her just before she crashed to the rocks at the bottom. I don't know what it is with Rachel. Somehow I always seem to save her in the air and from certain death.

There is the version where, in the depths of Deep Space, Ray was carrying out a mission near a Black Hole as part of some Probe and an agent of GARS was releasing his safety cable and sending him off floating, slowly, dude, very slowly toward the weirdness of oblivion. I saved him just before the end. When he was getting real close to the Black Hole and its terrible gravity, when he could see the alien sun set behind a planet that no human could ever call home. Floating slowly. I stopped time.

There's the version where Rachel has just had this shootout with 5 Ninja Dudes (from GovCorp?) in a fully functioning Nuclear Reactor and they'd wounded her badly and they were catching up on her fast—riding these cool three-wheeler trike things they have—but I used the slow-motion defense and flipped them all into slow-mo and Rachel could see the bullets coming right at her and she jumped midair to avoid them, jumped so high and twisted, bro—she looked so cool, like those photos of the high-jumpers in some high-jump event where they get pictured at the top of their jump, only Rachel had a gun blazing in each hand and this badass grin like she knew she was the best thing in the world and the bullets went straight thru the bad guys and I knew then that she had won the Level—totally defeated them and she looked so good in the air there, in the slow-mo, all like twisted to avoid the bullets that they were firing, I didn't want that moment ever to end. So I saved her. Midair again but this time absolutely triumphant.

And there's the version where Rachel is persuaded to work for GovCorp/GARS. I don't know what went wrong—but they made her an offer in a parking lot, and she just kind of transformed and after that she wouldn't cooperate on any missions I was setting and started in a conspiracy with some agents to destabilise Pakistan and start a global catastrophe. It was pretty incredible. I'd never heard of anyone else who had that happen—I don't know what I did wrong. But bro, I was being responsible—I mean, Chang with Rachel on its side is too powerful and too dangerous a Fate for the World and as soon as I figured out there was nothing I could do to keep the world away from her, I cut all losses and saved the game. I will not open that version again. Ever.

And there's the version where Ray and Rachel were shrunk to tiny and miniaturized size by some complicated machinery invented by Aliens and then the machinery is destroyed (by Cyborgs seeking revenge) and Ray and Rachel are left—together near the start of the game but reduced to approximately the size of a spider. They were certainly cute—Tory thought so—but they were never gonna win against Chang and the Zorda. Those were the days. Tory sat with me while I played the whole thing thru, a whole weekend protecting them, and we waited til we found a kind of safe home for them—in the skirting boards, cooped up with lots of supplies. And then she said, "Can you save them, keep them this way, keep them alive, they can be us, be like us, only there, living there?" Maybe she was stoned. I don't even remember. But I know that I said sure, why not, and we stopped time—saved the game. I think Tory liked that.

And there's the version where I let Ray get kind of distracted by other objectives—having fun and chasing Girls and making Bling. It was pretty funny for a month or two but you can imagine that GARS got really strong without Ray there to fight it. I mean, it's true that by the time I got Ray off his ass and with the AK47 in his hands it was too late. Just too much to do, the world was lost, all lost and Archduke victorious. So one night when the last battles were reaching their end before utter defeat and Ray was sleeping I saved the game. I don't know—I mean, I guess I put him in a kind of sleep inside a sleep. One layer of sleep on top of another. I cannot really think about it straight.

Dude. I could go on and on and on and on abt all the saved games in that folder—like frozen versions, all the worlds from which the flow of Time has been stopped. All the versions of Ray. Of Rachel. Their lives. It's like a collection of discarded ifs. If they ended here or there or had gone to X instead of Y or Z instead of whatever. It's like too much to calculate and I get thinking about my life also—like diff directions that it might have taken—if I hadn't moved to this city when I was looking for something— like if I had moved somewhere else. Or if I hadn't met Tory at the party that was organized by Michelle. Or whatever. It all can be so different. DON'T worry, I won't get too philosophical. Also. I have to start thinking seriously about what Ray *is* anyway. OR who Rachel is. Not like Ray in any one version of the game—or any one of Rachel—but in all the possibilities? And not just like these versions of them that are filling HAL til there is no freakin room to move there—I mean all the many many others on so many other C drives all over the world. Ray or Rachel are maybe not so much people as they are kind of containers, each one of them an assembly of some possible, an interlocking dream that many other people are having. OK. It's starting to get TOO philosophical. I'll stop it there.

*

I'm thinking about Brainiac. Like very simple—where is he now?

*

And now I'm gonna delete all those saved games and empty the Trash.

I say: Empty Trash.

HAL says: The Trash contains 42 items which take up 13.5gb of space. Are you sure you want to empty the Trash?

I say: Yes—Empty the Trash.

The disk in the C drive spins. And in those saved games the word starts to dissolve, in an instant, pixel by pixel, superrapid, very fast. Space and time ebbs away and breaks into shredded pieces, until nothing is left, no Ray, no Rachel, nothing—or just like this—in those saved games time stops again in different and terrible ways.

Tory left a msg that she cannot make the neutral coffee Friday coz "something came up." SO that is clear at least. She has other priorities now.

THE WASTEland/DIScovery

Now I can go back to where I WAS before all the *Hard Drive Melodramas*. No time to waste.

DECISION AT TRAIN STATION/FOUNTAINS. GUIDE/GUIDED ROUTE. TAXATION PUZZLE. RISE OF THE ROBOTS II AND III. Clues concerning Rachel.

Ray & Lao Pi make a route through the city (73rd Town). If not go back to GO and do not collect 200 dollars. Ha ha.

From ruin of train station to ruin of church, left at ruin of High Rise. Collect Radiation shield.

Ruin of High Rise to scorched park, scorched park to ruin of baseball stadium. Ruin of baseball stadium to flooded subway station (need aqualung).

Fight first Robot.

Ruin of Natural History Museum (check out the dinosaur skeletons, dude, they're still intact) to ruin of gymnasium to ruin of Hilton Hotel.

Fight second Robot.

Ruin of Hilton Hotel to ruin of Ibis Hotel to ruin of Sheraton Hotel to ruin of Holiday Inn to ruin of Best North Western Hotel. Collect Signal Flares.

Fight third Robot.

Ruin of Cathedral to ruin of Mosque. Ruin of Mosque to ruin of McDonalds to ruin of KFC. (It's funny, dude—I mean, all that war and in the end no one wins—it is ALL fucking ruins.)

Fight fourth Robot.

There's more. 12 Robots in all need to be defeated and then you can get out of town.

*

OK. OK. Now the shit has REALLY started to hit the fan and it's headed back across the room and it is really gonna blow me right out the door. Maybe you can remember what I wrote before about Me and Ashton making up names for Branimir and Miroslav etc—i.e. that writing all kinds of stupid abuse about them didn't really matter coz B&M don't use computers and would NEVER read this walkthrough.

Turns out that was a little bit way tooooo optimistic. I dunno exactly the sequence of events, but apparently some fucking nephew of theirs with an Internet connection thought of the brilliant idea of googling Domenico's. I don't know exactly how it happened, but B&M have now read everything I ever wrote about them here. They read it. They read it all—Everything. And it's pretty clear that they won't be able to take a joke. Oh man. Those two have such a glitch in the sense-of-humor department.

Ashton called to warn me. Now I'm just waiting to see if they'll phone to dismiss me or if the sadist in Branimir won't bring me in and do it there to make a example of me in front of the others. Anyhow. I think the final outcome is not in doubt one way or the other. It's probably enough to say that if Tory were still here she'd already be doing a calculation on how much money I have coming in and abt the bills and the back rent still owing on the apt and loan repayments and everything—trying to make a budget plan for us to survive. But I'm not Tory and I don't have a highscore in the stuff she Excels in. I think I'm more that kind of person with the special Skill to shrug and think "Oh no. The shit is getting so deep it's gonna be right over the level of the fan pretty soon."

*

On the edge of 73rd you reach a large radioactive wasteland. It looks a bit like my life is gonna look soon. Ha ha. Use the Geiger counter to find a way thru the maze of radiation pits and burning nuclear fires. Watch out for the Terrible Creature—I don't know the name of it—that you and Lao Pi must fight together, using combination attacks. I wouldn't like to meet the people that wrote and coded monsters for The Broken World—no offense intended but I think that would take a sick imagination.

Eventually you come to a crossroads by a single burned out farm building and here, once again, you must say farewell to Lao Pi. Like he says to Ray: "Each person must follow his own battles, the road will call us by name and we may only answer with a yes . . . "

With a successful exit from 73rd town and Lao Pi gone, Ray has to focus on one thing—finding Rachel. Strange the feeling that comes with this, like a free gift in the cereal packet you didn't ask for—Ray doesn't know what happened to Rachel of course, but you know it, saw it, watched her die. And now your job is steer Ray into Hell.

*

The landscape begins to get more normal and the Geiger counter calms down. Freaky plants start to appear in the ground which you can eat for Nutrition, the earth becomes less cracked, which means you can sometimes dig it for water. Finally you come to a security fence—high wire and concrete supports. Find a hole in this (or cut a new one using Cutters from Items) and you have succeeded in exiting the Nuclear Wastelands. A mile or more along the eastward track you come to the first in a series of small settlements (74th–78th Town) populated by an assortment of losers that mainly live by running salvage missions into the wasteland, then selling the radioactive and dangerous proceeds to suckers further inland.

Head right to the center of the THIRD settlement and look for a salvage operation called Big Joe's. Big Joe turns out to be a small Dude called Frank. I don't know why they make the game so confusing. Maybe there is a reason for it. Do NOT bother with the other settlements (cannibals). Trade Potions from the Colony with Small Frank and he will help you by providing a pre-owned (i.e. highly radioactive) Jeep and the name of the towns you have to go next. It's one piece at a time, one jigsaw fragment, one clue.

Take the jeep then hit the road.

*

I would like to know what the fuck is going on at D's now. Like what's Ashton saying to Stentson 2.0 and what's Branimir saying to Miroslav? Are they busy or not? Is Miroslav standing right by the phone and looking up at the wall where they pinned the list of everyone's numbers in different handwriting with various amendments because people got new phones or left or got fired or Miroslav didn't write the numbers clear enough in the first place? I mean, why doesn't he just call and get it The Fuck over with?

*

Thru the mountains you come to several towns. Most of them have some problem that Ray has to fix (a Monster, a criminal gang etc) but finally, at the end of a valley, you work yr way thru to another town, which in this case has no number. The town contains seven lonely and beautiful widows each of whom Ray must seduce in order to gain clues for the location of Rachel. It's a strange town, that much is for sure. The kinds of strategies and moves you have to use here are certainly different than the usual ones. I say no more than that. You'll know what to do.

I don't know if they do it like this just to make you feel bad deliberately—that in order to find Rachel you have to repeatedly betray her. I guess it could be coincidence. But effect is the same either way.

The widows are beautiful and with the seduction of each of them (Mrs A, Mrs B, Mrs F, Mrs I, Mrs K, Mrs M, Mrs O) Ray gets a part of the map that will lead him to the Far Lands. NOTE: The town will be scandalized by the arrival of Ray—a stranger apparently hell-bent on seducing ALL of its despairing rich lonely and attractive women. Way to go, bro.

Obviously there are various enemies that will try to stop you in completion of this task—the local priest and magistrate plus assorted do-gooders of the town and jealous old spinsters etc. Try to be discreet—it's not easy—it's a pretty small town, and like Mrs O says to Ray more than once when he visits her late at night "everyone knows everyone else's business round here, esp when it comes to matters of Grief and Desire." Go steady. You do NOT want to get drummed out of Town.

Only when all the widows have been seduced (IN alphabetical order) will Rachel's exact location be revealed to Ray. It's a mixed blessing, as they say—this is the info you have been searching for and you (Ray) NEED to complete the mission, but anyhow as a player you know already that what's waiting in the Far Lands is not so nice.

The last of the widows is a seriously HOT date, man. Jesus. Once you've slept with her a few times she will ask you to stay the night. In the morning when you wake in bed she will be up already, stood at the window, staring sadly out toward the Ocean. Ask her what's wrong, she'll tell you a story.

Apparently she lost her husband not long ago. He and his crew were sailing nearby. There was a terrible storm. They were headed home when they saw distress flares. There was an argument between her husband and the crew. The crew argued that it was most important to save their own skins. Her husband—a brave man with a good heart—said no, they had to go to the aid of whoever was shooting those flares, one blue, two yellow. They set off toward them—but as they got closer the sea got worse and they feared for their lives and again there was an argument about going in to help or turning back to safety. Later they capsized—they never reached the place where the flares were coming from—her husband died. Some other crew members survived.

Ironic is what Mrs O calls it. You can ask her what she means.

She will say that you are maybe the only person that can benefit from her husband's death. Ask her why.

She will hand you a piece of paper. It is the latitudes for the place where the Distress Signals were approximated to come from—the beach of the Island where Rachel died.

Take the paper. Mrs O will be doubled over by this point, crying in a soundless kind of way (it's not a defect with the sound. Just that empty retching kind of crying that doesn't make tears, like a guy with an empty stomach still cramping with the need to Vomit).

*

Some things missing here, sorry. Will try to come back.

*

And so it happens finally, as it must—that you as Ray step onto the shore of the lake where Rachel was before. Bad news hovering in the air. Horrible. Follow her footsteps as they meander up from the waterline and walk inland to the low concrete building that contains so much pain. Only now of course you are seeing all this for the second time—as Ray. Walk toward the building. Go to the door and open it. For you there's no surprise of course, but for Ray, trapped in the game, there's shock coming, and total heartbreak. Your task is to take him there, take him first to the edges of it and then to the very bottom of despair.

When you open the door to the bunker you lose control of the game and you watch it like a movie. They don't do this often in The BW—I mean, in some games they're ALWAYS stopping the action to show you a freaking movie, but not in *BW*. I guess the stop here is justified coz they want to make you really see what has happened. They want you (Ray) to truly weigh the consequence instead of just running and screaming and yelling with a gun and looking for Vengeance.

In the movie (scene) that unfolds, Ray looks down at Rachel's corpse and at the corpse of the anonymous kid. Ray looks down at the corpses, then staggers, sits, and weeps. Then he walks around. Pacing hard. Then he sits again. He looks at the walls of this dumb bunker/room that has become a morgue to his love. That is the start of the movie. It goes on a long time. They are stretching time here. It flows slowly. Irregular, continuous, and jagged, but in any case Terrible.

You're still not in control. It's way the fucking longest movie they do. Maybe the longest movie in any game—I guess Jo Bo might know that, or Scat. Cut scenes they call them. It's a cut scene alright—it cuts and cuts and cuts like a razor. Like they're teasing you—that what has happened is so bad, that this scene is so terrible, that for some time at least NOTHING can be done.

*

OK. SO now the call came already. And as of maybe 10 minutes ago I'm officially out of the human workforce. Branimir made a total vitriolic explanation/declaration down the phone like he was making an address to the Nation and in the background M was saying MOUTHFUCKER MOUTHFUCKER, which you know normally always makes me laugh but this time, oh fuck, this time I can't even raise up a smile.

On top of the fact that I don't have a job, they also owe maybe one week of back pay including three double/triple shifts, and which now, because of what has happened, I will for sure never see. It didn't seem to matter that I made with the apologetic tone and said sorry sorry and that the stuff I wrote in the walkthrough here was just Freedom of Speech—M&B were like two angry dogs barking at the sun when the heat is hot in summertime and they're trapped in a car, i.e. they weren't happy at all. I was a lamb to the slaughter. When I even mentioned the back pay Branimir just yelled that I am (according to him at least) liable for "theft of time" and "theft of Domenico's time" (is that a separate offense?) and threatening that they'll bring legal action. Doesn't seem likely, probably just a kind of warning/major incentive not to take the claim for wages too far.

*

After sitting there a long time by the corpse of Rachel just weeping and weeping, Ray finally starts to speak. Weird. Ray doesn't say too much normally, and his speech isn't very important. He says stuff like "GET DOWN, FOOL!" or "I AM back!" But here, in that concrete building, Ray does speak. The words come tumbling out, but they don't make much sense. It's the same kind of half-finished and incomprehensible sentence that Dieter's mom was sniveling when we went to see her, or the same kind of sad sad and circular stuff that Grieving Chelsea said to Tory when she was in that bar. I.e.—just a lot of words. As Ray speaks he seems less a Hero, more like just another ordinary, weak, fucked-up, downhearted, and broken person.

*

When you get back control of the game, Ray is still sat by Rachel's corpse. He needs to avenge her. He needs to kill whoever did this.

That's the new Mission. You don't need me to tell you that. But how to find out?

There's a method, but it's not nice. You won't like it, I promise that—they were cruel when they made this part.

Fuck. But like the kids say in 15th Town—the way forward is the way forward.

*

Cut out Rachel's eyes.

Also cut out the eyes of the kid she died with. Use the Scalpel from Items or if u did not collect it (from some Clinic, I don't remember where) there's a knife there somewhere, down among the rubble on the floor.

You need to do this. There's no other way.

Put the eyes in a jar (also from Items) and store it safe. Head out of the bunker. Don't look back.

*

Tory could never stand to watch me play this part. I guess it doesn't take a genius of psychology to figure out why.

I was thinking of calling her and twice times even had the phone in my hand. I meant to see if we could maybe figure out another date for the Neutral Coffee and to talk to her about the rent. ALSO I keep thinking that I should let her know how things stand with Brainiac i.e. there's still no concrete news except that people (BugMap's sister, Sleeptalk even) claim they saw him somewhere but they couldn't be sure (like in a crowded bar or across the street when they were on a bike). Just false sightings. Like people seeing UFOs coz they want to believe.

I've walked past B's place a few times lately—always no lights and nobody home. Last night when I passed by I saw the teenage kid from downstairs, the defective one built like a shotputter or something, and he was carrying the shopping into the house for his mom, and in one hand he held a red balloon that said SUPPORTING THE TOOPS. Surely it should've said TROOPS. Or maybe the TOOPS are something I don't know about—from the News or Internet or something, like the TOOPS are fighting a big Law case or fighting Corporate Libels. I'm out of touch. I don't know if the TOOPS are something real or just a spelling error. There was no one at Brainiac's, just the fucked-up kid. That's all I needed to say. I didn't call Tory. Maybe I'll get around to it sometime, but not now. Not tonight.

*

Wash your hands in the water at the edge of the misty lake—traveling with blood on your hands attracts these horrible winged creatures that you do not want to fight. FIND the boat where Rachel left it. Solve Navigation Puzzle using homemade compass made from floating needle and cork. Set sail for the mainland, away from these terrible islands. Steer S by SW.

*

One thing got clearer though. I guess the best tense for Tory came out just then without me thinking. She is slipping into the past.

*

Cross the lake. In the town you land at (19th), at the shore there's a small photography place—a studio and shop. In the window—wedding pictures, baby pictures, school pictures—all big smiles and stiff backs.

Use fake ID prove that you are FBI and tell the photographer that "you need to use his equipment for a couple of hours. No questions asked." The guy will then show you to a crude darkroom. Wait until he's gone, then lock and BARRICADE the doors. Listen: you don't want company in what comes next, or you will end your days paying dues in a hicktown Broken World jail. Life meaning life.

*

A text message from Ashton. "I AM SO SORRY BRO." What is it with Ashton that he can make even a text message sound gay.

*

Take the eyes from the jar. It's a hard thing to handle these eyes—those of a stranger and those of someone you loved. The eyes don't sparkle with light anymore now that they are dead and cut out. They are more like holes or wounds. Dead spaces. I cannot describe it. Or maybe I don't even want to. I mean—if I write it gets more real. Fuck it. So much for my watcher skills and writing-it-all-down skills. Hard to think that there, on the plastic-topped table in this makeshift darkroom, are the eyes that Ray once stared into, once fell into.

Put the eyes on the table. Take scalpel (or knife) from Items.

Flip the lights to the safe red.

Cut out the retinas.

Take each of the retinas (one by one) over to the photographic enlarger (that's the weird-looking tall thing with a lens that shines down on the flat table below). Place each of the retinas (again, one by one) in the tray of the enlarger—the tray that's supposed to hold negatives.

*

There is apparently a theory—thought up by lunatics, or witches, or scientists, or worse—that the retina of a human being will preserve the image of the last thing they saw before death. Like the eyes take a final Polaroid of the world.

In this case you want to "develop" those pictures from the retinas of Rachel and the anonymous kid. Light from the enlarger shines down thru the retina making an image on the board underneath. Focus the image. You won't be able to make it out clearly—the image in negative—but you can still see if it's sharp or not. When you think it's sharp turn off the enlarger. Place one sheet of photographic paper on the board. (You can find the paper in a box on one of the shelves.) Then turn the enlarger on again for 18 seconds. Take the paper to the red tray and place it in. Agitate the tray (rocking bwd and fwd) for 1 minute. And then a picture will slowly emerge. When the whole picture has come up take the paper out—place it in the yellow tray (30 seconds), then in the white tray (2 mins). Then the image is fixed. Repeat the process with each of the retinas.

*

The pictures will show you the clue. But be warned—when you see it you won't be too happy. Not many laughs around here.

The kid's eyes are useless—they don't show the killer, they just show clouds on a empty sky. Just some dumb unlucky dead kid. Doesn't matter. Just a kid whose eyes were fixed on the blue sky and those picture-book clouds at the exact moment she was dying. That's all.

But Rachel's eyes do show something. Someone in fact. A killer with dead eyes and gun raised. There will be something familiar abt the face of the killer tho. It is Ray. Your own face. Ray.

I guess it wasn't just a dream back there when Rachel dreamed Ray was killing her again and again and again and again.

The TIME Grenade

Of course even as the image of the killer is revealed at that terrible scene (Rachel dead) you will know straightaway that you (Ray) did NOT do this terrible thing. It's impossible, right? Ray didn't do that. I mean, not in real. Not with intent. Maybe it was a double (?) or an impostor (I don't think so)—that's certainly a theory some people are happy to chase. Clockwork said maybe Ray was hypnotized by Archduke against his will? Or somehow they got to him with messages secreted thru the Neural Tubes in cryogenic freezing on board the *spaceship*? Or Ray was forcibly cloned? OK, there's no scene or evidence that shows him actually getting turned into a mindless puppet of Chang or GovCorp, but maybe they have also destroyed a part of Ray's memory? Maybe GovCorp persuaded Ray that

Rachel is a traitor? Maybe she IS a traitor? That's what some people claim and there's like ten thousand words on blogs and other stuff devoted to all this and still no matter how you look at it one thing is CERTAIN. Ray has to figure this out Big Time and fast. Murdering the woman you love more than life itself sucks ass—this time it's Personal. If Ray were a coward you could make him give up now, but Ray is no coward.

Take a gd look at the photo of evidence again if you're having trouble processing all this. Ray with the gun, looking blurred with madness in his eyes = last thing that Rachel ever saw.

*

Later.

With no Domenico's shifts to break up the days and no Tory to make arrangements with, my life is just a big lump of hours I cannot make sense of or organize. Like I'm drifting on a sea that's not moving, in a breeze that hardly exists.

For about four days the mails from DrunkenApe stopped coming and I was starting to think he or she or it either found another project, or got moved to a more secure Unit and had email privileges revoked. Anyway. Then just now, 13 more mails came in one go and each one is longer and longer and even the Sender names are getting more and more messed up/hardcore. FukUDrillerKiller? Cuba Exonerate Saucer Eyes? I don't get it. Plus I'm really not gonna get freaked or lose sleep about crazy and unsubstantial threats against my person. No way.

I kept thinking that someone was trying to break into the apartment because of noises outside so I went out for a walk in the neighborhood instead. I looked in some bars and cafés to see if anyone is looking for skilled food workers like me. I'm an optimist. I can face a challenge.

*

But fuck it, I'm just distracting myself with this now—distracting myself from the murder of Rachel. Maybe one of the toughest parts of *The Broken World*. I mean here's a big philosophical question about Rachel's death. Man, I should have saved this for Joe.

Q: How can you stop something that has already happened?
A: It's impossible.

Let's have that one more time.

Q: How can you stop something that has already happened?
A: It's impossible.

NOTE: Don't worry. This walkthrough will get you all the way and EVERY time.

*

Ashton mailed with Domenico's gossip for today including the fact that Cookie (dayshift) totally lost her freaking temper with Miroslav again (over something like an aspect of the cleaning rotation) and basically resigned. She quit. Way to go.

The results of the first month's D Star assessment scheme looms, but it seems not everyone is going to make it that far. Bro, they got a new Cookie right away, who Ashton calls Cookie 2.0. Already. I guess soon the whole staff will be 2.0 or later series. Maybe they have a replacement for me there also, but Ashton wants to protect me from that. Or maybe Miroslav figured out they don't want a 2.0 of me. The 1.0 was more than enough and didn't really work.

*

OK. Here's my good advice. I will tell it quickly and deal with questions later:

1. First take the boat back to the island and the concrete building that you don't want to remember and probably cannot forget.

2. Throw a Time Grenade at Rachel's corpse. (I hope you saved one. There is no other way.)

3. Go back in time to where you (Ray) are going to kill her. It takes some trial and error to find the right scene. Be careful that you don't get NOTICED and when you get there immediately jump the Ray that is abt to kill her and tie him up (the other Ray) securely in a cupboard.

NOTE: Try not to let this other Ray see who you are—he'll just get angry and confused if he thinks that some dude that looks exactly the same as him is preventing him from success in his murder plans. ANOTHER NOTE: If you do get confronted there is no point in trying to reason with the Ray from the past—deal with him in silence because that will minimize the risk of time-contamination. Also be careful not to kill or injure this Ray—he is YOU but from the past and ANY damage you do to him will end up as damage to yourself. One time I got trigger-happy in this part and SHOT the past Ray in the shoulder. Man. We both got wounded. Freak-y.

4. When you're ready—and only then—stand outside the cupboard and throw a SECOND Time Grenade. (I hope you saved two of the grenades.)

Second grenade will take you back in time to an even earlier scene where another Ray is apparently being hypnotized and drugged by some agent of GARS, i.e. a "secret scene" as was suggested before. Your arrival will for sure interrupt the hypnotism, and then all you have to do is kill the guy who is doing it. Easy. I think he's called Norriss? Check how confused that Norriss MFKR looks when he is bending down to put the hypnotizing chloroforms over Ray's nose and mouth and then you (Ray from the future) come jumping out the doorway to attack him. Ha ha.

When you have done what you need to do with Norriss then take that other Ray back to his motel room (?) and try to get him to lie down. Everything will be alright. If he acts tricky just SEDATE him rapidly (use morphine or a solution of Sevoflurane which is a halogenated ether from Items) and tie him to the bed. You just need to get him out of the way and plz cause no trouble for an hour or two—you cannot make a good solution to the game if there are lots of Rays running about everywhere thru the vistas (?) of time all with their own confusing agendas.

*

I'm just taking a break to check that you are with me. I know this is confusing but you just have to concentrate for a while longer.

*

5. When you have dealt with the two Rays in the past it's time to take some Time Grenade antidote (hopefully you have some in Items. Otherwise you are trapped in the past). This part is complicated—do not fuck it up. Go FORWARD—using antidote—to the scene where the other Ray is locked in the cupboard and try to check up on him. See what happened? It's way cool—if things have all gone according to plan YOU WILL FIND THAT THE RAY THERE IN THE CUPBOARD IS GONE (i.e. he will not be there).

FAQ number one: Why will Ray not be there?

A: Because you have been back in time, asshole, and you have undone the hypnotism that supposedly took place before—therefore Ray was never hypnotized, therefore he never even went there to try and kill Rachel.

6. Wait in the room/bunker. Ten minutes later Rachel should arrive. Safe. You have found her—Ray and Rachel are reunited. This part is completed.

*

NOTE: Time Travel is dangerous, bro. Do not try it at home. You cannot mess with time.

*

Ashton just called, laughing so much having just ended his shift for the day. He said that Branimir and Miroslav assembled the whole shrinking team of Domenico's workers together in the yard out back just to explain the first month's scores in so-called D Star Assessment. Before the official results could be pronounced the Brothers Grim narrated the story of my sacking but made it seem like a big Warning concerning investigations and "regrettable blogs" on the Internet Web. Yes. It was only thanks to Miroslav's cyberdetective investigative bastard nephew and his brilliant skillful use of what Branimir called "the Google" that I was trapped down and justice meated out. Ha ha. If you google Domenico's this walkthrough ranks maybe ninth—it's not like his nephew joined *New Psychic Cops*.

Anyhow. When it came to the D Star results the whole thing was a farce of Justice in which Ashton (yes that same Ashton who is the Gay Slacker and who is frightened of the ovens) was crowned with the title Employee of the Month and whose efforts are now PROMOTED and rewarded with extra pay. He couldn't wait to tell me that, that's for sure. I cannot FREAKING WELL believe it.

Apparently Branimir made a certificate in Word complete with many typefaces, logos and icons—totally ridiculous—and they hung it on the wall near the swimsuit calendar. I guess for sure that THAT is the closest to Andrea Veresova that Ashton wants to get. Man, anything like that would be wasted on him—he would just try to swap pedicure tips.

*

Long silence when Ray and Rachel are reunited. Like neither of them can really believe that there on that terrible island is where it takes place. Check Ray's pulse in the health stats—like it hits 100 and stays there while he looks at her.

"Are you OK?"

"Yes," she says. "I got the code. The Replicant Code. I got it all memorized."

And Ray says, "OK."

But of course Rachel doesn't know what happened, cannot know a thing about the future that you (Ray) have anyhow prevented from taking place. Rachel looks at Ray, you looking back at her. I mean, I guess there's something pretty fucked up about the experience of once having BEEN Rachel and now she's right there in front of you . . . And now you are watching her and wondering if she seems the same she as she used to be when you were her. I don't know, it's a kind of mindfuck thing.

*

Something related, from 2nite, in that way the game can sometimes seem synced up with the world.

I went to buy milk/bagels/beer and I wanted the walk so headed to the far store—which is in anycase always cheaper than the near store. I had paid and was leaving already, just picking up the bags, and then I looked up and saw Tory next to soap, shampoos, and dental stuff, reaching for a box of something, maybe tissues. I guess I didn't really take it in what she was reaching for, I was in a panic, heart beating etc.

Like I was staring at her—watching her—but in those few seconds it was already more than watching. I was thinking (more like flashing across the topic at superhigh speed like a Japanese train but not in one direction)—thinking how could this person I was so connected to be there now, in front of me, like a few feet away, at the other side of the checkout, so TOTALLY unconnected, so separate. In a world without me. How could that be? I cannot explain it too well, it was just a kind of weird feeling for a moment and super superintense. To be so close and then not close at all. I watched her for a minute—maybe it was less—but she didn't see me. And then I left there just as quickly as I could.

 EATING a Meal Made of Words

It's time for an apology. Yesterday I wrote that long long explanation how Rachel can be resurrected from sudden death using the Time Grenade and "time flight potions" © and complicated plots involving various versions of Ray running backward and forward in time, and in and out of doorways. I swear on something important that this all worked for me before—I check everything in this walkthru a million times, maybe more. Ask Tory (before she left). But now I have major problems getting the same results again in this part. I had a proper chance to go back and check all this thru AGAIN and I admit that I cannot make it work. It's fucked up. I don't understand it, this worked for me before. I'm missing some step maybe. Several times I managed to get Ray all the way thru the procedure with the time grenade and the brainwashing and then get Ray back there etc, but then the Ray from the past captures or overpowers him (i.e. me, the Ray from the present) and ties HIM (me) up somehow and I lose control of the game. It's a freaking disaster. Several times I got thru the whole thing and got Rachel to the point where she did "survive" long enough to enter the room/bunker, and at first I thought OK good now I have the solution working again, just like it did before, but then she suddenly collapses and passes away again in a gray-looking heap and whispers to Ray how "You cannot mess with time." I DEFINITELY got sick to the stomach of that phrase in all the many times I heard it this morning.

All I can do is apologize. I mean, it's no use pretending something that's not true. It may be some fluke how it seemed to work before but for sure it doesn't work now. Must be a detail that I missed. The only honorable thing is to admit the mistake and to publish it here so that's what I'm doing. I take full responsibility. I DO NOT know any reliable solution to that part of the game and right now ANY WAY I play it AT ALL Rachel ends up dead. I'll do some research on the different blogs and see how other people solve this part. Maybe Grinning Cat has different solutions, or Miss Kittin or Helium. Apologies again.

*

Another note on the Kitchen table from Rolo. Now he's apparently wondering how it's gonna work with the rent now he gathers Tory moved out. He's such a stoner that this only now occurs to him. Jesus. He hopes I'm not counting on him, that we're gonna maybe just split it between the two of us, because he's not making that much right now etc etc so what are we gonna do?

It's a good question, but not exactly what I want to be thinking about now.

*

Four weeks to the day that Brainiac vanished.

Nearly five since Dieter died.

And just more than three since Tory left.

How much am I loving these anniversaries? I think you know the answer without me telling it.

When Brainiac first skipped out I would still sometimes call him, by accident, like somehow without thinking I'd press his number in the cell and only then remember that he wasn't around (whatever that means). Back then his number was still live, and you could still hear him on there saying "I'm not picking up—so if you got something to say, better say it now" (which was always his message, ever since I've known him). But like what freaking message do you leave when a person goes missing? "Er, hi, Brainiac. What's up?" It's ridiculous.

These days I never call him by mistake—I guess it's pretty fixed in my mind that he's gone. But sometimes I do still call him like I'm going to call him now, even tho I know already that there'll be no answer. I call mostly at night, like this, just to mark that I'm thinking of him. The phone is ringing now. Ring, ring, ring. No answer of course. A week or so back they closed up the phone account or the credit ran out or the Airtime Agreement or whatever got terminated and you cannot even hear him talking anymore—so after a time there's just a dead space/dead sound at the other end. That's what I'm listening to now. On the speakerphone. Just nothing at all.

I mean, the cops more or less told B's brother Paul and the rest of the family that there's no more they can do. The credit card is not getting used and there's no trace. They haven't gone for the posters at the subway tollbooths yet but they tried ALL THAT other stuff that cops do, talked to people, followed LEADS—just like in *Virtual Precinct 9*. No sign of him.

*

When I look out the window at this moment it just looks like shit in this city. It's just like they say in a movie—people are too busy running about anywhere they don't take time for another person. Plus the weather is exhausting and the air has that feeling I think it's maybe going to storm. There was a freaking flood unleashed already anyway of abusive emails concerning my Time Grenade Solution. Yeah, very funny BigBalls, HitlersBrother and all the rest—I put in big hours of hard work and countless vital solutions and then make one mistake that I admit straightaway and suddenly everyone wants to be the one that takes turns in kicking me. It's a feeding frenzy of nasty sarcasm (like Branimir said once, back in the day, about the attitude of Stentson 1.0), and some people suggesting that maybe I should get in a Time Grenade and go back to the point where I was just about to write all of that and quickly lock the me that's in the past into a cupboard sedated. OK, people, yes. I admitted already that I made a mistake—what more do you want? I'm eating my WORDS.

*

Still drunk and a taste of jalapeños.

Venter and Sleeptalk came round to take me out of my misery via beer and in a long story involving several locations we all sat playing *BW* til the early hours. When they first even arrived at my place Sleeptalk was already a bit drunk with dirt on his Converse and jeans where he had been hanging out at some bands/minifestival thing all afternoon at the park. There was no food in the apt here (like I said, the times are hard) so first we went over to BugMap's with a view to raiding his freezer, but he wasn't there so we ended up with some tacos at Venter's and we were playing *BW*. It was late and we were fooling around. Sleeptalk was playing Ray like a drunk—picking fights with very nasty-looking strangers for no reason in towns of no importance and getting Ray beat up pretty bad, heading off on totally futile missions into hostile GARS territory where he was guaranteed to lose health points if not worse. Then BugMap took over (he called and came by when he heard there were tacos involved, but again he seemed in a weird mood and wasn't so communicative). I was like Hi and he was like Er yeah Hi but then he broke off talking. What's his problem? On the game he was having Rachel play chicken in the traffic on an esp busy freeway near 63rd town and all these guys were leaning out the windows and yelling at her to get the freaking hell out of the way. And then Sleeptalk took over the controls again and he was mumbling to some extent and telling this long story about a place in some town where Ray could catch this really disgusting disease and how he was going to show us but it kept being the wrong town, or the wrong place in the right town, I don't know, not infectious enough or something—anyhow people were kind of losing interest like they do when you play the game like that to kind of destroy it or not take it seriously—I mean play it to lose, I guess, or just cause random destructions of Ray or Rachel. Like if you're just fooling around and you get Ray so drunk that he'll crawl along in a gutter of his own piss stains, or you get him sick for no reason and admitted to the "Poor Hospital" or you get him deliberately possessed by Demons from the crypt of a church. It's a blast for a while but the fun of it kind of wears off for some reason.

As Sleeptalk played on without caring who else was interested he was also on his cell phone a lot of the time trying to get some crystal meth off this guy and I was pretty drunk too because I was saying "yeah yeah I would be up for some crystal" which is ridiculous because I hate that stuff and otherwise yelling at Venter to put on the new Dominion tracks really loud until the neighbors were complaining.

After all the playing to lose and getting Ray and Rachel in all kinds of stupid situations and after all the complaints from the neighbors got so vocalized that they had to be taken more serious, there was some more talk about my Time Travel solution. (Give it a rest please, people.) So at maybe 2am there was a big argument about the best way to proceed in the game beyond this point with Rachel dead. Everyone has his favorite route and his favorite theory.

This guy Rick (I hardly know him) was saying that it's best to go into 12th town and get the suitcase of Zorda Embryos, kill McSham, then go to Swamp Town and wait for the attack of the various Swamp Monsters etc. BugMap was saying no, it's best to head to 119th Town and get the Ring of Power, use that to force a Recount in the disputed elections then form an alliance with someone (Lao Pi again?) to fight against the Vampires that are terrorizing the Midwest which (in turn) will bring you closer to the total defeat of GARS (he couldn't explain exactly how). Then this guy Venice (he was just hanging out at Venter's for no reason so far as I could understand it) he wasn't talking about the game at first he was talking about Tattoos but then he tuned in to the conversation and started saying that the most important thing was just to forget the death of Rachel and head off to do the big Magnetic Puzzle (54th Town) and then afterward do Time Traveler Diversion (#1): Fall of

Rome and Time Traveler Diversion (#2): Revenge of the Dinosaurs, then head off to some swamp I never went to. I mean, half the stuff people were talking about I never even heard of it or never went to those places and the stuff from the Venice guy esp was making me feel really stupid like I hardly know anything. Or like I was playing a different game this whole time. The game is so big and just when you think you know it all you realize that you've hardly touched the freaking top of the iceberg. It was all this level and that other level and I had no clue. By the end Venter was totally drunk (I mean even more than normal) and he was saying WHAT YOU NEED IS BIGGER WEAPONS, WHAT YOU NEED IS BIGGER WEAPONS, WHAT YOU NEED IS BIGGER WEAPONS until later a piece of innocent fooling around with stepladders and a watermelon in the kitchen that he BugMap were doing ended in a accident with the light itself getting broken and glass everywhere and he (Venter) had to go to ER. (It wasn't broken, they said it was just a sprain.)

*

I went with Venter in the cab to ER. I mean, someone had to go with him, WHAT YOU NEED IS BIGGER WEAPONS is not a good line to yell at a cab driver when he arrives.

Anyway. In the cab Venter was still drunk but somehow not saying much and I was just talking again to fill the air and to take his mind off the Pain. I was telling the latest on DeadHead80 and BodyCounter and the various abusive emails and how I wasn't freaking out about it, and how it took more than that to threaten me even if this person was constantly reporting that they knew where I lived etc. And Venter was kind of leaned with his head on the glass, I couldn't tell if he was passed out with the drink or the suffering or if he was just looking out the window. Anyway. I couldn't even tell if he was listening but when I finished he kind of turned his head more toward me, but still leaning against the glass, and had this expression on his face that looked like a "?"—I mean, just a question mark kind of look, I don't know what to call it and he said: "Bro, you know that shit is just BugMap messing with your mind," and I didn't know if I'd heard him straight but then he looked at me like "yeah" and I was like WTF, exploding in the taxi and started to cry, I think it was the drink, and I was yelling and demanding that Venter say more and at first he didn't want to but then he told me how it started with Dieter and BugMap and how they were just trying to yank at my chains about the walkthrough and then it got kind of out of hand and wasn't that funny anyway and then shortly after they started Dieter died and BugMap kind of carried on even though the joke was really kind of lost and he felt bad but he was always waiting for it to get to a good place of TOTAL ridiculousness and then tell me like on some dumbass Pranker show where they play the pranks on celebrities and use those hidden cameras to show the reaction when the Cops have neutered and impounded their Pit Bulls or when a errant construction guy has filled their (the celebrities) swimming pool with a truckload of steaming Horseshit. But apparently the moment didn't come. BugMap could see it wasn't funny but he was waiting and waiting and felt it was kind of impossible to stop until an appropriate Climax was reached. Like what did he want—that I impale myself on a bread knife? Or enter a Lunatic Aslyum? And then was he going to wait for Visiting Hours and get an appointment and sit across the glass from me where I would be all tied up with a straitjacket with my arms restrained behind my back and tell me IT WAS ALL A FREAKING JOKE?

That's what Venter told me when we were in the cab to ER and afterward he didn't say anything else about it and they bandaged up his foot and told him to take it easy. That is all.

Fuck. I guess anyone else would have spotted it by now, but I just took it like a sucker. Fuck. Apparently BugMap is feeling really bad about it (thanks, bro) and cannot even bear to be in the same room as me when I'm talking about the thing and the way Venter tells it it's like HE (BugMap) is the one you have to feel sorry for—like starting the project to torment me humorously with Dieter and then Dieter getting trashed and him feeling somehow like he should carry on—maybe as a TRIBUTE to Dieter?? WTF. Asshole. I don't think I can even be angry about it. I'm too tired and stressed. I started looking at all the old emails again and trying to see if there were like clues on the identity, but that's a freakin waste of time.

*

Bro, I'm not sure I can keep on with this walkthrough. Maybe that's just the time of night and the total dehydration talking, but I don't know. I think this may be the end of the road for all this. It's too much after this with BugMap and all that stuff with the Time Grenades and all. I'm too miserable about Tory also. I cannot continue. I forgot to say that Quitter is also one of my skills. Like when they're picking a mission they say hey yeah let's get that guy coz we can count on him to totally bail on the whole thing when it gets to the first freaking sign of difficulty.

*

Another thing. I don't really think Brainiac is dead. But I do think for sure sure sure by now that he's not gonna be found. Like I said, he can be so thorough, inventive/meticulous. Those are skills that really belong to him. I think if he wants to vanish he can do it. In the last week a few people still thought they saw him—the brother of Venter supposedly saw him in the distance, and Sleeptalk maybe saw him "on a bus" etc—I even thought I saw him myself in a crowd near the Markets. But to me these "sightings" are more like proof that he's NOT there than they are a suggestion he's ever gonna be found. Proof that he's passing over to the Zone of a fantasy, not even a real person anymore, something more like the UFOs I mentioned or like Elvis where ppl see him sometimes as a face on the planet Mars, or at a truck stop in Wisconsin.

Yeah. Brainiac at a Subway in Lowshore, but when Sleeptalk got over the street he was gone. Brainiac at the Ferry Terminal as spotted by someone or other that knows Venter. But it wasn't Brainiac, just some guy that looked like him. Brainiac in a Crowd at the football game and Clockwork supposedly glimpsed him there in the background on TV which is so fucking obviously BS. I.e. I'm sorry, Clockwork, but I cannot think of another person on the whole of the Earth that is not interested in Football as much as Brainiac is not interested in it. You think he went into hiding from his whole life just so he can start watching football? No.

I mean, Face It, he just wanted to go, get gone, disappear. That can happen in a life, I believe that's true. That it all stacks to a certain point and then like in one instant the only way out is by a previously invisible exit.

Like out thru a door, going to the EL.

# MORE abouT LAST NIGht

I was just sitting there at Venter's, listening to the various people, all the various theories, and just thinking too much. Meanwhile someone (it must have been Clockwork coz he stayed out of the other discussion) was trying to drag the whole thing bkwd and suggesting ways to avoid Rachel getting killed in the first freaking place—like by stopping her from going to the Island (she needs the Replicant Code, dumbass) or by Antidotes, Voodoo, and Potions to prevent Ray from ever becoming a mindless hypnoassassin. But I mean, I don't think that any of this is any kind of realistical solution. For me it seems Rachel is dead for good. I mean, that's how it is in the RW, just ask Dieter. Why should Rachel get more shots at it just coz she's in a freakin computer game?

About the walkthrough. I need some time to think about it, bro. I really don't want this to turn out like that old cartoon thing you see sometimes with the sword swallower where the guy is straining in an awkward posture in front of the TV and he has a sword all the way down his throat and the guy on the TV with like a big smile on his face has a speech bubble that says "And on next week's program we show you how to get the sword OUT again . . . " No—I don't want to leave it like that here but I need some time to think, that's for sure. My Quitter skills are coming thru on top.

*

Tory called. I guess to say sorry about blowing out the coffee gig the other day and also about Brainiac—since the various dumbass stories concerning people seeing him on the opposite side of a subway platform only now he has a beard etc are reaching her too and she wanted to check if any of that was true. But it also seemed like she was just using those topics for a reason to call coz she was asking how I was and I was confused. I mean—no real contact for so long and then suddenly calling. Plus I had that picture of her in my head, from the supermarket, near the checkout three nights ago. Like I have this secret knowledge of her that she doesn't know about.

*

I try to get on—if only for distraction purposes.
Even if you cannot resurrect Rachel for very long, bro, you still have to bring her back because you NEED her to pass on the Replicant Code.

Here is my solution. It's not pretty but it works and I checked it 3 times and it still works, and I don't think I can get further any other way no matter what anyone else proposes, drunk or sober. SO here goes. Get Rachel back to life with the time grenades etc just like I wrote before. Watch her eyes fill with Joy when she sees Ray again etc and then watch as she mysteriously collapses. Yes. Yes. I know it. YOU CANNOT MESS WITH TIME. Then take her in your arms as she's dying and have her speak out the code to you, dying, but whispering all that stuff.

> *A yacht on a sea that has no horizon coz the sea is the same color as the sky.*
> *Grinning corpses.*
> *Iris flowers.*
> *Rusted metal.*
> 74885909999999923
> 237534
> Etc.

It would be kind of beautiful, if it wasn't so freaking tragic and if it didn't take such a terribly long time. Anyways. Ray needs the code and once he has it he has the key to victory and you can let Rachel die in peace without these endless incompetent resurrections. It took me maybe five times to get the whole code out of her, bringing her back and bringing her back and watching her die and die again and then it's all over for Rachel. It's sad to leave her there, a gray ghost on the floor in that bunker, but there are no points to be gained by burying the dead in war like this against GARS. Ray has work to do. It's not good to be pulled the whole time by things from the past. Rachel is the past now. Only war and fighting is the future.

*

When Tory called to say sorry about the no-show we were in the middle of talking and then suddenly she said she didn't realize the time, had to go, and hung up immediately. She was always pretty good in the skill of Mixed Messages but that is taking it to the MAX.

*

For some reason there are gray areas here in this part of the game. I can hardly remember some towns. There is definitely some kind of trick or Magic Mystery level. And something about a sea monster. Then 69th Town. And 93rd with some kind of language puzzle. I'll come back to it.

But after those towns (and ONLY if you already have the Replicant Code from Rachel) you must for sure go after the main guy in NESTADO—the one they call Dindara. How come the bad guys get such weird freakin names? I mean, they're never called Ross Johnson or something like that, but I don't want to pick holes in the game. Dindara has a hideout in the mountains above 212th Town. To get there pass thru Blue Town—defeat the Hit Men. Visit Science Class of Dr Molloy to maybe find a way to double Energy (I don't know—some players say that this works but it didn't for me. I'm being more cautious in what I write from now on).

When you get to Dindara's hideout it's surrounded by a supermagnetic pulse fence plus 4 twenty-foot-high regular fences topped with razor wire and in between is a series of no-man's-lands with land-mine hazards, tripwire traps, laser-beam deterrents and dog defenses. You get the impression that someone doesn't want visitors? Correct. I mean, some folk just put a sticker on the mailbox that says No Junk Mail Please, but that is clearly not enough in this case. Dindara LIKES HIS FREAKING PRIVACY.

At the pulse fence find all the Output Phase Units and rig an improvised/adapted Microwave cooker onto them using some kind of focusable Macrotransmitter that runs off a Lithium battery. NOTE: I DON'T understand the science, (that's Clockwork's department)—I'm JUST writing down WHAT he told me but HE MAY AS WELL HAVE BEEN TALKING French (capslock). Transmitter somehow blocks out the receptors on the OPUs (sending False Positives) which means 1) you can get thru the fence without getting fried and 2) detector system cannot notice when you cut and crawl thru.

After this you just have the land mine, tripwire, laser beam, and dog defenses to get past plus the 4 regular fences. Time to rack and roll (that's a lyric from Skeleton).

*

Another thing about the call from Tory is that she didn't really add any personal details. I mean, like if there's anyone else on the scene and what about that Postcard Guy? I don't feel like I should be the one asking these questions, but then if she doesn't say anything it all stays a mystery.

*

Once you are thru the fences into Dindara's Mansion watch out for his taekwondo-trained personal bodyguards Girl One and Girl Zero, otherwise known as the Binary Sisters and oh yes yes yes they are cute in those catsuits. Aside from the obvious bodyguard stuff I have put a lot of imagination into thinking what other services etc they might have to do for him or each other on all those long lonely nights in that hideout. ANyhoW (capslock). I try to CONTinUe (CApslOck fucking CAPsloCK). Clockwork says these chicks must've got their names from the Binary computer code (all ones and zeros, on and off, yes and no)—so even the biggest cleavage fest in The BW has an educational dimension.

Head thru the Sliding Door Puzzle, secret lab, and "experiments chamber", Puzzle of Sealed Doors, etc etc. Keep on moving upward in the Mansion until finally you get to Dindara's Operations Room—a huge astronomical observatory on the very top of his Residence and defeat the obstacles you find there. Then put Girl One and Girl Zero out of action and into the fish tanks full of Piranhas—I'm so sorry, that's the only way. Now you have reached the season's big pay-per-view attraction—fight night with Dindara.

He will be sitting there smiling when Ray walks in. At first sight he's just a defenseless nerdy-looking guy with glasses in a wheelchair, but don't be fooled. He's a raving lunatic with a rocket ship intended to blast off into space so he can start Mankind again but only once he has taken control of the Earth for natural resources and total slavery. Guess what?—your task is to put him out of Action. But check it out— if you reach for your gun you cannot get your freaking hand to go there, like a great weight is pressing down on Ray's limbs or some kind of paralyze potion is working on you. Soon Dindara is laughing and wheeling himself around like he is really fucking great or something, practically doing a wheelie he is so totally delighted and Ray is powerless to stop him.

*

Tory called back again, a bit incoherent. After a while I was starting to wonder if she was high or maybe had some really bad news to tell me and was debating how to do it and suffering doubts or cowardice or maybe her parents just had some bigass question that they couldn't wait for an answer and now they know the truth (that Tory has moved out) they are somehow too embarrassed to keep using me like an information line for retarded suburbanites and they wanted Tory to ask me instead. Or none of the above.

Anyway. Now it turns out (from the second phone call) she's "kind of in the neighborhood." I don't understand (i.e. 1) what "kind of" in the neighborhood is, and 2) what she's doing "here" anyway—she cannot be temping unless her agency went seriously down downmarket, and the Grieving Chelsea Person certainly doesn't live close by. ANYway, she said she was kind of in the neighborhood and I thought it was best if I didn't say too much to interrupt because she wasn't formulating too well. There was an awkward silence and I said maybe we should hang up because it seemed kind of weird. Then she was wondering if I want to have coffee, in an hour or so. So at that point I gave up trying to understand what was really going on and said OK. Whatever. We need to do it sometime. I don't care what happens, it's too messed up. I'll try to complete the parts with Dindara before she arrives.

*

I'll tell you in one sentence what otherwise takes a long time to find out in the game, i.e.—Dindara's secret is mental telepathy.

That's how come Ray cannot reach his gun and why he gets that double-glazed look in his eyes and cannot press the trigger of the Laser Grenade. Also that's the reason how come some small inanimate objects—rope, chairs, and other stuff—have a habit of getting in your way when you try to attack him. Dindara can also somehow animate them by using his Mind Control power.

To beat Dindara first you have to break down his defenses. Have Ray use Concentrate (the mental power) and focus on the things that are important to him—stuff from the past or memories and things and ideas that burn bright in his mind. If you do this Dindara's strength and Powers will start to weaken.

*

I took a break to tidy the apartment a little before Tory drops by but soon it was clear it would take too long. I put the music on and was shoving things here and there, but ultimately it felt like a wasted effort. Too little too late. I cannot organize this stuff. I don't really remember where things live. I found a whole nest of beer cans in a box near the CD player—relics from sometime BugMap and Venter were here. Thanks again, BugMap. I have more to say to you some other time.

*

When Dindara is weakened use the Think Command to focus on pure cold ICE. Dindara is somehow sensitive to that. Like using his main skill against him—turns his strength into weakness. You can soon see his hands where they grip on the controls of his electrical wheelchair thing start to turn white and blue and pretty soon he cannot wheelie around anymore. You could almost start feeling sorry for that guy but plz do NOT—I'm just reminding you that Dindara is an evil deluded megalomaniac with ambition to enslave the Galaxy.

Back to work. Once D is shaking with cold the fight is nearly over—you can just pull the gun and blast his brains into non-standard arrangements all over the walls. Spare no mercy, dude, even when he is calling for Girl One and Girl Zero to come save him, or looking up at his Maps of the Stars and destiny and whimpering and trying to wheel away in his fucking wheelchair and everything. Empty the clip in his head (as Venter loves to advise) and watch the brains go EVERYWHERE. Bro, if you got that far congratulations—that is the end of Dindara.

*

Maybe an hour of waiting, trying not to wait, but really just waiting. Then Tory buzzed the door and came up (to the apartment). She was smiling and we kissed in a friends way and we said hi but I was already feeling weird, I guess about her being here since my efforts to clean up were so half-assed and Rolo's crap is piled Everywhere and Anywhere now and the few remaining plants that were still alive have died and in general it looks just like an apartment inhabited by a jobless loser that spends waaay too much time hooked up to *The Broken World* (I say no more about this). Anyhow she had only been here abt five minutes and I was already watching her looking around with a very critical expression i.e. that covering of clothes the hallway flooring has seemed to acquire, and that growth of some kind that started on a bowl near the sink. Then, while we were stood there in the kitchen, Rolo showed up all unexpected. It's like he has telepathic skills like Dindara, but only for Bad Timing. With Rolo there saying "Hi" and "How's it going you two, everything OK?" and just looking and staring at us the whole time, the scene moved steadily upward from the scale of super-awkward to super-super-advanced-awkward and in the end me and Tory said "OK, Rolo. See you later" and went out.

We walked and talked. The sun was kind of shining (OK, I exaggerate—but it wasn't raining) and we went thru the park, not saying much at first. Past the first part of the park where some people are playing ball games, and the next part with benches and homeless guys that are sitting on them listening to cassette tapes. I said to Tory NOW you know where all the TAPEs and tape players go—the homeless guys have got them—and we were laughing. We even saw one guy with a tape of the third Centurion album—that has the Cavegirl chicks all over the front—and we had to laugh a bit about that also, but only once we were well past the guy. Then we went on right past the big steps and the line of statues—where people are sitting on the steps, reading and hanging around—and from there into that part of the park where they are working on renovations and stuff.

We talked pretty much the whole time. At first it was me talking. I don't know, maybe I was just trying to prove that I can Communicate in words, or at least in words that don't have Next Level or Check the Cool Fight Options in every sentence. When I was done—how weird it was to be in the apt all alone without T, how I kind of missed her, how I never understood quite what the deal was anyhow with her whole moving-out thing, if that was permanent or not, or maybe I just wanted to believe that I didn't understand it when in fact I understood it so much it made me sad and crazy. Anyhow—I tried to say basically what I was thinking and what I was feeling about everything, about the whole situation, and when I was done with that, then it seemed to me it was like her turn, Tory's turn (to speak, or to say what she thought), and I waited and looked at her and at first she just went on in silence and I thought that I had overstepped the mark, that she would maybe just leave it all there while we walked up the rough hillside on the edge of the park and then wait til we got past the tree stumps that are all rotten where the trees were cut down before fall and say "Yeah" or "Yeah. Kind of" and leave it at that.

But she didn't do that. ANYONE THAT DOESN'T WANT TO READ JUST PERSONAL STUFF PLEASE GO AHEAD AND SKIP IT. You should know that by now.

So Tory didn't leave it at silence and instead when we did get past the rotten tree stumps she said that she had missed me too. That there had been something with the Postcard Guy but that that was nothing, not important, at least not important now, how it all turned out. That she HAD been mad with me about the Dieter Funeral thing (I know—I think I really figured that out without her having to tell me) but anyway that wasn't so important either, in any case, that the most important thing (the strongest) for her had been this sudden feeling of starting to panic— panic that this (me, her, Rolo, the temping, the weekends in the mad hole of suburbsia)—was starting to feel like "her life." That that was it, that she was done and dusted, trapped in a different way but in the end (?) just like Ray in that office unit they made into a prison cell. Anyway. She didn't resort to the Strength of Silence and chose instead to Talk, which I took as a good sign altho in truth she didn't talk as long as me, and left some stuff more unsaid or only half said, only hinted, between lines. It was kind of exhausting, caused also by the fact that we were climbing on that rough dirt hill that's not proper ground but more like earth and leaves that are falling to pieces, and at the top of the hill we finally stopped to rest and looked down, across the whole park and ever further. Seeing all the people coming and going down there. The joggers making big circles, the homeless and the picnickers appearing like these stationary features of huddled black coats and blankets or start-of-summer optimistic clothes, and all the games players—the baseball ones, and in the distance on the basketball courts—all the games players marking out patterns with the routes they traced on the ground, repeated shapes—circles, straight lines, twists and phrases, jumps and sudden stops, and the walkers walking, on the paths and off them, and to cap it all the occasional dogs that shouldn't be off a leash but which are off a leash anyway, going round in all directions in irregular patterns, going everywhere.

*

After the hill we somehow turned the topic back to other stuff, to Dieter a bit and how the Grieving Chelsea Person isn't grieving quite so bad now, to the losers at T's latest temping gig and to the ultimate and tragic fucking Low Score I personally achieved in becoming Domenico's Ex-Employee of the Month, to Linda, to her parents (there's apparently some big thing (?) out at their house on the weekend) and then in the end, around all the long, long circle right back around to Brainiac. OK, at first there was a bit about Tory and Paul (B's brother) and how that ended way back and how she still didn't really have feelings for him but that she thought of him sometimes, but mainly we talked about Brainiac and what the fuck, like where and why and what on Earth could any one of us ever do to help him or to figure out what has happened. I don't think of it like a Mystery or an Adventure or a Mission but still for me it's so hard to live in the world with an unfinished thing like B's disappearance hanging over everything and staying so fucking unfinished.

Later somehow, after it rained and we sheltered for a bit to get coffee while it passed, we decided to go over there, to Brainiac's. I don't know which of us suggested that or who really made that decision, I mean maybe it's one of those times when no one actually decides a thing but it just kind of emerges as a decision without anyone even saying "let's do that" or "yes, yes, let's do that," it's kind of clear and accepted that THAT is what's gonna happen. That's how it was with deciding to go over to Brainiac's and take another look, together.

MIRRORS of Truth and MIRRORS of UNTruth

We walked. It was early evening. (Skip ahead mouthfuckers if you don't like it.) For some reason a lot of firetrucks were going by and in the distance too, like there was a big fire over Redwood way. But we were headed in the other direction, to Brainiac's, and this time there were no dramatics on the fire escape and Venter's big Heroics climbing routine with the bleeding stomach grazes like the last time I came—it was a lot easier coz I had some actual keys, keys that Clockwork had had (all along, in fact, so we could also have been spared the earlier Dramas) from when he once stayed coz Brainiac had gone away and Clockwork's roommate of that time was kind of psycho and had started using again and Clockwork wanted to keep out his way. Anyhow the keys worked just fine.

When we got in there, well, it was the same as before, exactly the same and totally different. I mean, when me and Venter were there we kind of went through determined, looking for stuff, like we were On A Mission. But with Tory it was more low-key, more abstract. Like we met up in the Empty Level. The EL. We walked around the place (it doesn't take long, bro, there's just the tiny bedroom, living room, and the small kitchen (between) which has no windows. One of those thin railroad apartments. Tory looked at stuff—the same stuff I already looked at before—the things he has by the computer, the stuff he has pinned to a wall. The magazines. We walked around it quietly, like that feeling you sometimes get that if you speak you will break a mood of something or in this case like to speak might frighten some clue or evidence away. But there was nothing. The same nothing like before but also kind of different. We sat on the sofa. Tory didn't cry—she's not that type of person. And me neither, at least not in this instance. We just sat there quite a long time. And then we left. Locked the door on that room which is kind of like the saved game of Brainiac's life, everything there waiting, just like it was. I mean—at what point will someone (Paul? the landlord?) decide that enough is enough and like box it all up and take it to storage or convert it into a yard sale? When the rent runs out? When the police issue some kind of certificate? It's weird. Like the cops should make a statement to get rid of all the uncertainties, to end all ambiguities, but of course they can't do that. And B's place stays there in the meantime, an Empty Level that for one hour had me and Tory in it, sat together, mostly in silence.

*

Afterward, again without a discussion or like a sense of who was suggesting and who was following, we came back to the apartment. It was late. Rolo was sleeping already. We came in superquiet, neither of us speaking. I lay on the bed and Tory took her clothes off. Slow and without speaking. Just looking at me. With that look on her face and in her eyes that means the same thing in any language.

*

Hack the computers in Dindara's Mansion using Intelligence and some Software Apps from Items. They make it like a whole set of puzzles using patterns and math tricks and a vocal identifier thing that you have to fool by getting Ray to use his voice in different ways. You need deceptions and subterfuges. Computers hold the info to final stronghold of GARS—solve clues to find it. I cannot tell you more. What comes next is the hardest part of the game.

*

Tory went off to work this morning looking pretty beat since we were so late last night. There was no breakfast (sorry), but also no awkwardness, and for now no big conversation about the future or like "What was that that happened last night?" I don't know if she is "back" officially or even "back unofficially" or maybe not "back" at all or even what the fuck it was. I guess that's OK—reasons and the rest of it can wait somehow.

After a good morning came a depressing afternoon. First I was looking for BugMap to confront him about the aggressive emails which have now (not-so-mysteriously) stopped again. Anyhow Venter must have warned him already that he gave the "game" away. I don't know. But when I went there BugMap wasn't at his house, or at the University library (he works there) and he wasn't online. So I don't know.

Later I had two so-called interviews in not-so-local delivery places and one in a café/lunchbox kind of place that's closer, but it felt like I wasn't talking the right talk (or even to the right freakin person on the right planet) and all conversations ended with the phrase "we'll let you know" which sounds like the cue for Total Silence Forever. I thought Domenico's must be the most miserable and insanitary CCF place in this city but the lunchbox was worse. Maybe I can get a new job as a Health Inspector.

T called much later and asked me what's for dinner. By which she was 1) kind of inviting herself and 2) I guess letting me know in a subtle way something (?) about her future plans or intentions.

*

Once you hack the computers you know the location of GaRs/GovCorp's final stronghold and I guess Ray has a Big choice on what to do with this Info. He can give it to the Resistance and hope they make a good solution or he can go it alone. I think it's clear already how organized the Resistance is. I mean—Q: Are they exactly winning in the war against GARS? A: No. Another Q: Are they controlling any towns and bringing in an era of peace, equality and enlightenment? A: No. So the big answer is pretty clear—that Ray must go ahead and act alone. That's my advice. There are two roads—a hard one and an easier one. Ray must take the hardest road.

Now here is the really bad news. They have made that final Hideout a VERY hard place to get to. Very hard and it's not just a matter of electrical fences and guard dogs this time. I guess GARS had an idea that was a bit like the Elders or whatever from the resistance that Rachel talked with before. It's kind of like they fled to another dimension of reality. It will all become clear. And like I said, of all the parts in the game, now comes the hardest part, the hardest part of all.

*

Go to 45th Town. Take time on the train, bro. And take a good look at the scenery you pass thru. It will be clear why later. They make it fall in this part of the game. A kind of time-locked thing—it's always fall. No matter "when" you arrive. The way they do the trees is beautiful.

Check in at the Harborfront Hotel right by the sea. In this place of "faded opulence" the game will enter its Final chapters.

Check the room. Red velvets. The Regency-effect furniture. The four-post bed.

Once the Nightporter or whatever has showed you to your room and left you alone then head to the ensuite bathroom. Go straight to the mirror.

You are Ray. Ray is the tall one. The strong one. The one with darkest hair.

There is just a moment—the smallest of movies—where Ray will look into his own eyes in the mirror, but then you have control of the game again.

*

Tory says you can tell a person just by their eyes and there in the Bathroom you can look in the Mirror (Mirror of Truth/Mirror of Untruth) deep in Ray's own eyes and you can see that Ray is like a weird fucking combination of tired, exhausted, weary, and scared.

The scared or weary part is easy to get. I guess he is scared of running, sick of death, killing, and weary of the constant fighting. Just look in those pixel eyes. He looks the same, like sometimes in the TSZ or that look Rachel gets back there in Blood Corridor. A feeling like a kick in a pit of your stomach. Like deep down Ray wants no more Zombie killing, no more leading the attacks on spaceships that burn, no more slaughtering Zorda, no more smashing Agents and defective murderous Robots. No more. No more. No more. No more. No more.

But in there, with the scared and the weary, there is also Determined. Like you know that your missions aren't finished. That *The Broken World* needs you. That there's something more that you (Ray) must do to make sure that the Evil will never rise again to strike from the darkness of Time. Ray knows that there's one more stronghold of the Enemy to storm. He knows exactly what to do. Here is my advice:

Take the gun (Shotgun in Items, recovered from Warehouse, 14th Town). There, in the bathroom. Take the gun and bring it up to your mouth. Open Mouth and insert both barrels. Do NOT hesitate. PULL TRIGGER BOTH BARRELS and BLOW BRAINS OUT. This is my good advice to win the game.

*

OK. A lot of people take objection to this part of the solution. Hard to see where these Broken World coders and writers are coming from with this I admit. I mean, you spent all the time trying to keep Ray alive and now you're gonna kill him? What the fuck? It sounds completely psycho. Dude. I can understand the resistance and I know that there were some glitches in my recent advice. But listen—really, I think there is no other way. Trust me. You have to feel my truth on this, if you really want to succeed. Ray has one more Mission to complete.

*

For dinner there were Tuna steaks, salad, wine, and Coronas (I'm kind of working on the assumption that the rent crisis is over). Afterward we were just watching trash on TV and badmouthing the presenters and badmouthing the guests and badmouthing the actors and badmouthing the stupid fucking characters in the stupid fucking miniseries. Only once did I catch Tory looking at me in that way like she was thinking something that she didn't want to say, but when I asked her "what?" she didn't say anything, so I guess it was nothing that important and one look like that in a whole evening is not too bad in my opinion.

Later (when we lay on the sofa) T let slip some more abt the big lunch planned at her parents' on the weekend. Big celebrations. The lovely (and crazy) Linda will be there plus the Legendary Dental Mike—and Tory rumors that there's a surprise announcement in store. Bro, it SOUNDS LIKE I AM INVITED AND I think you know I really can't wait. Even T is not looking forward that much. Yeah. I mean who can possibly know what that big surprise announcement is gonna be?! Maybe Mike is going to do free dental work for the entire family? Barbara and Joe lucked out with that? Maybe Linda is gonna quit Secretarials and train to be a naked Circus Acrobat? Or that maybe they are going to get engaged? Only time itself will tell the truth. You cannot mess with time.

Joe is apparently preparing for the weekend already by asking T to ask me 1) what type of bbq fuels would be best to purchase? And 2) what ARE the health implications associated with eating bbq food? You read it here. You read it here.

*

Staring at computer screen. Like Ray back there, staring into the mirror.

I have been playing the game very long and writing maybe too long. Even Venter and Brainiac (wheresoever he is) said I played way too much, not to mention Tory (hi, Tory). Welcome back to the present tense.

It's late. I know what Tory's aunt used to say about too much thinking at night. But like I said already, the night can play tricks on you like that and then it's too late and you're thinking already before you even know it.

The QuALITY of LIGHT

Many times I have thought abt about the Quality of Light. For example the flickering of the screens way back in the TSZ. Or that kind of haze you see in a burning town or reflections in a pool of water. Or the glitter of pixels in Ray or Rachel's eyes or how steam rises from the subways sometimes in the towns, they make it so beautiful you have to stare. Or light in trees or stained glass in different Castles. How it flickers (the light) and how I even make Ray or Rachel stop to watch it for ages sometimes—it reminds me how Clockwork's sister's baby would stare at light, steam, and also shadows, staring and staring.

The final shift—to ghost mode, after the Mirrors of Truth/Mirrors of Untruth—is like the major transformation of the game. Weird. Weird.

As a ghost (i.e. after the shotgun blast) you have control and can drift through the streets. Check the neat new moves—floating and walking through walls. It's great. And as a ghost, of course, you are made of light—i.e. somehow you are part of the light in *The Broken World*, a part of its shimmering. You can see ghost Ray as he shimmers in the streets, moving fast, almost invisible.

Check out how fast you can move.

*

I don't know what it is with these things, but to me somehow that shivering of light is like the actual "soul" of *The Broken World*. OK. I'm not a religious person and I didn't have a religious upbringing. When Tory was a kid her parents sent her to Preacher Camp and the Preachers half scared them to death with all their study seminars of Hell and playing Heavy Metal Music backward and pointing out the various sinister words you could hear in there by listening with a lot of imagination, but I don't believe in that and when Rolo's brother came back from the army last time (not that long ago) Rol said he "believed in God now because HE HAD SEEN MEN DIE." But to me that doesn't seem like a good freakin reason to really believe in anything.

I said the shivering and shimmering of light is the actual "soul" of *The Broken World* and that Ray becomes a part of that, but I want to make clear this isn't turning into a movie by Walt Disney who 1) is dead and 2) had his head frozen people say. Cryogenically. As far as I'm concerned the shimmering of which Ray is a part (?) isn't even something that's good or nice or warm or kind. It doesn't make anyone feel better. It doesn't make anyone feel like "a part of the family of animals" or in "the circle of life" or other crap like that. The shimmering that Ray becomes part of is ANYTHING dead and alive. It's harsh and bloody and with death and pain just as much as it's with LIFE and what people like to call goodness. It's like Skeleton say in the last track of the album *Obvious*. They do the shimmering real well—in all its harsh and dead and also living sense. Bro—I think the graphics for the ghost mode are way way way the most cool of recent years. It's better even than the big fire of witches in *Bonecrusher 9*. Yes, the flicker is that good. *"It is obvious, that like I'm falling into you, just like you, you're falling into me."* (That is the lyric from the Skeleton song.)

*

Now we are getting INto the end. Getting right to the final crunches. This guide will help you beat the bad guy every time.

As Ghost RAY you must head to the biggest junction near the Harbor. To the North is a building/bunker, on the left of street where the Pool Hall stands. This bunker contains a store of entire materials for *The Broken World*. It is the storeroom, I guess, that I was imagining before. Clockwork says this "place" isn't in the game and I have read a lot of debate by gamers who say it's more a code dump or cache or holding place for the game's residues, and stuff. There was some thesis-type DUDE (my favorite) calling it "a temporary computational resting place for [the game's] mathematically written objects and properties and not an actual location." What the fuck do I know about it? I'm not an expert. I'm not a freaking computer scientist.

I mean, it's certainly true that that storeroom place doesn't appear on any map of *The Broken World* that I ever saw and I admit that I found it by accident. But there's another true thing about that storeroom also—it's true that the C4 explosive that Ray has in Items will blow the FUCK out of it. And from my way of thinking that means it IS in the game. I mean: if you can kill it, it's definitely alive. If you can destroy it, it's definitely real. That is LOGIC.

Hint: Use the C4.

Hint: You know what to do.

Bigger Hint: Blow the freakin storeroom place to bits. Only that can be the final final end and No More GARS, GovCorp, or NESTADO forever and ever.

*

Venter came by to say he had tickets for the Skeleton gig at Venus De Milo. Way to go, way to go. I had forgot that it was happening. Incredible—like Christmas came early (as they say). All me and Tory had to do was grab coats, put on shoes, and WALK.

Sleeptalk was there, Clockwork too, even Rolo, as well as BugMap. I had some words with him, but I don't want to make it a big deal like I can't take a joke. Nice joke, I said. Ha ha. Next time I'll call in the cops, and BugMap didn't reply. Venus was full to the bursting-out point. It was pretty well a *BW* crew reunion plus some other faces from past and present. I guess a Skeleton gig in this town is always going to do that.

Thru pretty much the whole set I was stood at the back of the hall and from time to time I could see Venter and even Clockwork in the pushing and shoving confusion at the front of the stage and coming out to rise above it and jump into the waiting arms of the crowd. I was watching them getting carried and jostled and flown to the edges before they would find their feet and return. I could see Tory too, with a beer in one hand, getting caught sometimes in the swirling edges of the crowd and pushing and shoving and then getting back to the edge, nearer the speakers where she could just lose herself in the noise, I guess, with an occasional wave back to me.

Skeleton played it pretty cool. They didn't speak between the songs and mainly did stuff off the new album. When they did "Night Ride" they did it with no lights on in the hall at all. Just this faint glow of LEDS on the amps and equipment and the huge wall of noise coming up and at you out of the dark.

When the set carried on I would sometimes see Tory or Jane or Sissy or BugMap's brother or whoever like heading to the bar and returning with an armful of Sierra Nevadas in those lame plastic glasses and they would nod to me at the wall and I would nod back. I was kind of aware that people had me and Tory on their radar, seeing that we were kind of together again, even if we weren't stood together, or even talking, like people just knew.

Dieter's sister (Angela) was there—I guess I hadn't seen her since that night outside the pool place where I decided she was cute. She came by and shouted to me over the music a bit but there was a moment when she saw me watching Tory instead of concentrating on her when she was yelling to me and she stepped away slightly, smiled and then once again did that small sad kind of laugh and shrug combination, the thing that people do when they're thinking about something that can't be translated into words. Then she left.

Stood at the back, against the wall, I was like a fucking cliché of myself. The classic position for someone with Watcher skills at the edge and looking at it, feeling the bass thru the floor and the concrete. Writing it all down. Like now. Fingers moving at the keyboard of HAL. Tory sleeping in the bedroom just meters away, her ears still ringing, I guess, with the sounds of all those Skeleton songs. I love Tory. Not like Ray loves Rachel—something else. I'm glad she's back.

*

Around the end of the Skeleton set—after "Mission to Run" and before they did "Echoes and Reversals"—I got a sense of someone new stood at the wall to my right. I was looking ahead and did really not look round. But I could tell there was someone there, stood by me. Closer than before. No prizes for guessing who. When "Stun Gun" finished Gresha moved off the mike to wipe sweat off his head with a towel and Neon made like a devil sign to the crowd and was grinning like crazy and there were cheers from the crowd and then a sudden silence.

Just then (in the silence and the dark) a voice came out from that new person stood next to me, saying:

"How ya doing?" which was kind of ironic. I mean, Brainiac is the one that everyone was worried about, the one that disappeared and never came back—but there he was grinning like a fool right next to me and asking How was I doing? How was *I* doing? Like he'd never gone running away, or dodged his fucking phone calls and scared the shit out of everyone for like a month or more.

Motherfucker.

*

Walk Ghost Ray to the Storehouse/Building/Bunker and lay the C4 all round it. Be slow and methodical, laying detonator, wires, triggers, and timers. No one will notice a ghost. If they notice they won't pay attention. Those monsters got other fish to fry. Zombies busy. The henchmen of Chang, reprogrammed Robots working for GARS, and GovCorp agents all searching the Town for signs of resistance. But soon they will have a much bigger bigger bigger and bigger problem than that.

When you're ready take the detonator and program it using the REPLICANT CODE. You need to enter fragments of the code in a sequence. That is the only way to arm the detonator. So Rachel's death is not in vain. Once you do all of that plz hit the SWITCH and Bring It On. Take out the storeroom, my Brother. Watch it all the way. The Storeroom is the big one. Let it go. Bring it on.

When you hit the switch the whole of *The Broken World* will blister, burn, and roar. It will shimmer and dissolve. That temporary computational resting place for the game's mathematically written objects and properties which is not an actual location can kiss my motherfucking Ass goodbye. Bring it on. Bring it on. Bring it on.

Then you will be free. Ray free. Rachel free. No more GARS forever. No more. No more. A voice sounds like before (it's not clear who it is) saying: *When I was small I thought that forests and the jungle were heaven.* I don't understand why they have that voice say that.

*

The Broken World goes falling into itself just like rain falling into rain on a plain of dissolving rain.

At the start of that C4 explosion you see flickering (like a dream). You see the crowds spilling into the streets of *The Broken World*, but at the same time EVERYTHNG is all exploding. And as explosions rip thru the fabric of everything you see Rachel (dead and somehow translucent) and she leans to the camera, flips back her hair and flips down her shades and makes a thumbs-up sign directly to you. Smiling. Flashback or premonition, I don't know. And then even the sky explodes. It's exploding in every direction with the deep red petals of fire that they do so well.

*

Of course all night people were gathered around Brainiac or just staring at him, and he was kind of not letting on that he thought anyone would have even noticed he was gone for nearly 5 weeks and was playing it cool, whatever that means in that situation. A mix of relief to see him and frustration (not the right word) with what he made people go thru, tho no one really said a thing about that, Tory calling Paul to tell him, but apparently he already got some kind of message from B.

No encores from Skeleton, which is just what you expect. Gresha jumping into the crowd at the end of the set, and carried this way and that, like he also wanted to disappear, at least for a while, in the sea of raised arms, tattoos, sweat, and spilling beer.

Brainiac's "big story" got lost somehow in a swarm of confusing details that I've only now half pieced together. Not even sure which parts of it are true. A Hitchhike ride to a city that could have been New Orleans. Several drunk nights walking streets he doesn't remember. Waking up in a field. Blank nights. Lost days. A week in a motel. Some time in a place down near the Car Refurb/Paint Job garages on 12th Street—not the gentrified part, the other part. Not leaving the room for more than a week except for finding food. More drunk nights. That part is true, I'm sure. Waking up in another place, outdoors, with the noise of machinery. Another town. More Lost Days. Deciding to head home.

I mean, what he said is one thing but also it was so strange to watch Brainiac there at the bar in Venus, knowing there's all this secret history inside him. Not like he's keeping it a secret but that a lot of what's happened in this time (and in his other breakdowns) is probably a secret even from him. What happened, its weight and EVERYTHING, can only ever get clear with time and maybe not even then. Memory coming slowly to the surface—like the pieces of a boat that got blown to pieces by a massive explosion. The pieces coming up to the surface at irregular intervals, caught up in black whirlpools of anything negative before spitting out to the top.

It reminds me of Rachel when she first loses her memory. Like you are Ray and you know the score, you know that the story is there inside her, just waiting to rise and flood out. I'm wondering what the algorithm for memory is. And then I'm wondering about other things. The algorithm for forgetting. The algorithms for grief and for peace. The algorithm for hope and the algorithm for love itself.

*

OK. I'm getting back to it. When you (as Ghost Ray) hit the switch it is Bang with the C4 and goodbye the Storeroom, and goodbye the sky, and goodbye Ray and Rachel, and goodbye GARS and all the conspiracy, and goodbye the everything, I guess.

You see it all go up and exploding around. The petals of fire. The voice rises but cannot escape. *Life is so precious even right now.*

Exploding, exploding. Going upward. And then the world is all raining down again in pieces. Glimpses. Pieces of locations visited. Pieces of items, weapons, potions. I cannot understand how it can be like that but it is like that, somehow. I'll check with Clockwork but for now, this one last time, you have to take my word for it. You can even see pieces of properties, skills, maps, and moods. You see pieces of the World. And tho it's technically not possible (?), as debris falls, I guess you also see parts of what's written here. The pieces of me. And pieces of Tory and Venter and Brainiac and Rolo and Sleeptalk and Clockwork's sister and her kid and Branimir and Miroslav and Ashton and even BugMap (freaking joker Asshole) and Stentson (1.0 and 2.0) and that Cookie who mainly did the morning shift and Cookie 2.0 and pieces of this city. And pieces of the place/s you live. And the way Tory smiles and stands and looks at the snow falling on the edge of 2nd Town and the way that light plays on the windshield when you stop at a junction and that expression of Ray when he first sees that HE is the hypnotized killer of Rachel and Rachel's expression when she first sees the Camps at 80th Town (I didn't write about that, I'm sorry) and pieces of desert, cityscape, and rain, and pieces of your breathing and of everything that you are thinking and of everything that you will think and of everything that you might have ever thought if a few simple circumstances had been different.

Then a huge whiteout and trembling. Then silence. And everything is gone.

*

Now it's very, very late. Late night. I'm alone. T is asleep—the lyrics of SKELETON'S SOng (capslock) drifting thru her mind, and on her face an echo of that wide Wide smile that she had when she first saw Brainiac in Venus.

T asleep and me at the keyboard. Like this scene became a default setting of my life. Yes, again I'm sat in front of HAL and the TV is turned down, just like so many times since I started writing this guide. I think maybe after everything I wrote in this walkthrough so far, I'm starting to believe that you cannot truly say it in words. A contradiction. But I'm doing the best job that I can.

APPoiNTMENT with LUNCH

Me and T hit the big big Lunch that was organized. Dental Mike was there with Linda, his eyes and hands all over her esp after the big "surprise" announcement, which didn't surprise anyone, that they're getting engaged. Joe proposed a toast but somehow managed to turn even that into a rambling kind of question about the true nature of modern Life and other stuff like that.

Oh man. By the end of the afternoon Mike was in the pool and Linda, Tory, and Barbara were sat by it, drunk and laughing with each other, reclining on the sunloungers and talking to Shay on the speakerphone while I was sitting far off to the side away from them, in the shade drinking whiskey with Joe. At some point thru all the laughter there was a kind of random silence falling.

How come, said Joe, looking out, how come that the reflections on the pool are so imperfect?

Then he pauses and looks over the pool (where Mike's on the air bed, belly up and floating), looks over the pool toward Linda, Tory, and his wife. Then Joe says:

How can one remain independent and still be loved?

I say I don't know what he's talking about. He kinda nods and looks at his glass and the ice and the sparkling light of the pool, takes in the whole scene for a while, then he asks another question:

How does one reconcile the need for privacy with the need for human warmth?

I tell you for the last and final, final time. They're going fucking crazy out there in the Burbs.

*

I guess after the explosion that's truly the END of the game.

You get black screen and credits. Maybe there are also some different ways to end the game other than to blow it all up, but I don't know them yet. Plz send me mail. I will Credit and keep adding good information. I need help for translations and the scenes when I couldn't find a way thru. I apologize.

Here are Sections I didn't cover—at least the ones I know—all in order but not necessarily geographical. I.e.—Depending on choice you make you may come to it all in a different way.

Bridge of Ice. Bone Stockade.

Machine Plant. Ray's House (Revisited). Firing Range.

Chinatown. Arctic Circle. (You cannot do both of these Levels.)

Labyrinth (Heating Duct). Labyrinth (Ventilators System). Labyrinth
    (Aztec Tunnels).
Secret Passage(s).
Black Ruins. Bowling Alley.
Forbidden Zone.
Spiral Bunker. Sinking Ship. Flood Plain.
Library. Forest.
Crackhouse.
Telepathy Lab.
Jujitsu.
Holding Camp. Crab Nebula.
Hardware Store. Hi-Jack Plane. Bunker.
Hallway near club entrance.
Plaza. Piazza. Lobby. Penthouse.
House: Cellar. Kitchen. Bedrooms. Hallway. Bathroom. Attic. Garden.
Vienna (I and II).
Island of Wishendor (where magic has ceased to function to the
    distress of all the wizards and sorcerers of that realm).
(More still to be added.)

*

Characters I didn't mention:

Cipher Expert.
Keith Savage.
Traven.
Hypnotist's Daughter.
Television-Handed Ghostess.

Mercenary Leader.

Elouise.

First Assassin.

Second Assassin.

Third Assassin.

Priest.

Girl in Lift #1.

Girl in Lift #2.

Zeus.

Kali.

Guys that are so old they leave a trail of dust everywhere they go.

You can tell where they've been and follow trail to get to the clues.

Hypnotized Boy.

"Shaky" Mo Collier.

Lost Lisa.

Billy.

Lt Col Snipe.

"Judas" Serial Killer.

Case.

The Android Girl.

Roman Totale.

Saskia.

Turner.

Jenna.

Joseph.

Marnie.

Zico.

(More still to be added.)

*

And scenes I didn't write yet (part alphabetical).

Acolytes of Shara.

Data Wars (I, II and III).

Dementia.

Dog Attack.

Destruction of Antwerp.

Execution of Hostages.

Exorcism.

Free Fall.

Gambling.

Helicopter Ballet.

Karate School.

Minefield Chase.

Makeover.

River Walk.

Rachel and Ray Flashback Love Scene.

Rachel Torture (not in all versions of game).

Relay Race.

River Crossing (Night).

River Crossing (Border, Day).

Flight Training.

Linear Algebra.

Safecracking.

Seagull Attack.

Snipers.

Telekinesis.

Underwater Discovery.

Virconium.

Whitewash of Political Aftereffects.

Interrogation/Polygraph.

Identification of Bodies.

Disruption Opera.

Pursuit Across Ice.

Pursuit in Desert.

Pursuit in River of Mud.

*

Also objects not fully accounted for:

Shield.

Rope.

Potion.

Wheatsheaves.

Penknife.

Bazooka.

Blue Paint.

Magical Flute (of Rohinora).

Smart Bomb.

Star Map.

Rune Scroll.

Sextant.

Snow Goggles.

Spiderwebs.

Stethescope.

GPS.

Hidden Microphone.

Ouija Board.

Wings of Icarus.

Code Book (photocopy).

Waterskis.

Treasure Map.

Hypodermic.

Chess Set.

Pebbles.

Painting of a Gothic Castle.

Rice.

Heroin.

Love Letters.

Crossbow.

Artificial Eyes.

Egg Timer.

Mousetrap.

Mantrap.

Videotape.

Grenade Launcher.

Cloak of Invisibility.

Dust Particles.

Vial of Hope.

Vial of Permission.

Spell Book.

Morphine.

Quantum Particles.

Page torn from *The Tempest* (Shakespeare).

Human Strength (in powder form).

*

That's all for now. Thanks for comments, thoughts, and encouragement to the end. I hope the guide can get you thru all missions and adventures and help you smash the bad guy every time. Take it to the Max. Big thanks to the people that wrote and coded *The Broken World*. Big thanks to Venter, Clockwork, Sleeptalk, Brainiac, BugMap, and all the *BW* crew for codes, hints, and cheats. Thanks to V. Thanks to D. Thanks to M and S for the beautiful and amazing Demon Maps. And, like I said before, this walkthrough is dedicated to Tory. Hi, Tory. Peace.

ACKNOWLEDGEMENTS

Along the way, many people gave their advice and support, or read versions of this book and made comments. My heartfelt thanks go to Hugo, Rupert, Tony, Mike, Victoria, Ruth, Mary Agnes, Astrid, Peter, Kate, Penny, James, Adrian and Michael, as well as to my colleagues at Forced Entertainment—Richard, Robin, Cathy, Claire, Sam, Eileen and Matt, and especially to Terry. My sons, Miles and Seth, spent many hours discussing The Broken World with me, enthusiastically suggesting new levels, weapons, skills and challenges for the game. I owe them, and their mother Deb, very much for their comments, love and support.

Much gratitude to my agent, Ivan Mulcahy at Mulcahy Viney, and my editor at Heinemann, Jason Arthur, both of whom were perceptive/thorough, patient and (best of all) inspiring in their input at different stages in the process. Many thanks also to Suzanne Dean at Heinemann for the vivid cover and sharp design.

I would like to thank my friend Aenne Quinones, who in 2002 asked me to write a short story including the line "life is so precious even right now" for a small publication she was working on in Berlin—a story that became an early sketch for The Broken World. My thanks and respect are also due to Edit Kaldor, whose amazing performance Or Press Esc inspired parts of the chapters "Subterraneans" and "Frozen Time".

Finally, my love and thanks to Vlatka Horvat who has been insightful and questioning through the whole thing, helping me navigate The Broken World and much else, reading the book piece by piece and then reading it whole, in several versions, in numerous locations, with numerous distractions. She was, and remains, the best inspiration anyone could wish for.

Tim Etchells, Sheffield, March 2008